108070

PS
3553
H79
I23

Chun

I am heaven

Date Due

Jac.			
2-27-4			
AUG. 09.1991			
MAY 1 0 '95			
FEB 2 8 2017			

CHABOT
COLLEGE
LIBRARY

i am heaven

JINSIE K. S. CHUN

MACRAE SMITH COMPANY
Philadelphia

Library of Congress Cataloging in Publication Data

Chun, Jinsie K   S
    I am heaven.

    Bibliography; p.
1. T'ang Wu-hou, Empress of China, 625?–705—
        Fiction. I. Title.
PZ4.C55934Iac [PS3553.H79] 813'.5'4 72-11101
            ISBN 0–8255–2410–5

To

My Father

His foresight in giving me a bilingual
education enabled me to write *I Am Heaven*

Author's Note

In the seventh century, while the disintegration of the Roman Empire was plunging Europe into the Dark Ages, China was at the height of its territorial expansion, culture and prosperity. This great heritage was usurped by a woman, whose self-assumed name was *Wu Tse-tien,* meaning "Wu is Heaven." In a country where women traditionally had no social, economic or political status except that which came by their own wits, this woman managed to sidle into the throne and create a dynasty of her own. How she did it is the story of *I Am Heaven.*

This novel is based on historical records. Only minor characters and incidents, consistent with history and the character of the protagonist, are fictitious. A bibliography and a list of historical personages, in Chinese and English, are appended.

I wish to acknowledge my indebtedness to:

Emma Lester Chase for exposing me to the beauty of English literature.
Saxon Carver for reading my first attempt at novel writing.
The late Dr. Hu Shih for his guidance to the source materials.
Benjamin Schneider and the late Beverly Tseng for reading the rough draft of *I Am Heaven.*

Morgan Harris and Molly B. Ritterband for their fine instruction in writing.

Virginia Bradley, a wonderful and selfless instructor in Westchester Adult School, for helping me with the manuscript and for giving me so much of her time.

My husband, Hongcha Chun, for his help in typing, for his criticism which often squashes my ego but enlivens my writing, and for having to live with a wife whose heart and soul are in her writing.

Los Angeles, California   Jinsie K. S. Chun

I
am
heaven

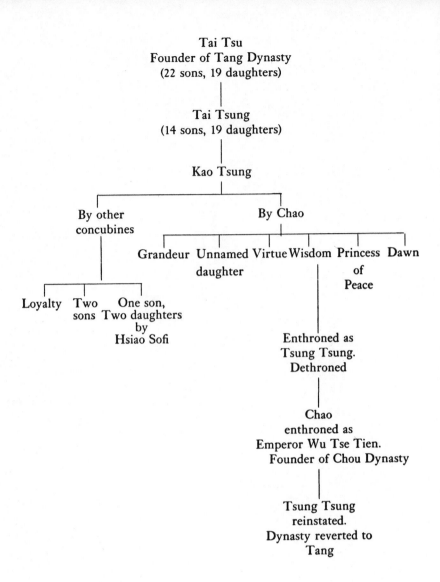

Tai Tsu
Founder of Tang Dynasty
(22 sons, 19 daughters)

Tai Tsung
(14 sons, 19 daughters)

Kao Tsung

By other concubines

By Chao

Grandeur Unnamed Virtue Wisdom Princess Dawn
          daughter   of
                                    Peace

Loyalty Two   One son,
         sons Two daughters
               by
               Hsiao Sofi

Enthroned as
Tsung Tsung.
Dethroned

Chao
enthroned as
Emperor Wu Tse Tien.
Founder of Chou Dynasty

Tsung Tsung
reinstated.
Dynasty reverted to
Tang

I

In the tenth year of Emperor Tai Tsung's reign (637 A.D.) Chang-an was the capital of the Tang Dynasty. It was a city of many walls—walls around the Palace City, walls around the Imperial City, walls around the city of the commoners. Even the street-blocks were enclosed in walls, each like a miniature rectangular citadel within the large rectangle of Changan.

The hub of the city was the trading mart, set back from the Street of Heaven by a beaten-earth flat. Here a motley crowd waited for the mart to open. There were the long-robed upper men—scholars, physicians, wealthy merchants—in maroon silk twill, royal blue satin, and gray damask, their topknots pinned with a wooden bar, their black, hemp-cloth shoes turned up at the toes like the prow of a junk. There were the short-garbed lower-men—farmers, laborers, servitors—in peasant blue dimity tunics and black dimity trousers, their hair pinned with a bamboo bar, their feet bare or shod in straw sandals. There were peddlers with bamboo baskets on their arms, selling candied crab apples, steamed wheat rolls, and toy monkeys that jerked by the contrivance of a string. There were ragged urchins seeking odd jobs and hideously deformed mendicants shocking people into giving.

Several in the crowd squinted their eyes at the sun; others

cocked their ears to listen; yet when the sun reached the zenith and the drum in the Wall Tower rolled three hundred times to open the tall arched door, none took notice of it; for two guards from the Imperial City had just ridden in, their metal pagoda-topped headgears and scalelike breast plates glistening in the sun, their horses pawing and neighing.

One of the guards tossed a coin to a dirty-faced urchin and bade him hold their horses. Ignoring the eyes of the crowd, they swaggered off with a small wooden bucket of soft starch and a leather cylinder containing the edict of the Son of Heaven. They unrolled the scroll and pasted it on the wall beside the entrance.

After they were gone, the fast-moving lower-men crowded in front of it. They gawked at the black inscription on yellow paper imprinted with the dragon, then at the red three-inch-square seal stamped at the lower left; but none could read to tell what it was about. When the genteel, slow-moving upper-men came at their heels, a pompous man in an ostentatious brocade robe said in a sarcastic tone: "Since you cannot read, will you make room for those who can?"

The lower-men backed away docilely. Pushed to the far back, a peasant with baskets of turnips and sweet potatoes dangling from his shoulder-pole called to the front, "Will some honorable teacher read it aloud for those of us who cannot read?"

"It is an edict to select ladies-in-waiting for the Palace," came a voice from the front.

This set strangers talking to strangers, upper-men to lower-men.

"Hmmmm, I wager parents with pretty daughters will wish they had ugly ones."

"Why?" asked a boy-servitor with a skein of pink silk thread dangling from his finger.

"Because only pretty ones are selected to the Palace," a scholarly man explained. "Parents would rather have their daughter ugly than have her waste her life working in the Palace."

"Imagine—never to get married but to sew, embroider, cook or wash in the Palace the rest of her life. It's against nature."

"Someone has to do the work in the Palace, just as soldiers have to be conscripted in time of war."

[2]

"I wouldn't grudge the Son of Heaven my daughter, if I had one. He is a benevolent Emperor. He should have selected his ladies-in-waiting ten years ago, when he first ascended the throne. Instead, he released the older ladies in the Palace to their homes."

"I would rather see my daughter in a nunnery. At least one could visit the nunnery. Once in the Palace, one would never see her again."

"Not if she is chosen to be the Imperial Concubine. Then, not only is her father permitted to see her, but he is elevated to a high official position."

"The odds are three thousand to one."

As people dispersed to make room for others, the boy servitor ran with the news to the House of Wu, the residence of the late Director Wu, of the Board of Works, and his clan. Its many one-story buildings and courtyards were set among flower beds, rock gardens, and bamboo groves, clustering around the Ancestral Hall like the petals of a gigantic narcissus bloom.

In the west pavilion of the late Director's courtyard his daughter, Chao, was reading at her desk in a sing-song chant. Her mother, a stout, sensual woman in her mid thirties, toyed with an unfinished embroidery on her lap and pouted. "A boy-servitor is never reliable. It must be an hour since I sent him to get the thread."

Chao knew why the man-servitor they had had was sent away. To use her sister-in-law's words, he and her mother had made the reputation of the House of Wu "stink worse than a cesspool." She did not blame her mother, whose flowery eyes and passionate nature were never meant for a widow.

"He is here at last," said Chao, as she saw the boy-servitor run into the courtyard.

"It's about time," muttered her mother. "What took you so long?" she asked the boy.

"I saw the guards post a decree on the wall, to select ladies-in-waiting for the Palace. Girls between fifteen and nineteen are to register their names at the Board of Selection."

"Aw-w-w?" said Chao's mother; then, "Thank Heaven you are fourteen."

Chao, however, frowned. She had wanted to go into the Palace ever since she was four. Emperor Tai Tsung had been a prince at that time, when he and his brother-in-law, Chanson Wochi, came to see her father. Her father had apologized for her presence there, but the prince had said, "A very pretty girl. We must have her in the Palace when she grows up." These words had stuck in her mind, and she dreamed about the Palace. How unfortunate that she was still too young for the selection!

As Chao brooded over her book, her mother said, "You read too much. Books are for men. For a girl, embroidery."

"I wish I were a man. A man's horizon touches the sky; a woman's, only the kitchen," Chao scoffed.

Her mother sighed and let fall the slipper she was embroidering. She, too, wished she were a man; then she would be married again. Being the widow of the eminent Director, she was doomed to a loveless life.

"Why the sigh, Mother?"

"Nothing. I was thinking that if your father had been alive he would have arranged your betrothal long ago. He said you were fit for a prince."

Chao was certainly a beautiful girl. Her high forehead, straight nose, and well-shaped mouth were perfectly proportioned for her oval face. Her black, glossy hair, rolled into a loop in front and tied with red twine at the back, set off her fair, fine-textured skin. Her most beautiful features were her eyes, scintillating like black gems cut in multiple facets to reflect her moods.

"Isn't it warm for the ninth moon?" said Chao, to cover her embarrassment at the mention of her betrothal. She reached across her desk to slide wider the papered, latticed window that opened onto a sunken granite court. Her gaze went to the padlocked east pavilion, her late father's study. How things had changed since he had died. Equipages of princes, nobles, prime ministers, used to crowd their door. Now, even bullock carts were seldom seen.

Following Chao's gaze to the court, her mother caught sight of a servitor cleaning a lantern that hung from the eaves of the center pavilion. "A new man-servitor!" she exclaimed excitedly.

She dropped her embroidery on the chair and walked over to watch him.

Chao's stepbrother came through the corridor, and judging from his blue silk official robe and his black gauze, cloven-peaked hat, he had come straight from his post. She wondered what brought him here, for her two stepbrothers and their wives despised her mother's loose behavior, and the family relations were strained. At her brother's sudden scowl she followed his eyes to where her mother stood. Her mother's eyes were ugly with desire as they shifted from the servitor's husky midriff, exposed in reaching for the lantern, to the mound below his groin. Chao's cheeks burned in shame. She rushed to the court to warn her mother of her stepbrother's presence, but his discreet cough had already brought her mother up to a semblance of dignity. Chao followed them to the center pavilion, sat apart and watched in silence.

"What wind blows you here?" asked her mother.

He held up an official envelope and said, "Chao is chosen to be a lady-in-waiting in the Palace."

"Impossible! The age is from fifteen to nineteen. Chao is only fourteen. Who reported her name?"

"No one. The Board of Selection says it is the Emperor's wish."

"You liar! You swine! You want to get rid of your sister because she is on my side, because she can outwit ten of you. What a horrible life you send your sister to. No husband, no children—not even the sight of a man. You turtle spawn! How could you do this to her?"

The stepson's face paled. He glued his eyes on the scrolls of calligraphy on the opposite wall, then let them stray to the circular marble-topped table in the center, to the mahogany chairs and tea-tables along the wall, to every direction except that of his stepmother. He tightened his hands on the envelope to keep from slapping his stepmother's face and bit his lips to maintain his silence. But his disdainful look showed he knew that back of her perversity was her frustrated desire. Without a word he laid the envelope on the table and left.

Chao's mother burst into tears. Chao, patting her mother's

shoulder, said, "Why cry like a child? How could it not be a blessing to see the face of the Son of Heaven?"

"I saw ladies released from the Palace, old, wrinkled and gray-haired, with life crushed out of them. Not once did they lay eyes on the Son of Heaven."

"Didn't Elder Brother say that in my case it is the Son of Heaven's expressed wish? Didn't you say Father said I was fit for a prince?"

"A prince, yes. Then you would have a husband and children and come and go as you pleased. But a lady in the Palace—you are one of the three thousand slaves, buried alive to work, work and work."

"Suppose I'm chosen to be the Imperial Concubine."

"You are too young, Chao. A man does not pick a green peach while he can have a ripe one. And the Son of Heaven is a man."

"He said I was beautiful, and I will not stay 'too young' for always."

"I hope you are right." Her mother sighed.

2

The day Chao was to enter the Palace, she woke early and speculated on what life would be like there. It would be strange and lonesome in the beginning, she thought, but once she became the Imperial Concubine . . . then . . . she could do so much for her mother, sister, and whomsoever she wished to favor. She would like to see her sisters-in-law dare to be disrespectful when her mother was made a duchess!

She raised herself on her elbow, scooped up the overlapping bed-curtain and draped it on the silver hook. As her eyes swept her familiar furniture, somehow the mahogany wardrobe, the carved dresser and the circular bronze mirror seemed to be adorned with writhing dragons and long-tailed phoenixes, emblems of the Imperial House. She blinked her eyes to shake off her fantasy and got out of bed.

Her mother came in and dropped into a chair by the dresser. "I couldn't sleep last night," she said. "All the time I was thinking that this is your last day home. How can I get along without you?"

She began to sob, and Chao could not keep back her own tears. Besides, a guilty feeling gnawed at her, that in wanting to go to the Palace, she had not thought of her mother's plight. Who would defend her mother from her sisters-in-law's barbs after she was gone?

"There, there, Mother," she said. "There's too much to do today to waste our time crying."

Later in the day, Chao's married sister came to assist with Chao's toilet. She parted Chao's hair into halves, lacquered them with mucous fluid of wood shavings, and rolled them into high loops like the uplifted wings of a dragonfly. She helped Chao change into a sky-blue flowing robe with wide sleeves and open neckline that overlapped like a scarf. She pulled the ends of a braided silk belt through a jade buckle, letting them fall gracefully between Chao's legs. She tied two embroidered fragrant pouches on Chao's belt, then turned her around for a last inspection. "You look beautiful. I wish the Son of Heaven could see you now," she said, her round, flat face beaming with admiration. She guided Chao to a chair. "There, you sit down carefully and stay as you are."

When the bullock cart from the Palace was announced, Chao linked her arms through her mother's and sister's, and together they went to the Ancestral Hall. Here the servitors had opened the paneled doors of the ancestral cabinet along the entire center wall; and Chao knelt to the tiers and tiers of wooden tablets carved with the names of the dead members of the House of Wu, to bid them farewell, then knelt to her mother and other elders gathered in the Hall. To those of her own generation, she bowed. The female clan went with Chao as far as the door, since it was unbecoming for a group of women to be seen on the street. Before the black double door with the lion-head knockers swung open, Chao's mother threw her arms around Chao and wailed.

"Why cry on this happy day?" said her elder sister-in-law. "Today Chao goes in a bullock cart; tomorrow she will return in an equipage of imperial yellow, drawn by four horses——"

"With pheasant plumes flying and dragon flag flapping," joined in the second sister-in-law.

Chao knew such an equipage was only for the Empress, and their derision infuriated her, but she kept her silence. She would show them when she became the Imperial Concubine.

[8]

When she was alone in the musty, heavily-curtained bullock cart, a suffocated feeling, like drowning, seized Chao. Fear and doubt joined hands to torment her. What if her mother was right? What if she was never to see the Son of Heaven? What if her brother had lied? He could not do it, she told herself. It wasn't his nature to lie. Besides, he would not dare. To cheat the Emperor was to ask for decapitation. She was fourteen, and the age limit was fifteen. If she had been summoned, it must be the Son of Heaven's wish.

The din of heavy traffic told her she was on the Street of Heaven, which cut the city in the center, dividing it into East and West Changan. She lifted the curtain and fastened her eyes on the moving, kaleidoscopic scene. There were carriages drawn by horses and dromedaries, riders on Mongolian ponies and slow-footed camels, traders, and students from as far as Persia and Arabia, Japan and Korea. Chao wanted to etch in her mind what she saw, for, once in the Palace, she would never see them again.

At the gate of the Imperial City, the driver stopped and exchanged a few words with the guards, then started again. Chao had never been inside the Imperial City, as it was exclusively for the administration of government affairs and the residences of the nobles. She stared curiously at the immense edifices on either side of the Street of Heaven, wondering which one was the Board of Work, where her father had worked. At the end of the street she faced a horizontal avenue, wide enough for two hundred horses to run abreast with ease; and there, in front of her, was the double-walled Palace City. She flung wide the curtain and gawked at the Gate of Heaven, with its high turret etched majestically against the sunlit sky.

She arrived at the Side-Palace through a less elegant wall-gate to the left. There she was taken to the receiving hall, where a portly eunuch in black robe examined her little bundle, a book of poems and a few sticks of color. He registered her name and handed her a pass, which designated the room she was to occupy and the places in the Palace she was permitted to go. Then the eunuch called in a loud voice, "Old Ancestor, your lady is here."

A eunuch about sixty, wearing a black robe and a black beret

[9]

with a black pompon, approached Chao; his wrinkled face wrinkled deeper and his rheumy eyes became compassionate as he saw how young Chao was. He bowed and said, "At your service, my lady."

Anxious to cultivate friendship in this strange surrounding, Chao bowed in return and said respectfully, "Do not stand on ceremony, Old Uncle."

Responding to the gracious address, the eunuch's face smoothed into a smile. "I am to take you to your quarter, my lady. Shall we proceed?"

As he led the way, he chatted to divert Chao from her obvious homesickness. He swept his arm and said, "All these buildings are for the administration of the Palace City; offices of the palace officials, guards' houses, slave quarters, and, far back there, the schools for you ladies."

Chao was not impressed by what she saw, but as she went through a tunnel-like passage beneath the wall to the Thousand-Pace-Corridor of the Main Palace, her eyes widened. Here the carved dragon on the railing and the medallion ceiling in red, green and peacock blue were magnificent beyond her imagination. As she stood looking down the long corridor that seemed to run into eternity, Old Uncle said, "This marks the perimeter of the Main Palace. Look to your right and you will see the Audience Hall." Chao squinted her eyes and caught a glimpse of the tiered roof in the distance, the glazed tiles glistening in the sun like sheets of gold.

"Have you been in the Palace long, Old Uncle?" asked Chao, as they headed north in the corridor.

"Since the defunct Sui Dynasty. Then, I held a high position in the eunuch hierarchy. Now, a different dynasty, a different hierarchy." He sighed.

"You must have seen history made before your very eyes."

"What I have seen could be of value to you, my lady."

"I am sure, Old Uncle." Chao, then confided to him the circumstances under which she was summoned to the Palace. She expected an enthusiastic response. Getting none, she shot him a sidelong glance. His bent head, his furrowed brow, together

[10]

with his silence, told her he did not share her hope and confidence.

They were entering a walled compound with a wide beaten-earth lane and side lanes branching from it like the legs of a centipede. There were rows and rows of low houses with gray brick walls and gray tiled roofs. No trees, no flowers, not even a touch of color, broke the gray monotony. "This," said Old Uncle with obvious reluctance, "is the ladies' quarter."

"It's like a . . . barrick," Chao groaned.

Old Uncle pushed open a door on a side lane to a tiny courtyard. The center-room and two side-rooms flanking the small open court were plain: white walls, black woodwork and no decorations. Old Uncle put Chao's little bundle on the table in the west room. "This is your quarter," he said. "A lady from the southern prefecture has the east room." At Chao's set face his tone softened in sympathy, "I will get you a pot of tea. It will refresh you and make you feel better."

Chao scanned with distaste the cheap, pine-wood bed, the square table that served as desk and dresser, the bamboo chairs, the tiny bronze mirror hung from the washstand. "Drab!" she muttered. She slid open the latticed window. A faint sob came from across the court. She listened, then went to the east room. She touched the girl sobbing at the table, whose large eyes, shaded in long lashes, looked up shyly. Chao studied the girl for a moment; her fine-textured skin was as fair as her own, her heart-shaped face was beautiful, and her black, glossy braids, coiled behind her ears, were becoming. From the richness of her dress and ornament, Chao judged she was from a family of an official or a merchant-prince.

"My name is Chao," she introduced herself.

"Mine . . . Beautiful Phoenix."

"I suppose you are a new lady, as I am. Things will be different once we see the Son of Heaven," said Chao, to console herself rather than Phoenix.

Phoenix shook her head emphatically. Blushing, she told Chao she loved her cousin and would have been married to him

[11]

next spring if the prefect of her district had not requisitioned her for the Palace.

"But is it not better to be the Imperial Concubine than the wife of a commoner?"

"I do not love the Son of Heaven. Besides, he is forty-one and my cousin is eighteen."

Old Uncle came with a wooden bucket of hot water. Scooping some into Phoenix's brass basin, he said, "You ladies had better repair your toilet, for the Head Eunuch will be at the dining hall to appraise you. Today the new ladies will eat separately from the old ladies."

As they approached the dining hall, Chao saw a short, stout man seated at the entrance. His rich satin robe made his prominent paunch even more prominent, and his heavy eyebrows shifted noticeably as he measured the ladies going into the hall. Behind him stood two young eunuchs, one carrying a tray of writing paraphernalia, the other recording the "can do" and "can not do" after the names of the ladies, as indicated by the Head Eunuch. When Old Uncle reported Chao's and Phoenix's names, the Head Eunuch pulled hard on his small, receding chin, a sure sign that he was pleased with what he saw, and a "can do" was entered under their names.

Chao found the atmosphere in the dining hall subdued, and conversations were in whispers. There was not the usual racket one would expect from the more than four hundred young girls seated on benches at square tables. Chao and Phoenix shared a table with four others. They eyed each other shyly, but no one spoke to get acquainted. Chao craned her neck to look at the girls at the other tables. As far as she could see, there was no "stork among the fowls." At her own table her gaze narrowed to Phoenix. In spite of Phoenix's swollen eyes she could be a competitor, and an uneasy feeling began to shake Chao's confidence.

Phoenix leaned close to Chao and whispered, "I have never seen so many females, except in a nunnery." Just then the shadow of the Head Eunuch fell upon their table, and Phoenix, caught whispering, fumbled and dropped her chopsticks. Her face crimsoned as she picked them up. The Head Eunuch paused to take notice of her, then moved on to the next table.

[12]

After he left the dining hall, the girls began to talk more freely. One of them said, "My name is Jasmine. I think I am the oldest among us. I am nineteen." She paused, then sighed. "We are passengers of the same boat, lonely, homesick, with no friends, no loved ones. We need each other. Let us pledge to be sisters." At their nod of approval she asked, "Shall we go to my quarter to talk this over after dinner?"

Chao liked Jasmine's squarish face, kind eyes and sisterly attitude, although her fleshy nose made Chao wonder how Jasmine got selected to the Palace. Chao knew Jasmine took to her too, by the way she smiled and held her hand.

When they were all seated in Jasmine's room, Chao said, "Since our elder sister's name is Jasmine, let us take our favorite flowers as our names and call our sisterhood the Six Flowers. My favorite is Chrysanthemum."

"Mine, Peony," said Phoenix.

"Queen of flowers. It suits you well," said a lady next to Phoenix.

As Chao scowled, Jasmine said in defense of Chao's flower, "I think the chrysanthemum has character, and it is loved by poets and scholars."

"I like Lotus," said another lady. "Coming out of the mire, yet unstained."

"I'll take Oleander," said the one who complimented Phoenix.

"And I, Magnolia," said the last of the six, "for I like its rich fragrance."

"Now, shall we tell each other something about ourselves?" suggested Jasmine.

While the others talked, Chao listened and watched each sister calculatingly. The more she looked at Phoenix, the more she wished Phoenix had not been summoned to the Palace. Chao's eyes hardened as they shifted to Oleander and Magnolia; their gravitation to Phoenix displeased her. Sycophants! If they thought Phoenix would be the Imperial Concubine, they were mistaken! But she would not put them wise that she was here on the Emperor's expressed wish. She would enjoy seeing their disappointment when the time came.

As the drum beat the hour of sunset, the ladies retired to their

[13]

own quarters, for sunset was the end of the day in the Palace.

Back in her room, loneliness wrapped around Chao like a mourning shroud. She could not remember being parted from her mother for even one day; now, each was in a separate world. Would their paths ever cross, or would they run in parallel lines, never to meet again? The drabness she saw made her yearn for her home even more, and her homesickness became an unbearable pain. Then came her tutor's words: "When in perturbation, read the book of poems." She untied her bundle, took her book and began to read.

The door creaked and Old Uncle came in. "Not in bed yet, my lady?" he asked outside her window.

"The sun has hardly set. Besides, I feel depressed."

"Perhaps some good news will brighten you up. I heard the Son of Heaven will hold an audience with you ladies tomorrow to choose his Imperial Concubine in person."

"This is good news! Now I cannot go to sleep from sheer excitement."

Long after Old Uncle left, Chao was still in the clouds. She was thinking of what she should say to the Son of Heaven. Should she mention their meeting many years ago? Should she mention her father? Should she . . . ? She stopped short as she remembered she was not to speak until spoken to, and she wondered what the Son of Heaven would say to her. The thought that tomorrow she would be the Imperial Concubine intoxicated her. Yet, would she? What if Phoenix was preferred over her? She sensed that Phoenix, if not prettier, was more desirable than she, perhaps because of Phoenix's full bosom and flowery eyes. If Phoenix should be chosen, how was she to survive in this drab place? She wished her father were living. He could speak to the Son of Heaven on her behalf. She missed him and the wonderful times they had together. Once he had even disguised her as a boy to ride alongside him and accompany him on his hunting trip. Those were free, happy days.

Wandering down the trail of her sunny past, she was lost to time and place, until the drumbeat of the next watch brought her back to the present. With a sigh she untied her belt and walked reluctantly toward to the unfamiliar bed.

[14]

3

Chao and Phoenix were among the ten chosen to have an audience with the Son of Heaven. The other ladies were assigned to work or be trained in special schools according to their aptitudes, Jasmine in the School of Medicine and Lotus in the School of Dancing.

Old Uncle took Chao and Phoenix to a pavilion in the Side-Palace to learn the etiquette. As they joined the other eight, there were the usual introductions, courteous smiles and greetings, but each measured the others covertly, wondering which would be the Imperial Concubine. They stopped talking as a middle-aged eunuch with a large paunch, heavy neck, small eyes, and a flabby face came and stood in the middle of the room. "Sit down, ladies," he said, indicating the straight-backed chairs interposed with tea tables on each side of him. Then he placed a chair in front of the square table in the top center of the room. "Let us pretend this is the dragon-throne. Now watch how I approach it." He bent his head demurely, folding his fat hands over his paunch; then in exaggerated, mincing steps, he walked toward the throne, knelt and bowed, then got up and backed away from the chair, graceful as a nymph in spite of his ponderous weight. "Remember to keep your eyes to the floor," he said.

"Now you do it." He turned to the lady nearest him and made her perform several times before he called the next one.

When it came to Phoenix's turn she managed to get down to her knees, but as she rose, her foot caught in her skirt and she fell to the floor. The ladies snickered, then laughed aloud.

"Accident does happen," said the eunuch, helping Phoenix up. "Watch the next lady and you can try again."

He complimented Chao on her first try. "Excellent. Do it once more. Watch, ladies. See how gracefully it can be done?" After they all had their turns, he dismissed them.

In the afternoon, Old Uncle brought two dresses, one pink and one green, and some gold and silver ornaments. Handing the green one to Chao, he said, "Be ready as soon as you can. The summons may come any time."

Chao eyed the pink dress and said, "Old Uncle, do you think pink is more becoming to me?"

Old Uncle hesitated, for it had been the Head Eunuch's order —pink for Phoenix. "I have heard that green was the favorite color of the late Empress, whom the Son of Heaven loved dearly," he hedged.

"Then I will take the green. Will you ask Jasmine and Lotus to help me dress?"

When they came, Chao put the green dress against herself. "How does this color look on me?"

"Beautiful," said Jasmine.

When Chao was dressed, they went over to see how Phoenix was doing. One look at Phoenix and Chao wished she had the pink dress. "Remember, Phoenix," she said, "to lift your skirt when getting up from your knees. It would be terrible to flop on the floor like a frog before the Son of Heaven." The ladies laughed, and Phoenix's face flushed to the color of her dress.

Oleander, scowling at Chao's patronizing attitude, said, "Never mind, Phoenix. You are pretty enough to get away with it. Besides, pink is not the color of a frog. Green is."

"This room is too small for all of us," Chao said to Jasmine and Lotus. "Let us wait in my room."

When the sun disappeared from the wall of the little courtyard, and still the summons did not come, Chao's animated talk lagged, then ceased. Her eyes flew to the door at the slightest hint of a footfall. She glared at the east room. "Do they have to prattle and giggle all the time?" She was annoyed that the delay did not matter to Phoenix at all, while her own nerves were worn thinner than spring ice. When the drum beat the hour of sunset, Chao knew the waiting was over for the day; and disappointment cut her to the heart.

After Jasmine and Lotus left, Chao waited for news from Old Uncle. When he shambled in, she asked, "Old Uncle, why didn't the summons come?"

"The Crown Prince's plot to usurp the throne was uncovered today. He is a wild one and lame in one foot, too. The Second Prince and a brother of His Majesty are also involved, and all three have been banished."

"And it has to happen today, of all days!" Chao wailed. "Who is the next Crown Prince?"

"The Ninth Prince. A good, kind-hearted prince but a little on the weak side. His Majesty wanted to give the succession to his third son, who is next in line according to age and has all the good quality of his father; but Chanson Wochi insisted it should go to the direct issue of the late Empress, his sister. The Son of Heaven defers to his brother-in-law, because whosoever succeeds to the throne needs Chanson Wochi's support."

"Now that everything is settled, will the Son of Heaven summon us tomorrow?"

Old Uncle shrugged his shoulders. "My opinion is that the Son of Heaven is too distressed to do it so soon."

No summons came the next day or on the days following. To Chao, each day was a day of suspense. Each day could be the day the summons would come; yet it never did. There were times when she could hardly contain her frustration. She wanted to let herself go—to scream, to kick, to vent all that was suppressed in her bosom.

One day a sudden gust, playing havoc with the treetops, carried a dried magnolia leaf to her room. Chao closed her window, picked up the leaf and twirled it by its short stem. An impulse

[17]

to write a verse on the leaf and send if off by the gale came to her, not without a far-fetched hope that it might reach the Son of Heaven. She dipped her brush in the ink and wrote:

Tears moisten her pillow, sleep will not come;
Songs from the distance deepen the silence in her room.
Why is one so young, so beautiful, unfavored and
neglected,
Waiting, waiting, forever waiting, till her hair is gray?

She slid wide the window, held the leaf high and let it go. The blast snatched it up, tossed it, and whirled it out of the ladies' quarter, followed by a flurry of other leaves.

When the gale was over, Chao watched the eunuch sweep the debris littered by the wind. She picked up a cone, and wondered how far it had come, and how far her magnolia leaf had gone. Was it, like the cone, being swept and burned, her poem never to be seen by any eyes?

A few days later, Old Uncle smiled proudly at Chao, and said, "Your ladyship's literary talent is very much admired in the Side-Palace."

"How is that, Old Uncle?"

"Your poem was blown to the Side-Palace and brought to the attention of Professor Hsi of the Literary School. He says if you wish to further your study, he will be happy to tutor you."

"But . . . the summons."

"When it comes I will let you know. I wouldn't miss this chance. He is such a well known man-of-letters in the Palace."

"Then take me to him."

The school was in a quiet courtyard, simply furnished. On the wall was a brushed image of Confucius, and in the center of the room there was an oblong table with stools around it. Professor Hsi was reading in the armchair at the head of the table when Chao entered. She knelt to the image of Confucius and to Professor Hsi. He bowed in return and then said, "I Like your poem. Very well written. I believe our studying together could be mutually beneficial. In fact," he added in a depreciatory tone, "I need someone to stimulate my foggy mind more than you need

[18]

a tutor. Shall we start on the three obediences and four virtues of a woman or is there any subject you are specially interested in?"

"History . . . economics . . . statecraft . . ."

"These could hardly be of use to a lady."

"But I am interested in them."

"Hmmmmmm, then I see no reason why we should not discuss them. However, we shall start with Confucius' and Mencius' teaching, then study Taoism and Buddhism. Philosophy and religion are, after all, the fundamentals. Then we shall ramble into whatever paths our fancy takes us."

Chao attended the school religiously. Without it, she could not have survived the long months of waiting. One day she asked Professor Hsi about the Crown Prince's usurpation and he said, "It is a regretable affair, a son attempting to kill his father for the throne. But in an Imperial Family love is often ruptured by power politics, a monster with no heart, no morality, only the will to succeed. Suppose you write an essay on usurpation or, if you prefer a broader subject, the rise and fall of the dynasties. You will find the one fundamental cause of all the downfalls is that the ruler has lost the hearts of his hundred-names* [people]. A nation is like a pyramid, with the throne its apex, the hundred-names the base. If the base disintegrates, where will the apex be? A ruler must have the welfare of his hundred-names in his heart. To oppress is to spell his own doom." Then he smiled, "I do not know why I am discussing this with you, or why you are interested. Sometimes I think your judicial mind should be in the head of a prime minister instead of in a slip of a girl."

Sometimes when he found her too impatient, he chided her, "You cannot plant a tree in the morning and saw planks from it in the evening. Learn to wait and deliberate. Remember, many good things come of waiting. You cannot hurry the will of Heaven. Why burn your energy unnecessarily? I know it is hard to master your own temperament, but you must, to survive in the Palace."

*The Chinese book of surnames has one hundred names

[19]

Chao spent more and more time in the school. She dreaded that dismal, miserable ladies' quarter. She couldn't think of a worse punishment than to have to live there all her life, and the endless droning of small talk from Phoenix's room did not help matters. One day, returning from school, she found the door wide open and the little court steeped in silence. How strange, she thought, for ordinarily the chatter of Phoenix, Oleander and Magnolia was the first sound to reach her. She looked in Phoenix's window. Empty boxes littered the floor, dresses were draped carelessly over the bed, and toilet articles were in disarray on the table. Had Phoenix gone to the audience and left her behind? She turned in panic and saw Old Uncle. "Where is Phoenix?" she asked.

"Congratulations, my lady. You are now a Lady of the Fourth Rank."

"Where is Phoenix?" Chao repeated.

"She . . . she is summoned to the Main Palace."

"You mean she is chosen to be the Imperial Concubine?"

Old Uncle nodded. "The Son of Heaven decided to choose from the ten brochures the Head Eunuch prepared."

Chao groped to a chair and sank into it like a soulless person.

Old Uncle, frightened, ran to the School of Medicine to fetch Jasmine. When Jasmine came, she squeezed the nape of Chao's neck again and again. As the knotted nerves loosened, a loud sob escaped from Chao. "What will become of me?"

"You are still young. Wait till you are seventeen; then the Son of Heaven will desire you." Jasmine cupped her hand over Chao's breast. "See, it hardly fills my hand. His Majesty must have a special eye on you. You are given a Fourth Rank, and none of the others is."

"I hope you are right, Jasmine. I hope you are right," said Chao, grasping desperately at the thread of hope Jasmine threw out to her. "Tell me about the summons . . . and Phoenix."

"Not much to tell," said Jasmine in a matter-of-fact voice, as if to spare Chao. "The edict came when you were in school. Then suddenly the courtyard was filled with eunuchs bearing trays of dresses and boxes of jewels, and with ladies jostling to wait upon Phoenix. They bathed her in fragrant water, dressed

[20]

her in embroidered robes, and combed her hair in high puffs."

As Jasmine went on, her excitement carried her away, and her voice became animated. "You should have seen the ornaments —Lapis lazuli, carnelian, malachite, coral, pearl, jade, set in filigreed gold! She looked beautiful when they were through with her, but frightened, clinging to Oleander and Magnolia for dear life. They are now her ladies-in-waiting. She was borne away in a sedan chair. Her tear-filled eyes told me she would rather stay on with us." Jasmine sighed, then added, "I wish it were you. You wanted it. She never did."

After Jasmine had left, the walls began to close in on Chao. She dropped her head in her hands and groaned. What if she was to live in this hovel the rest of her life? What if the Son of Heaven never wanted another concubine? *You will go mad if you do not get hold of yourself. Learn to wait. Remember, till seventeen. Two more years. Only two more years.*

She pressed her lips into a thin, determined line. She would live through those two years no matter what happened. And then . . . ? Her thoughts did not venture beyond that. All she could manage was to hang on to that slender thread of hope . . . until seventeen.

4

Chao walked with a set face to where she was to work.

"Cheer up, my lady," said Old Uncle. "Fourth Rank is a very high honor. Out of the three thousand ladies only seven are the Fourth Rank, and you are one." He looked sideways to Chao. No response; only a glum silence.

He tried again. "Think of the privileges you now have: a courtyard all your own on the lane where the other ladies of the Fourth Rank are, a serving woman to wait upon you, and no running back and forth to the dining hall with meals served in your own court."

"You know very well that even the highest rank is but a functionary in the Inner Palace," Chao snapped. "I hate this world. I hate His—" She checked herself. The blasphemy of hating His Majesty would surely bring punishment to herself. Perhaps her tongue would be cut off. She cast a look of apprehension at Old Uncle. "I am not myself today. I don't know what I'm saying. Please do not mind me."

"I understand. But be very cautious with your words when others are around. There is much pettiness and maliciousness in the Palace."

They entered an enormous oblong court paved with sheets of slate. It was flanked with buildings on three sides, with the

[22]

fourth side open. Here the ground sloped to a sunken field with low, spreading trees in even rows reaching to the horizon. Chao ran to the very edge and looked about her. With the wind blowing through the trees, the leaves billowed like waves of the sea lapping the bank she was on. After being hedged in by walls and tiny spaces, this openness was a sheer delight. Unconsciously her melancholy dissipated and an almost imperceptible smile softened her set face.

When Old Uncle caught up with her, he said, "These are Chia-Sang, the best variety of mulberry trees. Their yellowish-green leaves are the only kind tender enough for the newly hatched silk worms. About ten days after each spring festival, the Empress comes here to perform the rite of silk worm raising; then this court is packed with ladies and their attending eunuchs. From then on for two moons, the ladies in that department will be busier than bees. It is a sight to watch them pick the leaves, their colorful dresses against the green of the mulberry trees."

As they proceeded, he pointed out the buildings for spinning and weaving, for wood-carving, for "any craft you can think of," he said. He indicated the building in front with his chin. "That is where you will work."

The courtyard they were entering was similar to Chao's own at home, only many times larger and with blocks and blocks of storage houses behind it. Old Uncle shook his head at the noises coming from the east and west pavilions, and with a wry smile he said. "These chattering magpies are your ladyship's helpers."

Through the open windows, Chao could see rows and rows of ladies at their desks, talking, laughing, and cracking watermelon seeds. The lack of discipline flabbergasted her. She would not permit such slackness if she were running the department. "Old Uncle, who is the head here?"

"Pure Jade. She is sick most of the time. That is why the ladies are getting out of hand."

Not any more, she thought, now that she was here. She followed Old Uncle to a long, narrow room in the Center Pavilion, where six pinched faces eyed her curiously. A pale, sickly lady of twenty-seven came over to Chao. "My name is Pure Jade. I

[23]

am not really the head of this department, only I have been here the longest, so I am, in a way, taking charge of things." She took Chao by the hand to the desk of the other ladies of the Fourth Rank. "Peony, Fong Fong, Sooying, Mayli, Lulu," she said.

Chao bowed to each as their names were called, and wondered why they looked so old and languid in their early twenties, as if their spirits had gone through a press and only the dregs remained. Except for Peony, whose dark brown eyes, deep-set in a pretty face, still glittered, as if in bitterness.

"Your desk is over there." Pure Jade indicated a rectangular table with shallow drawers at the far back of the room. "We ladies of the Fourth Rank take charge of storing and distributing materials, silk, linen, cotton——"

"In the Empress's court only," interjected Peony. "We have nothing to do with the Emperor's court, and none of us ever gets to see the Son of Heaven."

As Pure Jade showed Chao the records in a tall cabinet, a violent cough overtook her. "You should have stayed in bed," chided Peony, while patting Pure Jade's back.

"I cannot bear to be alone; it makes me think of home all the more," said Pure Jade.

"I dreamed of my mother last night," said Mayli, her eyes shining with unshed tears. "A most vivid dream. I wonder if she is dead and her spirit came to tell me of it."

"They should at least let us write home," said Pure Jade.

"And let you disclose the secrets of the Palace?" Peony questioned sarcastically.

Chao forced a smile and went to her desk. Finding it covered with dust, she withdrew a sheet of rice-paper from the drawer to wipe it, making streaks of gray on the dark surface. She clucked in disgust, then tossed the paper in the wastebasket.

"The lazy hag must have forgotten to clean it," Pure Jade apologized. "I will fetch her."

"I will, if you will tell me where she is," said Chao.

"The last room down the hall."

Chao sailed down the hall, her wide sleeves flying like the wings of a bat. In the service room she found three old women seated on a bench, cawing like crows on a branch. "Which one cleans the room of the Ladies of the Fourth Rank?" she asked. When the two women pointed their chins to the third, Chao said, "Get some water and follow me."

"I have done the cleaning this morning," came the answer.

"One more word and you will be flogged."

The two friends jabbed their mate with their elbows, and the woman rose reluctantly.

Chao pointed out every crevice and corner the woman had carelessly overlooked. Unaccustomed to such fastidiousness, the woman was about to protest, but something in Chao's eyes intimidated her into silence.

As the door closed upon her, Peony said, "The hag has lost her tongue. You should hear her back talk when we ask her to do anything."

About suppertime, Pure Jade came to Chao's court and said, "It is lonesome to eat alone on your first night. Why not join Peony and me in my court?"

As Chao took Pure Jade's outstretched hand she said, "Your hand is hot. Do you have heat in your system?"

"Perhaps, but . . ." Pure Jade shrugged. "What difference does it make?"

"Why so morbid, Pure Jade?"

"You would be, too, if you had been here ten years."

"Ten years!" Five moons were an eternity to Chao.

During the meal they talked of their work, of the other ladies and of the eunuchs.

"Do not arouse their jealousy," warned Peony. "They can be more deadly than a serpent's fang. One of the ladies was involved in a triangle with two eunuchs, and she was found drowned in a water vat."

"You mean they still can love?" asked Chao.

"Why not? It is not their hearts that are tampered with; only their . . ." Peony giggled and left the word unsaid. "And they are the greediest breed you have ever seen."

"In a way you cannot blame them." said Pure Jade. "They can have no wives, no children, no official positions in the court. The only thing they can have is money . . ." A severe cough inter-

[25]

rupted her. She sucked for breath, and the handkerchief she pressed to her mouth came away stained with blood.

Frightened, Peony ordered the serving woman to send for a physician.

"No, Peony. Please . . ." said Pure Jade weakly.

"Why not?"

"Why prolong this wretched life?"

"Because I love you."

The physician was a scholarly eunuch in his early thirties, neither stout nor thin. He felt for Pure Jade's pulse with a gentle touch and his voice was soft, yet firm. "No more work for six moons."

As Peony accompanied the physician to the study to write the prescription, she asked anxiously, "How sick is she, doctor?"

"Her consumption has reached the third stage. It still can be cured if she has a will to live, which she does not seem to have."

"She is very unhappy . . ."

"Which is understandable. But one must learn to resign oneself and not to rebel or despair. If one's natural emotion is dammed, then one should seek an outlet in other meaningful pursuits: painting, writing, music, carving . . ."

"Please help her, doctor. I want her to live, for we are as sisters."

"If she will help herself."

After the physician left, Peony had her serving woman move her bedding to Pure Jade's courtyard. "I will watch her tonight," she said to Chao.

"I suppose she will need your care for quite a few days," said Chao. "I will help out by taking charge of the work room."

"Would you know how, since this is only your first day?"

"I have read the palace manual Old Uncle gave me this morning, and I have a clear idea what our duties are."

Peony hesitated then said, "I was going to ask . . . I don't really know who I was going to ask. We are more or less a loose body with neither head nor tail. We just do whatever there is to be done. From the way you managed the hag this morning, you are all right. If any tribute comes for storage, there is a catalogue in the cabinet. It will tell you what supplies we have, how they are stored, and where the new tribute should go."

"Thank you, Peony. I am sure I can manage. Now, where are the keys?"

"I will get them. Pure Jade keeps them beside her pillow."

When Peony came back with a large bunch of keys wrapped in an embroidered kerchief and tied with a red cord, she said, "I had better warn you, Chao, some of the eunuchs will steal. Keep your eyes open."

Chao was the first in the work room the following morning. By the time the others came, she had familiarized herself with the catalogue and the plan of the storage houses; her mind was already buzzing with possible innovations: a fresh inventory, a simplified book-keeping system, a new way of cataloguing, and strict discipline.

Later in the morning, a eunuch came with a tribute-tabulation folded like the pages of a book. Before Chao was out of her seat, Sooying was already beside him, asking, "What can I do for you?"

Handing over the paper he said, "Here is the list of the tributes from the southwest prefectures."

"I will take care of this," said Chao, taking the list from Sooying.

"You?" asked Sooying. "You came only yesterday. How do you propose to know more than I?" She snatched the tabulation back from Chao.

"How do you propose to open the storage without the keys?"

"And how do you?" asked Sooying in return.

Chao withdrew the bundle of keys from her drawer, then spread her palm to Sooying for the list. With a stunned look, Sooying let the list drop to the floor and stamped away to her seat, mumbling, "It's hateful of Pure Jade to hand over the keys to a newcomer."

Going to the East Pavilion to get the girls to help, Chao found them entangled in a brawl. She clapped her hands to stop them. "This is the Palace, ladies, not the marketplace."

"It is our *new* lady of the Fourth Rank," came a sarcastic remark from among the girls.

"So it is," said Chao, equally caustic. "And from now on, there will be *new* ways of doing things—no tidbits in the working hours, no galloping around, no talking. . . ."

"What if we do not go along with the *new* ways of doing things?"

"It will be reported to the Empress. The punishment for disrespect to superiors is ten lashes; disobedience, twenty." Chao knew from their silence that she had command of them. She noticed a girl sitting apart and writing quietly in a beautiful hand. "What is your name?" she asked.

"Golden Lily," said the girl.

"Will you take your brush and inkstand to the center-room to do the recording?"

To the rest Chao said, "There are twenty stacks of tribute materials in the center-room. Check them carefully, then follow the eunuchs to the storage to see that every bole and piece is stored in its place and nothing is filched. No need to remind you what the punishment for accomplice to theft is."

From then on Chao's orders were obeyed without gainsaying. Six moons later, even Sooying admitted the efficiency of Chao's management.

It poured and drizzled, day in and day out, throughout the eighth moon. In the work room it was so dark that candles were lighted on the pewter sconces. Chao stood by the window and watched the sheets of water drip from the eaves like liquid prison bars. It should let up soon, she thought, now that it was the ninth moon, if the usual weather pattern held. She peered at the sky. The ceiling was low; dark clouds rolled and shifted with no hint of sunshine. Dreary! How very dreary! On such a day at home, she would be cuddled in her counterpane, with her mother humoring her every fancy. Yet, if all the bars, liquid or solid, were let down, and she were free to go as she pleased, home would be the last place she would go. She could not face her sisters-in-law unvindicated; nor could she see herself married to an ordinary man, to raise his children and cater to his every whim.

Her thoughts turned to Pure Jade, so happy with so little, a different person entirely since she had met the physician; cheerful, animated, even radiant. What magic had wrought that miraculous change? Love? What was love? Was loving to Pure Jade what wanting to be His Majesty's Imperial Concubine was to her? A craving that gnawed at her vitals, awake and asleep? Was she herself in love with His Majesty? Would she still want to be his consort if he were not the Son of Heaven? She did not know.

The clouds shifted, then broke, and a puddle of sunshine peeped through, promising more for tomorrow. Peony came alongside Chao. "It looks as though the rainy season will soon be over."

"Then there will be a rush of tributes to be stored, which will keep all of us busy for some time."

"Pure Jade is worried about that. She feels she should come to help when the weather turns, since it is long over six moons, and she is really better than she ever was. But if she does, there is no more excuse to see the physician; and she loves him—lives for him."

Chao was silent, thinking that if she relaxed the discipline for Pure Jade, it would be a bad example to the rest.

Glancing obliquely at Chao's glum face, Peony tried again, "I told Pure Jade I would work twice as hard to make up for her share."

"It is not just the physical work. It is the principle of it; the right and wrong, the discipline."

"Forget about them, Chao. Happiness is a rare thing in the Palace. If one among us has found it, let her have it, by all means. Pure Jade's bliss is a sort of token to the rest of us. We want her to be happy. Mayli, Lulu, Fong Fong, Sooying—all of us—will work until our backs break in order to give Pure Jade the excuse of seeing the physician."

"So will I. But let it be between us; let the girls think she is still ill."

[29]

"Thank you, Chao. I wasn't sure how you feel. You are so strict with the girls."

"More so with myself—but she cannot stay sick for always."

"For as long as she can. Then they will resort to writing to each other."

5

One dismal year after another dragged its shackled feet over the
threshold of time, and at long last Chao was seventeen. She was
pleased with her transformation. Her bosom was full, her limbs
were rounded, her eyes were luminous with an irresistible al-
lurement. The realization that she was now a woman, possessor
of the secret power to which all men succumbed, made her
confident and happy. She laughed often and lightheartedly,
shedding her languidness like a silkworm its skin; for this was
the year the summons would come, this the year her life would
change.

The mirage buoyed her through spring and summer; but
when the autumn deluge came and still no summons, she began
to despair. Alone in her room one evening, with only a candle
for companion, she longed for her mother, for her dead father,
for someone to talk to.

She peered at the sky. Not a star glittered. A drizzle was
falling enveloping the little court in a haze. The wind whipped
the mist and moistened her cheeks, and with the wind came the
refrain of a distant flute, a soul-stirring, melancholy tune, calling plaintively to its mate in her heart. She dropped her head
in her hands, and tears seeped through her fingers.

She told herself that moans and groans would not get her

anywhere near the Son of Heaven. She must take destiny in her own hands and find a way to expose herself to him.

She went to see Lotus the first chance she had. "Lotus, when do you perform before the Son of Heaven?"

"I think soon. We are learning a new military dance interpreting His Majesty's victory over the Tufans. The master is so exacting, it makes all of us nervous. You can't wriggle a toe without his flaying you. Several girls have been dismissed."

"Is he taking others? Could you put in a word for me? I like dancing very much."

"I will see what I can do."

Two days later, Chao was among the recruits watching the ladies rehearse in the huge hall that was bare except for the master's desk and chair. Chao cast furtive glances at the eunuch dancing master. His small eyes were as cold and threatening as the bamboo whip in his hand. His arched nose and pointed chin were like those of a hawk.

One hundred and twenty dancers with wooden swords and pikes marched toward the master in single file, then turned alternately left and right to form two combat forces. One of the ladies missed her turn. Straightaway the bamboo whip cracked down on her feet. The girl uttered a cry and sank to the floor. The dancers flinched, the recruits pressed closer to the wall. Chao, however, stepped forward and asked to take the girl's place. The master scowled at her forwardness, but after measuring her from head to toe, he snapped, "You may try." Her dance impressed him, for Chao had learned the steps from Lotus beforehand. In dismissing the troupe, he said to Chao, "You dance well. Be here tomorrow at the same time."

The day they were to perform before the Emperor, the master warned in no uncertain terms that during their dance no one was to look at the Son of Heaven. "Even a Prime Minister keeps his eyes on his hu [the long, narrow tablet that was the official's badge of office] when in audience with the Son of Heaven," he said. "To let your eyes stray is to call for an unsparing whipping."

The dancers marched to the court of the main Audience Hall

in their silver-gray armorlike costumes, black leather boots and pagoda-topped headgear with flaps down over their ears. In spite of the master's warning, Chao's eyes took in the flags, the pennants, the legions of guards, the high officials on the marble steps, and the dragon throne in the center of the terrace.

As the troupe moved closer toward the throne, Chao's heart beat faster than the accompanying drum. She darted her eyes to the terrace, but with the swords and pikes thrashing all about her all she saw was a flash of the yellow satin robe and the embroidered dragons. The next time she faced the terrace, only the square, upturned toes of His Majesty's leather boots came in view.

Before Chao could attract Emperor Tai Tsung's attention, the dance was over. As the last row, which Chao was in, backed out to the exit, Chao was desperate. Had the Son of Heaven noticed her at all—one of the hundred and twenty nonentities with her face half covered with the military headgear?

"Merciful Buddha, make him see me, make him notice me, make him desire me!" she prayed. She lagged behind and was out of line, standing quite alone. Then, recklessly, she raised her head and looked to the throne. She saw the Son of Heaven talking animatedly to a minister at his left. She hunched in despair; she knew she had not made the slightest impression on him.

The last dancer, leaving, poked Chao on the back with her pike, and Chao came to herself and hurried out of the court. She sucked her breath in fright as she felt herself lifted off the ground and carried to the Side-Palace. There, stripped of her dancing costume, she was stretched out on the slate paving like a leopardskin. As the chains anchored in the ground clinched her wrists and ankles, a helpless feeling ran through her body. She lifted her head like a caterpillar and looked about her. The master was seated beneath the extending eaves, his face hard, his eyes pinpoints of anger. Two eunuch scourgers were stationed on each side of her, their hands on long bamboo whips, waiting for the signal from the master. In the terrible silence that followed, the master scanned the troupe of dancers summoned to watch, then raised two fingers to indicate twenty lashes. The bamboo slivers rattled and fell on Chao's posteriors as the scourgers counted alternately.

"One."

For an instant the lash froze Chao's nerve; then the pain came with redoubtable force, and she locked her jaws tight to keep back her scream.

"Two."

Her flesh was burning as if it were being cut into strips. She sank her teeth deeper into her lips; she would not scream and humiliate herself.

"Three."

"Four."

She felt the bamboo tear at her backside, her underpants sticky with blood. Swallowing to keep down her nausea, she heard Lotus scream, then silence.

"Seven."

"Merciful Buddha, let me die." No, she wouldn't. She'd live to pay back the world for what it had dealt her. She hated the master. He could have brought her to the attention of His Majesty, and she could make him the most powerful eunuch there ever was, yet he whipped her. For this he must pay, one day.

"Eleven."

"Twelve."

An awesome groan escaped from Chao in spite of herself, then came silence and merciful oblivion.

When she came to, she found herself in her bed. For a moment she thought it was all a nightmare, but the sharp pain brought her back to reality. She flinched when Jasmine bathed her wound with lukewarm water.

Applying the soothing salves, Jasmine said, "Stay away from the soya sauce until the bruise is healed; then your skin will be as good as when you came out of your mother's womb. Now take this herb and go to sleep."

As she raised her shoulder for the herb, the welts hurt, the pain spread until her whole body ached. When the herb finally took effect and she was asleep, Jasmine, watching by the bedside, mumbled a prayer. "Merciful Buddha, kill her ambition before she kills herself, or make the impossible possible for her."

In the three years that followed that humiliation, Chao often wondered if her mother was right. If she had not come to the Palace she would have been married long ago. Now, at twenty, she still had not known love; and she was her mother's daughter, with her mother's lust in her veins. Sometimes the urge drove her crazy, and the dreams of love at night made the reality of the morning even more hateful.

She entered the work room one morning in a bad mood. Her frown deepened at the gardenia on her desk and she dumped it in the wastebasket in disgust. Since the day she had singled out Golden Lily to do the recording there had been poems, flowers, and gifts without end. The girl's infatuation sickened her, and she avoid Golden Lily's very sight. She thrust the package Golden Lily left on her chair into her drawer and closed it with a bang. She felt the eyes of the ladies on her back, but why should she care?

Peony came over and said cautiously, "Pure Jade is sick again. She is worried over the physician. She hasn't heard from him for ages. It could be that he is sick."

"Perhaps Jasmine could find out from her School of Medicine."

"Will you ask Jasmine, then, Chao?" As Chao's mood softened, Peony ventured to ask, "Why did you throw away the gardenia Golden Lily sent you? And you didn't even look at the slippers she strained her eyes to embroider. Have a heart, Chao. A smile, a word, would set Golden Lily on the path to paradise. Do you like her even a little?"

"Like? If only she could be satisfied with that. I do not want her love, and she has no right to expect mine. What do I do with a person smothering me with unwanted love and gifts? I don't want to feel guilty that when I exert my freedom someone is hurt by it. I cannot and will not enter any sordid relation with her or any one. I despise tawdry imitations of the real thing."

"With only one man, the Son of Heaven, how does one get the real thing?"

[35]

"I suppose to find love from among ourselves is a release that keeps life going in the Inner Palace. I have no right to despise it, but for myself, I want none of it." She was thinking that if she gave her love it would be to a whole man, and the man had better be the Son of Heaven.

On her way back from work that day, Chao heard sobs. She followed the sound to a bush. Crouching beside it was a hunched form with the word "apprentice" circled in white on his black robe. She dropped beside the apprentice-eunuch and touched him gently. "Are you new here?"

A frightened but intelligent face turned to her. "I want to go home. I mean . . . to my sister's home. I have no home now."

"How is that?"

"Papa was accused of a robbery and murder he did not do. The real robbers must have slipped the gold in Papa's bedding when the Gold Guard came to search the Inn. Papa was on his way to visit my sister in Anhwei. Papa was exiled, and Ma and I became slaves. I do not know where she is." He began to cry again.

"Do not cry, little brother. What is your name? And how old are you?"

"Eight, and my name is Hung."

"Mine is Wu Chao, and I am a lady of the Fourth Rank."

"Lady of the Fourth Rank," he repeated in respect. "Please Lady, when you see the Son of Heaven, implore him to let me go to my sister."

"Alas, I do not see the Son of Heaven. Besides, to go back to your old life is not possible. You are a eunuch now. You would be out of place in the outside world. While here in the Palace you are with your own kind."

They walked in silence; then Hung looked at Chao and said, "My sister is about your age, only not as beautiful. You are the most beautiful lady I have ever seen."

"I wish this had come from the Son of Heaven," she muttered. Then she told him of her hope and ambition, and her despair when Phoenix was chosen, ending with a heartrending sigh. "I do not know why I am unburdening myself to you. You are too young to understand my frustration."

"But I do. And if I ever see the Son of Heaven, I will tell His Majesty about you. And if you ever see His Majesty, will you . . . ? I suppose it is no use. As you said, I will no longer fit in the outside world."

"I shall remember, anyway, little brother. Better days to both of us."

It was the autumn of Chao's twentieth year that Peony, Jasmine and Lotus came to her courtyard, each with a birthday present. They bowed to Chao and said, "May your life be as constant as the South Hill and your blessing as abiding as the East Sea."

Chao tried to smile, but her lips trembled and she turned to brush away her tears. A thousand bitter thoughts stabbed her. Six years! Six long years! How many more? Ten? Twenty? A lifetime? Was there no escape from this rut? A rut that was cutting deeper each year, its sides rising like perpendicular cliffs to imprison her? She was sick of the pinched faces of the lonely women, sick of the avaricious eunuchs, sick of the petty jealousies of the ladies. Life in the Palace was like a picture in a warped frame; nothing was in perspective.

She turned abruptly to her visitors. "Wish me death instead of long life. Six years . . . six years. . . ." She sank into a chair and sobbed.

Chao's outburst opened the wounds of the others, and they cried with her. Finally Peony said, "We came to celebrate your twentieth birthday. How stupid of us to cry like mourners."

The door squeaked and Old Uncle shuffled into the court with a large bamboo basket of food and a pewter urn of Moutai wine.

"Here comes Old Uncle with food. Let us drink today's wine today and worry tomorrow's worry tomorrow," said Jasmine, leading the way to the center room.

"I wish Pure Jade were here," said Peony.

"Will she ever get well?" asked Lotus.

"If the physician gets well," said Peony; then, turning to Jasmine, she asked, "How is he?"

"Let us talk about happier things," Jasmine said evasively.

"But Pure Jade asked me to ask you, Jasmine," Peony persisted.

"If you must know, he died two days ago."

"How shocking! Poor Pure Jade! It will kill her."

To change the subject Jasmine said, "Let us drink to Chao's health. Lifting her wine cup to her eye level, she said, "May your wish come true, and very soon."

When Peony was saying her little rhyme of well-wishing, there came a terrible scream and then the sound of running feet. For a moment, no one spoke or moved.

Probably the ladies are squabbling again," said Old Uncle. "I will go and see."

Peony turned her glazed eyes to Jasmine and said, "Something terrible must have happened. Feel my goosepimples."

Presently Old Uncle came back, his eyes moist with tears. "Lady Pure Jade has hanged herself. Her maid found her dangling from the door frame."

"No! No!" shrieked Peony. "No! No!" she kept screaming like a demented person. Jasmine slapped her quiet; then she and Lotus took Peony to her own court.

Chao stared at the untouched food and the half-drained cups, then paced the floor with her hands locked behind her back. "Poor Pure Jade!" she kept repeating. Six years ago she would not have understood. Now, she, too, began to see the attraction in a rope that could end all misery. She shook her head. She had to keep her sanity and her hope. "Is there somewhere I could be alone, away from all this for a little while?" she asked Old Uncle.

They wound through an unfrequented path, with grass knee high, to a low hill, bare except for a few pine trees and a summer house perched on its peak.

"This is a forgotten hill," said Old Uncle. "No one ever comes here. You will be alone up here."

Chao's legs were about to give out when she reached the top, and she sank exhausted on the bench in the weather-beaten summerhouse. Here the air was fresh and cool and scented with pine. A few paces from her, a lone pine tree stood sentinel on a crag. Its wind-blown branches bent in a bizarre but graceful shape; its classic pattern batiked on the ground. Its whisperings

[38]

made a lovely, lovely sound, purging Chao's soul of its rancor and its sting. Strange, how a single tree could transform the barren peak into a site of infinite charm.

She walked beneath the pine and felt the brown, resilient needles soft under her feet. Her eyes swept the scene below. To the east, the Wai River shimmered like a silver ribbon; to the south, the fissured Chungnan Mountain lay like a giant palm, its fingers pointing to Changan; to the west was the boundless plain, dotted with flocks of sheep. Space! Illimitable space! She loved space. And what a delightful change from the cramped ladies' quarter! Her eyes, however, rested longest on the Palace City, memorizing its every detail; the turreted double walls, the three audience halls, the many resident halls, the temple, the pavilions, the summerhouses, the pagodas, the gardens, the lakes, the zigzag bridge, and the Gold Water River, winding its way to the Imperial Park beyond the north wall. There, hidden amidst the mass of foliages, were green-tiled roofs, vermilion colonnades, and peacock-blue balustrades. Someday she would ride into that paradise with the Son of Heaven. There would be wine and music, and she would dance and sing to charm His Majesty. A possessive smile came to her face. Someday. Somehow.

6

The years piled up, and Chao was twenty-five. She was afraid to look in the mirror lest she find wrinkles, crowsfeet or even a gray strand. But the face looking back at her was still unflawed. She sighed nevertheless, thinking that if the mirror could reflect her soul it would be in tatters.

She heard footstep approaching her courtyard, not the slow, shambling gait of Old Uncle, nor the light footfalls of the ladies, but the impatient tread of a young eunuch. She leaned over her window expectantly. When the door opened she cried in surprise, "Hung!" and ran to the center-room to greet him. "How good to see you! What a handsome man you turned out to be. You must be . . . sixteen?" Pushing him into a chair, she said, "You are out of breath. Sit here while I get you some tea."

"No time for tea, Chao. You are to go to the Hall of Timely Dew to wait upon His Majesty." At Chao's dumbfounded look he said, "You see, the Son of Heaven was exhausted by the last Korean expedition. Then, on top of it, he caught dysentery. The Crown Prince wants a lady with light feet and gentle hands to serve in the sick chamber, and I recommended you. We must go as soon as we can."

"Let me change my dress. It will only take a moment."

As they hurried along the Thousand Pace Corridor Chao said,

[40]

"Tell me about yourself. I haven't seen you since that time we met."

"I am a personal attendant to the Crown Prince."

"What kind of a Prince is he?"

"A good Prince, kind to those who serve him and most filial to his Imperial Father. He waits at his father's bedside not because tradition requires him to but because he is truly devoted to the Son of Heaven. You will find him easy to serve."

As they approached the Hall of Timely Dew, Chao saw at the open court a three-tiered marble stairway with an exquisitely carved dragon relief in the center and stairs on either sides leading to a marble horizontal terrace. Chao quickened her step, but Hung directed her to the left of the building. "We use the back entrance," he said.

In the antechamber a eunuch handed Chao a bowl of herb broth on a lacquered tray to take to the Son of Heaven. She made her way to an enormous reception hall with steepled ceiling and golden rafters. Her eyes swept the captured standards, the arms on the wall, and the exquisitely carved red sandlewood chest, then rested on the throne seat behind the huge dragon desk for a long time. She crossed the hall, pushed open the jade-studded red lacquered door to the sleeping chamber. There in the center was an elegant dragon-bed, its arched panel ornately carved, its yellow silk curtain held up on golden dragon hooks. She moved noiselessly to kneel beside the bed but did not notice the Crown Prince dozing by the window. Thinking she was alone, she boldly raised her head and looked at the sleeping Son of Heaven. Her eyes bulged at the sick old man, his beard lusterless, his cheeks sunken, his hands sinewy like the talons of the dragon embroidered on his counterpane. What a cruel fate, to be brought to the imperial chamber when it was too late. Even if His Majesty could get well, he could never give her a son, and it was her dream to be the mother of an heir-apparent to the throne.

When the Crown Prince woke up and saw Chao kneeling with a bowl of brewed herb, he came over to take it from her. Chao withdrew her hands in fright and spilled the brown liquid on the Prince's hand. She sprang up and set the bowl on the

[41]

table, then came to wipe his hands with her sleeve. The commotion woke the Emperor, and Chao quickly fell to her knees. The Crown Prince took the bowl to the bedside and gestured Chao to help him. Chao slipped her arm gently under Emperor Tai Tsung's head to prop it up on her shoulder, while the Crown Prince fed him the brew spoon by spoon. When it was half gone, Emperor Tai Tsung sank back to his pillow, exhausted. Large beads of sweat glistened on his forehead. Chao wiped the Emperor's face with a hot towel; then, when taking the tray to leave, she heard the Crown Prince whisper, "Wait for me in the reception hall."

There, Chao held on to the back of a chair for support. Her head was reeling, her heart thundered. He liked her, she thought. It was far better to win the love of the Prince with a long reign ahead of him than the old Emperor whose sun was setting. Besides, he was young—he couldn't be more than twenty or twenty-one—and handsome, in his own soft way. But even if he were pockmarked, he would still be desirable to her because of his throne. He was kindhearted, Hung had said. Such a person would be much easier to manage than his forceful father. Her head whirled with schemes to worm her way into his heart.

Chao knelt at the Crown Prince's feet with the grace of a sprite as he settled on the couch. He tipped her chin toward him and asked, "What is your name?"

"Wu Chao, Your Highness. Lady-in-waiting of the Fourth Rank."

His eyes went from her oval face to her slender neck and her jade-white bosom, half revealed above the fold of her dress. "You are beautiful."

"If your handmaid pleases Your Highness, let her be your slave the rest of her days."

"Come, sit beside me."

In getting up from her knees, Chao contrived to step on her flowing sleeve and wrench it from her shoulder. The sight of her half-exposed breasts set his passion on fire. He grabbed Chao by her waist and kissed her breasts and the valley between them. His hand crept down to her thigh. A cough from his father made

[42]

him stop and drop his arms. He got up abruptly and walked to the sick chamber, his head hanging in guilt and shame.

That same evening, as the Crown Prince sat by an oblong table, watching the sickbed, his eyes wandered and came to rest on the candle flame knocked about by the air from the cracks of the windows. It bent far down almost to extinction, then suddenly flared again. He heaved a sigh as if the flame had signified his father's condition. He wanted his father to live, because he felt that he himself was not ready to reign. The thought of governing a vast empire crushed him. He felt tired, his head ached, and his eyes were red from lack of sleep. He propped his elbow on the table and dropped his head in his hands.

Chao, watching him, came to kneel at his feet and touched his knees lightly. "Could Your Highness trust your handmaid to watch His Majesty and take a rest yourself? Your Highness will not reproach your handmaid for having a bed prepared for you in the reception hall?"

The Crown Prince cupped Chao's face and looked tenderly into her eyes, "You are not only beautiful but thoughtful as well. I do need—" He hesitated as his eyes went to the patient on the bed.

"Your Highness will be better able to attend His Majesty after a much-needed rest," Chao urged.

"Perhaps you are right. Sit here in my chair and be comfortable. Forget the rules of standing and kneeling for the time being," he said, as he went out of the chamber.

Chao leaned her head on the back of the chair and looked about the shadowy chamber. The gabled ceiling seemed to lose itself in its own height, and it looked as though the dragons on the rafters were writhing in the flickering light. As her eyes came to rest on the sleeping Emperor, Chao's nostrils tucked up in distaste. Extraordinarily vigorous herself, she had neither understanding nor sympathy for infirmity. He could not live very long, she thought; but just let it be long enough for her to seduce the Prince! That should not be difficult. It had almost happened this afternoon. It would happen again. She knew that if they should be caught she would lose her head and he his inheritance. But the stake was worth the head.

[43]

She listened to the night-watchman's drum, unearthly in the dead silence. It was the third watch, with two more to go before daybreak. The night was fast slipping away. Should she go to the prince? Her insides quivered. With his gentle nature, his lovemaking would be gentle too, and an urge possessed her to slip into bed with him.

As his hands touched her shoulders from behind, she trembled in excitement. She tipped her head back and smiled dreamily into his eyes before vacating the chair.

"How is His Majesty?" he asked.

"Sleeping very well, Your Highness. I am sure the crisis is over."

"It is your turn to sleep now," said the Crown Prince. "I will watch."

Chao tossed her head saucily, "Where, Your Highness? In Your Highness's bed?"

"Where else?"

Chao flung her arms around his neck and kissed him with such passion that the Crown Prince forgot his sick father and his duty to his nation.

At the mahogany couch that was made into a bed, Chao stripped herself of her clothing and tumbled into it. The warmth of the comforter from the Prince's body made her tremble, and she waited breathlessly, wishing for him to come. He came, and she watched him disrobe in the dim light. Then she lifted a corner of the comforter to let him into her arms.

Tai Tsung's convalescence gave Chao and the Crown Prince opportunities to indulge in their liason. They often stole to Chao's secret hilltop for lovemaking. Afterwards, while the Crown Prince pillowed his head on her arm and slumbered, she stayed wide awake and reveled in her dreams. She saw the summerhouse as a luxurious hall lit with a thousand candles; music, dancing and a sumptuous feast celebrated her installation as the Imperial Concubine of the newly ascended sovereign. All this would come to pass when the old Emperor died. Chao cold-bloodedly wished for his early demise.

At Tai tsung's ascension-to-heaven two years later, while the

[44]

nation mourned, Chao was secretly happy. Hope arched over her like a rainbow after the rain. At last her day was here. She knew the tradition: ladies of the late Emperor were to be sent to a nunnery, lest the ascending Emperor commit incest unknowingly. But what was tradition to the Son of Heaven who had the absolute power to give and to take, to kill and to let live? He would not and could not send her away, not after what had happened between them. Tradition? She scoffed at it.

She waited anxiously for the newly crowned Emperor Kao Tsung's edict; but when it came, it stabbed her like a thousand knives. All the ladies under thirty were to be sent to the nunnery. She was no exception. "It can not be! It can not be!" she cried, her voice rising, her face blanched. With glassy eyes, she paced the floor like a caged tigress. Her rainbow of hope had turned to mist. She was wrapt in gloom.

It was Chao's last night in the Palace. She slipped out to the willow tree by the lake where she and the Crown Prince, now Emperor Kao Tsung, had had their trysts. Tonight she was alone. She looked longingly at the tiered roof etched against the pale moonlight above the treetop in the distance. The night was still. Not a sound. No whispers of love. No muffled laughter. Only a fish splashing in the water broke the silence.

A light breeze stirred the willow tree, breaking the silver reflection in the lake, and a thousand thoughts stirred in Chao's bosom, breaking her heart and her dream. She sat motionless, until the moon was gone and the shadows thickened, before she dragged herself to her room to a restless sleep.

The next day, Chao took a last look at her room. It was a simple room, yet it was a room within the Palace near the seat of the Son of Heaven. She fingered the pretty dresses she was leaving behind. Hereafter a gray priest robe would be her lot.

In the bullock cart, while the ladies murmured and wept, Chao sat in silence, her face hard, her eyes narrowed, her heart a lump of flint.

The summer sun blazed and the beasts were slow. When they finally reached the nunnery, the ladies got off in silence, subdued by the tedious journey and the heat. The Abbess welcomed

[45]

them at the gate, directing the nuns to guide the novices to the living quarter behind the main abbey.

Chao glared at the stern religious surroundings with repugnance. She had hoped to cradle a royal heir in her womb. Now this nunnery. What could she expect here? There was no lack of lovers, she had heard; for, as high as the walls of the Palace were, they could not shut out the gossip of the street. The eunuchs, cruelly denied sexual activities themselves, reveled in descriptions of voluptuous love affairs in the nunneries. Some of them were no better than brothels, they said. Chao did not belittle the need of the flesh. Endowed with more than a normal share of vitality, she knew too well the urge of love. Yet to her that was not all that life demanded. She had another, far deeper and greater passion crying to exert itself. She was sure she was made for a higher destiny. But what could she aim to be in a convent? An abbess?

On the day of Chao's head-shaving rite, her resentment reached new heights. Her pretty face was hard like a flower chiseled in flint; her lips were thin and silent. Dressed in a gray cotton robe, with her hair in braids, she was conducted to the Grand Hall of the main abbey. There fresh candles were on the altar and the air was redolent with sandalwood incense. While Chao knelt on a low, square stool facing the three golden Buddhas, the nuns chanted the sutra in sonorous tones. As the aged nun cropped her hair and the severed strand fell to her hands, Chao flung it away as if it were a live snake. Then tears gushed down her face.

She shunned the mirror; the reflection of the melonlike head nauseated her; but she was unaware of her more ugly inner change. The scissors had shorn not only the beauty of her hair but the goodness in her nature also. The irrevocable vow renouncing all worldly desires forced upon the unwilling acted as a poison, curdling her heart into a callous, brutal lump.

That night, when the rest of the novices were asleep, Chao slipped to the Grand Hall, where only a few wicks burned in a bowl of oil that hung from the center of the high ceiling. In the dim light, the spacious hall was eerie, and the images of the Bodhisattvas along the walls were bizarre and menacing, but she

[46]

did not notice. She knelt before the immense Buddha and poured out her fervent prayer that she be relieved of her crushing frustration, promising in return all she would do for the gods once she was in power.

She stepped over the high threshold to the open court, her hands behind her back, her face turned to the crescent moon. She was thinking of her trysts with the Crown Prince on other nights like this. But he did not love her enough to flaunt the court tradition by favoring his father's lady-in-waiting. Or was it mettle that he lacked? Pacing the court alone, with only the shadows for companion, the night was very long and the dawn very slow in coming.

7

When word got around that the ladies from the Palace were in the nunnery, an avalanche of curious worshippers came, some just for the day, others for religious rites lasting for a longer time. For such rites the worshippers, with their friends and relatives, lodged in the guest house of the nunnery. The Abbess was aware that the ladies were the cause of this sudden burst of piety; but far be it from her to complain, for she needed the windfall to replenish her sorely depleted treasury. However, she assigned old nuns to watch over the new ones, to keep the influx of the worldly world from contaminating the novitiates.

Chao and Lotus shared a cubicle with Clear Water, a broad-faced nun of sturdy farm stock. It was Clear Water's duty to snuff the candles in the main abbey and to keep the one oil lamp before the Buddha burning perpetually. One night, after going to bed early with a headache, she suddenly sat up and said, "I have not put oil in the lamp . . . or have I?"

Lotus giggled at Clear Water's senile muddle, and Clear Water retorted peevishly, "You wouldn't giggle if you had to get up from your warm bed."

"I will check it for you," said Lotus.

Clear Water told her how to lower the lamp, where to get the

[48]

oil and how much to measure out, and then she sank back to her pillow with a sigh.

Lotus made her obeisance to the Buddha perfunctorily, then did as Clear Water directed. As she knelt again to take her leave, a streak of silver traced on the tesselated tiles enticed her to push open a panel of the screenlike door. The beauty of the moonlight flooding the court into a silver pool made her suck her breath in sheer delight. She stepped over the high threshold and ventured into the court. With her face turned to the full moon and her palms pressed together in front of her bosom, her feet began to move irresistibly. Accompanied by the delicate orchestra of the nocturnal insects, she began to dance—a heavenly dance, transporting her to nirvana.

Suddenly she felt a hand clamp down on her mouth from behind. Another hand pinned down her arms, and a strong body propelled her out of the court into the guest quarter.

The next day Lotus wanted to unburden herself to Chao but the vigilant Clear Water never left them alone. "Lotus, if you have nothing better to do, help out in the kitchen," ordered Clear Water. "There will be ten tables of worshippers at noontime." To Chao she said, "Aren't you in the Rite of Eternal Life? It is starting—and you are still here?"

Chao gave her a chilling glare and walked out of the room in no apparent haste.

The moon had waxed and waned again before the nunnery worked off the reservations on its book and settled down to its routine. Clear Water finally relaxed her watch and left her two charges alone.

"What is on your mind, Lotus?" asked Chao. "You look worried."

"I . . ." Lotus swallowed hard to keep down the upsurge in her stomach. Then she bent over a spittoon and retched.

"Are you ill? Have you eaten something wrong?"

Lotus turned her moist eyes to Chao and shook her head, and the shame on her face made Chao ask, "You couldn't have . . . conceived?"

Lotus told of her rape by a military cadet. "He made me go

[49]

back to the guest house the next night—else he would have complained to the Abbess that my dance seduced him. I went. He had been called to duty, but his friend was there, a young, handsome scholar . . . and . . . very gentle. Even if I die, I will have that one night of love to remember. But right now I'm terrified."

"How far gone are you?"

"It happened the full moon before last."

"There is yet time. Do some heavy work. Help Clear Water to carry wood. It may drop."

Later in the day, the Abbess sent for Lotus. As she waited on a straight-backed chair for the erring nun, her high cheek bones flushed to the color of amaranth. She indicated a stool in front of the chest as Lotus entered. "Sit down. Clear Water suspects you are in trouble. Tell me about it."

Lotus told of the rape but said nothing about her night of love.

The Abbess mumbled "O-me-to-fo" several times, then declared, "Desire is the root of sin. A nun must put away all desires of the flesh. Your desire to dance has become your snare. Now may Buddha forgive you. May his mercy give you a chance to redeem your sin. Pray constantly for his mercy. You will have to be sequestered till the baby is born. I will tell Clear Water to look after you."

At the close of the day, when Chao saw that Lotus's bedding was gone, she asked anxiously, "Clear Water, what has happened to Lotus?"

"She has gone home. Her father is very ill. She will be back when he is well again."

"Hum!"

Clear Water knew she was not fooling Chao, so she continued sheepishly, "That is what I am to tell the nuns."

"Where is she?" Chao insisted.

"If I tell, it is only for your ears. I was ordered not to."

"Lotus is my pledged sister. Do you think I want others to know her shame?"

"Then you know?"

"Of course. Where is she?"

"In the old shed behind the pine grove."

[50]

"Locked in?"

Clear Water nodded. "Very soon she will be bulging. She must not be seen by anyone. What a scandal to live down if her condition is known!"

"The pine grove," said Chao thoughtfully. "Isn't it rather far for you to take food to Lotus, especially with your swollen legs?"

"I cannot let her starve. I have stocked some rice, beans, and dried vegetables there for her. She will not need any food for a few days."

"If you want me to, I will do it for you. My legs are stronger and faster."

Clear Water let Chao supply Lotus the first few months, but as Lotus became bigger and bigger she took over the chore herself.

"How is Lotus?" Chao asked one night.

"As well as anyone could be after her illness last month."

"You didn't tell me she was ill."

"She got well. No harm done."

"Is her time almost here?" asked Chao.

"Three days either this side or the other side of the half moon. I shall need your help when the time comes."

Chao watched the moon and counted the days. Then one night Clear Water woke her up, "The baby is coming. Hurry! Hurry!"

Chao dressed hastily and hurried after Clear Water. When she saw a glimmer of candlelight, Chao asked Clear Water for the key and ran ahead. She opened the door to the bare room with its plank bed, rough table and two stools, but there was no welcoming smile from Lotus, who was groaning in her bed, her face screwed up in pain, her brow wet with large beads of sweat. Chao knelt beside Lotus. "How bad is it, Lotus?"

Lotus's answer was an agonizing moan. When the spasm was over, Lotus's hand reached for Chao. "Do not leave me."

Chao cradled Lotus' head in the crook of her arm, crooning softly as she wiped Lotus's brow. "No, Lotus, I will not leave you. I have only you, and you me. Two lonely pledged-sisters, and I love you no less than my womb-sister."

"I am frightened, Chao."

[51]

"No need to be. It will soon be over."

Clear Water set a kettle of hot water on the floor, pulled a wooden tub from under the table, lifted it onto a stool and pushed it alongside the bed. She peeled off Lotus's trousers and made her sit on the edge of the bed with her feet extended over the tub.

"And you, Chao," ordered Clear Water, "Sit behind Lotus and hold her tight." Then she placed her large palms against Lotus's feet. "Bear down with all you've got."

Chao felt Lotus's body strain against her own, again and again. One final effort and the baby was in the tub. There was a strong lusty cry, then silence. Chao was horrified to see Clear Water's palm flat upon the little face. "No, Clear Water! Don't!" she cried.

"Don't be squeamish. What can one do with an illegitimate child? You were too protected to know the hard life of people like me. When crops are bad, farmers kill their newborns for want of food."

Chao heard Lotus sigh, then felt her body limp and slipping. "Clear Water, she is fainting!"

Clear Water quickly thrust the dead baby into a gunny sack and came to the bedside. She stretched Lotus out on the bed, burned some toilet paper and waved it in front of her, hoping the smoke might sting her back to life. But Lotus's eyes did not open. Her blood kept coming, and Clear Water was helpless to stop its flow.

"Lotus, don't go! Do not leave me," Chao wailed. But there was no answer; death had sealed Lotus' lips.

"She's dead, Clear Water. She's dead! It isn't fair. It isn't right! Why should she die? Why should she?" Suddenly she was silent, for something died in her with the death of Lotus. As she knelt by the body new with death, her eyes were dry; her face was passionless; her heart, her liver, her every organ felt turned to granite. Love, tenderness, compassion, all the finer feelings of life that had been dying were smothered entirely now. Only the determination to survive burned. Chao would live by fair means or foul. By cunning, deceit or murder she would hack her way to where she wanted to be—and let no one stand in her way!

[52]

The days in the nunnery were dreary and monotonous—the same lighting of the incense, the same chanting of the sutras, the same gray robe, the same chores, and the same vegetarian food. Like the beads in her hand, each day was like the one that followed. Time crawled, yet the years passed, and Chao was twenty-nine. The golden age of a woman's life was slipping by. A few more years and she would be as good as dead. She was in a state of deepest gloom when suddenly the nunnery buzzed with the most exciting news. Emperor Kao Tsung was coming to commemorate his father's third death anniversary in the nunnery. Chao was sure he was coming to see her. He couldn't have forgotten her—not the way she made love to him. But would he take her out of that drudgery into the Palace?

When the main hall was made ready to welcome the imperial worshippers, Chao slipped quietly to her room to make her toilet. It was against the canon to use toiletries, but she could not have cared less. She dusted her face with powder, touched her cheeks and lips lightly with carmine color, and darkened her shapely eyebrows. Then she adorned herself in a new robe. Even in this sober gray she must look her best.

As she joined the nuns lined on each side of the Grand Hall waiting for Their Majesties' arrival, she managed to stand near the large incense urn before which the worshippers would kneel. "Please, Buddha, make him notice me," she prayed.

When Their Majesties entered, followed by the Abbess and a retinue of eunuchs, a thousand emotions engulfed Chao like a tidal wave. She pressed her hand to her bosom to still the violent throbbing of her chest. She saw Kao Tsung step to the front of the incense burner, his eyes sweeping the Grand Hall. Was he searching for her? Could he find her in this indistinguishable gray mass? They were standing so close that she could almost touch him, yet so far apart that she could not make her presence known to him. If he should go without seeing her, she would surely die. While the nuns chanted in a resonant, melodic tone, accompanied by drums, bells, and wooden beaters, Chao struggled to keep her tears from running down her nose. Then it occurred to her that if she sniffled loud enough it could draw Kao Tsung's attention.

[53]

As Kao Tsung turned at the silibant sound their eyes met and held for a brief instant; yet in that instant a life story was told. Through blurred eyes each saw the sorrow in the other's heart.

The silent byplay did not escape the eyes of the Empress Wong, who had wondered why the anniversary was observed in this obscure nunnery. As her turn to worship came, she cast sidelong glances at the most beautiful nun she had ever seen. But Chao was too blind with tears to notice the Empress.

Long after the other nuns settled down to their routine, Chao still rode on the crest of her hope. Kao Tsung had seen her. His eyes had told her he loved her still. Surely he would send for her. Yet a month passed and no summons came.

The sky was a fiery glow in the west and the temple bell tolled for the evening meal. The nuns filed silently into the dining hall and took their places at the long narrow tables set on each side of the gilded shrine. The Abbess sat alone at a small, square table in front of the shrine, and she led the prayer with eyes closed and palms together, with the nuns joining in in a drawling chant. When a loud "O-me-to-fa" ended the prayer, the servitors came in to serve. They went from place to place with their wooden buckets of rice and mixed vegetables. At each place there were a pair of chopsticks and two inverted bowls, which each nun was to set right side up for service. But when it came to Chao's turn, she remained motionless, as in a trance. The hungry nun beside her nudged at her waist and the servitors knocked their ladles on the buckets.

Reversing her bowls, Chao suddenly felt hot food burn her hand and gravy spill into her lap. The sloppiness of the servitor was the last outrage. Trembling in fury, she snatched the bowl and dashed it to the wall. The pottery crashed and fell to the floor and the stringy vegetable splashed all over the wall. With a loud intake of breath the nuns stopped eating. The Abbess, however, was unruffled, and she said in a calm voice, "Go and meditate on what you have done before the Buddha in the Abbess's Hall." As Chao left, the servitors quietly cleaned up the mess and the nuns resumed their repast in silence.

Kneeling before the Buddha, Chao was unrepentant. It was cruel to confine a dragon in a well when its home should be the

[54]

sea. Blinded with tears she begged—no, demanded—from the gods release.

The Abbess sank into her usual chair by the square table. Fingering her beads, she mumbled "O-me-to-fa" many times. She called Chao to her side and said, not unkindly, "Not every one is made for a life of self-denial. If you wish to return to your home, I shall see that it is arranged discreetly."

Chao shook her head resolutely. To return and humiliate herself in the eyes of her sisters-in-law was the last thing she wanted. It was the Palace, the court, the Emperor that she craved. Short of that, nothing.

The Abbess was puzzled by Chao's decline, and she said, "If you choose to stay, then, remember there is discipline to keep. Learn to be resigned to your fate and you will find peace in your soul. May Buddha give you light and understanding."

A few days later there was a knock at the back door. The nun's eyes bulged to find that it was a eunuch, and she said apologetically, "The honorable messenger from the Palace should use the front door; the back door is for peddlers and servitors."

"I do not wish to call attention to my visit. I have private business with the Abbess. Please take me to her without disturbing the others."

Seated opposite the Abbess in the guest house, the eunuch placed a gold ingot on the tea-table, "Your nunnery is in the Empress's thought ever since her visit here. This is to provide incense and candles for your abbey."

"May Buddha bless our Empress. We are most grateful to Her Majesty." The Abbess sensed there was a reason behind the donation and she asked, "Is there something we can do to show our gratitude? A religious rite perhaps?"

"When Her Majesty was worshipping here, one of the nuns, named Chao, took Her Majesty's fancy. If the reverend Abbess will let her hair grow discreetly, it will please Her Majesty."

"It shall be done as Her Majesty wishes."

The news of the eunuch's coming swept the nunnery like a gale. The more curious among the nuns hung around the corridor waiting for the eunuch to emerge. But his forbidding face and silent lips gave no indication of his mission. Hope was dashed too often for Chao to get excited over a eunuch, since Kao Tsung's own presence had brought no change to her lot. When the Abbess sent for her, her steps were unhurried.

"The Empress has sent word to let your hair grow," said the Abbess. "Move your things to the room behind mine and say nothing to the other nuns."

For a moment Chao was dazed; then tears of happiness brimmed her eyes.

8

By the beginning of the next year, Chao's hair was long enough to manage a fairly high coiffure with the help of a switch; but she didn't think she would be summoned to the Palace in that wintry weather, snow, ice and howling wind. Perhaps in the spring, the season for love, then Kao Tsung would send for her. It surprised her when the eunuch came on one of the worst nights of that winter. But she did not mind; she would go through fire to be in the Palace. She scooped up the bundle of clothes the eunuch had brought and hurried to her room to change. The dress, the padded hood, the sheepskin-lined cape, were those for a serving maid in the Inner Palace, yet her spirit soared as she discarded her gray robe for the dress. As she came to bid the Abbess farewell, she was radiantly beautiful even in such plain apparel. With palms together she bowed reverently, "O-me-to-fa," she said.

"O-me-to-fa," replied the Abbess. "May Buddha protect you and guide you."

The eunuch untied the horses, and Chao rode behind him, not conscious of the wind whipping the snow into a frenzy, nor of the traffic and the pedestrians struggling against the cold. She rode with her head high, her eyes sparkling, happy that she was soon to be with Kao Tsung. She would make him promise never to send her away again. This time her seductive web would be so tenacious that he could never get away.

They dismounted at the stable in the Side-Palace, then went on on foot. Chao knew the Palace City well. From her secret hilltop she had engraved in her mind every inch of its ground. Today, instead of going by the Thousand-Pace-Corridor, whose long, narrow roof would shelter them from the snow, the eunuch took an unfrequented bypath. Was she being smuggled in? And where were they heading? She tried to ask, but the howling wind drowned her voice. Besides, this eunuch was forbidding and secretive, with none of the friendliness of Old Uncle.

Chao's heart leapt when the Hall of Timely Dew came into view. She noticed the West Wing was brilliantly lit, while the East Wing was a mere shadow. She was disappointed when they passed it by and headed for the dim East Wing. There the eunuch knocked cautiously at an unobtrusive back door. A lady-in-waiting opened the door a crack and whispered a few words with the eunuch, then pulled Chao in furtively, giving her no time to shake off the snow on her hood and cape.

Chao followed the lady to the Empress's chamber, but it was not the magnificence of it that impressed her; rather, its desolation. She knelt at the Empress's feet and stole a glance at the unhappy royal mein. Then she heard Her Majesty's cold voice order her to rise and felt a slender finger turn her face from side to side.

"Jasmine," said the Empress. "Roll up the sleeves."

Chao, surprised, turned to Jasmine, but her pledge-sister's eyes avoided hers. Jasmine pushed up Chao's sleeves to the shoulders, revealing two perfect arms. Chao, although sensitive of this humiliating inspection, as if she were a chattel or a slave, hid her resentment deep within herself. She would submit to any indignity, even crawl, to gain her end.

"Send her to the eunuch who brought her," said the Empress to another lady-in-waiting. Jasmine started to accompany Chao, but the Empress stopped her. "Not you, Jasmine. My head is aching again."

Jasmine went to massage Her Majesty's head, and her chance of speaking to Chao was lost.

[58]

With the Empress's strict order to conceal Chao, the eunuch put her in a discarded cell. In the following days, the only person she saw was a woman who brought her food. Puzzled at this unexpected turn, Chao tried to question the woman, but no amount of sociability could draw the slightest response. Desperate, Chao grasped the woman's arm and pleaded, "Have pity. Speak to me. Where am I? Why am I here?"

The woman turned a compassionate look at Chao, then pointed to her lacerated tongue. Horrified, Chao covered her face and sobbed.

One day the door opened and Jasmine came in. Chao stared; then her eyes blazed. "Why do you come? Little do you care that your pledge-sister is rotting in this hovel."

"I could not come any earlier. I did not know your whereabouts. It is Hung who found it out for me. Believe me, I love you," said Jasmine, as she came to sit beside Chao.

"Why am I here? What does Her Majesty want of me?"

"I do not know for sure. Her Majesty is a person of few words. She never speaks her mind to anyone, certainly not to her ladies-in-waiting. I guess she needs someone pretty like yourself to divert His Majesty's affection from Hsiao Sofi."

"Is Hsiao Sofi His Majesty's favorite? Is she more powerful and influential than Her Majesty?"

"The Son of Heaven does love her above his other concubines, and naturally the eunuchs and the palace officials revolve around her. But she herself pays no heed to power or influence. She loves His Majesty for his own sake and she only wants to be a good concubine and mother. Hung says—Hung is still attending His Majesty—that the West Wing is warm and unconventional, like the home of a hundred-names. She even cooks His Majesty's favorite food herself. She mothers not only her two daughters and her son but her ladies-in-waiting as well. She is not pretty, but she has a most wonderfully soothing and pleasant disposition. His Majesty feels relaxed in her company."

"And the Empress is jealous of her?" said Chao.

"Who could blame Her Majesty? When the wind blows in our direction, we can hear their happy voices, laughter, songs, and music; while in the East Wing, the Empress reads alone. Besides, the four Imperial Concubines all have children; only the Empress has none. Yet in Her Majesty the maternal instinct is specially strong. Every dawn Her Majesty prays to the Goddess of Mercy for a son, but in this matter even a goddess is powerless without the cooperation of the Son of Heaven. For all I know Her Majesty may still be a virgin. His Majesty comes for his courtesy call every new moon. They bow to each other, enquire after each others' health and sip tea in silence. Before leaving, His Majesty invariably asks if there is anything the Son of Heaven could grant to His Empress. But how could Her Majesty ask for the one thing she wants the most, one night of His Majesty's love to bear a son?"

"If Her Majesty wants a rival for Hsiao Sofi, why does Her Majesty lock me in this hole?"

"Perhaps Her Majesty doesn't want your presence in the Palace known till she is sure of her ground. Even Hung had a hard time locating you."

"Jasmine, speak well of me to Her Majesty. Tell Her Majesty I am entirely at her service and she could trust me to be discreet."

"Let me think of some way. I must be extremely careful, for Her Majesty has a suspicious nature. If she should learn of our relationship it would not fare well for either of us. Your affair is as my own affair. Trust me to do my best. My heart often ached for you and Lotus. How is Lotus faring?"

"She is dead." Chao recounted the tragic death of Lotus and her baby.

"Poor Lotus!" said Jasmine. "What a price to pay for one night of happiness! The years exacted their tolls in the Palace too. Old Uncle is dead. So is Oleander. Phoenix and Magnolia are well. They live in the Hall of Eternal Spring. On festival days, when the entire Inner Palace assemble, I have a chance to see them, but not close enough to talk to. Now I must go. Her Majesty may want a massage. Her head aches whenever she is upset. Recently, she is so obsessed with the fear of losing her throne to Hsiao Sofi that her head aches often."

A few days later, Jasmine brought Chao to the Empress's

[60]

study. It was a spacious room, lined with bookcases and open shelves but with little furniture—a couch at the near end, a rosewood desk and a chair with a half-moon back at the far end. The Empress was at her desk, and a brazier glowed beside her. Jasmine discreetly backed out of the study, while Chao dropped to her knees.

"Rise," Said Empress Wong, without taking her eyes off her book. She kept reading till she finished a page; then she put the book down and turned to Chao.

"How old are you?"

"Thirty, Your Majesty."

"Can you sing? Dance?"

"Yes, Your Majesty."

"You may wait upon me with Jasmine. But you are not to step out of the East Wing. Remain in your room whenever you are not on duty."

"Yes, Your Majesty. Your handmaid will obey Your Majesty's every command faithfully."

Kao Tsung came to the East Wing on one of his customary visits. He was in his ordinary robe of yellow satin with large dragon medallions embroidered on the bosom, lap and shoulders, with narrow sleeves wrapped tightly around his wrists. After the usual courtesies were exchanged, Kao Tsung placed his hands on the arms of his chair to push himself out of it. Chao entered, then, with two cups of tea on a golden lacquer tray. She knelt before Their Majesties and held the tray high above her head. When the cups were taken she dropped her arms and smiled into Kao Tsung's face. Kao Tsung turned his astonished eyes to the Empress.

"If my lady-in-waiting pleases Your Majesty," said the Empress, "I shall command her to be at Your Majesty's pleasure." She ordered Chao to sing and dance, and for once, the lifeless East Wing came to life.

Kao Tsung stayed on, forgetting his promise to Hsiao Sofi to return early. When Dinner was over and the evening aged, two ladies-in-waiting holding red candles led the way to the suite the

Empress had prepared for them. Alone in their room, Chao rushed into Kao Tsung's arms. "I missed you . . . How I missed you!"

"I missed you, too . . . terribly," said Kao Tsung. "Heaven knows I did not want to send you away. But what could I do? How could a newly ascended Emperor defy tradition to take his father's lady-in-waiting as his own without alienating the court?"

"I understand, Your Majesty," said Chao; but in her heart she was unforgiving. She despised his weakness. If she had been he, she would have told the court to stretch their necks on the chopping block. Aloud, she said, "As long as I am in Your Majesty's arms I feel safe and happy. Do not ever let me go. Tell me you still love me." Kao Tsung's hungry lips upon hers told what she wanted to know.

Hsiao Sofi was puzzled when day after day Kao Tsung did not return, and she sent for Kao Tsung's attending eunuch. "What is keeping the Son of Heaven in the East Wing? Has some magic suddenly transformed the Empress?"

"No, Your Highness. It is not the Empress. It . . . it . . . it is the Empress's new lady-in-waiting," he blurted out. "She is beautiful although no longer young. She has His Majesty entirely in the hollow of her hands."

"Tell His Majesty privately that I wish to see him," said Hsiao Sofi.

When Kao Tsung came to Hsaio Sofi and found her crying, his conscience pricked him. "There! there! Who has offended our Imperial Concubine?"

"When Your Majesty is happy with your new love, does Your Majesty have no thought for your old love who weeps because of her loneliness?" said Hsiao Sofi.

Then Kao Tsung studied Hsiao Sofi's bloated face and untidy hair and wondered what he had seen in this homely woman to have loved her at all. Ashamed of his own unworthy thought, he averted his eyes. After all, he had had three children with her. The thought of the children made him ask, "Where are our daughters and son?"

"They have been asking for their Imperial Sire every day," said Hsiao Sofi. "Tell the prince and princesses," she said to her lady-in-waiting, "their Imperial Father is—at long last—here."

The children swarmed around Kao Tsung, and the commotion they made relaxed the tension between their parents. Kao Tsung swept them into his arms. Hsiao Sofi smiled at the happy reunion of father and children. Even if His Majesty no longer loved her, he still loved her children. At least she had that for comfort, and she prayed that her rival would be barren.

Kao Tsung's eunuch came to ask if His Majesty would have dinner in the West Wing.

"Of course you will, Father," urged the children.

"Some other time," said Kao Tsung. It hurt him to see the children's faces fall, but to be away from Chao a single moment was like three autumns. He walked to the door with the three hanging around him and Hsiao Sofi following behind. She watched him go down the corridor with a sinking heart. By his not staying for the night, she knew she had lost him for always.

From then on, Chao alone had Kao Tsung's love, but she remained as a protégée of the Empress. She had no intention of being an adjunct of Her Majesty's for good, but she bided her time, for she needed Empress Wong's connivance to keep her presence in the Palace a secret. If it should become known prematurely, the court could bring pressure to bear on the weak-spined Kao Tsung to send her out again. But if she waited until she had a son, then her position would be legalized in spite of her background. So each dawn, after she saw Kao Tsung off to the Audience Hall, she placed fresh flowers on the altar table of the Goddess of Mercy and prayed for a son. Two months later she conceived, and she nurtured the seed in her womb with the greatest care, for it was her emancipation.

The wearisome months of carrying the baby passed and Chao at last was in labor. If the picture of Lotus's labor came to her mind, she pushed it aside, and not a cry of pain escaped her lips, only a prayer that the baby be a boy. To Chao, a son meant an heir to the throne, giving her the right-of-way to power. Although there were four other princes in line of succession, she was confident that she could dispose of them with a little strategem. As her head tossed on the hard porcelain pillow, she kept mumbling, "Let it be a boy."

Empress Wong drank cups and cups of tea to still her agitation. For once, a child was being born in the East Wing. She considered Chao's child to be her own, since it was she who had brought her to the Son of Heaven. She kept looking toward the door till Jasmine finally burst in. "Your Majesty, it is a boy."

"A boy!" cried Empress Wong, and her placid face rippled with joy. She went to Chao's center room to see the newborn prince. Cradling the little bundle of pinkish flesh in her arms she experienced a peculiar fulfillment to her maternal yearning. As the baby snuggled its head against her bosom a warmth seeped through her body. She touched the round, bloated face tenderly, then bent down to sniff the intoxicating baby-scent.

"He is a lovely prince," said the midwife.

"He is," replied the Empress. "How is the mother?"

"She is faring well. It has not been an easy labor, since it is the first child and she is thirty-one. But she has a marvelous constitution."

To legitimize the son, Chao was made an Imperial Concubine, and the Hall of Prosperity was renovated for her abode. The court raised no voice against it, since raw grain had already become cooked rice.

When the baby was one month old, the Hall of Prosperity was ready and Empress Wong watched with a stony face as the eunuchs moved Chao's belongings. When she saw the cradle carried away, she called Jasmine. "Tell the wet nurse to bring the baby prince here."

"Yes, Your Majesty."

Empress Wong took the baby from the nurse and pressed her cheek to his, then swayed him tenderly on her shoulder. She took him to her bedchamber and beckoned the nurse to follow her. Then she handed the baby back to the nurse and ordered her not to leave the room. Back in her study, Empress Wong said to Jasmine, "Tell the Imperial Concubine the baby prince stays here with me. He is too young for this sudden change of surroundings."

Chao, when told, shut the chest she was packing with a bang and headed for the Empress's study.

"Where is the Prince?" she demanded unceremoniously.

"You forget your manners," said Empress Wong, offended by Chao's sudden arrogance.

"You forget that I am no longer your humble handmaid. Give me back my son."

"He is staying here."

"He is my son, and he goes with his mother."

"I am the Empress Mother of all the princes. Besides, if I had not elevated an insignificant nun to the imperial couch, you would never have your son."

"And you would never have your revenge on Hsiao Sofi. You had your vengeance; now let me have my son."

As Chao started for the bedchamber to look for her baby, Empress Wong cried to her ladies-in-waiting, "Stop her!"

"Whoever touches me, I shall demand her head from the Son of Heaven," threatened Chao.

Empress Wong stepped in front of her door, but Chao thrust her aside, opened the door, took her baby, and sped out of the chamber like a junk at full sail.

Chao made the nurse hold the baby right in front of her eyes while she packed her remaining possessions. When the lid of the last trunk was closed, she sat with her hands folded and brow gathered, thinking how foolish it had been of her to antagonize the Empress. She could easily have gotten the prince back through the Son of Heaven. Now she had made an enemy of the Empress. On second thought she ceased to blame herself, for eventually the Empress would hate her as she did Hsiao Sofi. She must be watchful from now on, for since the Empress had smuggled her in to foil Hsiao Sofi, she could do the same thing again to her. But she would not be caught hands down like Hsiao Sofi. She would make Hung and Jasmine her eyes and ears.

[65]

9

Empress Wong woke from a restless sleep with a splitting headache. "Jasmine!" she called. "My head. . . ." She felt Jasmine's
thumbs press to her forehead and rub down to her temples again
and again. They were soothing but could not reach within to
ease her turbulent mind. She realized, too late, that the weapon
she had employed to hurt her rival was double-edged, hurting
herself as well. What stupidity not to see through Chao's mask!
Now the real face—the hard, arrogant, cunning face—made her
shudder. She had brought in a viper. How to bag this viper was
a problem.

Her thought turned to her uncle, the Deputy Secretary of the
Imperial Secretariat—Liu Shih, her mother's elder brother. His
counsel had been helpful in the past. That time, when she had
feared that Hsiao Sofi's son would inherit the succession, he had
advised her to take Kao Tsung's first born, Prince of Loyalty,
under her guardianship and sponsor him as the Crown Prince
to forestall Hsiao Sofi's son. It had been an astute move. Loyalty's mother was a disfavored concubine; she had nothing to fear
from her; and since Loyalty reached the Crown-princeship on
her support, she could count on his obedience. Perhaps her
uncle could come up with an equally ingenious move to contain
Chao. She pushed off Jasmine's hand. "That is enough. Tell the

eunuch to summon the Deputy Secretary to the Palace at the hour of the goat [1-3 P.M.]."

When the Imperial Uncle had been conducted to her study, Empress Wong told him of Chao's impossible behavior. "She should be whipped for biting the hands that feed her. Cunning, treacherous, ungrateful and . . . ambitious. She is the kind who stops at nothing—far more dangerous than Hsiao Sofi. I cannot rest until she is out of the way."

"Your Majesty should have let well enough alone," said the Deputy Secretary, with disapproval evident on his broad, bony brow.

Empress Wong took his reproach in silence. It had been her mistake not to consult him before smuggling Chao into the Palace.

"I would not do anything in haste," the Deputy Secretary continued. "Oftentimes one fares better by doing nothing. Sooner or later His Majesty will be tired of her as he was of Hsiao Sofi. A wrong move could cause irreparable damage to Your Majesty."

"Nip the bud while there is still time. To wait might be too late."

"It is unwise to act in hast. Wait for an opportune time."

Empress Wong waited for a year, and still no measure had been taken by her uncle to dislodge Chao. During that year she and Hsiao Sofi joined forces, and they spared neither effort nor opportunity to disparage Chao in Kao Tsung's ears. Chao used that year to win the loyalty of the ladies and the eunuchs. She went out of her way to be approachable, dispensing favors and gifts especially to those in the East Wing, so that every depreciatory word said of her was reported to her. Yet she spoke of them to Kao Tsung in the friendliest terms. This made Kao Tsung discredit Empress Wong and Hsiao Sofi even more, attributing their complaints to their catty jealousy. Annoyed by their nagging, he even ceased his proprietary visits to them.

This so worried Empress Wong that she summoned her mother to the Palace. "Has Uncle come up with any plan yet?" she asked her mother.

"He says to wait."

[67]

"I am sick of this word. Would he wait if a viper was in his sleeve?"

"He says the Son of Heaven is so infatuated that it would take superhuman power to disenchant him."

"Then look for superhuman power."

"You are right, and why didn't I think of it before? I heard there is a Taoist priest who could invoke any curse, even death, on any one. He could stick a pin in the effigy's eyes and he will be blind; in his legs, crippled; in his heart, dead."

"Does it really work?"

"You remember how insanely jealous our neighbor was of her husband's favorite concubine? She went to this priest, and in less than a month the concubine was dead."

"It must be done secretly. No one must ever know I have a hand in it."

"No one needs to know. I'll go to see him myself. But he will want a dress worn by the person he is to cast the curse upon."

"You shall have one. She left several discarded ones in her room when she moved."

Spring was cold that year, and Chao lounged in the murky sunshine let in from the window. There was not a sound about her, for all the ladies had gone to the rite of silkworm raising. She was left behind because she had recently given birth to a daughter.

"Your Highness," said Hung in a cautious tone.

"You startle me. Why are you here?"

"To warn Your Highness that Her Majesty's mother has engaged a Taoist priest to invoke a curse upon Your Highness."

"How do you know?"

"A chair-bearer in the House of Wong is an agent of mine. He says a straw effigy of Your Highness's likeness is hidden in a secret room in an out-of-the-way temple. It wears Your Highness's purple robe, with Your Highness's name, age and date of birth on its back and two pins pierced through its heart."

Chao's pupils dilated in fear, for in spite of her extraordinary intellect she believed in sorcery, wizardry or any other occult power. "No wonder there is a strange, oppressive feeling in my bosom lately," she said. Suddenly she felt as if she were suffocating, and she said to Hung, "Hurry to the Son of Heaven. Tell him his Imperial Concubine is dying."

When Kao Tsung saw Chao groaning in her bed he asked anxiously, "How does this sudden illness come about? Has the physician been summoned?"

"Your Majesty, the physicians have no power over the evil spell cast by my enemy," said Chao between groans. "Your unfortunate concubine is doomed to die."

"How is that?" asked Kao Tsung perplexed.

"Hung will tell Your Majesty."

Hung's report so incensed Kao Tsung that he fumed. "The audacity! Summon the Empress's uncle and mother to the Palace immediately."

"Shouldn't Your Majesty leave this to the judicial department? If you handle it yourself and are lenient, the court will say Your Majesty favors the Empress; if you are not lenient, they will say you favor your Imperial Concubine. Either way, it will draw censure upon yourself." Chao thought it was time the court knew of the Empress's cattiness.

"Then we shall instruct the Chief Secretary of the Judicial Department to attend to this."

Later, when the verdict was pronounced, Chao was displeased. The temple was sealed, the priest was imprisoned, and the Empress's mother and uncle were banished, but the Empress herself was unscathed. She had hoped that the court would recommend the dethronement of the Empress. There was not enough room in the Inner Palace for both of them. One would have to go, but it was not going to be Chao. She had climbed too strenuously, with too much heartbreak, to where she was. She would let no one dislodge her. She had sheathed her shaft so far; now she would let it go with a deadly shot. From now on, she would work for the downfall of the Empress.

One day, watching the innocent face of the infant in her arms she saw the face of Lotus's baby with Clear Water's hand bearing down upon it. And it came to her that her baby could be more useful dead than alive. As the baby's grasp tightened on her finger, she wrenched it away and thrust the baby to its nurse. She paced the floor, back and forth, but the insidious thought persisted that she could kill her baby and blame it on the Empress. Others had done so for lesser reasons, she argued to herself—a poor peasant for one less mouth to feed, a nun to cover her sin. Surely she had a far better reason than they. The road to power was never paved without bodies. A fierce glint came into her eyes.

She walked briskly to her chamber and shook a little brass bell. "Tell Jasmine privately that I want to see her," she ordered her lady-in-waiting.

When Jasmine came, Chao said remorsefully, "Jasmine, I have been thinking how foolish it was to antagonize Her Majesty. It is always better to have a friend than an enemy. Do you think a reconciliation is possible? Tell me how I could get back to Her Majesty's good grace."

"Her Majesty loves your children very much. She misses the Prince of Grandeur and also asks about the baby Princess. Could you take them to see her?"

"Not till after the baby's one-moon birthday. Could you get her over to see the baby before then?"

"If I tell her about the baby's peculiar birthmark do you think she will want to look at it?"

"Not likely; but if you tell her I pinch its arm blue she will come over fast enough."

"But that's no way for a reconciliation."

"Once she is here, I know how to appease her. I will apologize. I will promise to let her take the baby for her own."

"Will you really? She'd love that."

"Why not? After all it is only a girl. With a son it is different."

Later, when Jasmine sent word of the Empress's coming, Chao went to the nursery to receive Her Majesty. "Your handmaid is honored by Your Majesty's visit." Chao bowed.

"I heard that the baby Princess is not faring well, and being the Empress-mother to all the imperial children, I am concerned," said the Empress.

"She is well enough. Your Majesty can see for yourself. Give the baby to Her Majesty," she ordered the nurse, "And you may go."

[70]

The hard crust of the Empress's face cracked into tenderness as the baby cooed in her arms. She coddled it and pressed its soft cheek against her own. Then remembering what she came to examine she pushed the sleeve up. At the sight of the blue spot she turned her angry eyes to Chao. "How could you do this to her?"

"She is my daughter. I can do as I please."

"You are unfit to be a mother."

"The gods do not think so. Otherwise why should my womb be fertile and yours barren?"

Touched on the raw, the Empress put the Princess on the bed and swept out of the nursery. Chao ran to the door, slammed it shut, and leaned her back against it. Her plan had worked. The Empress had come and gone. Now all she had to do was to smother . . . a sudden revulsion stopped her. To do this to her own flesh and blood? No, she couldn't. She looked about the room. It was quiet, too quiet. From the distance a temple bell tolled, but there was not a sound in the nursery. Was the baby asleep? It would be that much easier if she was. She started for the bed. The baby cooed, a sweet, happy, contented coo. Chao shrank back. She couldn't . . . yet . . . she must.

The drum was beating the noon hour of the horse. At any moment Kao Tsung would be back for his midday meal. It was now or never. She pressed her lips to a thin line and stepped to the bed, her face a grotesque mask, her eyes murderous. She looked beyond the baby's waving arms to the comforter folded like a fan at the inner side of the bed. With one swift motion she swept it over the baby and pressed her hand on the blanketed face. She felt the little bundle quiver, then became still. She let down the bed-curtain. The sound of the silver hooks banging against the bed-posts made her tremble. She cling to the bedpost for support and stood rooted as if paralyzed; then, exhaling a long sigh, she left.

Back in her chamber, she sat still as a statue until she heard Kao Tsung coming, then she forced her taut face into a warm smile and hastened to welcome him with extended arms. She took the ginseng tea from her lady-in-waiting and served it to Kao Tsung herself, then pulled up a footstool and sat at his feet.

[71]

"I am happy Your Majesty is here. Your presence dispels the gloom cast by Her Majesty." She told him of the Empress's visit. "Her Majesty said I was unfit to be the mother of our daughter." She laid her aggrieved face on Kao Tsung's knees, her eyes moist with injury.

"She is jealous of your child," said Kao Tsung. "How is the little Princess?"

"Tell the nurse to bring the Princess here," said Chao to her lady-in-waiting.

Suddenly there was a terrible scream from the nursery, then the lady-in-waiting came running back. "Your Highness, the Princess is dead!"

Chao ran to the nursery with Kao Tsung following close behind. She sank by the bed and wailed, "My poor baby! My poor baby!" Kao Tsung tried to get her away, but she kept wailing. When he finally dragged her up to her feet she accused the nurse. "How careless of you! You've killed her!"

Frightened, the nurse stuttered, "She . . . she . . . was alive . . . when I put her in Her Majesty's arms, and I haven't been near ever since."

Chao's eyes widened as if a sudden realization had dawned upon her, and the horror on her face accused the Empress more eloquently than words ever could.

"So her jealousy has driven her even to this," said Kao Tsung. "I will talk to her."

"What is the use? She will blame the nurse. It is between the two of them. There is no witness. But Your Majesty can see she is bent on destroying me and mine. First the imprecation, now this."

"She is depraved, unworthy of her throne!"

"The Inner Palace under a depraved Empress! What is Your Majesty going to do about it?"

Kao Tsung sighed. "I wish I could make you the Empress. I know our Imperial Concubine is more worthy, and nothing could make me happier than to have you share my throne. But the court . . . It is of a different mind; the Empress's family is highly esteemed, with a wide circle of influential friends in the court."

[72]

"They cannot be more influential than Your Majesty's uncle, Chanson Wochi. If Your Majesty would solicit his support, perhaps he could change the mind of the court. Let us pay him a family visit."

The day before the visit, Chao went to the storehouse to select the presents herself; a watermelon with jade rind, ruby meat and onyx seeds, a three-foot-high coral Goddess of Mercy, a pair of ivory phoenixes exquisitely carved; also ruby earrings and strands of pearls for Chanson Wochi's concubine, since his wife was dead. She weighed out many ounces of gold and ordered the eunuchs to fill ten cartloads with brocades, satins, linens, gauzes, porcelains, bronzes, and lacquer wares; also embroidered tapestries, robes, shoes, and table covers; for the best was none too good for the person whose support could put her on the throne.

On their way, the next day, Chao was quietly speculating on the outcome of this consequential visit. Much would depend on Kao Tsung's strategem, and she hoped he would remember the approach they had agreed upon. She wondered what Chanson Wochi looked like now. He had been a slender, scholarly man when he and the late Emperor Tai Tsung had called on her father almost twenty years before. Would he be as feeble as Kao Tsung's father was in his latter years?

Chao was surprised to find him still alert, his eyes keen, his hair and beard unspeckled, his body lithe in spite of his sixty years. Kneeling beside him at the gate was his concubine, a pleasant-looking woman about forty. Chao went to her to raise her from the ground, while Kao Tsung helped his uncle up with both hands, saying, "It is not the Son of Heaven who is visiting; it is only your nephew."

Chao took the hand of Chanson Wochi's concubine and together they followed their menfolk to the center chamber. There a chair was placed for Kao Tsung to receive the three kneelings and nine kowtows, but Kao Tsung waived the rite and went with his uncle to the east side-room to talk casually of the family affairs and to reminisce about his mother.

In the evening a feast was spread in the center chamber. The atmosphere was gay at the table, with Chao exerting her utmost charm for the benefit of Chanson Wochi. When Kao Tsung

[73]

deemed the time proper to speak of the purpose of his visit, he said, "Our uncle is the pillar of the nation. Any issue proposed by our uncle the court is bound to approve. Therefore——"

"Not any issue," interrupted Chanson Wochi. "Only if righteousness is on the side of the issue."

Kao Tsung, unexpectedly distracted, was silent. Chanson Wochi's concubine quickly raised her silver wine cup to drink Chao's health. Directing a significant glance at Kao Tsung, Chao asked her hostess about her three sons.

"They are in His Majesty's service," said Chanson Wochi's concubine. "We hope His Majesty is pleased with them."

"Their work is most commendable," said Kao Tsung. "And I intend to promote their ranks three grades. Do remind me of it," he said to Chao, then turned to his uncle. "You are fortunate to have three sons. It is my great regret that our Empress has no son——"

"Since Your Majesty has five sons," Chanson Wochi interrupted, "and since the question of succession is duly settled on Your Majesty's firstborn, it is immaterial whether the Empress has an heir or not." Chanson Wochi knew that barrenness was a lawful cause for divorce.

Again and again Kao Tsung led the conversation to what was in his mind, but Chanson Wochi swerved it to another direction. Chao knew that Chanson Wochi realized what the Son of Heaven had come for, yet he shrewdly headed him off. But as long as he did not come out openly against her, there was hope.

Back in the Palace, Chao fretted. "Your Majesty should be more direct. How is anyone to know Your Majesty's mind if Your Majesty does not voice it?"

"Tomorrow I will speak to our uncle," said Kao Tsung, patting Chao's cheek.

The next day, Chao waited at the veranda when Kao Tsung returned from the audience. "What did our Imperial Uncle say?" she asked breathlessly.

"Too many weighty matters of the state to get to it," he said sheepishly. At Chao's pout, he tipped her chin and kissed her. "Tomorrow I will speak to him for sure," he promised.

Many tomorrows went by, and still Kao Tsung did not speak

[74]

to Chanson Wochi. Chao knew that with Kao Tsung's timidity and procrastination her hair would be gray before she could reach the throne, so she took the matter into her own hands. She sent word to her mother by Hung to approach Chanson Wochi's concubine to influence her husband to be on Chao's side.

Chao was impatient when several days passed and no report came from Hung. Waiting, waiting, waiting, she thought. It seemed that all her life she was waiting. She wished she could make a quick end of the Empress—a little arsenic or a sudden fall. But out of the past came Professor Hsi's advice: "Many good things come by waiting."

When Hung finally came, she learned that although Chanson Wochi's concubine had received her mother graciously and showered her with valuable gifts, nothing had come out of the visit. Chao's shoulders sagged, then straightened to attention as Hung added, "Her Grace said that a Director of the Board of Rites had visited her and offered his good services to prevail upon Chanson Wochi——"

"Aw-w-w!" said Chao surprised. "What kind of man is he?"

"Shrewd, lustful, unprincipled and ambitious. Even at seventy he is still eagerly seeking for advancement. He has unusual literary talent. His pen can make black white, white black."

"Did he prevail upon Chanson Wochi?"

"He was practically thrown out of the house. 'What is the world coming to,' Chanson Wochi said, 'when even the Director of the Board of Rites stoops to fawn upon the handmaid of the late Emperor?' "

"If that is the Imperial Uncle's attitude, we shall see."

"The Director wants Your Highness to know that Your Highness can count on his service. He will rally others in the court to support the dethronement of the Empress."

"Tell him he shall be well rewarded."

10

Long after Kao Tsung's cortege left for the Audience Hall, Chao stood on the veranda gazing in the direction of the East Wing. In the early hour before dawn, its tiered roof was a shadow in the distance; yet she could not turn her eyes away from it, because traditionally it was the abode of the Empress.

She sighed. A month had passed since her baby had died, and she was no nearer the throne. Was that sacrifice made for nothing? She hated Kao Tsung's timidity—afraid of his uncle, of the court, of his conscience. He could have made her his Empress with a brush of his pen if he had had the mettle. But he had not; and she had to create crises to prod him into action.

A faint gray appeared in the east, and the canaries in the aviary at the far end of the veranda exploded into songs. The ying-wu (parrots) in hoops along the veranda squawked. Chao listened, and then a sudden cunning came to her face. She clapped her hands for a eunuch. "Summon Hung," she said.

When Hung came, she told him in a conspiratorial tone, "Poison all the birds on the veranda."

"Even the two white ying-wu Your Highness taught to say *'Wen sou, wen sou, wen wen sou'* [ten thousand years to His Majesty]?"

"Even they."

By noon, when Kao Tsung returned, instead of the parrots' raucous "*wen sou*" an eerie silence greeted him. Startled to see two rigid white bodies dangling from the chains, he swept his eyes over the veranda. All the parrots were dead. He hurried to the aviary. Stiff little birds were all over the cage. A shudder ran through him. Had sorcery turned the Hall of Prosperity into a hall of death? He sped to the sleeping chamber to look for Chao. "Thank Heaven you are all right. Uncanny! All the birds are dead."

"The birds dead? How could that be?" said Chao, and she rushed to the veranda. "How ghastly! They are poisoned!" She turned a horrified face to Kao Tsung, "This time it is the birds; next time it could be me. Send me back to my mother, Your Majesty, that I may escape a violent death!"

Kao Tsung folded her in his arms. "No harm shall ever come to you. Whosoever imperils our Imperial Concubine imperils the Son of Heaven. Your life is my life, your death my death."

"But Your Majesty, I cannot bear a life of constant fear."

Kao Tsung sighed. If this kept up, he would have no peace of mind to attend to the affairs of the nation. He said reluctantly, "I shall issue the edict of dethronement tomorrow."

"And Hsiao Sofi, Her Majesty's ally?"

"She shall go with the Empress."

The next morning, long before the Emperor was due, guards in pheasant-plume headdresses, dark red waistcoats and embroidered trousers lined the open court of the Audience Hall. Their swords, spears and halberts gleamed menacingly in the torchlight. In the hall, ministers in robes of purple, crimson, green and blue with belts of gold, silver and brass waited in reverent silence before the dais, which was raised seven steps above the floor, guarded behind by gold dragons embossed on seven gold panels. The ministers stood according to their ranks, the purple-robed near the dais, those in black to the rear.

When the drum in the east tower and the bell in the west tower announced the arrival of the Imperial Cortege, like the graceful fall of the waves the rows and rows of officials descended upon their knees and crouched to the floor. The protocol officer then called for peacock fans to screen the throne, for

[77]

the seating of the Son of Heaven was not for common eyes to see. When the fans were removed, Emperor Kao Tsung was on his throne, behind an oblong table skirted with an embroidery of maroon and dark green dragons in purple clouds, traced in gold and silver threads.

Kao Tsung's eyes swept the minister uneasily, his face wearing a harassed expression, his shoulders hunched. It had seemed an easy task, yesterday, to decree the dethronement of Empress Wong. Now, before the court, difficulty loomed in monster size. He was worshipped as a god, loved as a father, held up as a model. How was he to let down this god-image, to permit his love for Chao to override his consideration for the dignity of the throne? Chao, after all, was his father's lady-in-waiting, while Empress Wong was of noble birth. How could he expect the court to approve the displacing of one by the other? As much as he wanted to, he could not get the decree out of his mouth. Yet how was he to face Chao without redeeming his promise? As a last resort, he summoned the three guardian ministers to come to the Palace for a conference.

Those three, Prime Minister Chanson Wochi, Preceptor Li Chi, and Deputy Secretary of the Department of State Chu Saliang, had served the Tang Dynasty since the time of Kao Tsung's grandfather. In the eyes of the people they were pillars of the nation and were revered next to the Son of Heaven. To all three the purpose of Kao Tsung's summons was obvious. Preceptor Li Chi, unwilling to displease Kao Tsung, excused himself on the pretense of sickness. He was a valiant warrior, an able tactician, with many victories to his name. Yet he had a tender heart, easily touched by kindness and friendship. Once when he was ill and the prescription had called for human beard, Emperor Tai Tsung had cut his own for Li Chi's cure. After that, neither heaven nor earth could alienate Li Chi's allegiance to Emperor Tai Tsung. Li Chi had been banished just before the late Emperor died. Later he was recalled by Kao Tsung at his ascension. This was intended by Tai Tsung to win Li Chi's gratitude and friendship for his son.

Chu Saliang, in contrast to Li Chi's giant stature, was short

[78]

and compactly built. He was a native of a tropical southern prefecture. But if he was a dwarf in body he was a giant in spirit. He never lacked courage to speak his mind to the Son of Heaven. His memorials were candid and fearless. That day on his way to the Palace, he said to Chanson Wochi, "His Majesty is determined to dethrone the Empress. To oppose His Majesty's wish is to court death. Yet, since the Late Emperor appointed me as one of His Majesty's guardian ministers, I cannot evade my duty. If I do not remonstrate with His Majesty, how can I face the Late Emperor in the next world? I intend to protest."

"I am of the same mind," answered Chanson Wochi. "Let your words be forceful, and I shall follow yours with mine." As they stepped into the reception chamber of the Hall of Timely Dew, Chanson Wochi noticed that Chao was behind a screen to the left of Kao Tsung's desk. He scowled and cast a significant glance to Saliang.

Kao Tsung, in the presence of his father's trusted ministers, found it hard to find words. He shifted in his dragon throne and looked uneasily at his uncle. Then in a low, uncertain voice he said, "Of all the failings in a woman the greatest is her inability to bear an heir. Our Empress has no son, while our Imperial Concubine has given us an heir. Our wish is to dethrone the Empress and exalt our Imperial Concubine."

"Has Your Majesty forgotten?" said Chu Saliang. "The Late Emperor on his deathbed took Your Majesty's hand and said to Chanson Wochi and me, 'I entrust my good son and my good daughter-in-law to your hands.' The Empress was chosen to share Your Majesty's throne by the Late Emperor and therefore cannot be removed without a serious offense having been committed. Besides, if Your Majesty desires to change an Empress, the choice should fall on someone worthy of this supreme position." Then he put his hu aside, removed his headdress, knocked his head on the floor and said, "Your servant in opposing Your Majesty's wish deserves death. In returning this hu, your servant humbly begs Your Majesty to spare his life and permit him to retire to his village."

[79]

"Take him out!" cried Kao Tsung to the guards, his face flushed crimson with anger and shame.

"Why not decapitate this southern aborigine?" came Chao's infuriated voice from behind the screen.

Chanson Wochi intervened. "A minister guardian cannot be executed for his censure."

"Even a minister guardian has no license to be impudent. The severest punishment is called for, lest no one respect the throne," Chao persisted.

Kao Tsung was alarmed at the unexpected turn of events. He certainly did not want Saliang to die. So he said, "Banish him to Aichow."

Chanson Wochi heaved a sigh of relief that Saliang's life was spared. In view of the tension sparked by Saliang, he kept his silence.

That disgrace for a minister of Saliang's stature set the court in turmoil. There were outspoken ministers who presented memorials to defend Saliang, opportunists who secretly worked for Chao, and others who wanted to take no side until the direction of the wind was clear. But because of the opposition, Kao Tsung postponed the dethronement, much to Chao's chagrin.

Chao noticed that among the guardian ministers Preceptor Li Chi had not openly opposed her, and she asked Kao Tsung to summon him for a secret audience. Kao Tsung received Li Chi in a garden pavilion where he could talk to him informally. "We have summoned our Preceptor for advice as a friend, not as a minister," said Kao Tsung. "Our heart is sorely troubled. . . . In view of Saliang's objection to the dethronement of Empress Wong, should this matter be dropped?"

"Why trouble to ask outsiders, since this is Your Majesty's private affair?" Li Chi understood Kao Tsung's wretched state of mind, his love for Chao and his reluctance to override his ministers. Besides, he was a military man, not a statesman. He saw no inauspicious implications for the reign in changing an Empress.

After Li Chi left, Chao stepped out from behind the screen and said, "At last we have a minister of stature on our side. Is

Your Majesty convinced it is Your Majesty's heart that dictates who shall be the Empress?"

Empress Wong heard the rumors of her dethronement but gave them no thought. Surely the court could not permit the handmaid of the Late Emperor to displace her. But when Saliang was disgraced she knew her own fate was sealed. She blamed no one. After all, it was she who had brought Chao into the Palace.

The day the edict came she was alone in her study. She leaned her pensive face against the window as she surveyed the bleak scene—roofs and trees dusted with snow and not a sign of life. The landscape was desolate like her heart. The sound of sudden footsteps made her turn to the door. Jasmine came in.

"Your Majesty, a messenger from the Son of Heaven is here . . . with guards."

Empress Wong's steps were slow but steady as she walked to the center chamber to receive the edict, which the messenger pronounced in a loud voice. She was now reduced in station to a commoner and was to be confined in a remote hall in the Palace City.

"Is Your Majesty ready to leave?" asked the captain of the guards.

"Proceed," said the Empress. She had no one to say farewell to, and this was the only time she was glad she had no children. It would be doubly hard if she had to leave them behind.

Jasmine brought a fur cape and draped it over the stately shoulders. As she tied the cords of the hood beneath Her Majesty's arrogant chin, she saw that the Empress's eyes looking into hers were suffused with gratitude, which had not been her wont in other days. Jasmine lowered her head and stepped aside, tears blurred her eyes.

Empress Wong followed the guards, her head high, not in her usual haughtiness but in majestic regality. Never had she been more the Empress than she was now.

Hsiao Sofi, too, heard the rumors of the Empress's possible dethronement. Not wishing to be involved, she secluded

[81]

herself in the West Wing to pass her days with her children.

That day, she and her older daughter were at either end of the rectangular wooden frame, each embroidering a peony petal while her younger daughter stood and watched.

"One more stitch here," she said, smoothing the crimson petal with the nail of her thumb.

The door flew open and a lady-in-waiting rushed in. "The guards!" she said. "They are in the antechamber with an edict from the Son of Heaven."

Startled, Hsiao Sofi pricked her finger. A tiny bead of blood oozed out, staining the peony petal a dark red. Without noticing the blood or the pain, she gathered her son from his desk, then her daughters, and pushed them into another room, shutting the door after them, as if a door could be a protection in a palace.

When she learned that she was to be confined with the Empress, she could not believe her ears. Had the Son of Heaven forgotten that she was the mother of his children? What had she done to deserve this? It was all because of Chao. Life had not been the same since Chao came. It was as if a sorcer's spell had been cast upon the Son of Heaven.

She ground her teeth as if to tear Chao into shreds. She tried to rise, but her children swooped down upon her. Locked in one another's arms, they wept.

The guards shoved the children aside and yanked Hsiao Sofi to her feet. She freed herself with dignity and brushed the sleeves the guards had touched.

"Think you are still the Imperial Concubine?" scoffed the brute of a guard.

Hsiao Sofi, ignoring him, looked sadly at her wailing children. "Take care of them for me," she said to her weeping lady-in-waiting; then she turned and went with the guards. As the cries of her children became fainter, her hatred for Chao increased, and she called down a curse in a loud voice: "Let Chao be transmigrated into a mouse and I a cat, that in life after life I may tear at her throat."

II

Chao's coronation was a simple affair confined to the Inner Palace, in which neither Kao Tsung nor the public participated. In the morning the edict making her the Empress came to the Hall of Prosperity, followed by the presentation of the Empress's costume: a robe of dark blue brocade woven with five pheasants in their natural colors, a crown of gold lacework with twelve sprays of filigreed flowers and five phoenixes, each dropping a string of pearls from its beak.

In the afternoon, dressed in this costume, Chao held audience with the court at the Gate of Majestic Significance; a triple, elevated, bridgelike entranceway between the courtyards of the Inner Palace and the Outer Palace, which women are forbidden to go beyond and men forbidden to enter. In the evening a feast was spread in the Inner Palace to present wives of kings, nobles and high-ranking officials to the Empress. Every detail of these functions was prescribed in the book of Rites and directed by the protocol officials. All Chao did was sit and receive their kowtows. Yet at the end of the day she was exhausted, burned out by her own excitement. The thought intoxicated her that at last she was Empress, supreme among women, subject to no one but the Son of Heaven. Besides, with Kao Tsung's weak nature, she knew she was as good as supreme.

[83]

Next day, going through the long-coveted East Wing, Chao touched a table here, a chair there, possessively. She ordered a complete renovation—tapestries changed, furnitures rearranged, potted plants and flowers brought in. There must be nothing to remind Kao Tsung of the past to prick his oversensitive conscience.

The West Wing she changed into a nursery; she could not permit another "Hsiao Sofi" in the West Wing or any other wing. If she could displace Empress Wong, someone could also displace her. Suppose Kao Tsung should favor another pretty lady? Suppose, as the years went by, he should want to select new ladies younger than herself? After all, she was four years his senior. She could not see herself sent back to the ladies' quarter or, worse still, confined like Empress Wong and Hsiao Sofi. Death would be preferable. But it would not happen to her. She would be vigilant and permit no one to oust her. She would make Hung her head eunuch so that the entire eunuch hierarchy would be her eyes and ears. She had once thought that when she became Empress her struggle would be over. Now she knew that was only the beginning.

During the following month she planned and worked with Hung to buttress her position. She reorganized the works of the ladies-in-waiting to increase their efficiency and familiarized herself with the functions of the Side-Palace: the administrative offices, the palace guards, the slaves, the schools, and the department that attended to Kao Tsung's personal needs. In each, she had Hung place a confidant to report to him.

When she was sure she had the management of the Palace firmly in her hands, she turned her thoughts to the court. She could not believe that Chanson Wochi and his faction were reconciled to her ascension. She supposed that they were waiting for Kao Tsung's affection to cool; then they would maneuver for her dethronement. She needed confidants in the court to counterbalance their influence.

Her thoughts turned to the Wu Clan, her natural allies, since their fortune was contingent upon hers. Already, because of her ascension, a posthumous title of Duke had been conferred upon her father, and her mother had been made Duchess of Splendor, her sister Duchess of Han, and the official ranks of her brothers and cousins had been promoted several grades.

A ghost of a smile tugged at the corner of her mouth. Never in their wildest dreams had her sisters-in-law thought that their taunt would become reality. But it had, and she would go to visit them riding in the very equipage with which they mocked her. She had sworn, then, to grind them under her heels. She could do it now, easily, but she wouldn't. In her position she could afford to be magnanimous; besides, she needed their help. She would elevate them to high positions, even to premierships, if they would do her bidding.

"Jasmine," she called, on an impulse. "Order Hung to prepare an equipage for me to visit my mother's house tomorrow, and to spare neither expense nor effort to make it elegant."

The following afternoon, Chao was pleased with the equipage. Leading the procession were two large gongs. The red dragon-bars from which they hung were borne on the shoulders of men in embroidered short coats and trousers. Then came a group of musicians in blue robes, with five-string lute, moon guitar, reed organ and flute; foot-guards in glittering steel armor; and cavalrymen on white horses caparisoned with red and green silk nettings. The carriage, drawn by four horses, was light green and embossed with gold pheasant plumes. It had crimson wheels and yellow silk damask curtains. Bringing up the rear were uniformed men carrying flags and pennants embroidered with dragons and phoenixes, eunuchs carrying boxes of gifts, and ladies-in waiting bearing trays of the Empress's toilet articles.

As the procession entered the Street of Tranquility Chao searched for familiar faces among the neighbors who were jostling to get a glimpse of her. She noticed that the young faces she knew before were now wrinkled, the once black hair was now mottled with gray, and she recognized in the young men the toddlers she had known. She sighed. Eighteen years is a long time.

Stepping out of her carriage she saw her two brothers and five cousins and their many sons crouched on the ground. She graciously stretched her hands to raise them up, and they, with

[85]

their heads still bent reverently, followed her into the open court. She saw her mother kneeling there with the other women. She wanted to rush over to her, but she had to follow the protocol and proceed to the Ancestral Hall.

There a eunuch placed a throne-chair in the center for the Wu Clan to kneel to their Empress. When that was done, Chao knelt to her mother as a daughter. Chao's mother held Chao's hands, too choked to speak. Chao patted her and said, "We will talk later, Mother." She turned to the rest of the clan then, singling out her sisters-in-law to inquire after their health and welfare. She bent down to a little boy holding on to Elder Sister-in-law's skirt, "And who is this?" she asked.

"Shensi," said his mother. "Born after Your Majesty entered the Palace."

She tipped his face up, with her hand under his chin. "This one will grow into a shrewd man, I can tell. And we need shrewd men in the court."

Other mothers propelled their offspring toward Chao, scolding them for their shyness and lack of manners. Chao pressed her cheek against that of a pretty girl, ruffled the hair of a boy, and promised the older boys she would recommend them to the Son of Heaven when they grew up. Sweeping her eyes over the hall, she said, "I don't see Second Uncle."

"He passed away several years ago," said her cousin.

Chao sighed. "Time does take its toll."

When a eunuch came to remind her it was the hour of the goat (1–3 P.M.), Chao said regretfully, "Even the Empress has to bow to the whim of time. It flitted when it should have crawled. Talking to you has been like old times. I wish it could be longer." To her brothers and cousins she said, "I should like to talk to you after I have a little time with Mother."

When mother and daughter were alone at last, Chao's mother cried. "You don't know how hard it has been. Your stepbrothers' fists are tighter than a dead man's. Not a single servitor in my court."

"Now, now, Mother. It's all over. You are Duchess of Splendor, with an income of your own. You can have as many servitors as you wish. And if anyone mistreats you, all you have to do is to come and tell your Empress-daughter. I shall petition the Son of Heaven to let you come to the Palace as often as you wish." Chao coaxed her mother to smile before she went to her old schoolroom to wait for her brothers and cousins.

Seated at her desk as in the days of old, she realized she had come a long way from the innocent girl of fourteen. How ridiculously naive she had been to think that her beauty could open the way to where she wanted to be. She was a different person now, wiser if harder. The relentless school of life had compelled her to live with cunning, deceit, treachery—even slaying—without a twinge of conscience. After all, she thought, power politics is a brutal game; not to kill is to be killed.

Her contemplative mood gave way to a smile of welcome as her brothers and cousins entered. "Please sit down and do not stand on ceremony. Remember, the Empress is your sister who has your interest at heart. Tell me what I can do for you—and how is the family financially?"

"We are a frugal family," said Elder Brother. "If our income is low, our expenses are, too."

"That shall not be from now on. I will elevate the House of Wu even higher than in father's time." Without mincing words she told them of her intention to grasp power and said that she needed their help. When they made no reply, her eyes bored through them. Their discomfiture told her that they disapproved of her scheme. Remembering their incorrigible rectitude and traditionalism, she realized her own lack of insight in expecting them to be her pawns. In their opinion a woman should display no ability or ambition, ask no questions, have no interest besides her household affairs. What she asked of them was revolutionary, like making the moon the sun.

Elder Brother finally broke the awkward silence. "We—I . . . will only speak for myself. I know my meager capacity is unequal to this great responsibility Your Majesty has in mind. However, Your Majesty can count on my loyalty in my present lowly position."

Chao's penetrating eyes questioned the others.

[87]

"Elder Brother has spoken for all of us," they said.

Chao forced a smile. "Your humility is most touching." With eyes flashing, she swept out of the study.

A few days later Chao's mother came to the Palace bristling like a fighting cock.

"What is it, Mother?"

"What else but your brothers and cousins? Remember the lichi you sent me? Out of my good heart I gave them some to taste. You should have seen their pleased faces as they relished that rare, delicious fruit. I told them they are tributes from the south, brought in bamboo trunks flung on each side of the postal horses and rushed to the Palace, and that because they spoil easily, no commoner in the north has ever tasted them . . . and our family would not have, either, if it had not been for you. Isn't that the truth? Yet they acted as if they wanted to throw up the lichi at me, so I threw back at them. I told them that in the old time they did not put you in their eyes, yet now their ranks have been promoted because of you.

"You know what they said? 'We are descendants of an official family who for generations have served the Empire. We expect to be placed in positions commensurable to our abilities and do not hope to be favored simply because of our relation with the Empress.' They forget that even your father's dukedom is because of you. Show them, Chao; show them you are the Empress!"

Chao's brow rose in ridges. Curse their precious pride! Where would she be if she had not swallowed her pride and groveled? It had not been easy. She had had to claw every inch of her way to reach power. Let no one belittle it!

The anger on Chao's face prompted her mother to say, "Chop their heads off, Chao."

"Don't be childish, Mother. Even the Son of Heaven cannot decapitate a person without a cause."

Chao looked up as Jasmine entered. "What is it?" she asked.

"Hung has been waiting for some time. Should he come later?"

Chao turned to her mother. "Leave them to me, Mother. You

[88]

go home and forget about them. Jasmine will take you to your carriage."

When Hung entered, Chao asked, "What have you found out?"

"Your Majesty, from the reports I gathered, the court are of three opinions. One group approves Your Majesty's enthronement, one is against, and the third wants to wait."

"For what?"

"They say that in the past when an ambitious Empress has aimed to usurp the power of the Son of Heaven she usually began by aggrandizing her own clan. They are waiting to see whether Your Majesty will do the same."

Chao chuckled, then laughed aloud. Here was a heaven-sent answer to her situation, "one arrow to shoot two yees [wild geese]." She went to her desk and brushed a memorial to be presented at the morning audience that to preclude nepotism her kinsmen should not hold positions in the capital but should be sent to distant prefectures.

12

Chao wondered if she had conceived again, since her moon-path was late. She hoped not; she needed a rest: in the four years since she had returned to the palace she had given birth to Princes Grandeur and Virtue and a princess who had died before a name had been given to her. The memory of that odious episode brought furrows to her brow. She should not think about it. What was done was done. There was no use regretting or spending energy in recriminations.

She started for the nursery, but on the way she tarried at the rock garden to enjoy the enchanting snowy scene. The camel-backed bridge was an arch of powdery white, and a glaze of ice skimmed the goldfish pond. She inhaled the brisk air, thinking that it was a beautiful day and life was good.

She entered the nursery unnoticed. The nurse was sewing; Grandeur and Virtue were bending over a goldfish bowl on a round stool. Both wore padded garments, apple green silk tunics and red silk trousers. Grandeur's hair was parted in the middle and tied into a loop on each side. Virtue's head was shaved, except for a patch of hair in the center, which was combed into a stiff braid and tied with red cord. Virtue, two but tall for his age, stuck his finger in the water. Grandeur grabbed Virtue's hand to stop him. "You'll frighten the fish." Virtue struggled loose and plunged his whole hand in.

"No, No, Virtue!" said Chao, coming toward them. She ordered the nurse to dry Virtue's hand, while she swept Grandeur into her arms, pressed her cheek against his and crooned "My little precious!"

She was partial to her firstborn. Ever since she had first entered the Palace at fourteen, she had dreamed of conceiving him. She could still feel her heart expand with joy when the midwife announced that the child was a "dragon seed." Now she held the boy on her lap and peered into his pale, delicate face. "Has he been eating well?" she asked his nurse.

"No, Your Majesty. He just will not eat," said the nurse.

"We will see about that. Perhaps some birds' nest soup will tantalize his appetite."

Virtue toddled to his mother and pushed and pulled at his brother, trying to dislodge him from Chao's lap. Chao slapped his hand lightly. "You are a little *Pa-wang* [bully]!" Then, grabbing his fat arm, she lifted him up to her other knee, thinking that this one had none of his father's meekness but all of his grandfather's dominance. Whoever was in power had better keep a sharp lookout for him.

"Your Majesty," said Jasmine, coming into the nursery, "a eunuch is waiting in the East Wing with an urgent message."

"Aw-w-w!" Apprehension leapt to Chao's face and her thought flew to Chanson Wochi. Was he trying to cross her again? As long as he was in the court she could not feel at ease. She got up abruptly and went to see what the message was.

"Your Majesty," said the eunuch, "the Son of Heaven has gone to visit Empress Wong and Hsiao Sofi in prison."

"What made him do that?"

"Your servant does not know. Probably because of a memorial. As His Majesty read it, his eyes were filmed with tears. Suddenly he called for the palanquin."

"The memorial . . . whom was it from?"

"The exiled Minister Chu Saliang."

"Go and bring it to me."

Chao frowned when it came. "Your Majesty," she read. "Your servant kowtows again to thank Your Majesty for sparing his life. Wherever Your Majesty sends him, your servant has no complaint, even though Aichow is an outlandish place, hot, humid and swampy, insects come in swarms, lizards crawl all over the walls, natives are uncivilized . . ."

"What does he expect?" Chao muttered. "He deserves decapitation."

Further on, the letter said, "Does Your Majesty remember the time the Late Emperor Tai Tsung died, and Your Majesty threw your arms around Saliang and cried?"

So, Chao thought, playing on His Majesty's tender heart to wheedle a pardon! Hmm . . . Even if he gets it, I will see that he does not reach Changan alive.

Suddenly she realized she had ordered the doors and windows of the prison blocked, with only a slit open to let in food and air, because eunuchs in the past had smuggled prisoners out of the Palace for bribe or other reasons. She could not have that happen to Empress Wong and Hsiao Sofi.

"Hasten," she said to the eunuch, "tell Hung to divert His Majesty from his visit. Say that his Empress is suddenly taken ill."

She drummed her fingers on the tea table. She knew Kao Tsung's mind had been uneasy since the dethronement. It had taken all her ingenuity to quiet him, and now Saliang's memorial had stirred up the sediment of anxiety in Kao Tsung's squeamish conscience. She asked her ladies the time again and again and strained her ears for footsteps.

A eunuch finally came running, breathless. "Your Majesty, the Son of Heaven has already been to the prison and is on his way here."

"What happened at the prison?" she asked.

"His Majesty was horrified at the blocked entrance and kept repeating, 'Not in there. It couldn't be!.' He walked to the slit and called, 'Empress! Hsiao Sofi! Are you there?'

"As His Majesty heard their voices, his face turned white. His eyes burned. Never in my years in the Palace have I seen His

Majesty so angered. Hung arrived then. His Majesty ordered him to move Empress Wong and Hsiao Sofi to a comfortable hall immediately. As His Majesty stepped into the palanquin, Hung whispered to the chair-bearers to walk slowly to give your servant the headway to report to Your Majesty."

Chao dismissed the eunuch, paced the floor, and pummeled her fist into her palm. How was she to explain this to Kao Tsung? She could deny it. She could say she knew nothing about it. She could resort to tears.

She stopped pacing when she heard Kao Tsung's footstep. She straightened her robe, put a smile on her face, and went to meet him. "Where has Your Majesty been in this fouled weather?" Your Majesty's hands are icy cold. Come and warm them at the brazier. Let your Empress take your cape."

Brusquely, Kao Tsung brushed off her hands, dropped his cape on the chair and sank into the fur-covered couch, his eyes blazing, his face knotted into a terrible scowl, and not a word came.

Chao pulled up a stool to sit at his feet and looked up with eyes wide with feigned bewilderment, "Why is Your Majesty displeased? Who has offended Your Majesty?"

Kao Tsung glared, then looked away to the ceiling.

"Is it something your Empress has done? You know I would rather die than displease Your Majesty."

"Inhuman!" he muttered. "Even a swine cannot survive in that hole."

"What hole?" asked Chao. Her face was bland and innocent, and she managed to look straight at him.

"The prison of Empress Wong and Hsiao Sofi. Horrible! No door, no window!"

"Impossible! My order was to confine them in the Hall of Eternal Peace, which is a comfortable hall. No window, no door —It couldn't be! It must be a mistake. Whoever is responsible shall be severely punished——"

"An Empress is the head of the Inner Palace," interrupted Kao Tsung. "How could this be perpetrated without your knowledge?"

[93]

"If Your Majesty deems your Empress is responsible, confine her with them—even though her heart breaks for the love of you." She covered her face and broke into sobs.

Kao Tsung tried to look away, but Chao's sobbing held his eyes. Finally he said, "You know I hate to see tears. I only want to know how this terrible thing happened."

"Does Your Majesty think your Empress could purposely do such a heartless thing?" Said Chao, between sobs. "Shouldn't Your Majesty allow your Empress time to look into it before blaming her for it?"

She stole a glance and saw his expression soften. Then she felt his hands lift her face to wipe her tears. "There, there!" he said. "No more tears."

She tossed her head loose of his hands and pouted. "I can see Your Majesty's heart is still with them. Your Majesty no longer loves me," and she began to cry again.

"You know this is not true. You know I love you and only you. But it cuts me to the heart to see them penned like . . . like . . . animals. My heart cries out in compassion."

"Then promise me you will not visit them again."

"I have no desire to. I could not, even if I wanted to, I have no face to see them." His voice was laden with guilt. After a pause he continued, "I only want them to live out their lives in comfort and dignity."

"I shall see to it myself." She turned to Jasmine. "Send for Hung."

To Kao Tsung she said, "I shall order Hung to correct this immediately. Rest assured, Your Majesty, that your Empress will get to the bottom of this and punish the culprit." Inwardly she was planning to surround Kao Tsung with her trusted eunuchs so that thereafter he would see or hear nothing she did not want him to.

After Kao Tsung left, Chao's eyes blazed with fury. The scheming vixens! Even confined within solid walls they could contrive to have the Son of Heaven visit them and cause this near calamity. If she had not had her wits about her, what might have happened to her? "They shall pay for it," she muttered. When Hung came, she ordered him to give a hundred lashes to

[94]

Empress Wong and Hsiao Sofi, have their hands and feet cut off and their bodies soaked in wine. "Let them get drunk in their bones," she said, her voice harsh with vengeance.

For fear the eunuchs might have spared the real culprits and buried unknown persons in their places, Chao went to see the bodies of Empress Wong and Hsiao Sofi before she gave instructions for their burial. She found the blocked entrance torn open, the stench from it piercing. She turned away and followed the eunuch to the ground behind the prison. Here stood two vats side by side, filled to the brim with wine, now darkened with blood. She saw two gruesome heads propped against the edges of the vats, their distended bodies submerged in reddish fluid. Hsiao Sofi's dead eyes were wide open, burning with hatred. Empress Wong's face was etched in agony, indelible in death. Chao shivered in revulsion. She wanted to retch, but she could not show her weakness in front of the eunuchs. She swallowed hard to suppress her rebellious stomach, drew her face into an inscrutable mask, then said, "Let it be known that whosoever breathes a word to the Son of Heaven shall pay with his head."

Walking back to her palanquin, she heard a caw. On a bare branch, a crow cocked its head ominously at her and cawed again. She shuddered. She believed a crow was an evil bird casting curses upon people. And she spat on the snow to dispel its malediction.

Back in the East Wing, she bathed in fragrant water, but no amount of water or scent could cleanse the contamination in her soul. She kept seeing the grotesque faces of the two murdered women, and whichever way she turned, their eyes were there staring. The tapestries became replicas of the horror scene, the ivory statues their likenesses, the candle flames the glint of their eyes. Lurking in the shadows were their faces, blurred into astronomical multiples.

As day after day the hallucination persisted, Chao decided to fill the Palace with people so that the *yang*, the living world, would overpower the *yin*, the nether world. "A time of revelry —a noisy, boisterous fête—that should do it," she said softly to herself. "Jasmine," she called. "Tell the Son of Heaven we will have a feast in the Palace to view the new dancers. Summon His Majesty's kin and my own and the nobles and their wives to attend."

At the feast, Chao forced herself to be in high spirits, laughing and drinking excessively. While the party dined, sixty child dancers filed in, accompanied by fifes, lutes, bells and cymbals. The dancers' wide sleeves, purple silk robes, and skirtlike surcoats moved like drifts of evening clouds as their black leather shoes tapped in unison. But when they came forward two by two, Chao's hands tightened on the arms of her chair, for she saw in the two leading dancers the faces of Empress Wong and Hsiao Sofi. They moved away from her, but as they reached the far end of the hall and turned to face her again, Chao stood up in spite of herself, and leaned far away from the table. She saw two fearsome heads floating in space, looming larger and larger as they came toward her. She screamed in terror, and her hands flew to her eyes; then she sank unconscious into her chair.

"Summon the physicians!" cried Kao Tsung.

The terrified eunuchs scampered in every direction, the music ceased and the dancers immobilized themselves in their poses. Chao's mother and sister, forgetting their etiquette, rushed in an unmannerly way to Chao's side. Her mother pinched the trough of Chao's upper lip with her thumb and index finger to revive her, calling repeatedly, "Chao! Chao! Come back!"

"Thank heaven she is coming to," said Kao Tsung. "What caused this sudden illness?"

Chao heard Kao Tsung's question as from a great distance. Then, as it came to her that she had fainted, she immediately took control of herself. "It is nothing," she said. "Maybe one cup of wine too much."

She retired to her chamber and dismissed everyone except Jasmine. She would let no one know of her fears. When the court physicians came, she dismissed them too, for she knew her own state of mind better than they.

When Chao was finally asleep, Jasmine, keeping watch beside the bed, sniveled quietly. She knew what was harassing Chao.

[96]

She had watched the naive girl of fourteen become a brutal, vengeful woman. She hated the change in her, yet her heart went out to Chao as to a perverse child from her own womb.

She sprang up at Chao's shrieks. "Your Majesty! Your Majesty!" she called.

Chao flung herself into Jasmine's arms. "Horrible! Horrible! They haunt me. They will not let me be!"

"Your Majesty is overwrought. A bowl of ginseng tea will steady Your Majesty and drive the nightmares away."

Although no one dared to tell Kao Tsung of the gruesome killing, the story circulated in whispers all over the Palace. In time it reached the East Palace of the Crown Prince of Loyalty. He was a shy, sensitive lad of thirteen with a nervous tic around one corner of his mouth. His mother was one of Kao Tsung's four concubines but not a favorite like Hsiao Sofi, nor from such a powerful family as Empress Wong.

Loyalty had often been slighted in the Palace. Once, when he had complained to his mother, she had advised him to keep himself in the background. "You are the firstborn," she said, "by right the first in line for the succession. But others, more powerful, coveting it, would want to harm you. Your mother would rather see you alive without the throne than dead contending for it."

Later, when Empress Wong had taken him under her wing and sponsored him as Crown Prince to prevent the succession from going to Hsiao Sofi's son, Loyalty had gained a sense of security and prestige. Now that the Empress Wong was dethroned, he felt exposed and unprotected again. When the court officials began to shy away from him, he knew the wind had shifted again.

One morning, oppressed with an inexplicable fear, he woke up earlier than usual. He heard whispers drift in from the window, as one eunuch recounted to another the murder of Empress Wong and Hsiao Sofi in gruesome details. Loyalty shivered. When the portly Eunuch Wong came to dress him, he flung himself into the eunuch's bosom and asked, "Is it true that my Empress-mother was murdered?"

Eunuch Wong put his arms around his charge. "I wish Your Highness had not heard of it," he said.

"Will she kill me too?"

"Have no fear, Your Highness. Your Imperial father will not permit it," said the eunuch; but his words sounded hollow even to his own ears.

That morning, although Loyalty bent his head over his book, his ears were cocked like that of animal, listening for the footfalls of the pursuer, and he started at the slightest sound.

At night he was afraid to go to sleep for fear he would be taken unaware. He yawned, and his eyelids drooped, but he would not let them close. The drum sounded the third watch. It was midnight, but still he forced himself to stay awake.

"There is nothing to fear, Prince." Eunuch Wong said. "I will keep watch and wake you if anything untoward happens."

Prince of Loyalty turned his sleepy eyes to Eunuch Wong, then closed them gratefully.

Eunuch Wong let down the bed-curtain, snipped the candle-wick, and sat by the bed to read. His eyelids grew heavy too, but he did not doze. Now and then he took his eyes off his book to look at the bed. A sudden motion of the bed-curtain made him lift it up. The Prince sat bolt upright, gasping in his sleep.

Eunuch Wong shook him gently. "Your Highness! Your Highness!"

Prince of Loyalty opened his frightened eyes. "Have they come for me? She will kill me, I am sure. I do not want my hands and feet cut off. I don't want to die!"

"Sh-h-h! The walls have ears. You can save your life by renouncing your succession. She wants it for her own son."

"Will she let me live then?"

"Probably, like Hsiao Sofi's son, you will be sent away from court to live in a distant prefecture."

"The farther away the better."

"Then make your intention known to your Imperial Father."

The next day Prince of Loyalty went to his father's study. Nervously he crouched at his father's feet. Kao Tsung pulled him up and put his arm around him, "What has brought you here?"

"I . . . I . . ."

"Hasn't your tutor taught you how to speak?"

Prince of Loyalty wanted to tell his father about his terror, but, warned by Eunuch Wong, he said only, "Father, I wish to renounce my succession to the throne. I know I am unworthy of it."

Kao Tsung was surprised at the perspicacity of Loyalty in divining that Chao wanted the succession for her son. But succession was the affair of the state, and he was not sure the ministers would agree, especially so soon after his contention with them in making Chao his Empress. So he said, "We will see what the court has to say."

Kao Tsung, as usual, procrastinated, until one morning Director Hsu petitioned to change the succession to the Empress's direct issue, Prince of Grandeur. Kao Tsung then made Loyalty King of Yi, with his domicile at Liangchow, and Grandeur the Crown Prince.

On the day of Loyalty's departure, he took a last look at the East Palace that for a few short years was his abode. The forsythias were in bud, and in another month the garden would be a galaxy of spring flowers, but he would not be here to see it. The emptiness of his vacated hall brought a tremor to his young face.

None of his former officials had come to bid him farewell, not even his tutor. He mounted his horse with a sigh; then he saw Eunuch Wong by the vermillion colonnade wiping his eyes on his sleeve. With the reins in his hands he lifted his fists to the level of his eyes to bid his one friend farewell.

13

Jasmine came to Chao's sleeping chamber, silent like the fall of dew. "Your Majesty," she said. "Hung is here. Does Your Majesty want to see him?"

"No, Jasmine," said Chao. "I will see no one. My mind is like an ocean lashed by storms. What is he here for?"

"To report to Your Majesty that Prince of Loyalty has left for Liangchou."

"Hm-m-m!" muttered Chao, too harassed in mind to be concerned with Loyalty at present. Later she would take care of him. She knew that to permit anyone to live who had claim to the throne was to nurture trouble for the future, like cutting the weed without digging up the root. It would be easy, in far-off Liangchou, to eliminate Loyalty without showing her hand. But . . . later.

"Your Majesty looks tired," said Jasmine. Spreading the comforter she asked, "Will Your Majesty rest in bed for a while?"

"No," Chao replied in ill humor. She dreaded the bed. Every time she closed her eyes she saw the faces of Empress Wong and Hsiao Sofi.

Jasmine took the counterpane and laid it over the couch. "Then will Your Majesty rest here?" After making Chao comfortable on the couch, she said, "I will get Your Majesty some ginseng tea."

"No. Do not leave me!" Chao cried, her face suddenly contorted with fright. She gripped Jasmine's wrist and asked, "Who is lurking in yonder corner?"

"No one; only a plum blossom plant."

"No plum blossom plant was there before."

"It was brought in this morning when Your Majesty wanted some flower to brighten the chamber."

"Take it away. It looks too much like a human form." Then, "Let it be, but do not leave me."

She sat up all of a sudden. "What is that noise?" Her eyes flew wide at the cat that leaped from the rafter and disappeared beneath the chest. "Hsiao Sofi!" she cried, her hands flew to her throat. "Kill the cat! Kill every cat in the Palace!" She collected herself and said in a low tone, "The curse is working on me, Jasmine. I am losing my mind. I must get out of this place before their evil spirits destroy me."

Chao cudgeled her brain for a place to escape. She paced the floor to drive her mind to work, and the harder she drove, the tighter she locked her hands behind her back. Up and down she paced with Jasmine watching helplessly.

Chao stood still, as she recalled what her father had once told her about the Palace in Loyang—how the pleasure-loving Sui Emperor, forty years ago, had conscripted tens of thousands of men for its construction; how its huge timbers, rare marbles and ingenious works of brass and iron had been collected from all over the empire and across the seas; how roads, canals, ships and carriages had been built for their transportation; and how the Sui Emperor had finally paid with his crown as the impoverished people had risen in revolt and flocked to the standard of Kao Tsung's grandsire. Loyang had caught her fancy then; now she saw it as a haven for her escape.

"Jasmine, petition His Majesty that I am now well enough to welcome His Majesty's visit," said Chao as she lay down on the couch.

When Kao Tsung entered, Chao pushed aside the counterpane to rise, but Kao Tsung was already beside her in a few long strides. He sat on the edge of her couch and looked at her pale, strained face. Touching the hollow cheek gently, he asked, "How is it that the physicians have not been able to cure our Empress?"

"It is not an illness that herbs can cure. It is that the water-and-earth of the Palace City does not agree with my constitution. Neither has it agreed with Your Majesty. Your Majesty's cough drags on from autumn through winter; and even now, when it is almost spring, it is still persisting. See how loosely the robe fits you now. If we could move out of this dankness to a milder, drier climate like . . . Loyang, we both would fare better. I know I would get well in no time."

Kao Tsung was silent, his eyes avoiding Chao. Finally he said, "The Son of Heaven is not like a commoner who can move as he pleases. If the Emperor moves, so must the court, and the expenditure will be so considerable that the court will surely object."

"Is the nation's coffer more important than Your Majesty's health? Besides, Loyang commands a more strategic location than Changan for a capital, protected on the north by mountain ranges, bounded on the south by the Lo River."

"We could move to the Summer Palace, on the Dragon Hill outside the East Wall; then there would be no need to move the court. It is very pleasant up there in summer."

"But not in this weather. It is in winter that Your Majesty's delicate health needs the change. As to the court, Your Majesty will be surprised how a little firmness can override their objections. Since the move is for the health of Your Majesty, who would have the audacity to oppose? In case anything happens to Your Majesty, who is to be responsible?"

Chao's reasoning so convinced Kao Tsung that he said, "I shall issue the edict tomorrow. I hope there will be no objection."

"If Your Majesty permits none, there will be none. Surely the court will put Your Majesty's well-being above all else. As for myself, the very thought of the mild weather has already made me feel better."

"But the Crown Prince Grandeur; you know, traditionally he is to supervise the court in his father's absence, and he is only five, much too young to be left alone in Changan."

"I shall ask my sister, the Duchess of Han, to move to the Palace to take care of him. I shall not be surprised if she becomes more of a mother to him than his own mother. Ease your mind, Your Majesty, I will see to everything." With an escape in sight, Chao's spirit returned and she said excitedly, "Jasmine, tell the necromancer to choose a date to start the journey as soon as the snow is melted and the mountain pass is open, and tell Hung to make the necessary arrangement."

The preparation for moving the Inner Palace and seven tenths of the court took longer than anticipated. The packing, purchasing and conscription of help, the assembling of carriages, carts, horses and camels, and the renovation of the Palace in Loyang and the travel-palaces along the road required so much time that before everything was ready Chao was too big with child to travel.

Impatient to leave, she rebelled against her woman's lot. While men wallow in their carnal pleasure, she thought, the woman's share is only frustration; or was she alone a victim of this one-sided bedroom affair because of Kao Tsung's debility? She longed for the day when she could refuse his love-demands. She conceived easily. Virtue had been born after Grandeur. Two sons were enough for her purpose; another one at this particular time was an inconvenience. She counted the months on her fingers. It would be the eleventh moon (December) before the baby would come. By then the mountain passes would be snowbound, which would mean further delay. How aggravating!

It was in the second moon, after her third son, Wisdom, was born, that the journey finally started. Encumbered with a long procession of guards, eunuchs, ladies-in-waiting, palace officials, ministers, nobles and their families, with caravans of provisions and cartloads of slaves, with the li-recording cart to measure the distance traveled and the compass cart to indicate the direction, the progress was slow, and it was the third moon when the Imperial Cortege approached Loyang. As the equipage rolled

[103]

over the Tientsin Bridge that spanned the Lo River, Chao had an inexplicable feeling of liberation, as if the water they were crossing had completely washed away her excruciating memory. Going up the wide Tientsin Avenue lined with double rows of pink cherry blossoms and green pomegranite trees, she saw that Loyang was as beautiful as she had imagined. It was a city of many gardens, of tall poplar trees and pink peonies, of lazy streams and rushing rapids. Loyang was like a young girl, frolicsome and romantic, while Changan resembled an old dowager, wise but austere.

As soon as she saw Kao Tsung and the children settled to rest, she went to look over the Palace. The library, the treasure vault, the theatre and some of the resident halls were nothing but rubble, destroyed during the overthrow of the Sui Dynasty, but the remaining buildings showed the Sui Emperor's exquisite taste, as well as his extravagance. The immense size, the beautiful proportions, the artistic carving, the colorful ceilings, all were to Chao's liking. She could well understand the Sui Emperor's obsession for building. His enthusiasm struck a corresponding cord in herself, but she would not make his mistake in overtaxing the hundred-names. A ruler should keep his ears open and listen to the heartbeat of his nation, as she had been taught by Professor Hsi. To strain the people beyond their strength was to ask for trouble. She ran over in her mind the repairs that had to be done. But she would wait till the huge expenditure incurred from moving to Loyang was forgotten. For the time being she could manage with what she had. The princes could share a hall. She hoped she would not be pregnant again this year. There just was not room for another child.

Four months later, she conceived again, and the next year, in the month of Shao Yao (the *Paenonia albi flora*), a daughter, Princess of Peace, was born. Chao said to Kao Tsung, "We need more space. I cannot put our daughter in the same hall with the boys."

"I know we are crowded, and the ruins are an unpleasant sight. I have hinted to the court that the wrecked halls should be rebuilt; but our uncle said that with two capitals, two palaces, and two courts to keep up, the treasury is almost depleted; to drain it further is inadvisable. He has conceded our need for moving; we should not go against him in this."

"Your Majesty talks as if the Imperial Uncle were the Son of Heaven!" Chao laughed good-naturedly to tone down her sarcasm. Inwardly, she was furious. Must Kao always defer to Chanson Wochi? She could never have her way as long as the Imperial Uncle was in the court. He must be eliminated; otherwise she would be as powerless as a crab with bound legs.

However, she kept her thoughts to herself. To Kao Tsung she said, "Your Empress has heard that the harvest is good this year. Perhaps the Director of the Board of Agriculture could raise the fund."

"We will speak to him," said Kao Tsung.

It took two years to build the Hall of Harmonious Jade the way Chao wanted it. It was the first building entirely her own to plan and to supervise, and during its construction she was constantly at the site to watch the artisans carve the marble that paneled the veranda, watch the painters lacquer the enormous columns a brilliant red, and watch the artists sketch medallions of multicolored flowers on the ceiling. It was smaller than the Hall of Timely Dew in Changan, but everything was done to her taste. There were the usual open court for the equipage to gather each morning, the huge reception hall, the wide veranda, the rock garden, and the living quarter.

Here the architectural alteration was noticeable. Instead of three divisions, there were only two, the Dragon Pavilion to the east with Kao Tsung's sleeping chamber, book chamber, lounge chamber, guest chambers, and the respective antechambers; the Phoenix Pavilion to the west for herself; and between them a spacious family chamber for their meals and lounging. Behind these were the service quarters.

When they moved in, Chao was as excited as a child going to her first lantern festival. She led Kao Tsung to the horizonal door in the reception hall, with its twelve panels fitted in pairs into the dowels on the high threshold. "Remember these panels?" she asked, pushing one pair open to let the light shine upon them. "Feel them. The carvings are so smooth and fine! I

[105]

took these from our old hall, which is now Princess of Peace's nursery."

"Hum," Kao Tsung responded lackadaisically.

Pointing out the gold floral chandeliers, she said, "Look, Your Majesty, doesn't the pale gold make them look like real yellow chrysanthemums? I found these in an out-of-the-way pavilion in the Imperial Park. Also these cloisonne-topped tea tables— aren't these battle scenes realistic? The Sui Emperor must have had wonderful master artisans working for him."

Kao Tsung's answer was a silent nod.

Chao excitedly took him to the west wall. "What does Your Majesty think of this? Instead of the usual tapestries I have the scrolls of calligraphies written by the Emperors of the past. I spent days going through the scrolls to pick the best of each Emperor's."

"Mmmm," said Kao Tsung, reading the scroll.

Puzzled by Kao Tsung's "Hum" and "Mmmm," Chao turned him around to face her. "Is Your Majesty displeased with your Empress's taste?"

"Far from it. It is beautiful, but . . ."

"But what?"

"I am afraid the court will think this is too extravagant."

"But Your Majesty, all these things were already in the Palace. I only chose the suitable ones to decorate this hall."

"But it is so exquisite, so elegant, that I would have a hard time explaining it to the court."

Chao sighed. She knew if Kao Tsung got worried he could sulk for a long time and thus spoil her joy, so she said, "Could Your Majesty invite the court to see it and get their reactions over with?"

A few days later, Kao Tsung opened the hall to the court. Chao was not present, for it was a man's affair. On such occasions, Chao resented being a woman, always in the background, never in the center where she wanted to be. She wanted to see the minsters' expression, but she had to content herself with waiting for Hung's report. She sat up at the sound of footfalls. "Is it Hung?" she asked Jasmine.

"It is a eunuch sent to get His Majesty's cape. The Son of Heaven is taking the ministers to see the marble lanterns in the rock garden."

Chao returned to the book, but not a word entered her mind. When Hung finally entered, she dropped her book and asked anxiously, "What have you gathered?"

"Your Majesty, the ministers compared the hall to an exquisite gem, to the abode of heavenly beings. They especially liked the idea of the scrolls—said it was an artistic and scholarly innovation."

"What did Chanson Wochi say? What did he say to the Son of Heaven and the Son of Heaven to him?"

"Nothing . . . in particular. The Son of Heaven was surrounded by the more enthusiastic ministers. Chanson Wochi stayed apart with a few other, more reserved ministers. They read the scrolls and discussed the brush-strength of each. While admiring the chandeliers, one of them repeated an old saying, 'The track of a broken carriage ahead is a warning to the one behind.' "

"Aw-w-w!" said Chao puzzled. Then "Hum" as she realized its implication.

Next day, impatient from waiting for Kao Tsung in the family chamber, Chao went to him. She saw Kao Tsung hunched over his desk and she said, "Your Majesty is working too hard. What is so important that Your Majesty forgets your midday meal?"

He tapped the memorial in his hand. "This is from the Chief Censor, upbraiding the Director of the Board of Agriculture. It says the land tax is the blood and sweat of the hundred-names. Its surplus should be a reserve for the lean years. To appropriate the fund for the Son of Heaven's resident hall is to encourage him into a habit of extravagance, which was the cause of Sui Emperor's downfall. 'The track of the broken carriage——' "

"I know," interrupted Chao. "I heard it last night before the memorial was even drafted." At Kao Tsung's surprised look she did not explain but said, "Evidently it is an indirect barb for us."

"The Censor recommended banishment. How can I banish

[107]

the Director for doing what I asked him to do? If I don't, how can I justify myself to the court, who are in accord with the Censor?"

"Your Majesty could demote him now and later recall him or even compensate him with promotion, when the incident is forgotten." Chao was sure Chanson Wochi was at the back of this, and an intense hatred burned within her. She could easily manipulate Kao Tsung to let her have her way. To be hampered by Chanson Wochi was something she could not stand. She must get rid of him without further delay.

Next day she summoned Director Hsu to the Hibiscus Pavilion for a secret conference. She saw him enter, his head bowed, his eyes lowered, his hands gripping his brass circular belt hung loosely from his waist, and she ordered "A chair for Director Hsu," then dismissed the eunuch with a wave of her hand. Her eyes went from the Director's black cloven-peak-hat to his small crafty eyes, his long horselike face fringed with white scanty beard. The Director squirmed at the long scrutiny; his knuckles paled in tension. An imperceptible sigh of relief escaped from him when Chao finally spoke. "We have long appreciated our Director's devotion. His service is so satisfactory that we will entrust him with a most confidential mission."

"Your humble servant is at Your Majesty's service."

"Our Director will agree that no one who has insulted the Empress should go unpunished; neither should his humiliation to our Director go unrevenged. We intend to remove Chanson Wochi with our Director's assistance."

"Your servant pledges his honor to obey Your Majesty's command."

"He is well respected in court, therefore his removal must be justified and our motive concealed. Perhaps . . . our Director could implicate him in a plot of treason."

The Director shuddered at the gravity of Chao's retribution, because for this unforgivable crime the punishment reached to clansmen even nine steps removed. However, he concealed his discomfiture and managed to say in a steady voice, "Permit your humble servant to look for an opportunity. It may take some time."

"We can wait." Then she added, "In view of our Director's invaluable service, we shall petition the Son of Heaven to elevate our Director to be the Chief Secretary of the Imperial Chancellery."

Three months later, Hsu received an order to investigate two minor officials accused of forming a cabal. He grasped this chance to implicate Chanson Wochi. By promising clemency, he induced the two men to sign a confession that they were instruments of Chanson Wochi in his plot to revolt. With the confession in hand, he threw Chanson Wochi in prison, then presented a devastating indictment of him at the morning audience.

"Impossible!" said Kao Tsung. "Our uncle has had some differences with us lately, but a revolt is out of the question."

"Your Majesty, your humble servant could not believe this of our august Prime Minister if the two accused had not confessed. They said his very reputation blinded their judgment, and they beg for Your Majesty's mercy to spare their lives. Since they were misled, your servant humbly entreats Your Majesty to grant their supplication. As to the Prime Minister who wilfully plotted to overthrow the throne, your servant cannot but recommend the supreme penalty."

Kao Tsung looked about the court. "What is the opinion of our other ministers?"

No one spoke, as each was afraid the ax might fall upon himself; for a minister of Chanson Wochi's stature could not be impeached unless someone more powerful than Secretary Hsu was directing from behind. But several opportunists, who, like Secretary Hsu, staked their fortune on the Empress, spoke in support of the recommendation. Confounded, Kao Tsung, as usual, dismissed the court without making a decision.

Back in his study, he paced with Hsu's memorial clutched in his hand. He read and reread the memorial but was still unconvinced. Why should his uncle revolt? If he had wanted the throne, he could have seized it the time Kao Tsung's father had died. Why wait until now?"

Chao found Kao Tsung brooding at his desk, and her arms went round his shoulders in a caress. "What distresses Your

Majesty? Since I share Your Majesty's throne, let me share Your Majesty's worries too."

Kao Tsung thrust the memorial to her. "I cannot believe it. He has no reason to betray us."

Chao gave the memorial a cursory reading, since she knew its contents. Pretending to agree with him, she said, "Indeed he has not, but . . . could it be that he fears his opposition to the dethronement of Empress Wong has offended us? How unfortunate if he does; how fortunate for Your Majesty that the plot is discovered."

"You think fear could have perverted our uncle to betray us?" asked Kao Tsung with disbelief.

"What else could Your Majesty suggest?"

"It could be calumny. My father once warned me not to let slander come between our uncle and ourselves, as many are jealous of his power and wish to be rid of him."

"Whosoever dares to malign our uncle deserves the supreme penalty. Your Majesty must look into this. Shouldn't Your Majesty order another minister to review the case?"

"I was just thinking of that," said Kao Tsung. "I shall appoint . . . Judge Huang . . . No . . . Judge Ting . . . perhaps . . ."

"Your Empress has heard Li Nienfu is a loyal, fair, judicious magistrate."

"Then we shall appoint Li Nienfu."

Chao heaved a sigh, as Li was an accomplice of Hsu's.

Li petitioned to have two other judges sit on the bench with him, but he saw to it that they were of his clique. He delayed the indictment till the case was no longer in the center of the court's attention.

However, even with Li affirming the accusation, Kao Tsung refused to sentence his uncle to the supreme penalty but banished him to Kweichow instead. This displeased Chao, for nothing short of Chanson Wochi's death could vouch for the safety of her power. She decided to bide her time, but die he must.

The day before Chanson Wochi was to depart for Kweichow, Chao's brow creased into a frown. The hundred-names revered Chanson Wochi as much as the Son of Heaven, and tomorrow he would be exposed to them on the street. Would the sight of

[110]

him incite them to demand a reprieve, or even stir up a riot? Drumming her fingers on an open book, she ordered, "Jasmine, tell Hung to send word to Li Nienfu to get the prisoner out of Changan before the break of dawn. Plant a confidant among his guards. Order them to take the unfrequented bypaths and permit no one to come in contact with him."

The next morning, before anyone was astir, Chanson Wochi, with cangue round his neck and shackles on his wrists, was escorted out of the city gate by two guards. He was a changed man—his shoulders were stooped; his hair was completely white; his eyes were epigrams of tragedy. The commutation of his death penalty to banishment did not lift him. He knew he was a ruined man whether dead or alive.

The rugged journey on foot was slow and laborious. It was late summer when he and the guards started but autumn when they reached his destination, a one-street village beside a deep ravine in mountainous Kweichow. The guards reported him to the local post, then billeted him in a hut facing the chasm. They had taken compassion on the old man and befriended him during the journey. Now they removed his cangue and shackles and bade him farewell. With blurred eyes Chanson Wochi watched them cross the bamboo bridge spanning the ravine, watched them recede out of sight on the narrow path chiseled from the mountainside. They were returning home and he was left behind. He had never dreamed that he would envy a mere guard.

He surveyed the perpendicular cliff imprisoning him from across the chasm, listened to the water down the gully dashing over the boulders to join the Yangtse River to the sea, watched the native Miao tribe, large-boned, handsome, but illiterate and uncultured, with whom he had nothing in common. An indescribable desolation descended upon him; he would be friendless in this rugged place.

Yet Chao could not permit him to live, even in this remote village. She sent a judge to retry the case and sentence him to hang himself before the break of another dawn. That evening Chanson Wochi, after burning his writing, sat and watched the tears of the candle drip, then flow rapidly down its side, thinking that his own life, too, was burning low and tears were

[111]

flowing fast. His thought turned to his colleague Chu Saliang, whom he would soon meet in the next world. Would Saliang forgive and understand that remorse was cutting him like a scythe? Why had he not backed Saliang's protest with his own? Fear? Expediency? Poor judgment? Whatever it was, he could not escape the blame of permitting his Imperial Nephew to fall into the clutch of a vicious, ambitious woman. What false security he had entertained! He should have known she was coiled like a snake waiting for an opportune time to strike.

It was the fourth watch and he was to die before the fifth. He listened to the night watchman's drum and gong as to the tolling of his knell.

On the watchman's next round, all was quiet in Chanson Wochi's hut. Only the rapids roared and dashed, chanting the requiem for a lonely, disillusioned old man.

14

Two months after Chanson Wochi died, Kao Tsung suddenly took ill. Chao was having her hair dressed when Jasmine came to inform her of it. "Your Majesty. The eunuch says that while His Majesty was adjusting his diadem he suddenly staggered. Before the eunuchs could help him to his dragon bed, he swooned."

Chao waved aside the hairdresser and hastened to Kao Tsung's sleeping chamber, her hair hanging to her waist. She knelt by his bedside and called in a low, soft voice, "Your Majesty." No response. "Merciful Buddha," Chao prayed. "Make him well."

She slipped behind the screen when the physicians came. There she listened to their diagnosis and their decision to perform acupuncture. After an interminable wait she heard Kao Tsung groan, and she herself heaved a sigh of relief. After they were gone she went to Kao Tsung. "Does Your Majesty feel better? Your Majesty has given your Empress the fright of her life." She stayed till Kao Tsung had taken his herb medicine before she went back to her own chamber.

At her dressing table Chao stared into the mirror unseeing, her mind on more consequential matters. Kao Tsung's illness alerted her to the precariousness of her position. If he should die, with four other sons older than her own, there would be a mad scramble for the throne. Who could she count on to support Crown Prince Grandeur? Perhaps even the opportunist, Director Hsu, would shy away. She had to cultivate the court's loyalty to herself and grasp the rein in her own hands.

She had made a start by being with Kao Tsung often in his book-chamber to familiarize herself with the affairs of the nation. She had even helped him make decisions which otherwise he would procrastinate over for hours. Sometimes, when a simple solution eluded him, she wondered why she was not the ruler. She would be in her right element, like a dragon in the expanse of the sky, like a whale in the depth of the ocean. She saw Kao Tsung's indisposition as an opportunity to get her wedge in for governing, and she congratulated herself on her foresight in eliminating Chanson Wochi, who would surely be an obstacle.

When her hair was done, she went again to Kao Tsung's chamber. Touching his forehead she said, "Your Majesty's brow is moist. A good sign. The toxin is out of the system."

Kao Tsung gathered his worried brow and said, "The Mongolians——"

"Do not bother about them at this time," interrupted Chao. "I know they threaten the border, but permit Your Empress to take care of it for you. The court could be summoned to report and get their directions here at the reception hall. In matters of small consequence, your Empress could dispose them; in matters of importance she could refer to Your Majesty for decision. This way Your Majesty's health will not be unduly strained nor the affairs of the nation neglected. Shall your Empress issue an edict to this effect?" With Kao Tsung's nod, Chao left for his book-chamber.

On her way she said to a eunuch, "Tell Hung to prepare the reception hall for me to receive the ministers, and summon the Keeper of the Seal."

When he came with a yellow brocaded box containing the seal, Chao said, "Leave the seal here. We have use of it. You may go." He hesitated; it was his duty never to let the seal out of his keeping.

"We said you may go," Chao repeated. Her sharp voice and penetrating eyes so intimidated him that with trembling hands he placed the box on the desk, then backed out of Chao's presence.

In the reception hall, a phoenix throne was placed on a dais behind a twelve-paneled screen. Eunuchs were stationed to transmit memorials to the Empress and palace guards were placed along the walls and in the open court. As the ministers arrived, they questioned each other with their eyes, but no one spoke. When Chao was announced, they crouched before the screen, concealing their astonishment from Hung's searching eyes.

"The Son of Heaven is indisposed with severe vertigo," commenced Chao. "His Majesty does not wish to delay affairs of importance; therefore petitions and memorials are to be brought here for decision. His Majesty is worried over the Mongolian situation. Will our Prime Minister report the latest development?"

"Your Majesty, the tribe is restless and there have been skirmishes along the border. If not attended to immediately, it could develop into a major war. The ministers have advanced two opinions. One is to punish them with a speedy expedition; the other, to bribe them into submission. As yet the Son of Heaven has not made his decision."

"An expedition would be foolish if it could be avoided. Send twenty cartloads of valuables to the Mongolian Chief and confer upon him the title of Right Brave Marshall General, Lord Keeper of Border Peace. Select an eloquent envoy to go with the gifts and to make it plain to the Chief, much as we value his friendship, we value a peaceful vassal even more; and we would not hesitate to annihilate anyone disturbing our border with all the might of our Empire. At the same time inform our generals to be on the alert in case our gifts are not accepted." She then called on the head of each board to report. She listened, asked questions, weighed the facts, then made her decisions.

Chao went through the pile of memorials painstakingly, not wanting to make an error in her first attempt to rule. After they were finally dispatched, she sent for Hung, to hear his report.

"Your Majesty," said Hung, "the court was surprised at Your Majesty's skill in handling the affairs of the nation and the expeditious disposal of so many pending issues in one audience."

"But tell me of the dissident opinions."

"The Deputy Secretary of the Secretariat quoted an old saying, 'Inability is virtue in a woman.' He thinks an able Empress is inauspicious for the nation, as she could overshadow the Son of Heaven."

"Aw-w-w," was all Chao said, but the Deputy Secretary's penetrating insight alerted her to keep a close watch on him.

In the third moon of the next year Kao Tsung held audience again. It exhausted him, and he hurried to Chao as soon as it was over.

"How did it go?" Chao asked.

"I am out of touch. The many knotty, confusing issues make my head throb with pain."

"Then lie down and rest. Your Majesty must not overexert yourself. Why not let your Empress continue to read the memorials for you?"

"But you are big with child and it is almost time . . ."

"Three more moons yet. Besides, it is of no consequence. What is important is Your Majesty's health."

In time the court learned that although it was Kao Tsung who sat on the throne, it was Chao who made all the decisions. But since it was far easier to work with the decisive Empress than the procrastinating Emperor, they proffered no objection. In the beginning, Kao Tsung enjoyed his leisure. He read, composed poems, played chess, watched ball games, and practiced his calligraphy. But as time dragged on, idleness began to irk him, especially when he saw very little of Chao, who spent hours in her book-chamber and left him entirely to himself. On rare occasions when they got together, he found that she no longer catered to his wishes but was dominant and authoritative as if she were the Son of Heaven.

One evening when he was reading by the candlelight, his

[116]

loneliness depressed him. He looked up from his book and saw no one but the cringing eunuchs. Their very sight aggravated him. He wanted to have young ladies-in-waiting around him, as he had before.

His thoughts wandered to that happy night on the hilltop with Chao. She was lying on the soft pine needles, and with the moonlight etching pine tree shadows on her bare bosom she was a lovely sight. He could feel again her arms reaching up to him, her lips pressing his. He pushed back his chair and headed for Chao's book-chamber.

Chao was bending over a map on her desk when Kao Tsung entered. From time immemorial, the protection of the vast boundary extending from the sea to Tibet and India was the most difficult task facing every ruler of the Empire. Now it faced her. It was impossible to station an army along the entire border, and the uncivilized tribes could not be trusted to respect a treaty. She had to treat them like children, sometimes whipping them into submission with a crushing military expedition, sometimes playing one tribe against the other. So far her tactful diplomacy had kept the border in peace. Now the Manchurians were upsetting it.

She ignored Kao Tsung as her finger kept tracing the map. She knew what he wanted, but to demand her love at this time irritated her. How could he expect her to play a sweet, dutiful wife when there was so much on her mind? When she finally looked up, her face was hard, her voice brittle. "What does Your Majesty wish?"

Kao Tsung's sensitive face fell, his burning eagerness of a moment ago frozen into icicles. Too hurt to trust his voice, he turned and went away without a word, his eyes wells of deep pain.

Later in the evening, Chao's mother sent a bowl of meat paste and some home-brewed wine to the Palace, two specialties of the House of Wu that Chao and Kao Tsung liked. Jasmine felt the bowl and asked, "It is still warm. Will Your Majesty have some now?" At Chao's nod she set two places on the table.

"Jasmine! Who is the other place for?" asked Chao.

[117]

"The Son of Heaven likes——"

"The presumption! Clear it away. I am in no mood to humor the Son of Heaven after a day's hard work."

Jasmine beckoned Spring Willow, a new lady-in-waiting, to clear off the dishes.

"Wait," said Chao to Spring Willow. She spooned some meat paste onto the plate, "Take this and a jug of wine to the Son of Heaven."

Spring Willow's tilted eyes widened in awe. To see the Son of Heaven was to see a god, and she was to wait upon him. In the antechamber she refused to surrender the tray to the eunuch. "It is Her Majesty's order that I take this to the Son of Heaven."

With a lift of his brow the eunuch opened the door to let her in. Spring Willow found Kao Tsung at the table, his elbows propped, his chin on his locked hands. Noiselessly she crossed the chamber to kneel at his feet. Then, gathering her courage, she said in a shaky voice, "Your Majesty . . ."

Kao Tsung turned. For a moment, he thought the roundish, ivory face was Hsiao Sofi. "Who are you?"

"Spring Willow, Her Majesty's lady-in-waiting."

"And she sent you with these?" Kao Tsung laughed, a bitter, sardonic laugh. So he was to be palliated with a dish of meat paste and a jug of wine. Then a mischievous smile crossed his face. It had been a long time since he had been waited upon by a pretty young lady like this, and why not make the most of it? He propelled her backward to the other side of the table and down into a chair. "There. Now you shall eat and drink with the Son of Heaven." He ordered his eunuch to set another place. When he saw Spring Willow's dumbstruck face, he said, "Have no fear. The Son of Heaven is but a lonely man. He does not want to be feared. He wants to be loved." At Spring Willow's blush, he laughed, "How lovely! Your name should be Spring flower. Drink, Spring Flower."

With a few sips of wine Spring Willow began to relax. Encouraged by Kao Tsung, she told him of her life in Soochow before she had entered the Palace. When the jug was empty Kao

Tsung came to her on unsteady feet and led her to the dragon-bed, his hands fumbled around her waist to untie her sash.

The candle had burned low and the imperial chamber was dim and shadowy. Spring Willow stole down from the bed and dressed stealthily. She smoothed her hair, cast a tender glance at the sleeping Son of Heaven, then tiptoed to open the door. She saw a mean-faced, cruel-eyed eunuch staring straight at her. Beside him were two others, equally malicious-looking. Frightened, she tried to back into the imperial chamber, but a heavy hand clamped down on her mouth and two steely arms lifted her from the floor and carried her to the Side-Palace.

Next morning Spring Willow was chained to the ground where once Chao herself had been chained; and in the chair where once the dancing master had sat, sat Chao. Her eyes swept the faces of the ladies summoned to watch, and in the silence her voice sounded harsh and awesome. "Whip her . . . to death."

Jasmine pleaded at Chao's feet. "Spare her, Your Majesty. I am to blame that Spring Willow was sent to the Son of Heaven."

Chao ignored her and signaled the eunuch to proceed. Then, ordering Hung to oversee the whipping, she left.

15
૨

It was a beautiful day. Kao Tsung, wanting to stroll in the Park with Spring Willow, ordered his eunuch to fetch her. The eunuch hesitated, then scurried to Chao for instruction. He returned to say that Spring Willow was ill.

Kao Tsung went to the Park alone. He found spring everywhere—peach blossoms blooming, butterflies flitting, and the air redolent with the scent of many flowers, and spring began to pulse in his veins. He saw a young lady reach for a bunch of purple lilac, and the sight of her bare arms made the years roll off his back. He felt like seventeen instead of thirty-seven. He strode toward her. But when the lady saw that it was the Son of Heaven, she dropped the lilac and disappeared.

Kao Tsung sauntered to the bridge that spanned a small lotus pond. He leaned on the vermillion rail to watch the lotus leaves, some large, holding liquid pearls of dew, others half opened and curled on the edges. Following the voices he heard coming from behind the willow tree, he saw two ladies reaching for the lotus leaves with a long bamboo pole. One quietly slipped away; the other flung the pole in the pond and was about to run when Kao Tsung stopped her. "Why is everyone running away from the Son of Heaven?" he asked.

"Please, Your Majesty. Spare your handmaid's life. Your

handmaid does not want to be whipped to death like Spring Willow."

Kao Tsung stumbled to a bench and dropped his face in his hands. "How horrible!" he muttered. "How ruthless! What has come over her?" Where was that sweet, charming Chao whom he loved and who, he thought, loved him? Had he been fooled? Was it not love at all? Had she bewitched him only for his throne? And he had dethroned Empress Wong for her? His remorse made him physically ill. He swallowed hard to keep down the nausea. His head throbbed and ached.

Back in his study, he brooded over the course of his marriage. Somewhere along the way it had changed—or rather Chao had changed, so changed that he could hardly recognize her as the same person, this woman so distant, unapproachable, dominant and cruel.

He had been piqued for some time. This latest episode clinched his decision to be rid of her. But whom could he trust? Even his own eunuchs were in her confidence, lying to him and spying on him. How cleverly and insidiously she had isolated him from the court, with no one to turn to in time of need. He had trusted her with his power and she had used it to envelop him. He should have known that duty and power were inseparable. In shirking one factor he had lost the other. He went down the list of ministers in his mind and paused on the Deputy Secretary of the Secretariat, who, he sensed, was not wholly in favor of a woman's meddling hands in the government.

The next day, after the morning audience, Kao Tsung summoned the Deputy Secretary to the antechamber of the Audience Hall. He dismissed his attendants and lowered his voice. "Your Emperor is like a fly in a spider's web," he said, and he told him of the extent of Chao's domination.

"If Your Majesty is displeased with the Empress, all Your Majesty has to do is to depose her," said the Deputy Secretary.

"Then draft a mandate to that effect," commanded Kao Tsung.

The Deputy Secretary composed the declaration of repudiation immediately after he reached home and presented it to His Majesty at the next audience in a sealed memorial, which traditionally only the Son of Heaven could open, and Kao Tsung took it to his study to read.

One of the eunuchs informed Chao of the sealed memorial and she swooped down upon Kao Tsung like a bird of prey. She snatched the paper from him and began to read it. She chuckled in contempt. "Depose the Empress! What does this mean?"

Kao Tsung exploded. "The Son of Heaven can dethrone or enthrone whomsoever he pleases."

"Not without reason."

"Your jealousy and your cruelty. You whipped Spring Willow to death."

"As Empress I can punish anyone in the Inner Palace for misconduct."

"She only obeyed my command. Even a farmer with a good harvest can have as many concubines as he wishes, and is the Son of Heaven to have no one to warm his bed? You have neglected your duty as a wife and thus have failed as an Empress, too."

"Failed as an Empress?" Chao sneered. "Who do you think burns the candles late into the night so that Your Majesty can sleep in peace? Who bears the burden of the reign so that Your Majesty's delicate health may be spared its weight? Does Your Majesty not know how often your Empress lies awake at night racking her brain to solve the unsolvable problems? Does Your Majesty not know what long hours she works at her desk forgetting to eat and drink? And is this Your Majesty's gratitude?" She slapped her palm upon Kao Tsung's desk and peered at him with a murderous squint.

For a long moment they stared at each other. Kao Tsung's eyes were the first to drop, for he saw in Chao's deadly glint a demon that would stop at nothing. He shuddered at what she would do to him. Poison? Assassination? His hands began to sweat and his determination ebbed. He knew that if he yielded now he would be tightening his own fetters, never to be freed of her. Yet he was born not to fight but to yield. He could not do what it was not in him to do.

"Besides the Deputy Secretary of the Secretariat," came

Chao's hard, metallic voice, "Who else in court would agree to such a mandate?"

Without waiting for an answer, Chao suddenly softened her voice, for as smoothly as the court had worked with her, they would not accept her outright reign. She still needed her imperial spouse as her facade. "Your Majesty has been ill advised by the Deputy Secretary. Let us forget our differences." She tore the mandate in two, crumpled the pieces in her hands, and stalked out of the room.

Before Kao Tsung realized that she was gone, she was back again. She stood looking at him contemplatively, then said, "To prevent the ministers from giving Your Majesty further inadvertent advices, hereafter your Empress will accompany Your Majesty to the Audience Hall."

"That is unheard of!"

"Your Majesty forgets that there were other Empresses in the past who listened to the affairs of the nation behind a curtain."

The next morning, Chao sat behind the throne and wiped her moist palms on her perfumed handkerchief again and again. What if the court should object to her presence there?

She scrutinized the minister's faces through the gauze curtain, but they were impassive, with no indication of their reaction. She wished the audience would draw to a close. If a precedent was established today, she did not have to worry about tomorrow or hereafter. Had time stopped? Would it never end? When it did, she heaved a sigh of relief that another barrier was crossed.

To hold her power she knew she must win the hearts of her hundred-names with a good reign. She solicited men of ability to serve in her court and went out of her way to show respect and consideration to outstanding ministers. As for those who manifested the slightest sign of disloyalty to her, she disposed of them without mercy. In spite of this, men of integrity made their way to the capital, as they recognized in Chao a ruler of perspicacity and discrimination.

In the following years, supported by capable ministers, she promulgated statutes to improve farming and mulberry planting, to reduce tax and labor conscription, to restrict waste and immorality, and to economize public spending. She encouraged expressions of public opinion, forbade calumny, increased the emolument of higher officials, and reevaluated the low-ranking officials for promotion.

Her skillful diplomacy ensured a long stretch of uninterrupted peace. There were skirmishes at the border here and there, and troops were sent to quell recalcitrant tribes occasionally, but there was no major war. This gave Chao time to turn to peaceful pursuits. She encouraged commerce by keeping the trade routes open. Caravans came from Siam and India, ships from Korea and Japan. She summoned men of letters to the Academy of Literature to compose and compile literary works; she nurtured poetical talents to foster the flowering of a golden age; she encouraged women's education by giving recognition to female authors, enlarged the dormitories for foreign students to three thousand beds, and increased the books in the library to three hundred thousand volumes. Even the gods seemed to favor her reign by bestowing bountiful harvests upon the nation; and she had granaries built in all the big cities, filling them to the brim. "Every grain is nurtured with the sweat of the peasants," she said. "And Heaven would surely punish us if we, in our foolishness, do not provide for the lean years." With prosperity, her hundred-names were content, and they referred to her and Kao Tsung as the "Two Holies."

16

Chao was proud of her reign and wished she could say as much of her private life. Her relationship with Kao Tsung deteriorated steadily, then came to a head in the year her sister died. Her sister left a son and a daughter. The son was made heir to the Wu Dukedom when Chao's brothers and cousins were exiled. He was a libertine living in sin with his grandmother. Chao, indulgent to her mother, closed her eyes to this. The daughter, the Duchess of Way, was a homely girl looking much younger than her sixteen years. Now, left alone, she was summoned to Loyang to live with Chao.

When the Duchess arrived, Chao was preoccupied with the Korean expedition, and she left the girl to herself. When the expedition was finally over, Chao relaxed in the garden, admiring the chrysanthemums. Suddenly she paused and strained her ears at the sound of a girl's voice and a man's suggestive laughter. She hastened toward the pavilion. Through the green cascade of willow trees, she saw Kao Tsung lying on the bench that verged the veranda, his head pillowed on the Duchess's lap, with her hand caressing his face. Something in the girl's face told her they had known love between them. Her breathing quickened. Her own niece, doing this to her! She waited till her heaving bosom was still, and then approached them with an innocent smile.

The Duchess of Way's body stiffened, then shook with fright, for behind Chao's affable smile were the rapier points of her overpowering eyes. The tremor of the Duchess's body made Kao Tsung sit up. He touched his head sheepishly and said, "My head is heavy and our niece is giving me a massage."

"You should have summoned the physician," said Chao.

When the Duchess of Way was sent to her room, she was in misery. Had her aunt guessed their secret? Would her aunt kill her as she had killed Spring Willow? She shivered, wishing she had not heard the terrible story of Spring Willow's death.

The next morning, awakening from a restless sleep, the Duchess stretched her tired body and lifted her bed curtain listlessly. She let it drop at once, for seated by the table facing her was the notorious Nurse Chang, tall and husky like a man, with the milk pouches of a cow. It was her abundance of milk that brought her to the Palace to be wet nurse to the Princess of Peace, and later she had been retained as a maid. Her blind devotion to the Princess and the Empress and her callous cruelty to the others made her a useful henchman to Chao.

Nurse Chang lifted the bed curtain and stared down at the Duchess. "The Empress has ordered my humble self to wait upon Your Highness," she said in mockery.

"I . . . I thank Her Majesty . . . but I . . . I already have ladies-in-waiting . . ."

"They are assigned to other duties," Nurse Chang interrupted. Thenceforth she followed the Duchess more closely than the Duchess's own shadow.

The Duchess was still ordered to appear in the Palace banquets, but with no more freedom than in the solitude of her room, for Nurse Chang's eyes were like poniards against her ribs. Kao Tsung noticed the Duchess's silent pleading, but he knew that the slightest attention from him would hasten the end of the Duchess's life.

Then, the following spring, Tai Shan was consecrated as a holy mountain and prefects throughout the nation were summoned to attend the sacrificial rites. Afterwards, they accompanied Their Majesties back to Loyang to report on their respective prefectures and to present tributes indigenous to their localities.

Going through the list of tributes, Chao came upon those from her cousins expatriated to Szechuen years ago. They were netted silk, hand-woven cloth, sugar, candied plums, wine, and two jars of meat paste, the Wu specialty.

"Bring us the tributes from Szechuen," she told the eunuch, as a scheme evolved in her mind. She had never forgiven her cousins for not cooperating with her when she needed them. Now she could borrow their hands to kill the Duchess, thus killing two wild geese with one arrow.

Chao distributed the silk and the cloth to the various ladies-in-waiting she wished to favor. Then she ordered Nurse Chang to take a bolt of silk and a portion of the meat paste to her niece. "See that it is the last thing the Duchess will ever eat," she said.

After a long while, a eunuch came and said in an agitated voice, "Your Majesty, the Duchess of Way is dead."

"Dead!" she said in feigned surprise, then went straightway to the Duchess's suite. She asked the court physician, coming out of the Duchess's sleeping chamber, "What caused this sudden death? We have not heard of any illness."

"There is arsenic in the meat paste, Your Majesty," said the physician.

"Arsenic in the meat paste! Then it was intended for the Son of Heaven." She turned and said to her eunuch, "Order the Gold Guards to arrest the prefects from Szechuen." Then in a sorrowful tone, she said, "Poor Duchess. To have died in the place of the Son of Heaven."

When Kao Tsung heard of the Duchess's death, he knew it was Chao's doing. Her ruthlessness horrified him. He felt responsible for the Duchess's death and he shut himself in his chamber to drown himself in remorse. In the afternoon, he did not go to play chess with his favorite son, the Prince of Virtue, as was his daily wont.

Virtue was a handsome boy of eleven, with his grandfather's heroic mein and powerful physique, his father's benevolence and rectitude, his mother's intellect and iron will. He was also gifted with an extraordinary memory. Kao Tsung, to show him off, often made him recite classics before his ministers.

When the drum beat the hour of the monkey (3–5 P.M.) and still Kao Tsung did not come, Virtue said to his eunuch, "Find out why His Majesty is not here yet."

The eunuch left but presently returned. "Your Highness, His Majesty is busy today."

"About what?" asked Virtue sarcastically; he knew it was his mother who ruled the nation. He resented his mother's dominance over his father, reverting the natural order of Yang (man) and Yin (woman).

When several days had gone by and still his father did not come, he went to his father's study. He saw his father hunched in his chair with a book in his hand which he did not read, his eyes vacant, his thoughts far away. "Father . . ." he called, then ran to his father's outstretched arms. "Why have you not been to see me?"

With a deep sigh, Kao Tsung said, "There are times when my thoughts are like tangled flax. I need solitude to comb them out."

They looked up together as the door was flung open and Chao stormed in. At the sight of his mother's scowling face, Virtue slipped to the door and was about to leave when he heard her say in her harsh, metallic voice, "You have not shown your face in the audience for days. What will the court think of their sovereign who neglects his duty in an irrational whim of moodiness?" She pounded her fists on her husband's desk to emphasize her words.

Virtue wanted to cry at the sight of his father's strained, humiliated face. How could she do this to him? How could she berate the Son of Heaven? His eyes blazed; his hands gripped his belt till they hurt.

"There is fighting in Manchuria again," Chao continued. "It would be well to show your face at the audience tomorrow." She stalked out of the chamber and came face to face with Virtue. Mother and son stared at each other in silence. Then Chao shut the door after her with a bang, but she could not shut out Virtue's face; hatred, resentment and reproach were all so plainly written there.

When Virtue was fourteen and Chao forty-six, there was another confrontation between mother and son. Chao's mother
died, and because she had laid so much importance upon osten-
tation Chao wanted the funeral to be something her mother
could boast of in the spirit world. She wanted her sons and
daughters to be dressed in Taoist robes in the funeral procession. That day a eunuch brought to Virtue's chamber a
folded Taoist robe topped with a black headgear that looked like
the roof of a house.

"Her Majesty wishes Your Highness to wear this for the
funeral," said the eunuch.

Virtue lifted the robe, looked at it, then hurled it over the head
of the eunuch. "No! I will not look ridiculous before the court
and the foreign emissaries."

The eunuch folded up the robe and was about to leave when
the Prince's attending eunuch took him aside and whispered,
"Leave it here. Perhaps the Son of Heaven could persuade the
Prince."

But the eunuch's report aggravated Chao and she came to
Virtue's chamber herself. When she saw father and son sitting
side by side on the couch, their intimacy further aggravated her
and ridges rose on her forehead. "What is this I hear?" Indicating the robe on the chair she ordered, "This you shall wear. It
is my command."

Prince of Virtue stood up at his mother's entrance, looked
defiantly at her and said, "It is not said in the Book of Rites that
a prince should wear a Taoist robe in mourning for his maternal
grandmother."

"It does say that a son obeys his mother. If you have not
learned this filial duty you shall be made to learn." She grabbed
a long-handled duster to thrash the Prince, but Kao Tsung
stepped between them. Chao glared at Kao Tsung. "Is this the
way you discipline your son?"

"He will obey. Leave him to me."

"See that he does." Tossing the duster on the table, Chao
swept out of the room.

17

After working late one evening, Chao rubbed her tired eyes and went to the antechamber. She found the eunuch dozing on the floor and Jasmine embroidering on a square frame propped between two tea-tables. Jasmine covered the frame with a blue cloth while her foot reached out to wake the eunuch.

"What are you embroidering?" asked Chao. She lifted the cloth and saw a heart-shaped breast cover in imperial yellow satin with the character of longevity repeated in purple embroidery along its border.

"It's for Your Majesty's fifty-second birthday," said Jasmine.

"Fifty-second birthday," Chao repeated. "How swiftly the years roll by." She was thinking that even if she should live to be a hundred, half of it was gone. She walked the long corridor to her sleeping chamber with no other attendants besides the eunuch lighting her way with an octagonal gauze lantern and Jasmine following behind.

When in bed, she said to Jasmine, "Leave the bed curtain up and hand me that book."

"It's late, Your Majesty."

"Just for a little while. Go to bed and do not sit up for me."

Soon Chao yawned, let drop her book and stared at the ceiling of her bed curtain. Fifty-two . . . eleven years since she had first governed behind the throne. And much had happened in that time. Secretary Hsu and General Li Chi were dead. They had served her well, and she had decreed that their official emolument be granted to their families for ten years.

Then, before she realized it, her three sons had grown up. Busy with the affairs of the nation, she had had little time for them, while Kao Tsung had all the leisure to mother them. Their closeness to him piqued her. She wanted their love and confidence too, but somehow there was a gulf between her and them too wide to bridge. She was nostalgic for the time when they were little, when love was unalloyed with politics. Now she saw them through the eyes of a ruler. Would she be able to rule through the son as she did the father? That was the question.

Thank Heaven for Princess of Peace! At least her daughter was close to her, and between them there was no conflict of interest. She knew Princess of Peace's plump, squarish face was not beautiful, but the girl had intelligence and was as jealous as she of the powers denied to women. Chao could bare her mind to her daughter as to no one else. She knew it was time to arrange the Princess's betrothal, but she wanted to keep her daughter with her for as long a time as possible.

Her thought drifted to Kao Tsung. She noticed that he had aged. He had never been strong, but now at forty-eight he was already an old man, frail like a sere reed that would snap at the lightest touch, his vitality sapped, his skin dried, his hair and beard gray. She would outlive him, she was sure; then the throne would go to Grandeur, her firstborn, whom she loved above her other sons, but she did not really know him well, as he had been left in Changan as a representative of his father since he was five. They had corresponded often and Chao had tried to instill in him obedience to herself. But how much could she know from letters? She had enjoined the ministers in Chang-an to send minute reports of him. Lately the reports had been excellent, which should make a mother happy and proud in any ordinary sense. But Chao was not an ordinary mother. The

[131]

better the reports, the more worried she was. She wished it were spring so she could summon Grandeur to Loyang to watch him at close range.

In Changan, Crown Prince Grandeur also wished for spring to come. He was a pale, slender man, married now, but with no children. Like his father, he had a weak constitution and a kind heart. Confined indoors during the severe winter, he was impatient for the warm weather to come to get into the open.

On the first warm day in spring, he ventured out to the garden and filled his lungs with invigorating air. He noticed branches rough with leaf buds, pink magnolias bursting from their brown shells, and ants running up and down a tree trunk. A splash of yellow drew him to the forsythia bush. There he stood to watch an early butterfly, solid brown edged with yellow, flitting among the flowers. At the swishing of a bamboo broom he turned and saw Eunuch Wong, who had been relegated to working in the garden after Loyalty had been deposed. At the approach of Prince of Grandeur, Eunuch Wong dropped to his knees, then stood at attention with his hands on the broom.

"I like welcome-spring (forsythia)," said Grandeur. "Their little gold trumpets seem to promise good things to come."

"There is a whole bank of them in the Imperial Park. In their full bloom they look like a cascade of gold."

"Take me to see them," said the Crown Prince.

Eunuch Wong leaned the broom against the trellis and led the way. They turned from a tessellated brick walk to a narrow path overgrown with weeds, passed a bamboo grove, and came upon a glade, in back of which there was a small house, barred and locked. Guards squatted beneath the locust trees, their swords and javelins laid carelessly beneath the projecting eaves.

"Stay!" called the Crown Prince. "What is this? Who is in there?"

"Two disfavored daughters of the Son of Heaven," said one of the guards.

"Why are they confined?"

"We do not know."

"Open the door."

[132]

The guards looked at each other; they had orders from their captain not to admit anyone.

"Open the door!" the Crown Prince repeated. He did not raise his voice, but there was authority in his tone and the guards obeyed. As he stepped into the cell from the sunshine, a sudden darkness enveloped him, and the chilly, musty air pushed at him like a dirty hand. He blinked his eyes and found himself in a bare room with two emaciated women crouching on a straw pallet. They were deathly pale, and their skinny limbs looked like sere branches of a dead tree.

For a moment, no one spoke. The women's fear-filled eyes looked timidly into the Prince's compassionate ones. As the Crown Prince was too shocked to speak, Eunuch Wong said to the Princesses, "Do not fear. Our Crown Prince here is good and kind."

With encouragement and questions from the Crown Prince, the two finally told their story, how their mother, Hsiao Sofi, had been killed, how they were confined, and what they had suffered. "Days, moons, years have passed by," they said. "We have lost count. We do not know how long we have been here."

"I shall petition our father to set you free," said the Crown Prince.

On his way, the Crown Prince was oppressed with a sense of guilt as if he were responsible for this injustice, and an empty, sickening feeling churned within him. He leaned against the wall for a moment, then retraced his steps to the Palace, despising his original notion of seeing the forsythias as a frivolous whim.

He sat at his desk, painstakingly preparing his memorial, calling his every literary faculty into play. If he had not seen it with his own eyes, he would never have believed this warped facet existed in his mother's character. But she was his mother and he was not to judge her. So in his petition to his father he blamed no one, only set forth how he had come upon the women and in what a deplorable condition they had been found. "If Your Majesty had seen them with your own eyes, Your Majesty's heart would have broken as did that of your unfilial son. I humbly beg Your Majesty's forgiveness in calling this to Your

[133]

Majesty's attention, and in importuning for their immediate release." He sent his memorial to Loyang by a relay of the fastest horses. The injustice, he felt, must be corrected at once.

When the memorial reached Chao through the Senior Guardian of the Heir Apparent, whose department handled the affairs of the Crown Prince, she was infuriated that Grandeur should dig up what had been buried years before and force her hand to release the Princesses. She tapped the memorial repeatedly on her palm. "The presumption! Meddling into the affairs of his elder." If this was a foretaste of what was to come, she could not expect to rule after Grandeur came to the throne. She ceased to see him as her son but regarded him as an arch enemy; and she summoned him to Loyang to be under her close observation.

The months slipped by, and it was New Year. Eunuch Wong, in hanging the lanterns for the celebration, saw a cluster of eunuchs talking in low voices and long faces, and he went to join them.

"The Crown Prince is dead!" they said.

"Dead? No!" cried Eunuch Wong. "How did it happen?"

They looked at each other, then lowered their voices. "We heard a rumor that he was poisoned. Is it possible?"

For a long moment Eunuch Wong did not answer; then, with his voice choking with tears, he said, "Who knows? Another one of those insolvable mysteries in the palace history."

18

When Virtue became the Crown Prince, Kao Tsung came to see him. "I should be happy that you are now the Crown Prince," he said. "I always have had the greatest hope in you. I know you will be a credit to your ancestors. Yet . . . I am worried. Do be very careful. Watch your every step. And obey your Empress-mother implicitly. Do not let your obstinacy forfeit your birthright. The day will come when you will sit on the throne to reign as you see fit. Until then, be submissive to the Empress in every way. Be patient. Time is on your side."

"Ease your heart, Father. I will do as you say."

"You understand why I ask this of you?"

"Yes, Father. I am no longer a child. I am twenty and a married man. I understand."

Chao, too, was worried, now that Virtue, the most intractable of her sons, was Crown Prince. She was positive that in time, if she did not clip his wings, he would soar like an eagle to snatch her off her seat of power. A sigh of regret escaped her. She thought it a blackhearted affair to plan the downfall of one's own son, once and again. But there was her own survival to think of.

Then the Tufans' revolt pushed Virtue to the back of Chao's mind. The old chieftain, with whom Chao had had a long and cordial relationship, had died. His sixteen-year-old son had lost his power to an ambitious general, who with a formidable army was threatening to throw off the Tang suzerainty. Chao ordered General Si to the Tibetan border and then sent General Loo to reinforce him.

She hated war. It always worried her, and this time she had a strange premonition of impending disaster. It shouldn't be! she consoled herself. General Si was an excellent tactician, and with Loo's reinforcement his victory should be certain. Still, she was restive, waiting for the news from the front. When it finally came, she quivered with rage, for seven-tenths of her expeditionary force had been annihilated. It had been General Loo's disobedience to Si's order to leave heavy arms behind that had brought on the disastrous defeat. The clutter of armaments at the mountain pass had revealed the army's position, and instead of surprising the Tufans as planned, they had been surprised by them with a catastrophic slaughter.

Chao dropped the report on her desk, locked her hands behind her back and paced the floor. She could not permit this rout to impair her prestige. It would encourage other vassals to revolt. Neither could she send another expedition, for to conscript further men and money would surely cause discontent among her hundred-names. Wracking her brain for a way out, she decided to employ dissimulation.

She issued a decree to the Board of Defense to make it known with great fanfare that the celestial empire was mobilizing its entire army to punish the presumptuous rebels; and to spread rumors that all the generals were ordered to converge on the Tibetan border. At the same time, she rushed a courier to General Si instructing him covertly to settle the conflict as best he could. Her threat worked. A treaty of alliance proposed by Si was agreed upon and the Tufans withdrawn to their Himalayan strongholds without pushing their advantage into her territory.

But she had not heard the last of the Tufans. The next spring, an emissary came requesting an audience. Chao watched him curiously from behind the curtain. He was a tall, rugged man, and the woven-wool conch-shaped hat perched high on his head made him look even taller. Chao admired his powerful physique as she watched him stretch full length on the floor Tibetan fashion. She wished Kao Tsung had some of his brawn. She wondered what his mission was—To affirm the treaty, to dissolve it, or to bargain about their tribute. The Tibetans had been sending musk, white fox pelt, cow hide, wool, medicinal herbs, cattles, rhubarbs . . . Going down the list, Chao knew she would not forego any of them.

After the audience, impatient to know the purpose of the emissary's visit, she summoned the Director of Border Relations to the antechamber of the Audience Hall. "What is the emissary's mission?" she asked without preamble.

"Your Majesty, he is requesting the marriage of Princess of Peace to his Chieftain to consolidate the ties between the two neighbors."

"The presumption! The Princess of the Great Tang Dynasty to marry a barbarian and live in a tent? Never!"

"Your humble servant begs to remind Your Majesty that the Tufans, sensitive of their inferior station, might construe a refusal as a slight to be vindicated by war. And it is not without precedent to suggest that a princess of the empire be married into a tribe for reasons of the state. Princess Wenchen, His Majesty's sister, was married to the grandfather of the present Chief."

With the defeat of General Si fresh in her mind, Chao did not want to precipitate a war, neither did she want to appear selfish to the people in putting her daughter above the welfare of the nation. She sat thinking; and then suddenly her eyes twinkled, as she remembered that at her mother's funeral, Princess of Peace had been dressed as a Taoist priestess in full view of all the foreign emissaries. With a wry smile she said, "Inform the emissary that Princess of Peace took the vow of a Taoist priestess when her grandmother died. We know how devoutly religious our esteemed neighbors are. We presume they do not want her to recant the vow. Convey our regret to the Chieftain in the most courteous tone and send the emissary home with valuable presents." Then she added, "To convince the Tufan Emissary, we shall remodel the priory in the Palace for Princess of Peace to move in."

[137]

With the borders quiet, again Chao turned her thought to Virtue. She summoned a noted soothsayer, Ming, to the Palace to divine which of the princes would eventually succeed to the throne. Ming sensed that the Empress did not favor the present Crown Prince; otherwise why should such a prognostication be sought? After the usual Taoist rite he said hesitantly, "Your Majesty, the omen is from Heaven. Your humble servant is only the mouthpiece."

"Be of no fear. The will of Heaven is what we want to know."

"Alas, the Crown Prince is not ordained to succeed the throne."

Chao saw to it that the prognosis was widely spread. By the next spring it had reached Changan. Even eunuchs in the Crown Prince's Palace were talking about it in their eating hall. When the omen reached Eunuch Wong's ear, he suspected it had been spread with a purpose that did not bode well for Crown Prince Virtue. When the meal was over, he went to potter around the hydrangea garden outside the Prince's study.

"For a moment I mistook your head for my white hydrangea bloom," said Virtue, as he sauntered into the garden. "Are you the new gardener? I have not seen you before."

"I work in other parts of the garden. I came here hoping to speak to Your Highness."

"If it is something I could grant, it is granted before your asking. Your white hair speaks in your favor."

"It is not for myself I wish to speak. It is to warn Your Highness of the gossip I heard. They were repeating an omen that Your Highness will not be the prince to succeed to the throne."

"Aw-w-w?" said Virtue scowling. "Your prince appreciates your concern for him. And if you have further reason to speak to him, it is his wont to stroll here at this time of the day."

During the four years Virtue was in Changan, he was cautious and submissive. He wrote to his mother regularly, deferring important decisions until he received her directions. He worked conscientiously with the court in Changan and was well liked by them. Their reports to his mother had all been to his credit. Yet his mother's letters had twisted his words to construe

[138]

insubordination and had upbraided him scathingly. And now this omen. What was in his mother's mind? What could he do to placate her? He wished he knew.

A year passed before Eunuch Wong came to see Virtue again. "This time," he said, "the rumor is that Your Highness was not born of the Empress but of the Duchess of Han."

"Was I?" he asked, wondering whether his bastardy was the cause of his mother's animosity, or whether it was his mother's animosity that was making him out to be a bastard.

"Your Highness was born twenty-five years ago, two years before the Duchess of Han came to live in the Palace."

Virtue put the pieces together—the omen, the illegitimacy, and the upbraiding. They fell into a definite pattern indicating his mother's intention to depose him. He wondered when the ax would fall. Even if he should be deposed, he would lie low. Time was on his side, as his father said. Yet tension gripped him.Sometimes he woke up sweating; other times he talked in his sleep. One morning when the stars were still bright, his wife nudged him awake, and he asked sleepily, "Did I groan again in my sleep?"

"No. But listen . . . Footsteps and noises . . . It sounds like the feet of many people."

Virtue threw on his robe and went to the antechamber. There he saw a eunuch just coming in. "Your Highness," the eunuch said, "the guards are disarmed, and the messenger with Her Majesty's edict is waiting in the center hall."

The edict accused Virtue of plotting to seize the throne, as three hundred suits of armor had been found hidden in his stable. He was whisked away and thrown into prison before he could have a word with his wife. Virtue was stunned, his mind a blank, his eyes staring into the dense blackness. When the gravity of the accusation penetrated his consciousness, he cried, "Treason! No! Punishable by death! How heartless!" He knew there never had been any armor in his stable. If there had been, it was planted there purposely. He was resigned to waiting for his time, but not for death. Did his father know? Would he extricate him?

He gripped the iron bars, lifted his anguished face to the slit

[139]

of blue sky and called upon the spirit of his ancestors to wreak vengeance on his mother and protect the Tang heritage from her grasping hands.

The news of Prince of Virtue's treason struck Kao Tsung like a sledge hammer. He felt limp, as if all the blood were draining from his veins, and his head swam. But he managed to reach Chao's book-chamber.

"He could not have done it!" Kao Tsung repeated again and again, his voice rising with emotion.

"Read this yourself," said Chao coolly, thrusting the report toward him.

"I do not have to read. I know Virtue." As Chao refused to absolve Virtue, he pleaded for his life, "He is our son. I love him dearly."

"If you permit your love for your son to interfere with justice, how can you expect justice to be done in the empire? Is not every man someone's son?"

"If you kill him, you kill me also. I have given you my love, my throne, and what have I got in return besides pain and remorse? I do not care what you do to me. But Virtue . . . my son and your son . . . who came out of your womb, suckled at your breasts . . . How could you do this to him? Have you no heart? For heaven's sake, absolve him."

"I have no power. It is up to the Judiciary Department. If he is innocent he will be absolved."

Words, words, empty words, futile words. What was the use of saying any more? Hopeless, defeated, Kao Tsung stumbled out of the study.

Chao ordered three high officials from the Judiciary Department to review the case. The judges endorsed the indictment but recommended to spare his life, reducing his sentence to banishment. When this decision came to her desk, Chao was worried. To spare Virtue's life was to prolong her agony.

"Your Majesty," said Jasmine, as she entered timidly. "They are ready to light the bonfire to burn the three hundred suits of armor brought from Changan."

"We shall watch it from the tower above the wall gate," said Chao.

[140]

At the watch tower Chao stood by the ledge alone. Behind her stood Jasmine, then the Captain of the guards, rigid in attention. Below the tower, a wide avenue ran from the palace to the bank of Lo River, straight as a carpenter's line. At the far end, near the foot of the bridge, a huge crowd had gathered around a mountain of faggots topped with the leather armor. A column of smoke rose and swayed eastward like a plume. Then came an explosion of red sparks and pointed tongues of fire.

The northwesterly wind made Jasmine shiver; but Chao remained motionless, unconscious of the cold, her eyes narrowed calculatingly, thinking that the burning of the armor before the hundred-names should convince them of Virtue's guilt and should destroy his popularity and vindicate his deposal.

[141]

19

Chao did not realize what a pall Virtue had cast on her until it was thrown off. She had not felt so lighthearted since the day Virtue had become the Crown Prince. Returning from the Audience Hall, she had a frivolous impulse to skip and run as she had when she was a child. She chuckled to herself, thinking how shocked her entourage would be if she should act on her whim. Yet the urge was so strong that she dismissed the carriage and walked.

It was a beautiful day. A golden light glowed in an azure sky specked with a few fleecy clouds. The aspens were shimmering like myriads of silver coins caught in the shifting light, the gray-white eucalyptus trunks towering to touch the sky. Today everything seemed to take on a rosy tint. The peonies were of a brighter hue; the jasmine exuded a more heavenly scent. As she listened to the mating songs of the birds, a desire for her own mate overwhelmed her. Unconsciously her feet led her to Kao Tsung's study instead of her own.

She found him hunched over his desk. If she had not been blinded by her own effusive spirits she would have noticed the sudden change in him. His face was an artist's sketch of sorrow; his eyes were an eloquent witness to his weariness of life. He was writing to Virtue, brushing rapidly up and down the rice-paper. Chao circled her arms around Kao Tsung's shoulders from behind and laid her face against his head in a caress. Kao Tsung stiffened.

"Such a beautiful day!" said Chao. "It must be lovely at the Palace of the Ascending Sun. Let us take a day to relax and summon our daughter to meet us there."

"I am in no mood," he said. "As to our daughter, she is twenty-three and should have been married years ago."

"I need her. If it had not been for my ruse, she would be living in a tent with the Tufan Chieftain."

"Even a Tufan Chieftain is a husband," said Kao Tsung.

"She is happy. Let us not worry about her. Let us take advantage of this beautiful day and seek today's pleasure today." Sensing his resistance from his rigid body, she leaned against the edge of his desk to face him with her old, winsome smile; she smoothed his hollowed cheeks and cajoled, "Will you go just to please your Empress?"

"Have it your way. You always do."

The Palace of Ascending Sun was Chao's favorite retreat. The small, exquisite Palace, cut like a gem to suit her taste, was situated along a tributary of the Lo River outside the west palace wall. She had chosen that site for the sound of the running water, and had nine halls built on the right bank and five on the left, with a rainbow bridge connecting the two.

Arriving at the Palace of Ascending Sun they went to the Peony Pavilion, where the pink and white flowers bloomed in profusion. "Heavenly!" said Chao. "Sniff the air. So different from that of the Main Palace . . . fresher, sweeter, and . . . free of restraint. Jasmine, cut some peonies for the vases." As Chao saw the flash of a gray, satin priestess's robe, she said, "There comes our daughter."

Kao Tsung took a peony bud and playfully placed it between the loops of the Princess's hair. But she brushed it aside irritably. "A peony is hardly an appropriate ornament for an austere priestess."

Chao looked up at her daughter's bitter tone. *Hum*, she thought , perhaps the girl did want a husband.

At dinner, Chao filled Kao Tsung's cup and said, "Drink to

the roundness of the moon; drink to the fragrance of the many flowers; drink to this happy evening."

Kao Tsung drank perfunctorily, with none of Chao's cheerfulness. When his moodiness persisted, Princess of Peace whispered to a eunuch and left the table. After a while, she came back in an oversized costume of the Captain of the Guards, with the sleeves flapping and the headgear slipping down to her eyes. Her droll appearance and her caricature of a warrior's dance made Kao Tsung laugh in spite of himself. When Princess of Peace came, flushed and puffing, to sit beside him, Kao Tsung patted her hand and said teasingly, "Our daughter would make a handsome general."

"Would Your Majesty have chosen this handsome general to be your son-in-law?" the Princess said artfully.

At the words "son-in-law," Chao turned to her daughter, but the Princess's head was bent. Chao shrugged. She could not be bothered, even if it was a hint. Not tonight. She clapped her hands for musicians. Accompanied by a moon-guitar, a flute and a reed organ, she sang the song she had sung long ago to Kao Tsung when she was a lady of the Fourth Rank. She was pleased to see his mood soften as the familiar tune carried him back to the time when he first fell in love with her.

Retiring to the Hall of Immortal Abode, Chao looped her arm through Kao Tsung's, her hand holding his. She rubbed her face against Kao Tsung's shoulder, humming a love song, and veered Kao Tsung toward her own sleeping chamber; but he let her hand go, untwined her arm, and said, "Sleep well, my love." Then he walked to his own sleeping chamber, closed the door, and latched it.

Chao, blazing, cursed. "A decrepit Emperor! An impotent husband! What is he good for?" She stalked to her room, grabbed the vase of peonies and flung it out of the window. The loud crash brought Jasmine to the room, but she hastened to retreat as Chao thundered, "Get out!"

Her own frustration made Chao realize her daughter's need of a husband. The next day, she ordered the Director of the Board of Selection to prepare a list of eligible nobles. Her choice fell upon Si Shaw, the youngest son of Kao Tsung's sister, and

[144]

she set the wedding date for the twelfth day, seventh moon of the following year.

Two months before the wedding, the Imperial Family started for Changan where Si Shaw resided, as traditionally a marriage took place at the domicile of the groom's family. As their procession drew near Changan, Kao Tsung could see the Summer Palace from the distance. Perched high on the hill, half hidden in the cloud, it was beautiful like the abode of the immortals, and the wide granite stairway leading up to it was like the tail of a monster dragon. His thought went back to his mother and his carefree days in the Summer Palace. He wished he could spend the rest of his days on the Dragon Hill.

His eyes clouded as he saw Crown Prince Wisdom ride out to meet them. Wisdom brought his bay gelding abreast of his father's carriage and bowed. "The Crown Prince inquires after Your Majesty's health."

"Wisdom, my son, how good to see you."

"Father," said Wisdom after the formal greeting was over. "I hope the long journey has not tired you."

"I am tired. But we are almost there. Have you seen your mother yet?"

"Presently, Father."

"You had better go now. We can talk later. Peace is riding with your mother. Dawn is further at the rear."

When they arrived at the Summer Palace Kao Tsung went straight to the terrace, where directly in line in the distance was the Temple of Great Benevolence built in memory of his mother. It was a ritual with him that whenever he came to the Summer Palace, he would bow toward the temple in respect. Now he held his folded hands to his eye level and bowed reverently, and an inexplicable peace descended upon him.

On the morning of the wedding the Imperial Family went to worship in each of the seven temples of the Imperial House so that Princess of Peace might bid farewell to her Imperial Ancestors. That evening, as Princess of Peace, in her bridal robe of red silk gauze, came to kowtow to take leave, tears and smiles mingled on Chao's face. Murmuring auspicious words, she took her daughter's hand and walked with her to the bridal chair. When it was borne away on the shoulders of eight uniformed men, she went with Kao Tsung to the terrace, where they could see the bridal procession, lit with lanterns and torches, snake its way down the hill like a fiery dragon. Chao did not know how long she sat and mused until she heard Kao Tsung say, "If you intend to return to Loyang after the wedding, I want to stay behind."

"Why?"

"I began my life here and wish to end it here."

"Why those inauspicious words on this night, of all nights? However, if your Majesty wishes to stay, we shall stay." Chao consented readily, for she did not intend to return to Loyang right away. She wanted to familiarize herself with the court in Changan and to ascertain its loyalty to herself.

Down below, the bridal procession had entered the city gate. Chao could see people surging along the Street of Heaven, their torches forming walls of fire, turning night into day. Then as the nuptial chair finally entered City Hall and disappeared from Chao's view, a sudden loneliness enveloped her. She realized now how her mother had felt that day when she left for the Palace forty-four years ago. Forty-four years! Such a long time!

Letting her thought meander down the vista of the past, she forgot Kao Tsung. When she finally turned to him he was no longer there and his empty chair made her feel lonelier still. In the city the torches were gone, the people scattered, the streets dark and silent, and the stars were bright again. She wished she were a star. At least she could wink to the other stars. But she was a sun, and there was no other sphere of equal brilliance to nod to. The pinnacle is a solitary place. Sighing, she pushed herself up from her seat and walked to her resident hall. The grating of her feet on the gravel walk seemed to echo her lament, "Lonely, lonely, so very lonely."

It had been late summer when the wedding took place. Now it was spring. In all these months, not a drop of rain had fallen. Usually the downpour before the ninth moon would provide enough water for the year. Then, when the fourth moon came, the house tops would be hidden in luxuriant foliage, the Hibiscus Park would be a solid block of green, and the plain outside the city wall would be dotted with wild flowers, scampering sheep, and barefoot herdsmen on buffalos' backs. But this year the sun scorched every blade of grass from the face of the earth. Trees were dying, their leaves crisp and curled, and the land was cracked in deep lines, like the face of an old woman.

From the terrace Kao Tsung saw two skeletonlike beings fighting over a root dug from the hard-crusted earth in the outlying field. He turned away in revulsion and went to the Palace. There the table was replete with delicacies from different parts of the Empire, succulent roast duck from the northeast, spring bamboo shoots from the middle east, tonic herbs that looked like dried caterpillars from the west, seaweeds and shellfish from the coast. Kao Tsung let his chopsticks drop. The sight of food sickened him.

"Is Your Majesty ill?" asked Chao.

"How can we eat when the hundred-names are starving?"

"How can our not eating help the hundred-names?"

Kao Tsung eyed Chao's gusto with repugnance. He pushed back his chair and left the table. Chao cast a contemptuous glance at Kao Tsung's back. "All heart and no head," she sneered. "Behaving like a squeamish woman instead of taking action like a man."

She walked briskly to her study, stopping on the way to feed the parrots. "Summon the Superintendent of Granaries," she ordered her eunuch. When he came, she asked, "How many granaries are open to the hundred-names?"

"Six, Your Majesty."

"Open the rest, all of them."

"But, Your Majesty . . ."

"A decree has been sent to the southern prefectures to transport part of their grains to the north," interrupted Chao. "And to relieve Changan from providing for the court we will leave for Loyang."

She went to inform Kao Tsung of her decision. "We are returning," she said, "in . . . three days. Princess of Peace and Si Shaw will go with us."

[147]

"Is it safe to travel at this time? The highways are infested with outlaws. Hunger has driven even our good citizens to be marauders and the jails are packed with them."

"What is the nation coming to, if even the Son of Heaven cannot journey in safety?" She ran over the possible candidates in her mind for a man to escort the Imperial Cortege safely to Loyang, and decided on Way Yuan-chung, for she knew he was a resourceful man.

Chao's command weighed heavily on the tall, slender Yuan-chung. His deep-set eyes were worried, for to fail in his mission was to lose his head. His first thought was to look over the Left and Right Gold Guards, the usual convoy on such a journey. He found none of the usual boisterousness in the guardhouse. The men's faces were pinched, for hard times hit all. Even the guards' rations were drastically cut.

With his narrow, clean-shaven face puckered in a scowl, yuan-chung gave his horse free rein. Suddenly he jerked his reins and turned round about, heading for the city jail, as he remembered that a bandit chief had been arrested. If "poison is an antidote to poison," why not use the bandit chief to restrain the bandits?

As the warden opened the door of a large cell, the inmates slunk to the wall and gawked in fear. One prisoner, on a straw pallet, kept screeching his operatic tune unconcerned. The jailor shoved him and said, "On your feet, brother. His Eminence is here."

The man got up in a leisurely way. He was tall, muscular, and brown in skin. His uncringing manner showed that he was accustomed to command. At Yuan-Chung's inquiring look the jailor nodded. Yuan-Chung then took the key from the jailor to unlock the man's manacles.

The man eyed Yuan-Chung curiously. Flexing his wrists, he asked,"To whom and for what does the lower-man owe this freedom?"

"We will discuss this in my house," said Yuan Chung.

The man shrugged his shoulders and followed Yuan-Chung out of the prison. Yuan-Chung installed the man in the guest chamber and assigned two servitors to wait upon him, with orders to treat the man as an honored guest.

[148]

The Bandit Chief fingered the silk robe, square headdress, and leather boots his host sent him and shook his head in perplexity. He stripped himself and plunged into a wooden tub full of hot water. Then, adorned in his new outfit, he walked around to get accustomed to the cumbersome costume. He noticed that everything in the room indicated wealth and high position; but why was he, a Bandit Chief, brought into this elegance?

Dinner was served in Yuan-Chung's study. Unable to contain his curiosity further, the Bandit Chief said, "The lower-man is overwhelmed with Your Eminence's kindness. But what does Your Eminence want of the lower-man?"

Yuan-Chung then told of his commission to escort the Imperial Cortege to Loyang and his fear of not being able to conduct the journey safely without someone like his guest to help him. The Bandit Chief, amused at his host's strategy, said, "At Your Eminence's command."

During the journey Yuan-Chung and the Bandit Chief rode side by side. They both were in scaly armor and rawhide headgear adorned with long pheasant plumes. Yuan-Chung, to win the Bandit-Chief's loyalty, treated him with utmost respect, sharing with him his food, his tent, his all.

They were out of the drought country, and the lush verdure on the distant hills, like a milliard green ostrich feathers swaying in synchronization, was a balm to their sore eyes. When dusk came, they still had a mountain pass to cross before reaching the next travel-palace, and the road ahead, cut through a deep ravine, seemed weird and mysterious. Kao Tsung stopped the procession and sent a eunuch to Chao's carriage to inquire if they should cross the pass the next day in broad daylight.

"And cramp ourselves in a tent instead of resting in comfort in the travel-palace?" scoffed Chao. However, she asked Yuan-Chung for advice. Assured by the Bandit Chief, Yuan-Chung answered with confidence, "Whichever way pleases Your Majesty."

"Proceed," said Chao with a majestic motion of her hand.

They entered the pass with Yuan-Chung riding beside His Majesty's carriage and the Bandit Chief bringing up the rear. Struck by the sudden change of scene, Yuan-Chung studied the

[149]

terrain with concern. On his right the cliff rose upright like a wall. Along its base a little stream murmured, and between clumps of overhanging bushes he could see flashes of foaming water rushing over the boulders. To his left were jagged crags, layers and layers of them, with clumps of thickets and clusters of pine trees scattered here and there. Yuan-Chung did not like what he saw; the place was too ideal for bandit lairs. His muscles tightened as he saw a flash of red in the distance. It could be the red bandanna on an outlaw's head. He squinted his eyes for a better view, but it was gone.

The procession jogged along, the guards groggy with fatigue. But Yuan-Chung was alert to every sound and movement. He saw a large flag suddenly appear behind a crag, then smaller flags behind other rocks, all with the emblem of a wild boar. Then the valley resounded with a wild clamor of *"Sha!* (kill) *Sha! Sha!"* As the red-turbaned outlaws swooped down the hill, Yuan-Chung and the Bandit Chief raced to the head of the procession. The Bandit Chief thrust his headgear aside, wrapped his head in a red bandanna, unfurled a long streamer in the emblem of a centipede, and waved it above his head. When the Wild Boar Band saw the flag of the Centipede, they disappeared among the crags. The clamor of *"Sha"* died down as suddenly as it came, and only the flapping of the imperial flags and the gurgle of the stream were heard. To Yuan-Chung's questioning eyes the Bandit Chief said, "It is our code that one band does not plunder the spoils of another."

20

A few days after the imperial cortege arrived at Loyang it began to rain, then poured. Chao stretched out her hand from the veranda to feel the rain, letting it seep through her fingers. It was good to see the downpour after the drought in Changan. The splashing sound was pleasant to her ears. She wished Chang-an could have some of this downpour. She could just see the parched land soak up the water.

But after it had poured continuously for a month with no sign of letting up, Chao's joy turned to anxiety. The high palace ground was a sheet of muddy water. Eunuchs waded with their robes tucked high to their waist, their pantaloons rolled up to their knees. The first landing of the marble stairway to the Resident Hall was submerged, and each day, as Chao counted, one more step was gone under. The ministers petitioned for her and Kao Tsung to move to Sunshan, a mountain southwest of Loyang, but she would not think of leaving at that time, when a quick decision might be necessary in case of emergency.

She dispensed with the morning audience, and reports were sent to her by messengers. She dreaded to read them, for they invariably contained calamitous news. First the Lo River over-flowed; then the lowland became a vast lake and wheat and millet rotted in the fields. She impounded the temples on the hill to store grains moved from the granaries on the lowland, but much was already spoiled. Then came the devastating news of the break of the Yellow River dike, flooding the countryside, taking a heavy toll of lives. Prices soared even higher than those of Changan; rice was dear as pearl and firewood cost as much as cinnamon.

Water! Water! Water! Would she ever see dry land again? Distressed, she went to pray in the temple and pledged before the three golden images to hallow Sunshan. She believed that by propitiating the spirits of mountains and rivers, one could ward off calamities and ensure prosperity.

Eventually the water subsided, and the sun, as if to make up for its previous improvidence, blazed with a redoubtable force. The air became hot and humid, steam rose from the ground, and a fetid odor permeated the capital.

Hung came to report with furrowed brow. "Your Majesty, Loyang is in for more trouble. The gaseous stench rising from the streets has become a blight, sickness is taking a heavy toll of those surviving the flood, and dead bodies pillow upon each other on the roadside. It is feared that pestilence is on its way."

"Then we must prevent it." She issued a decree to the Director of the Board of Health to conscript men to clean the streets, to bury bodies in lime, to forbid travel and social gatherings, to quarantine the ill. In spite of these precautions plague reared its head, crawled insidiously, then sprang with a vengeance.

Loyang was like a dead city. Trading was at a standstill. Only bullock carts heaped with bodies plied the streets. Laughter and merriment were silenced. Only groans, wails and weeping were heard. It was not until the northwest wind began to blow that the death rate showed a decline, but by the first snowfall normalcy finally returned.

In the first audience after the long recess, Chao issued a decree to hallow Sunshan and to construct a palace named Heavenly Devotion as residence during its consecration.

"Your Majesty," a censor boldly remonstrated. "The nation's back is broken under the heavy burden of drought, flood and plague. To add this enormous expenditure to the already

[152]

stricken nation is inadvisable. Your servant humbly petitions Your Majesty to reconsider."

"We commend our honorable censor for his forthrightness. We know this is untimely, but we have vowed to the gods in our hour of distress and are in honor bound to redeem our pledge. Our Empire is vast; the resources of the southern prefectures can still be tapped."

The Palace of Heavenly Devotion took a year to build. When it was completed, Chao said to Kao Tsung, "The necromancer has chosen the twentieth day of the eleventh moon for the consecration. Let us start early and be there before the fifteenth. I can imagine Sunshan would be like a fairyland under a full moon."

Kao Tsung dreaded to travel, for every bone and tendon in his body felt tired. He wanted to rest . . . rest . . . rest. "Must we be in such a hurry?" he asked. "Could it be next moon?"

"But why?"

"My head . . . it aches more often now, and the pain is more severe."

"Your Majesty's headache is capricious. We cannot be sure it will not come if we go next moon, nor that it will not leave if we go this moon. But one thing we can be sure of: the mountain air will do Your Majesty a world of good."

They traveled to the foot of Sunshan by carriage and were carried up in sedan chairs, arriving at the Palace of Heavenly Devotion in the evening. It was too late to go through the Palace, but Chao liked what she saw of her resident hall, the Hall of Enchantment, especially the marble terrace. With the moon shining full upon it, it was as though carved out of the purest white jade, and she named it the Terrace of Gentle Breeze Teasing the Moon.

Early the next morning, Chao slipped out to the terrace again, and the scene took her breath away. Below her was a sea of fleecy, milk-white clouds. She felt exalted, as though she were a goddess living above the clouds. She sat on the low marble balustrade, marveling at the magnificence of nature's handiwork.

As the sun rose, spots of green began to puncture the fluffy

[153]

whiteness. Gradually the clouds drifted apart, then vanished entirely, as a golden light flooded the sky. Looking down, Chao's eyes followed the sheer drop to fathomless depths. The view below was frightening, yet fascinating. Tearing her eyes away from the sight of it, she turned to the hills behind her. Perched on the high peak was a red summer house, like a butterfly poised on the tip of a tree. She named it The Summer-house of Heavenly Brilliance.

After breakfast, she roamed the woods, enjoying the trees. Some cascaded like waterfalls, others were erect like marble columns or spreading like giant umbrellas. Their exposed roots gave the illusion of dragons and serpents gliding beneath the firs and pines. Coming to a lake, she watched the light and shade play upon its placid surface. She felt at one with nature, and her fear, anxiety, and guilt dropped away like a discarded veil.

So this was what she missed; this was the cost of power! She wished that the path to the throne had not been strewn with blood, that her conscience did not need to be burdened with the ghosts of her victims.

Wishing. Wishing. Only wishing! Peace, after all, belongs to the gods. For a human being like herself, she thought, there could be only an illusive glimpse of it—a flash, and no more. If only she could hold this moment in her hands and not let it go . . .

A fish splashed and a bird cawed, breaking the magic moment of her abstraction. She retraced her steps to the Hall of Enchantment to find Kao Tsung shivering with a chill, his head drooped in pain as if the whole Sunshan were on his neck.

Staring blankly, Kao Tsung cried, "I cannot see. My sight is gone!"

"Summon the physician," said Chao. Her tone betrayed her annoyance that he should be sick at this particular time. She glanced at her groaning spouse and then looked away. She could not bear the sight of him. She had nothing but utter contempt for a weakling.

The physician pressed his fingers on Kao Tsung's pulse, then hesitantly intimated that to let out some blood from His Majesty's head could relieve the pressure on his eyes.

"To puncture the head of the Son of Heaven!" Chao cried.

"You have our permission to proceed," said Kao Tsung. "Anything is better than this pain."

As blood was let out and the pressure was relieved, Kao Tsung said weakly, "My sight is returning."

The consecration of Sunshan was called off, and as soon as Kao Tsung was able to travel, they journeyed home. They reached Loyang on a bitter-cold day. Kao Tsung was bundled up in his cape of white fox, and only a small circle of his pale face was exposed from his fur-lined hood. As the court knelt at the south pier of Tienstin Bridge to welcome His Majesty, they could sense that death was hovering near the dragon throne. And the fast-falling snow seemed to portend the white of the mourning shroud.

Kao Tsung knew he had not long to live and he wanted to grant an amnesty as his last act of benevolence to his hundred-names. On his way to the Gate of Heaven for the announcement, he became breathless and could not mount his horse, so he announced it in the Audience Hall instead. When the cheers of "Ten thousand years to the Son of Heaven!" had ceased, Kao Tsung said to the ministers beside him, "If the gods in heaven could prolong this life for a moon or two to permit me to return to Changan, I shall then die with no regret." But the last journey had exhausted him. He was at his lowest ebb that evening.

Kao Tsung was delirious, and in his delirium the bars of his conscious mind were let down. His incoherent words became peepholes to his inmost soul, revealing his inhibited thoughts, his hidden fears and his ingrained remorse. For this reason Chao permitted no one in the sick chamber besides her most faithful eunuchs. She herself sat by the charcoal brazier and watched, her face inscrutable, showing no feeling for the man who lay dying, the man who had made her his Empress and abdicated his power to her. She had known he would die before she did and had been prepared for the inevitable. Now she just waited for the end to come.

Kao Tsung's heavy breathing was the only sound in the quiet room. He tossed his head and murmured, "Forgive me . . ." and

[155]

then sank into a deep sleep; but suddenly he screamed, "No! . . . No! Not I . . . She is the murderess . . . !"

The night was almost gone, and a loud gurgling sound told Chao the crisis was near. She sent for the physicians. The gurgling became louder, as if life were struggling with its captor in Kao Tsung's throat; when it subsided, an ethereal light came to his eyes and he whispered, "Empress! Hsiao Sofi . . ." then "Mother . . ."

When warned that the last thread of Kao Tsung's life was about to snap, Chao summoned Prime Minister Payi to the Imperial Chamber to receive the Emperor's will and last command. Payi knelt by the foot of the bed, clutching the will Chao had thrust into his hands. He had been summoned too late, as Chao had intended, for Kao Tsung's senses, like the windows and doors of a house about to be vacated, were already closed; only the last exit of a heartbeat was open for the soul to depart.

Kneeling by the head of the bed, the Chief Physician kept his fingers on Kao Tsung's pulse, which faltered and then was still.

21

According to Kao Tsung's will, the succeeding Emperor, Tsung Tsung, was to refer matters of importance to his Empress mother for direction. Thus Kao Tsung passed on to his son the very yoke under which he had writhed.

The court ministers, however, were not surprised at this reservation, without which, they knew, the will could not have passed Chao's hands; neither were they displeased, since with Chao's experienced grip on the helm, the continuity of the state policy was assured. But at Tsung Tsung's first audience, they were surprised to find the curtain behind the throne dismantled and the Emperor sitting on the dais alone. Chao's retirement was what it should be, yet tension tugged at the court, for now they were to serve a new Emperor whose policy was an uncharted sea.

Chao knew the court took for granted that she would rule behind her son's throne, but she was tired of manipulating a marionette. She had had enough of that with the father, and did not want to repeat it with the son. If she ruled, she would sit on the throne in her own right, Emperor of a dynasty of her own creation, perpetuating her own name. Why not? After all, she had reigned well for nearly thirty years. She knew tradition would never permit a woman to desecrate the holy throne. But tradition had not been confronted by a determined woman like herself. She would wait, she would retreat, but she would never cease to strive for her goal. She would inch her way slowly, carefully, to the throne, then sidle into it before the court was aware of it. If the court thought she had relinquished her power for good, they were due for a surprise. She knew Tsung Tsung had no judgment, in spite of his twenty-eight years. Sooner or later he would come into conflict with the ministers, who would turn to her for help. Then she would emerge to rule, with the support of the court.

In the meantime she occupied herself with the preparations for Kao Tsung's burial, which would take place later in the year. One day, tired from bending over the plan of the mausoleum, she called, "Jasmine, my cape and hood!"

She found the Palace of Ascending Sun still covered with snow; the rainbow bridge was a powdery arch over a frozen stream. With the sun casting a magic sheen over all, it was a breathtaking scene. She walked in the garden in childish delight, her leather boots leaving a track of deep imprints on the fluffy carpet of white. She felt cheerful, almost gay. For the first time in many years she was released of responsibility.

Yet, as she crunched up over the rainbow bridge, her mood changed. She paused and gazed thoughtfully toward the Main Palace. She wondered how her daughter-in-law enjoyed being the Empress. To forgo power, even for a while, was irksome to her. Then an insidious thought beset her. What if her perspicacity had been wrong? What if Tsung Tsung could get along with the court, making her retirement permanent?

She crossed to the other side of the stream and came upon a Lamei grove covered with tiny, yellow cups of waxlike flowers. She stood there inhaling their exquisite fragrance, and their courage to blossom in the severe winter inspired her with renewed confidence. She broke a sprig for her vase as a symbol of intrepidity, then made her way back to the Palace.

Hardly had she removed her cape and hood when Prime Minister Payi was announced. Chao raised her eyebrows in astonishment. She had not expected Tsung Tsung to be in trouble that soon. Payi entered with his head bowed, his sinewy hands holding onto his gold circular belt, hanging loose from the loops of his purple robe. He was a small man but did not appear so, for his dignity gave him stature.

Chao granted Payi permission to sit down and ordered the eunuch to move the brazier closer to him. "We are pleased with our Prime Minister's visit," she said. "How is the Son of Heaven faring? His inexperience will need the counsel from able ministers like your worthy self."

"Alas," said Payi, smoothing his scanty beard. "The Son of Heaven is not prone to accept counsel. This morning His Majesty issued an edict to elevate the father of his Empress to be Chief Secretary of the Imperial Chancellery. Your humble servant petitioned against such flagrant favoritism——"

"The Son of Heaven is indeed fortunate to be guided by the wise hands of our Prime Minister," Chao broke in, while inwardly amused at her daughter-in-law's foolishness. She remembered that when she had first become Empress she had almost made that same mistake. It had been Hung's report that had alerted her to send her brothers and cousins to distant prefectures.

"Unfortunately," Payi continued, "the Son of Heaven rebuffed his minister's advice. His Majesty said, 'If we give our father-in-law the entire empire, who is to stop us? Why quibble over a mere secretaryship?' "

"What wantonness! How injudicious of him!" cried Chao.

"Your humble servant fears that if unchecked, His Majesty tends to become an irresponsible despot."

"Such an Emperor would be a disaster to the nation. If only the younger Prince were the older. Our fourth Prince, Dawn, is by nature studious, judicious, and openminded. He welcomes counsel from his tutors and ministers and goes out of his way to seek them. It is a misfortune for the nation that the more amenable of the two is the younger."

"Perhaps a few words from our Empress Dowager could effectively restrain the Son of Heaven," said Payi.

" 'Rivers and mountains could be removed, but the nature of man cannot be changed.' However, we will speak to him."

As Payi left, Chao smiled complaisantly. Judging from Tsung

[159]

Tsung's first mistake it would not be long before she would emerge to reign. In that happy mood she went back to the plan for the monumental mausoleum she had started building three years ago for herself and Kao Tsung. On the Liang Mountain northwest of Changan, the new shrine extended over three hills, the solitary north peak for the crypt, the two low, south hills for a natural gateway to the mausoleum. Encircled by a wall the tomb site had the shape of an elephantine armchair, which according to geomancy portended blessings to posterity. Chao, however, had chosen that location because of the poplars and aspens that covered the hills, which gave out sounds like rainfall when swayed by the breeze.

Because she wanted the mausoleum to be the grandest that had ever been built, she spared neither effort nor expense. There were temples and memorial halls, with marble terraces and exquisitely carved railings. Colossal stone columns and giant statues of men, horses and quaint birds stood sentinel along the wide avenue leading to the crypt, and huge stone lions guarded the wall gates and temple doors. When Kao Tsung died, it had not been finished, but now the people ungrudgingly came forth with money, material, and labor to hasten its completion, because they loved their Son of Heaven. Despite the scourge of recent calamities, they considered his reign good. Even the neighboring tribes sent thousands of men over to build the tomb. To show her appreciation to the tribes, Chao wanted to have sixty-one stone statues, inscribed with the names of the sixty-one Chiefs, placed in front of the temple of worship in the mausoleum, and she marked on the sketch where these were to stand.

In the autumn, Kao Tsung's coffin was transported to the Funeral Palace in the mausoleum. On the day of the burial, his catafalque was carried on the shoulders of 240 men wearing white tunics, white trousers, white sandals, and white hoods. Following the catafalque on foot were the Emperor Tsung Tsung, the Imperial Family, the Kings, the Nobles, the Court, the Emissaries, the Prefects, and the Representatives from every city, town and village, all in white mourning robes. Preceding it were the musicians, the drums, the gongs, and six sacrificial animals (a horse, an ox, a cock, a dog, a goat, and a hog) carried on open, sedanlike stands. Behind them came the Right and Left Gold Guards, the foot soldiers, the Mongolian horsemen, the Taoist priests, the Tibetan Monks, and the protocol officers who directed the procedures with hoarse whispers and silent gestures.

Chao noticed the crouching mourners on the hills, the scent of sandalwood incense, the pouring of the sacrificial wine, the burning of written prayers by kinsmen and high officials, the endless kneeling and bowing of mourners, the plaintive blast of the trumpets, the mournful boom of the drums, the sobbing of people, the soughing of the trees. Yet all these were nebulous impressions. Predominating was her awareness that it was her son, the new Emperor Tsung Tsung, who was the central performer of the rituals and not herself.

After the burial, Chao's mind snapped back to razor-edge sharpness; her eyes became shrewd and cunning. Tsung Tsung had better make another blunder soon, she thought; else she would have to create one for him.

Chao did not have to wait long. Shortly afterward, Tsung Tsung issued a decree conferring the official rank of the fifth grade upon the son of the wet nurse of the baby Crown Prince.

"Your Majesty," Payi remonstrated, "the ranks are for rewarding the meritorious officials. To bestow it on the son of a wet nurse is a favoritism that will discourage loyal functionaries."

"Are you the Son of Heaven or are we?" Tsung Tsung asked in sarcasm. "We have spoken and will tolerate no objection." Gesturing for the peacock fans to screen the throne, he swept out of the hall. Payi's face burned. Instead of returning home, he headed for the Palace of Ascending Sun.

Chao listened to Payi's account with her brow furrowed, her head lowered in thought. "It is regrettable!" she said finally. "We wish we had the magic to change the Son of Heaven's nature into that of his younger brother." Suddenly she looked

[161]

up as if struck by an idea. "If we cannot change nature, we could change . . ." she left the sentence unfinished.

There was an awkward silence, then Payi asked, "The Emperor?"

"For the good of the nation," said Chao.

With Chao's eyes provoking him to obey her will, Payi said, "No one knows the son better than the mother. If our Empress Dowager thinks the youngest Prince is more amenable to the counsel of the court, it is not the place of your humble minister to dissent."

"We know our Prime Minister would put the welfare of the nation above all else." She then discussed with him the procedure for dethroning Tsung Tsung. Payi was to solicit the assistance of the Deputy Secretary of the Imperial Secretariat and the Left and Right Generals of the Wing Guards, and the latter two were to come to Chao for instruction early in the morning on the tenth of the month.

When that day came, Chao was nervous, although she anticipated no problem in deposing Tsung Tsung, yet her hands shook as she took the bowl of bird's nest soup from Jasmine. After a spoonful or two she pushed the bowl aside.

"Your Majesty is not eating," said Jasmine, concerned.

"Take it away. When one's mind is troubled, one's bowels rebel."

Chao got up and made her way across the center chamber to the veranda. She peered into the blackness of the garden, squinting her eyes at the glitter of lanterns coming closer and closer. Then, as the two Generals came into view, she heaved a sigh and went to wait for them in the center chamber. As they knelt at her feet she said, "It is painful to have to depose the Emperor. But the Prime Minister must have explained to you why it is necessary. We are entrusting to our Right Wing Guard General the duty of leading his men to surround the Resident Hall of the Son of Heaven and disarm the guards, then take the Empress and the baby Crown Prince to the Hall of Tranquillity, there to await our order. To our Left Wing Guard General we assign the duty of escorting us to the Audience Hall."

As Chao stalked onto the dais of the Audience Hall there was

[162]

an audible intake of breath, then a sudden silence. Riveting her angry eyes on Tsung Tsung, Chao ordered Payi and the Deputy Secretary to remove him from his throne. Tsung Tsung's startled face paled, and he stuttered, "What . . . what . . . have I . . . done?"

"You wanted to give the Empire to your father-in-law, and you ask what have you done," reprimanded Chao.

"But . . ."

At Chao's signal the Left Wing Guard General stepped up to the dais, his hand on the hilt of his sword, drawing it out inches from its scabbard. Tsung Tsung shuddered, and without finishing what he intended to say, he let Payi and the Deputy Secretary help him step down from his throne.

Chao, then, turned to the court and said, "The injudiciousness of the Son of Heaven has been brought to our attention. We regret that his mother and his Grand Tutors have not instilled in him the precepts necessary to a ruler of a great empire. We are as much to blame as the Son of Heaven. However, just as the early repair of a crack saves a dike from complete destruction, so in removing the Son of Heaven, we hope to forestall the despotic rule that his wanton nature portends. And we charge our court to serve with loyalty the fourth Prince, Dawn, who will be crowned as Emperor Jui Tsung. Emperor Tsung Tsung will be demoted to a commoner and exiled to Fanchou with his wife and son."

Chao knew that her twenty-four-year-old son Dawn, devoted to books and philosophy, had no inclination to seek power or to rule. She had nothing to fear from him; yet, since the court might want to instigate him to exert his right, she should take precautions. Therefore, immediately after he was proclaimed Emperor, he was confined in a remote hall, to live a sequestered life with his wife. On record he was the Emperor; in fact he was a prisoner, his every movement watched, his communication with the court completely severed.

The next day, to avoid appearing too brazen, Chao held her first court in the Purple Hall instead of in the Main Audience Hall. The court was appalled to see her on the throne and Jui Tsung nowhere around. They expected her to rule from behind the throne, not outright upon it. However, not a voice was raised. Chao herself was unperturbed. With a slight wave of a large envelope in her hand she said, "This letter is from Emperor Jui Tsung, and we wish to have it read."

"August Empress-mother," read the Secretary. "Your unfilial son petitions at your feet. Overwhelmed by the great responsibility of ruling a vast empire and cognizant of my youth and inexperience, my head cannot rest at ease on my pillow for fear my inadequacy might jeopardize the affairs of the nation. After a long and serious deliberation, your unfilial son deems it is in the best interest to petition his august mother to reign in his stead and permit this unfilial son to devote his time to further his learning until he is better prepared."

"Our son has shown wisdom in knowing himself," said Chao. "And we deem it our duty to assent to his request until such time as he is ready to rule for himself." Then she proceeded to issue orders with her usual alacrity. She sent her trusted generals to the outlying prefectures to preclude possible reactionaries and shuffled the cabinet to ensure complete loyalty to herself.

In the process of shifting the cabinet, her thoughts turned again to the House of Wu, her logical supporters. Her brothers and cousins were dead, and so far she had shown little favor to their sons, for she saw no reason to arouse the jealousy of Kao Tsung's kin and the suspicion of the court. But now, since she aimed to usurp the throne openly, it was time to reduce the powers of Kao Tsung's kin and elevate those of her own. So she recalled the Wus from exile and made her stepbrother's son, Shensi, heir to his grandfather's dukedom.

She summoned Shensi to the Palace one day to look him over. His pale, sickly, unimpressive appearance disappointed her, and his rich attire only accentuated his inelegance. But she approved of his shrewd aggressiveness, which she had noticed when he was a boy.

"Your Majesty," said Shensi, sitting reverently on the very edge of the chair. "Permit your unworthy nephew to thank Your Majesty for your copious favors. Your nephew wishes to assure His Imperial Aunt that he is willing to go into boiling water and to walk on fire, to requite Your Majesty's kindness to the House of Wu, whose loyalty and devoted service Your Majesty can be sure of."

"Hum," Chao grunted. She could see that Shensi had neither his father's pride nor his rectitude. In fact she sensed that he was intensely ambitious, and probably unscrupulous too, in gaining his ends. That was the kind of man she could use to serve her purpose. She said, "For such loyalty we shall promote our nephew to be the Secretary of the Board of Rites."

Then she asked about the family, each in detail, and before she dismissed Shensi she had a clear picture of her twenty-odd nephews and grandnephews, their capabilities and their inclinations, and what part each could play in her scheme of things.

Shensi, who had been suspicious of Chao's ambition before, was now certain. It excited him, for if a Wu Dynasty was established, he, a Wu, would be the logical heir, and he saw himself as the Emperor-to-come. He began to devise means to abet Chao to hasten the usurpation. He petitioned Chao to confer posthumous honors upon the Wu ancestors five generations back, and to establish seven temples for their worship. He knew such were the prerogatives of the Imperial House; to confer them on the House of Wu was to get a wedge in for usurping the throne.

When Payi objected to the petition as a danger to the continuity of the Tang Dynasty, Chao overruled him. "The dead could not possibly endanger the living," she said.

Payi's zeal in guarding the interest of the Imperial House aroused Chao's suspicion. She saw on which side Payi's allegiance would lie when her interest and that of the Tang Dynasty should come into open conflict, and she began to be on guard with her Prime Minister.

22

As Chao did not summon the rest of the Wus for an audience, they were restless. The young Wus did not have their fathers' rectitude but were rapacious, self-seeking and unprincipled. They resented their late elders' refusal to cooperate with Chao, which had brought on the hardship of exile. Now that they had been recalled, their expectation of Chao's favor was reckless. When months passed and nobody except Shensi was given anything other than a minor post in the court, they were disappointed, especially San Szu (meaning "threefold deliberation").

When Shensi gathered together the men of the clan and told them that their Imperial Aunt had finally summoned the entire clan to dinner at the Palace, Three Deliberation said, "It's about time." His small, cruel eyes glinted in his broad, robust face in resentment of Chao's preference for Shensi. According to family sequence he should take precedence, since he was the son of Chao's elder brother.

Shensi's cunning eyes bore through Three Deliberation before he spoke. "Let me warn you not to show the slightest impatience or bitterness to the Empress Dowager. There are far greater things at stake than we could possibly imagine. Although our aunt has not spoken in so many words, I can tell she intends to usurp the Tang Dynasty throne to establish a dynasty of her own. When she does, it will be a Wu Dynasty, which means that the House of Wu will be the Imperial House; and if she wants to perpetuate her dynasty, one of the Wus will have to be the Crown Prince. Think of it; one of us will be the Emperor and the rest Kings! It is to our advantage to help our aunt to the utmost."

The listeners were awed into silence, and then Three Deliberation said under his breath, "It is a prodigious stake!"

"I don't need to warn you," continued Shensi, "That an inadvertent word to an outsider could mean the loss of our heads. Keep your mouth shut and your eyes and ears open and follow my directions. Tonight I want every one of you to get on the best side of the Empress. Show your best manner, oil your tongues and pledge your undying loyalty, and leave it to me to puff the bellows of her ambition."

In the Hall of Harmonious Jade, the Wus gaped in awe at the grandeur and elegance of the reception chamber. Mothers quieted their fidgeting children in whispers, menfolk spoke in undertones when asking Shensi their last-minute questions about palace amenities. When they saw Chao and Princess of Peace enter, they crouched to the floor. But Chao said affably, "You may rise. This is a family gathering. No formalities! She patted her daughter's hand and said nostalgically, "The last time I was home, thirty years ago, Princess of Peace was not born yet, and neither were some of you younger ones." She turned to a little boy standing by Shensi and said, "This, I suppose, is your son."

"Yes, Your Majesty, the second one. His name is Extended Heritage."

"A good-looking boy," said Chao. Then she turned to the other Wus, who were nudging each other for position to be noticed. Chao did not overlook a single one, Three Deliberation's two sons, Shensi's three sons, Shensi's brother's two sons, her cousins' son, and their sons. To each she said a word or two. Neither did she neglect the women. She talked to them as if their household problems were more important than state affairs.

Then came the feast. Five round tables were set on the left side of the reception hall, one at the head, two on its either side.

At the head table were Chao, Princess of Peace, and a few outstanding Wus. During the dinner Chao paid special attention to Three Deliberation, who agreed obsequiously to everything she said. A born syncophant, she thought, who could be useful to her. Then seeing Princess of Peace's eyes rested admiringly on Yu-chi, the son of Chao's second cousin, her own gaze shifted to him. He was a tall, handsome man with large, kind eyes in a roundish face. His manner was attentive and respectful but with none of Three Deliberation's obsequiousness. Of all the Wus, he alone had the dignity worthy to be the scion of the late Director of the Board of Works. Chao thought that if she had seen him years sooner, she could have chosen him as the imperial son-in-law—which would have pleased her daughter, judging from the way she doted on him.

After dinner, while Princess of Peace entertained the clan, Chao said to Shensi and Three Deliberation, "In the few months you have been in the capital, what have you heard from the court and the hundred-names regarding our reign?"

"Your Majesty," said Three Deliberation, "Your unworthy nephew, in talking to his fellow-officials, heard them praise Your Majesty's good reign. In fact, some even wondered why Your Majesty does not rule on your own."

"Aw-w-w? But do not put weight on what the brass-belt officials say. It is the opinion of the gold-belt ranks that should be taken seriously."

Gripping his brass-belt, Three Deliberation replied, "A brass-belt official could hardly mingle into the gold-belt ranks to fathom their minds."

Chao chuckled. "There is truth in what you said. We intend to elevate the ranks of the Wu clan." Of Shensi she inquired, "What do you have to say?"

"Your Majesty, your nephew heard that many in court are staunch supporters of Prince of Virtue. They deplored his exile to Pachou and regard him as the only prince who can face up to Your Majesty."

A glint of apprehension leaped to Chao's eyes. Lately Virtue had been constantly on her mind. He was the problem she dreaded to face. She concealed her concern and said casually, "That is why he was exiled."

After the clan left, she walked meditatively to her study. She slid open the mother-of-pearl window and looked out to the darkness beyond, then muttered, "Virtue! Virtue! Why were you ever born? Why were you not born a dullard, that your mother would have no compulsion to despatch you?" She stood motionless for a long time; then wrenched herself away to her desk, and began to brush rapidly a summons to General Chur for a secret mission to Pachou.

In Pachou, Virtue grieved over his father's death. His father's missiles had been the only link between him and his old life. Now they were never to come again. He placed a soul-tablet carved with "Kao Tsung the Great Holy Emperor" on the altar table in the center room. Each day he lighted the white candles, burned sandalwood chips, and prayed to his father's spirit to protect the Tang heritage. One evening, alone by the altar, Virtue saw his father's face, lined with unspeakable sorrow. When he looked again, there was only the soul-tablet with the twin dragons at its edges writhing in the flickering candlelight. Something must be terribly wrong that his father's spirit could not rest in peace. Had he died of foul means? Was the Dynasty in danger? Was this a foreboding of evil to come?

The next morning, when the news came that a General Chur from Loyang was on his way to inspect the house, Virtue divined what his father was warning him of. With the last restraining hand gone, his mother probably wanted him despatched. He was resigned to whatever might come, but his wife's worried face grieved him. He laid his hand on hers and said, "It would have been better if you had married a commoner. You have shared little of my honor and much of my grief."

"I have Your Highness's love. That is honor enough for me."

Virtue received Chur in the center room, hoping that his father's soul-tablet would remind him that he, a prince, had the blood of the late Emperor pulsing in his veins. Chur knelt perfunctorily before the altar. Then, with a set face, he led Prince of Virtue to another room. He extracted from his pouch a red silk scarf folded into a square. Prince of Virtue paled at the sight of the red, the color of blood, of condemnation, of death. Criminals on their way to the execution block wore jackets of this red, and he knew it was Shih-Pai*.

Chur flung the scarf to the Prince, "A gift from the Empress Dowager."

Virtue's eyes did not waver. He let the scarf drop to his feet. He calmly measured Chur, who stood with his feet wide apart, his face hard and cruel. He was thinking that his mother could not have chosen a more brutal man for this brutal mission.

"Be grateful that it is silk instead of steel," mocked Chur, as he locked the Prince in the room to end his life.

When the news of Virtue's death reached Chao, she sighed in relief as if a knife at her neck had been removed; yet at the same instant waves of remorse flooded her. She shut herself in her study. A force stronger than she propelled her into perpetual motion . . . pacing, pacing, pacing.

With Chao's terrible mood, the atmosphere in the Palace was on the verge of explosion. Jasmine, worried, sent for Princess of Peace in the Empress's name.

Peace's empathy for her mother told her the very thing to say. "Why torment yourself, Mother? You know Virtue would have done the same to you."

Chao stopped pacing and turned to Princess of Peace, "He would?" Then with a grateful smile to her daughter, she said, "Of course he would."

She did not hold audience for seven days, in mourning for Virtue, and she honored him with high-sounding posthumous titles and buried him in his father's mausoleum, which he had not been permitted to see during his lifetime.

When Chao held audience again, she spoke without preamble in a brittle tone, "We sent the Left Gold Guard General, Chur,

*"Shih-Pai" means the bestowing of silk on offenders of royal blood or high-ranking officials to hang themselves in lieu of the disgrace of public execution.

to Pachou on a routine inspection. If evidence of the Prince's rebellious intent was found, it should have been reported to us and submitted to the Judicial Department for trial. To press the Prince to take his own life is a gross overstepping of authority. Even decapitation is too light a punishment." She paused and swept her eyes over the court. No one spoke.

Then Three Deliberation, recently promoted to the silver belt rank, stepped forward and said, "Your Majesty, it is, no doubt, an unpardonable offense; but the General's intention is to protect the throne. His fault is in his overzealousness. Therefore your servant recommends reducing his punishment to exile. With our extensive border, the General's military skill could be of service on the battlefield. When occasion arises, Your Majesty could command him to redeem his offense with a victory."

"What is the opinion of the court?" asked Chao, with eyes still blazing.

Although no one was fooled by the play-acting of Chao and Three Deliberation, yet silence hung over the court; for who had the audacity to strip the mask from the Empress Dowager's face?

When no dissent was voiced, Chao said, "Then we shall accede to the petition and exile General Chur to Tachou."

Payi realized that he was a pawn in the Empress Dowager's crafty game. He had helped her depose Tsung Tsung for a better Emperor in Jui Tsung, but he had not bargained for Chao's outright reign. Now Virtue's death confirmed his fear that Chao aimed to usurp the Tang Dynasty. But how was he to prevent it? While it was easy to pluck a young sprig like Tsung Tsung from the throne, it was another matter with an old tree like Chao whose root sank deep in political strategems. After the audience, he tarried on the marble steps and looked after the backs of the departing ministers, wondering to whom he could unburden his mind.

His gaze fell upon the broad back of the crimson-robed Deputy Censor, Ti. Payi had known Ti since he was a young official starting his career; now he was over fifty, and his squarish face was deeply lined, and his three-pronged beard was gray.

[171]

In all those years he had been known as a conscientious minister unafraid to censure his sovereign, and his counsel often had borne weight with Chao.

Payi touched him on the elbow and said, "I would like to have a word with you." Lagging behind the crowd he continued in a low voice, "In view of our friendship I shall take the liberty to speak to you of what is plaguing my mind. However, I would be putting my life in your hands, for if you should report me to the Empress Dowager, my head would roll."

"Then deliberate it three times before you speak."

"I trust you. I remember when your colleague was sent to a border post, you felt sorry for his aged invalid mother and went to that outlandish place in his stead. If you could be compassionate to a mere colleague you could be no less to a friend of long standing. I am worried over the recent turn of the state events. The confinement of Emperor Jui Tsung, the sudden influx of the Wus in the court, and now the death of Prince of Virtue, coming one upon the other—they seem to presage a threat to the Tang Dynasty. Shouldn't there be a consorted action among the loyal ministers to restore Emperor Jui Tsung to the throne?"

"I do not condone the way the Empress Dowager disposed of her sons," said Ti. "Neither Am I unmindful of her other shortcomings, but the one significant consideration with me is her statesmanship, which neither of her sons can equal. To me, it is to the advantage of the nation to have an indomitable but capable sovereign rather than a pliant but indiscriminate one.

"Our Empire is vast," Ti continued. "Without a strong hand at the helm, pretenders would rise to disturb the peace of the nation. Besides, it is all within the family. The Empress Dowager cannot live forever. After her death the throne will, in the natural order, revert to the legitimate heir. You and I may live to see that day, while if we act unheedingly now, either we will lose our heads or plunge the nation into a civil war, at the end of which she might still come out the winner."

As they reached the wall gate where their carriages were waiting, Payi said no more. But on his way home he mulled over what Ti said and was unconvinced. He, too, would go along with Her Majesty as long as the throne was kept in the Tang

Dynasty. But if Chao should displace the Tang Dynasty, that was something to which he could not acquiesce; and he was not sure that that very thing was not what Chao intended to do.

To forget his worry he loitered to the flagstone court outside his bedchamber and watched the fantail goldfish in the large earthenware vessel. Their leisurely movements, graceful like the swing of a dancer's skirt, relaxed him. He looked up when a servitor approached.

"Your Eminence," said the servitor. "The secretary is here with an urgent report."

Frowning in apprehension, Payi said, "Show him to my study." His tiredness came back and he dragged his feet in a slow, labored gait; but he did not have far to go, for his residence was a small, simple house. Despite his high position he lived frugally and unpretentiously.

"Your Eminence," said his secretary. "Six disemployed officials have captured Yangchow as a base to start a revolution. They claimed in their manifesto that their purpose is to restore the legitimate heir of the Tang Dynasty to the throne. They denounce the Empress Dowager in scathing language. Many have flocked to the rebels' standard, and their army has already swollen to ten thousand."

"Hum," grunted Payi. "If there is further news, deliver it to me immediately."

Payi's thoughts were tugging in opposite directions. It was treason to rebel against the reign, yet he could not help endorsing the rebels' cause. If only there were more hot-blooded champions for the Emperor in the court, the Empress Dowager could not override the Son of Heaven. He, the Prime Minister, was the first to blame. Now, in this crisis, he must petition the Empress Dowager to restore the Emperor to the throne, so that the insurgents would have no cause to rebel. But before he had had time to write his memorial, he received a summons to attend an urgent conference in the Palace.

In the Council Chamber Chao stated tersely the purpose of her summons, then asked for plans to suppress the rebels.

"Your Majesty," said Payi. "The rebels' cause is to restore the Son of Heaven to the throne. Once the Emperor is on the

[173]

throne, the uprising should dissipate by itself and no expedition and bloodshed would be necessary. Your minister humbly begs Your Majesty to consider his unworthy opinion."

"And to traffic with the rebels? Ridiculous!" said Chao. To foreclose further petitions of that nature she speedily appointed General Li Hsiao-i to command the expedition and Way Yuen-Chung to be the Chief of Staff. She also took the opportunity to recall Chur and promote him to the office of Assistant Chief of Staff.

With Chao's rejection of his counsel, Payi knew he had signed his own death warrant, but at least he had been true to his own conviction. He was not surprised when, a few days later, a Tribunnate of Censor accused him of treason in the morning audience, and before Payi could defend himself, the Captain of the Guards whisked him out of the hall.

The court was aghast. Recovering from their astonishment, Payi's colleagues, one after the other, defended him; but they were drowned out by the loud incriminations from the Wu clique.

"Silence!" Chao cried. "We have reports that our troops have suffered a bad reverse and the rebels are sweeping north like the waves of the sea. At such a time we cannot take the chance of being undermined by rebels from within the court. Decapitation to the Prime Minister, and banishment to those who have defended him!"

Chao stared around the court, then added, "We command General Si to hasten his soldiers to attack the rebels from the rear. Let none of the six leaders escape."

Three days later, Payi's head hung on the city wall.

23

It took two years to suppress the Yangchow insurrection. They were nerve-wracking years for Chao. The fighting was on her own territory and the challengers were her own hundred-names. She believed the nation as a whole considered her reign good and was not against her, yet as long as there was an abscess, the inflammation could spread. She bent her efforts to clear it up, but the rebels were more tenacious than she thought.

She was relieved when the sentence of the six rebel leaders finally came for ratification. Reviewing the documents, she asked, "Which of the six wrote the condemning proclamation?"

"Loh Ping-Wong, Your Majesty," said the secretary. "A talented member of the literati but also a wanton gambler."

"It is the negligence of our Prime Minister that such literary talent was not made available to our court." She admired his brilliant style so much that she sent a messenger to Yangchow to collect his work. However, she did not confuse her admiration for his talent with the political situation at hand. In her usual bold handwriting she brushed, unhesitatingly, the fatal word "decapitation."

From then on, Chao was obsessed with suspicions that there were other factions plotting for her downfall. Secluded in the Palace, she had no way of knowing what was brewing in the

[175]

remote parts of her empire. She was determined to devise a means for her hundred-names to report to her directly, so that every man could be her eyes and ears to ferret out insurgents.

She issued an edict to have four receptacles made in four colors, each with a narrow slot for depositing memorials. These were to be placed in the Judiciary Hall, the green for personal advices to the Empress Dowager, the red for political criticisms or suggestions, the white for redress of injustice, and the black for information concerning conspiracies against the reign. They were to be made accessible to people of all walks of life, even to the lowest peasants and the meanest workmen. Those in far-off districts who had secret information to impart were to be provided with postal horses from station to station, with food and lodging all the way to the capital. If the information was factual, the informant would be rewarded with an official rank; if not, no punishment would be meted out to him. Proclamations to this effect were to be posted throughout the nation.

At the marketplace in Hochou of the western prefecture, a crowd gathered in front of the proclamation. A man holding the hand of his seven-year-old son paused at the outer perimeter and craned his neck to see what it was about. Suddenly the boy howled "Ah-yah! He stepped on me," pointing to a broad, robust man in black robe and a black beret with a blue pompon who was elbowing to get to the front.

"Who do you think you are, pushing and stepping all over people!" said the boy's father.

The man flashed his small, cruel eyes on the speaker and rolled up his sleeve to fight.

"Get out of his way," someone whispered. "He is the notorious ex-convict Lan Chinzen."

Father and son quickly lost themselves in the crowd and Chinzen walked overbearingly to the front, with the people backing away to make way for him.

Chinzen was the son of a gambler. His mother had been sold to pay his father's gambling debt while Chinzen was still in her womb. As a child he was clever but brutal; as a man, sagacious but profligate. Now, reading the proclamation, he muttered, "Everything to gain and nothing to lose."

He drew up the corners of his mouth into a sly quirk and headed for the magistrate's office. He said importantly to the secretary that he had secret information to impart. The secretary eyed him dubiously, but since it was not his duty to verify the informations, he dispatched Chinzen to the capital without ado.

Chinzen was the first to come forth wtih incriminating information. Curious about this first informer, Chao summoned him to an audience. Chinzen reminded her of Secretary Hsu. In appearance they were very different, Chinzen broad and strong, the other tall and slender; but there was something alike in their small, cunning, avaricious eyes. She knew Chinzen could be bought to serve her purpose as Secretary Hsu had been. Therefore, even though the information was of little consequence, she rewarded him with a secretarial post in the Judicial Department.

From Chao's queries, Chinzen gathered that the Empress Dowager was susceptible to suspicion of rebellion, and he took advantage of it to further his own end. He exacted confessions from innocent people to prove his loyalty and efficiency. He rose in favor, and before long he was a Deputy Censor. Other unscrupulous officials quickly followed his example, and soon a group of ruthless officials evolved, to abuse justice and abet the Empress Dowager to a reign of terror.

Racing down the main avenue one day, Chinzen's carriage ran into a bullock cart. As he got out of his carriage, he heard a man's groan from the bullock cart and a girl's frightened voice asking, "Are you hurt, Father?" The father's answer was drowned by the violent curses of the two drivers, each atop his seat.

Chinzen opened the door of the cart and out came an old man and his young daughter not quite eighteen. Chinzen's lecherous eyes bulged at the sight of her pretty face. The girl hid behind her father and lowered her head. Nursing the bump on his head,

[177]

the father murmured, "What an evil day! A broken head and a broken cart!"

"What have you done to my carriage, old man?" asked Chinzen in a severe tone.

The old man, a minor official in the Board of Rites, recognizing Chinzen's high rank by his official robe, apologized profusely, "It is the fault of my careless driver. I hope this does not inconvenience Your Eminence too much. Your humble servant will pay for the repair of Your Eminence's carriage," he offered, as he saw that the damage was slight.

"Hum!" said Chinzen. "Three hundred ounces of gold may well repair it."

The old man's jaw dropped. "But—but it only needs a few splints," he stuttered.

"Three hundred ounces of gold," repeated Chinzen.

"Even if I sold my old life I could not get three hundred ounces of gold."

"But you have a young life in your daughter. I will take her in place of gold."

"Purple Orchid is already betrothed. Even her wedding date is set."

"Send her over tomorrow," said Chinzen, stepping into his carriage; and his driver, giving the other driver a contemptuous stare, flipped his rein grandiosely.

"Give me a few days; I will raise the gold," the old man called after the departing carriage. But it was gone, raising a trail of dust behind.

The next day the old man gathered his family and friends together to raise the gold. One of his friends said, "It is not the gold he wants. Gold he can easily get by other means. It is your pretty daughter."

"Why not drop a memorial in the white receptacle in the Judiciary Hall and petition Her Majesty for redress?" said another.

The old man waited until it was dusk; then, with the petition hidden in his sleeve, he trudged to the Judiciary Hall. Going up the steps to the hall, he tripped. Before he could pick himself up,

[178]

he was dragged away to a dungeon by Chinzen's henchmen. There he was pressed to sign a confession of treason. When he refused, he was tied to a board and whipped. At each welt the old man's teeth sank deeper into his lips till blood dripped down his chin. When he still refused to confess, Chinzen's men called for the finger rack.

"Confess, old man," a torturer advised. "Even younger and stronger men than you have succumbed. How can you hope to withstand the tortures here?"

"Heaven be my witness. I have not conspired against the throne," the old man groaned. "I am prepared to die, but I cannot confess to a crime that will banish my sons and enslave my womenfolk."

As the rack pulled harder and harder on the old man's fingers, he could no longer stand the pain and he agreed to sign whatever confession they drew up for him.

With the confession in his hand, Chinzen executed the old man and took Purple Orchid as his spoil.

When Shensi found that Chinzen's rapaciousness and deception were not only undetected but lauded by his aunt, he began to wonder if Chinzen could not be a useful instrument to himself. One day when the court was dispersing after the audience, he came alongside Chinzen. "I heard you have taken possession of a new beauty. Judging from the lengths you went to, she must be a worthy prize."

"Rumors of such things spread faster than fire," said Chinzen evasively.

"Rumor? Her father was a minor secretary in my department."

Chinzen laughed to cover his discomforture. Unable to fathom Shensi's purpose in bringing up this subject, he threw out a line speculatively, "If Your Eminence has eyes on some beauty, your servant is at your command."

At Shensi's negative gesture, Chinzen angled again. "Perhaps some enemies I could sweep out of Your Eminence's way?" At the flush of Shensi's pale face, Chinzen rubbed his avaricious hands in delight. What could augment his prestige and power more than to be in league with the Empress Dowager's nephew? "Your Eminence needs but to give the word and I shall do the walking and the running."

Shensi's aim was to hasten Chao in her plan to defy the law and establish a new dynasty, so that he would be the heir to the throne. He had persuaded Chao to place the other Wus in important positions. However, although the influence of the Wu Clique was getting formidable in court, they were opposed by a number of high officials, whose hostility to the clan was as unquestionable as their loyalty to the Empress Dowager. To gain his objective, Shensi would have to eliminate them. He named six to Chinzen, among them Way Yuan-Chung, recently promoted to Deputy Censor, and Ti, then Chief Censor.

"Leave them to me and Your Eminence shall see their heads tumble," said Chinzen.

When the accusation against the six high officials came to Chao, she was flabbergasted. Treachery even in high places in her court! If Way and Ti could not be trusted, whom could she trust? Was she hated by everyone? Were they all plotting to restore her son to the throne? It could not be—not with Way and Ti. Yet... without the wind, there could be no wave. Something was back of this accusation. She must look into it. She ordered Chinzen to investigate the case and rush his finding to her.

Chinzen himself supervised the exacting of the confessions of the six officials. They were shoved into the torture chamber in a dungeon. There were men hung upside down there, weighted with mill stones. The air was foul with the stench of burning flesh, and the walls echoed the mad ravings of men in pain. There were pumps to squirt vinegar into culprits' nostrils, and racks to stretch their limbs.

"This is worse than the eighteen layers of purgatory," Yuan-Chung cried in horror. "What kind of monster are you?"

Chinzen's cruel eyes glared as he signaled a henchman to slash a whip across Yuan-Chung's face, sending him flat to the ground. When Yuan-Chung got back to his feet, Chinzen swept his arm around the torture chamber and said, "This is for recalcitrants like yourself." Turning to the others he said, "For those who confess, I promise special consideration."

[180]

To throw Chinzen off his guard, Ti said, "If it is a choice between whipping and confessing, I will take the latter."

While the five stared, Chinzen smiled, "I see that at least one of you has sense." He turned to his henchman and said, "Take him to a cell and give him food and drink. These others need more inducing, but they will come around."

When the goaler brought his food, Ti asked anxiously about the other five.

"A mule has more sense than they," the goaler said. "They refuse to confess even when hung by their feet. Where do they think their stubbornness will get them? No one ever leaves here without confessing."

"I figured as much," said Ti. Then, revolving the heavy jade ring on his thumb, he sighed. "I am a doomed man and this will be of no value to me in the spirit world. To someone living it can fetch a good price."

With his greedy eyes on the ring, the goaler asked, "What can I do for Your Eminence? Perhaps a pot of wine?"

Ti shook his head. "I have an old mother at home. She is over seventy. I would like to write a few words of farewell as my last filial duty to her. Could I trouble you to deliver a son's last letter to his mother?"

"I can slip out after dark. I will get Your Eminence some paper and ink and a brush."

Before the note to his mother, Ti wrote one to his son and hid it inside the fluffy cotton padding of his coat. When the goaler came back, he said, "The weather is getting too warm for a padded coat. Will you ask my family to take off the padding and send back the coat? And here is the letter to my mother."

Chinzen rushed the indictment to Chao late in the evening. Reading it in the candlelight, Chao's face blanched. "Decapitation to the six ingrates!" she muttered. She had trusted them—personally placed them in high positions—and they had plotted against her. Yet, on second thought, she could not believe this of Way and Ti. Her knowledge of human nature could not be that amiss. Malediction? Intrigue? Someone wanted to get rid of them to clip her wings? "Hum-m-m. This bears looking into."

[181]

She brushed an edict to appoint a special inspector to reexamine the six culprits.

Chao now imagined herself to be surrounded by conspirators. Where there were only shadows she saw assassinators, and she, who had always loathed a retinue, now surrounded herself with many attendants. On her way to her sleeping chamber there were eunuchs in front, behind and on either side of her, each holding a silk lantern dangling from a bamboo handle. At the veranda, she heard the snap of a twig. "Who is there?" she shouted. "Call the guards!"

In the antechamber she caught the ladies drowsing. "Stay awake and watch," she thundered. "Whoever dozes shall receive a hundred lashes."

She ordered the ladies to throw a cordon around her bed. When she saw Jasmine's gray head among those of the ladies crouched on the floor, she said, "Jasmine, you may be relieved."

"Permit me, Your Majesty, to watch with the rest. Their young eyelids will droop in spite of themselves, while I, at my age, will need little sleep. Besides, my anxiety for Your Majesty's safety will keep me wide awake."

The next day Princess of Peace found her mother slouched in her chair, her eyes closed in troubled thought, and, on her desk, the papers in disarray.

"So you have come at last," said Chao straightening up. "I need to talk to you." And she motioned her daughter to pull up a chair.

"You look tired, Mother. Had you not better take a rest?"

"Not until I get this off my mind." Searching among the papers, she told Princess of Peace of the accusation of the six and the subsequent indictment. "Here it is. Read it."

"Convincing," commented Princess of Peace, as her eyes went up and down the lines.

"I sent a special inspector to the prison to question them. Not only did his report confirm Chinzen's finding, but on top of it came Ti's confession. What further evidence could I ask? Then this morning a sealed memorial came from Ti's son. He said his father and the five others were victims of someone's malicious false accusation. And here is Ti's letter, smuggled out from the

[182]

prison, asking his son to appeal for redress. Is Ti guilty or not guilty? He is too important to be set free if guilty, too valuable to the nation to be executed if innocent. The sentence is here for my signature, and the indecision is driving me to distraction."

"It is a weighty decision, Mother. Let me dwell on it a moment." Princess of Peace realized that her mother's indulgence was making Chinzen into a dangerous weapon that could cut down anyone, even . . . her husband, whose obvious sympathy with the confined Jui Tsung was a constant worry to her. She decided that she must watch Chinzen, to strike before he struck. Perhaps she could talk Purple Orchid into being her spy in revenge for her father.

"Do not keep your thoughts to yourself," said Chao, impatient of her daughter's silence. "Let us hear your opinion."

"I think there is more than what appears on the surface. Why not question Ti yourself?"

At the audience next morning, Ti was brought before the throne, and Chao's first question was about his confession.

"Your Majesty," said Ti. "If your humble servant had not confessed, he could not have lived to appeal for redress." He then told of the horrible torture chamber and what the other five suffered.

"The inspector we sent said nothing of the torture in his report; neither did he find any counter-evidence to vindicate the accused," said Chao.

Justice Hsu of the Judiciary Board stepped out of his rank and said, "Your Majesty, if the inspector's report did not coordinate with Chinzen's indictment, he, too, would be accused of treason and thrown into prison. It is my humble opinion that in view of Ti's record of meritorious service to Your Majesty, he is incapable of what he is accused of. Besides, from my humble association with him, I have known him as a man of integrity who could not be disloyal to a friend, far less to Your Majesty."

"Your Majesty, if Ti's confession is not an evidence of his guilt, what is?" Shensi argued.

"Your Majesty, a person under duress will confess to any crime," said Judge Hsu. "To assure Your Majesty of Ti's innocence, your servant will pledge with his head."

[183]

Chao knew Hsu was a just judge, loved and revered by the people of his jurisdiction. His courage and gallantry convinced her of the six ministers' innocence. But on second thought, if they were innocent who was behind this accusation? Her searching eyes went from face to face and came to rest on Shensi's. Was he contriving to hasten the usurpation? Foolish, she thought. A dynasty cannot be won by eliminating pillars of the nation, but by winning their loyal support. Then she said, "In view of Justice Hsu's vouching, we will spare the lives of the six. However, they will be banished to distant prefectures, since their calling suspicion upon themselves is in itself a crime. But because of their past merits we shall recall them in due time. To our good informants we warn them not to let their zeal override their prudence."

Since his false accusation of so great a personage as Ti had left him unscathed, Chinzen became rapacious without limit. He convicted many innocent officials and confiscated their properties to enrich the Imperial Treasury and line his own pocket. Justice Hsu, who offended him and the Wus by his fearless defense of Ti, became his prime target. Twice Chinzen made his henchmen accuse Hsu of treason, and twice he was banished. But each time Chao reinstated him, much to the joy of the people. On his second reinstatement, he pleaded with Chao to release him from office. "Your Majesty, your humble servant is a deer surrounded by hunters. If Your Majesty does not release him, eventually he will be the venison in their cooking pot." Chao did not let him go.

Chinzen's wanton brutality became such a terror to the court that several memorials were presented to Chao to restrain him. Chao tossed them aside. She chose to hold in one hand a mighty whip in Chinzen to beat the insubordinates into line, and in the other an equitable scale in Hsu to ensure justice to her hundred-names.

24

Chao sat sideways on the bench that bordered the veranda, one day in late spring, wondering what to do in the long afternoon. With Chinzen, her watchdog, baring his teeth to her enemies, she could relax and have time for pleasure. But what pleasure could she have with only ladies-in-waiting and eunuchs in the Inner Palace? She wished she had a man to love—a strong, robust man, not a weakling like Kao Tsung.

She wondered if she had ever loved Kao Tsung. If she had, it had been for his power, and not for the man. Now she wanted to love for love's own sake. But set apart in the Palace, how was she to find love? How was any woman to find love when she could not be seen by men, could not hand anything directly to a man, lest the touching of hands incite passion? How was she, the symbol of all womanhood, to sidetrack tradition and find love without drawing discredit to herself? Was she doomed to a loveless life in spite of the power she held in her hands?

She pushed herself up from the bench and went to the Bamboo Pavilion. On her way, the warm, scented air, as sensual as a courtesan's breath, heightened her desire. She found birds chirping and fleecy clouds sailing lazily in a blue sky. A soft breeze touched her cheeks like a fluffy powder puff. The butterflies flitting in pairs made her painfully aware of her own solitude. She tossed an acorn playfully into the placid pond. As the water spread wider and wider, with the center the prisoner of the very circles it engendered, she wondered if she, too, were not the prisoner of her own power, with no freedom to love and be loved.

Waiting for Princess of Peace and Princess of Gold she asked irritably, "Are they not here yet?"

Princess of Gold, several years younger than Chao, was Kao Tsung's aunt. While the other kin secretly resented Chao's usurpation of the Emperor's power, she shamelessly fawned upon Chao; for she knew if ever the antagonism between the kin and the Empress should come to a head, the Empress Dowager would come out the winner, and she wanted to be on the winning side. She was often summoned to the Palace, for her tattling kept Chao's finger on the pulse of the other kin.

When Chao saw Princess of Gold's round, freckled face approach the box hedge, followed by Princess of Peace, she stepped out to meet them. "What makes you so late?" she asked sharply. She led the way to the summer-house, sank down on the bench, and indicated the stools at the table for the other two. Jasmine came with a tray of black-dragon-tea, dried lychee, candied pine seeds, honeyed figs, and salted watermelon seeds.

Princess of Peace, sensing that her mother was not in a good mood, occupied herself in cracking the watermelon seeds. Princess of Gold babbled about the kin—whose husband picked what wild flower and how jealous the wife was; whose children were sick, whose bouncing; which boy was clever, which stupid; and who said and did what. Chao, usually amused by these bits of gossip, today showed no interest. With her eyes on the birds among the trees she said wistfully, "Even a bird has a mate to warm its nest; yet the Empress Dowager must keep vigil with her own shadow night after night."

The yearning was so transparent that it occurred to Princess of Gold that if she could find a lover for Her Majesty, wealth and honor would be hers the rest of her life. "Will Your Majesty trust your humble aunt to be your 'old man in the moon'?" she asked.

"Your Empress Dowager is hard to please," Chao parried.

[186]

"Perhaps someone like . . . ?" Princess of Gold waited for the Empress Dowager to supply the name.

"Someone like the Tufan Emissary," interrupted Princess of Peace, as she remembered how her mother had admired his robust physique.

"What was he like?" asked Princess of Gold.

"Tall and sturdy like a tree, with the muscles of a lion and the heart of spring," said Chao dreamily.

"I shall find someone like him, even if I have to comb every street and house in Loyang," said Princess of Gold.

In the following days both Princesses searched for a tall, sturdy man. But, confined to the company of women by convention, they found little opportunity to see any man besides their own families.

"Why not ask your second Cousin?" said Princess of Peace. "He is a general. Perhaps he knows a warrior or two."

"He is indiscreet. You do not want to smell like mutton before you have even tasted the meat."

One afternoon while Princess of Gold was away at the Palace, her maid, Autumn Fragrance, studied her own reflection at her mistress's dressing table and sighed. Her pointed face and long, sensual eyes were pretty, yet she was just a slave, while the flat, ugly face of her mistress was that of a princess. She changed into an apple-green skirt and lavender blouse, then slipped out of the mansion. When she saw the sun fast slanting towards the west she quickened her steps. She must reach the mart before the closing gong struck at sunset.

There were a great variety of stores in the mart with merchandise that could delight the eyes of a nineteen-year-old girl, trinkets, jewelry, carved ivories, silk brocades, and exotic goods from foreign countries. But Autumn Fragrance did not give them a glance; she headed straight for the apothecary shop. Behind its counter men were gathering dehydrated herbs, seed pods, flowers, insects, snakes, toads, and other medicated substances from tiers upon tiers of square drawers along the wall. Among these men, Wenyi towered like a giant. Autumn Fragrance watched him pull a string from a reel above his head, tie the bundle of herbs in a cross-knot, and hand the package to a

[187]

customer. Then, aiming at a vertical hollow bamboo at the corner, he tossed the coins into its gaping mouth. Autumn Fragrance sidled up to him before another customer could claim his attention. Wenyi's handsome face broke into a smile, and his pitch-black eyes burned like a blacksmith's forge. He leaned across the counter, his elbow touching her bosom. Autumn Fragrance pushed him aside. "Have you no shame? In front of those people?" she chided, stepping back, although her eyes were inviting.

He laughed in a base note of passion, then asked, "Has she gone to the Palace again?"

She nodded.

"Then I can come tonight? At the same time?"

"I shall wait inside the garden gate."

"How will you know to let me in? Shall I bark like a dog?"

"Silly! How would I know whether it is you or a real dog?"

"Throw a stone over the wall?"

"That's better. But be very careful. If we are caught, it is to meet again in the spirit world." Her fragrant water intoxicated him, and he pinched her cheek. She thrust his hands aside and ran away from the store. He chuckled. His eyes followed her until she was lost in the crowd.

When Wenyi came, Autumn Fragrance led him into a cave beneath an artificial hill in the rock garden. Here, locked in each others' arms, they made love. Lying side by side, his hand exploring her body, he whispered, "Someday it will be on a soft bed. Someday I will take you away to a far-off land." They talked and dreamed, forgetting time.

Suddenly Autumn Fragrance said, "It is time she should return from the Palace. You had better go."

As they walked stealthily towards the gate, they saw it open, and Princess of Gold's carriage rolled in. Wenyi darted behind a tree, but with the lanterns and the torches that accompanied the carriage shedding a flood of light his way, he was seen.

"Thieves! Thieves!" cried the gatekeeper.

Wenyi was trussed like a hog and brought to the Princess.

Autumn Fragrance pleaded at her mistress's feet. "He is no thief. He is my cousin."

[188]

"Cousin!" scoffed Princess of Gold. Why should your cousin meet you in stealth in the garden? If it were not for my soft heart, you would be whipped to death this very moment." She turned to her servitor. "Lock her up and send her to our manor in Changan tomorrow.

Princess of Gold's eyes swept Wenyi from head to foot. His sturdy physique and animal strength proclaimed him the very man she was looking for. "Untie the man," she ordered. To Wenyi, she asked, "What is your name?"

"Wenyi, Your Highness. I am no thief. You can search me. I have taken nothing."

"Hum!" said Princess of Gold. "No doubt nothing can be found on you. But you have stolen Autumn Fragrance's virtue. I should hand you over to the Gold Guards and put you in prison, but I—I will see what to do with you tomorrow," she said enigmatically.

Next day Princess of Gold sent for her steward. "Take that Wenyi in your hands and teach him the court etiquette. Tell him the sooner he learns the better it is for him, and get him some presentable robes."

Wenyi was puzzled at this unexpected turn of events, but why should he care, so long as he was well fed and well clothed? He did not like the kneeling, the cringing and the conventionalities, but it was better than the prison.

When the rough edges were polished off, Wenyi was brought into the Princess's presence. Princess of Gold sent her attendants away; then in a low voice she explained what she intended for him. Wenyi's eyes popped.

"If you please Her Majesty, wealth, position—anything you desire—will be yours," said Princess of Gold.

"How old is the Empress Dowager?" asked Wenyi.

"Sixty-two."

"Your mother!" ejaculated Wenyi. "A grandmother!"

"Watch your tongue. No vulgar curses," chided Princess of Gold.

"What if I refuse . . . What if I cannot . . ."

"Then you go to jail where you should be in the first place," said Princess of Gold.

[189]

When Chao was told about Wenyi she wanted to see him herself. Since no man was permitted to enter the Inner Palace, she decided to visit Princess of Peace on some pretense and see Wenyi there.

Princess of Peace sent her husband, Si Shaw, away. She did not want his silent censure to strain the atmosphere. Then she installed Wenyi in the guest pavilion. When Chao came, Wenyi crouched at her feet in a big awkward heap. He felt Chao's eyes appraising him, and he stole a glance at the Empress Dowager to whom he was to sell his love. He had imagined her to be wrinkled, perhaps toothless too. To find her a woman of beauty, who looked no more than forty-odd years, with virility equal to his own, was an unexpected stroke of good fortune. His eyes twinkled with relief. He stole another glance. This time his eyes met Chao's and saw he was desired, and he closed one eye in a roguish wink.

Chao chuckled at this bold rakishness. Patting her daughter's hand, she said, "Tell Shaw he has an uncle in Wenyi. I shall see that Shaw is well rewarded."

Wenyi emerged in court as Si Wenyi, uncle of the imperial son-in-law, and Shaw was pressed into attending Wenyi at Chao's command. Even then, Wenyi had no access to the Inner Palace; neither could Chao visit him. Chao racked her brain for a way out. Should she pretend to be sick and have Wenyi come as a physician? The eunuch physicians could easily see through that ruse. Besides, she did not savor the idea of simulating illness. He could come into the Palace as a religious teacher. She could make him an abbot of . . . the White Horse Temple. Then she could worship in his temple, and he could come to hold religious rites in the Palace.

The White Horse Temple, located twenty lis east of Loyang, was so named because the forty-two volumes of the first Buddhist sutras were borne to the capital on the back of a white horse. It was the oldest temple in the Empire, built when Buddhism was first introduced into China, six hundred years before. Now it was defaced by weather and blackened by incense smoke. But through the centuries the trees around it had grown to towering heights, and a rare mellowness permeated the place, giving it the dignity of a bearded sage. It was an ideal sanctum for a recluse but nothing that an apothecary could desire. Chao chose it because of its out-of-the-way location, where there were neither visitors nor neighbors to pry. Soon after Wenyi was installed as Abbot, Chao went to the White Horse Temple to worship. Going through the grounds, Wenyi kicked a loose brick from the moss-grown walk and pouted. "It is coming apart. What can I do with a broken-down place like this?"

Chao laughed. "It shall be rebuilt to your heart's content, and you shall be permitted to draw on the Imperial Treasury for its construction."

Overwhelmed with happiness, Wenyi impulsively swept his benefactress into his arms, and spun round and round with her before he set her down. Laughing at his crazy action, Chao chided indulgently, "You must be taught better manners." Then surveying him with adoring eyes, she said, "How very strong you are."

In ten months a magnificent temple stood in place of the old. The glaze of the roof tiles, the vermillion lacquer on the columns, the bas relief on the stone balustrades—everything was the best human hands could shape. The three gold images and the eighteen Boddhisattvas were unparalleled masterpieces of art, breathing with life. But it was in the Abbot's abode behind the main temple that Wenyi's extravagance and ingenuity had their greatest fling. Here Chao came to spend long hours with Wenyi, to sip fragrant tea under the ancient ginkgo tree, to listen to the tinkling of tiny bells on the temple eaves, to forget that she was an Empress, to be only a woman in love, to experience the exquisite sensation of falling in love for love's sake.

Wenyi, catapulted from a nobody to the exalted position of the Empress Dowager's paramour, began to have preposterous ideas. He imagined himself, if not an Emperor, at least a king. He wanted disciples to fill the dormitory built for a thousand monks. But where could he recruit them? From other temples? Their sanctimonious ways made him puke. No meat, no women. What was life for? They were not his kind. Scratching

[191]

his shaven scalp, he thought of Pockmark, his colleague in the apothecary shop, who was definitely his kind. He would ask him to help.

At the counter of the apothecary shop, a clerk caught sight of Wenyi's rich priest robe, and his jaw dropped, "It's you, Wenyi."

"Abbot of the White Horse Temple to you," Wenyi swaggered. "Where is Pockmark?"

"In jail. His creditors caught up with him."

"How much does he owe?"

"Three strings of cash [three thousand coins]."

"I will get him out."

"You have that kind of money?"

Wenyi laughed and left for the prison.

As Wenyi stepped into the cell he asked, "In trouble again, Pockmark?"

Pockmark's eyes bulged at Wenyi's gorgeous priest robe. "Have you joined a troupe or something?"

Wenyi chuckled, then told of his temple and his plan to recruit disciples. "I have room for a thousand and more," he boasted. "I will make you a squad leader, and do not worry about no women, no meat. In my temple I make the rules."

Pockmark's cell mates, listening in silence, now joined in, "Honorable Abbot, how about taking us into your temple?"

"Why not? The more the merrier."

Words got around among the riffraff and the outlaws, and soon the White Horse was packed with them. Although Chao provided large tracts of land for the support of the temple, Wenyi's ever-growing, insatiate band, accustomed to outlawry as their trade, still pilfered, robbed, and killed. And with Wenyi under the shield of the Empress Dowager, the Gold Guards were helpless. The Secretary of the Board of Censor, however, decided to brave Chao's anger to bring the band to law. When Pockmark learned of it through a servitor in the Secretary's office, he said to Wenyi, "If our Abbot is going to the Palace, put in a word with the Empress Dowager——"

"What about?"

"I heard the Secretary of the Board of Censure is going to bring our band to law."

"We will dispose of this matter ourselves."

That night Pockmark and a few of his squad disguised themselves in bandit outfits—black short coat, loose trousers, and red bandanna. They hid on both sides of the street where the Secretary would pass on his way home. When they saw him coming, they threw a rope across the street, pulled it tight to trip his horse, and then beat the fallen Secretary half to death.

One day, Wenyi galloped to the Palace dressed in a gray satin priest robe, a vermillion cape brocaded in gold, and a gold miter that was perched rakishly on his head. As he came upon a peasant laboring under a heavy load of faggots, his horse reared and threw him off his saddle. Raging like a mad man, he grabbed the peasant by the collar and dashed him against a rock, then hopped on his horse and rode away, leaving the half-dying peasant on the road.

Wenyi stomped into the Palace City with no regard for the protocol providing that certain entrances and passages were for certain officials, and he got into everyone's way. He even jostled the Prime Minister. For this impudence the Prime Minister ordered the attendants to smite Wenyi's cheeks. Burning with shame, Wenyi hastened to Chao to air his grievance. Chao touched his cheeks tenderly, but she only said, "Our religious teacher should avoid the south gate, which is for the use of the Chief Ministers only. Use the north gate hereafter."

The court closed its eyes to Chao's private indulgences. But since Wenyi's overbearance made him a nuisance and his band was becoming more impossible day by day, several memorials were presented that censured him.

Chao had been dallying with the idea of lodging Wenyi in the Palace. Their intermittent meetings whetted her desire, leaving her unsatisfied. Now the memorials clinched her decision. She issued an order that because of his artistic ability, shown in the renovation of the White Horse Temple, Wenyi was to supervise the building of a resident hall in the Inner Palace.

[193]

While the rest of the court was content to have Wenyi out of their way, the Director of the Board of Censure petitioned to castrate Wenyi to ensure the chastity of the Inner Palace. Chao dropped the memorial on the dormant pile.

25

Chao installed Wenyi in the sumptuous Wisteria Pavilion, in a sequestered part of the Imperial Park, where ladies could not haply run into him. Chao herself seldom came there. She preferred to meet Wenyi in the Lotus Pavilion, a small three-room pavilion in the center of an elongated lake. A zigzag bridge connected it to the shores, and weeping willows and peach trees shaded the bank. Chao chose that pavilion because, with the eunuchs guarding both ends of the bridge, no one could possibly chance upon them.

One night, as Chao watched a full moon hung over the Lotus Pavilion, golden like a setting sun, she flashed her love-light upon Wenyi and said, "Such a lovely moon. Shall we row out in the boat?"

It was quiet on the lake. Besides the rise and fall of the oars there was only the sound of Wenyi's breath coming fast and short. He gave the oars a few quick pulls, shooting the boat beneath a cascade of willow trees. Dropping the oars into the boat, he moved toward Chao and untied her belt to feel her body, smooth and pale in the moonlight as if carved in white jade, yet hot and tingling with passion. Time stood still for the lovers; they forgot where they were or how long they were there, insulated within a scintillescent bubble of love, floating

[195]

away from the rest of the world. Eventually with a sigh, Wenyi picked up the oars and rowed toward the pavilion.

Days and nights passed in an idyllic dream. For months Chao neglected her work, until the memorials accumulating on her desk were like the ridges of the Chungnan Mountain. But in time her sense of duty returned, and she began to work again with a savage determination.

Wenyi, left to himself, was bored to distraction. He began to hate the perverted order of things—that he, a man, was obedient to a woman's beck and call. He was vexed by the restrictions of the Palace—the things he could not do or say, the places he could not go or stay. Bursting with animal energy, footloose and independent, he strained like a wild horse confined in a corral.

He longed for his free life in the White Horse Temple, where the days flew by with the daily excitement of raiding the villages. And the thought of the luscious peasant girls made his bowels tingle. There were pretty girls in the Palace too, but just let him cast his glance in their direction and the jealous wrath of the Empress Dowager would be upon him. He wondered how his monks were faring, and he ached to steal out and visit them.

He stretched his arms and legs, one afternoon, as if to break the shackles that fettered him. Then he sent the eunuchs away, one by one, on some unnecessary errands. When the last eunuch was gone, he saddled his horse and rode to the White Horse Temple.

During Wenyi's absence, the Temple had become more a fortress than a temple. The monks, afraid of being surprised by the Gold Guards, posted a sentry in the drum tower above the gate. When the sentinel saw a rider approaching in the distance and recognized Wenyi, he called down to the monks, "Our Abbot is returning."

The monks dropped whatever they were doing and rushed to the gate to welcome Wenyi. They led his horse to the Abbot Hall as if he were a general returning from a triumphant campaign. Wenyi sat grandiosely on a dais, with his monks seated cross-legged on the floor.

"How have you fared?" he asked.

"Not so well," said Pockmark. "We have scraped the bottom of the villages. We should plunder the city. But curse the Gold Guards! They guard the wall gates as carefully as their mothers' virtue."

"Our band is dwindling. Several of our brothers have gone back to the hills," said another.

"The shortsighted swine!" Wenyi cursed. "How could the hills provide better than the White Horse Temple?"

Wenyi knew he was despised by the court and hated by the people. He was in power only because of the Empress Dowager's favor. If anything should happen to her, he would immediately be torn to pieces, and those who fawned upon him now would be the first to stab him then. To protect himself he intended to train his monks into a fighting force. He imagined that with enough militant monks he could even seize the throne for himself. He summoned his twelve squad leaders and plunged into plans for training the monks.

While Wenyi was playing the truant, Chao was fingering the few remaining memorials with a frown. Work, work, work! There was no end to it. Somehow, she could not concentrate today. Her mind kept wandering off in a tangent to Wenyi. She dumped the papers into a drawer and closed it with a bang.

"Tell the Abbot to be at the Lotus Pavilion in an hour," she ordered the eunuch.

Excited like a child let off from school, she hastened to her chamber to make herself desirable for Wenyi. She bathed in fragrant water and dusted herself with jasmine powder. She put on a sky-blue floating robe with a sash of a darker blue. Her hair, dressed in high puffs, glittered with ornaments. Her fuss in dressing and the radiant excitement in her eyes made the ladies-in-waiting exchange significant glances behind her back.

She reached the Lotus Pavilion early and waited on the veranda. She kept glancing at the zigzag bridge from whence Wenyi would come. When he did not come, she fumed. "Where could he be? What could have kept him?"

As she saw a eunuch running across the bridge, she went to meet him.

"Your Majesty," said the eunuch out of breath. "We cannot

find the Abbot anywhere in the Palace. He must have gone to the White Horse Temple."

"Fetch him back, you fool!" she thundered.

The afternoon was almost gone before Wenyi came. With a surly salute, he sank into a chair with his back toward Chao.

As Chao came over to face him, her anger dissipated at the sight of his handsome face, boyish, defiant, yet adorable. Her tone was caressing as she asked, "Why did you leave the Palace without our permission? Do you know that, waiting for you, a day is like three autumns?"

"Then how many thousand of autumns have I waited? What am I to do when you shut yourself in your study—count my beads for a better reincarnation?"

When Chao realized that Wenyi was bored with idleness, an idea to keep him occupied came to her and she said, "If you knew for what purpose I sent for you, you would not have tarried."

Wenyi's face quickened with curiosity, judging from the Empress Dowager's tone, a prize worth having was in the offing.

"How would you like to supervise the building of the Hall of Great Brilliance?" asked Chao.

"Hall of Great Brilliance?" echoed Wenyi.

"It is not an ordinary hall," explained Chao. "Its design is prescribed in the historical records. Both Emperor Tai Tsung and Emperor Kao Tsung entertained the idea of building it. But the disagreement among the scholars and ministers over the interpretation of its plan in the ancient record forstalled it. Now I shall build it. I shall permit no quibbling. I, myself, shall be the sole interpreter of its plan. According to the record, it is to be a three-storied structure, two hundred ninety-four feet high, square at the bottom, round at the top, with a dome supported by nine enormous pillars of gold dragons. Above the dome is to be a cupola, where a huge phoenix will stand with extended wings flying to the clouds. The square Audience Hall on the first floor is to symbolize the four seasons; the Hall of Libation, on the second floor, the twelve signs of the Zodiac; and the third floor, the twenty four vapors constituting the elements of the

[198]

weather. You can go on from there and make it the grandest and most elegant structure human eyes have ever seen."

"I will, my love," said Wenyi excitedly, counting in his mind the gold that would flow into his hands, which he could divert to recruit more monks. His eyes glittering with greed, his laugh a satyric roar, he swept Chao into his arms and carried her into the inner chamber. When Wenyi was happy, his lovemaking was passionate, making Chao forget her throne, her empire, and her schemes for usurpation.

The Hall of Great Brilliance was completed a year later. It was a structure of superb beauty and grandeur. Inspecting it with Wenyi, Chao said, "You have done well. We are pleased with your artistic taste." Her eyes, sweeping the hall, came to rest on Wenyi's face. "For this we will confer upon our Abbot the title of Left Brave Guard Marshall General; also, the rank and emolument of a Duke. We will open the Hall to our hundred-names for three days so that they, too, shall see how well you deserve your rewards. We will have an inauguration of such splendor that none will ever forget it," said Chao, her eyes dreamy with images of pageantry, ritual, and display. "We will summon all the prefects, all the nobles, all the Kings——" She paused on the word "Kings." She stood still in the center of the elegant hall, deep in thought, unconscious of what she had been admiring a few moments before. Wenyi, accustomed to Chao's utter absorption in things beyond his comprehension, left her alone to her brooding.

With a distant look in her eyes, Chao repeated, "The Kings . . . the Kings. . . ."

There were thirty-odd feudal Kings in the nation. Scattered, they were of no consequence; but if a righteous cause should combine their forces they could be a formidable foe. They would have a righteous cause if she should try to displace the Tang Dynasty with her own. In the eyes of the hundred-names, she would be the malfeasor, and they would side with the Kings to oppose her. Because of this, she had procrastinated, brushing aside Shensi's urging to establish her own dynasty. The Kings

[199]

would have to be eliminated, but it would be foolish to gamble on a frontal attack while the goal could be won by cunning and subterfuge. She had been waiting for a chance, and now she saw it in the inauguration of the Hall of Great Brilliance. She would summon the Kings to come, as was traditional; then, shorn of their guards, they would be her easy prey. If they refused to come, she could legitimately punish them for disobedience. Eager to talk it over with her daughter, she clapped her hands for her eunuch. "Summon Princess of Peace."

Si Shaw watched Princess of Peace leave for the Palace with misigivings; whenever an urgent summons came, something sinister was brewing. He despised his wife, truckling to and scheming with the Empress Dowager; mother and daughter had worked like two blades of scissors to cut the young Emperor, Jui Tsung, out of his power. He would not have married the Princess if he had had his choice.

One day Shaw received a letter from his cousin, the King of Lanya. He slipped it into his sleeve to read it in his study. The King of Lanya suspected that the Empress Dowager's summons to participate in the inauguration was a device to lure the tigers from their lairs, and he was in a dilemma as to whether he should come or not come. "Perhaps you could assay Her Majesty's intention through your honorable wife," he wrote. "I pray to heaven that my fear is unfounded. I shall wait for words from one close to the throne before I make my decision."

Shaw read the letter again and again. The responsibility of deciding for his cousin overwhelmed him. His intuition told him that to come within the Empress Dowager's reach was to stretch one's neck on the block. But he couldn't base his judgment on mere intuition when his cousin's fate depended on it. He sat at his desk in a quandary. With the brush poised in his hand, he did not know what to write.

The candle flame fluttered at the sudden inrush of air. He looked up and saw Princess of Peace at the door. He quickly laid his arm over the letter he was writing, but her sharp eyes had already caught the salutation.

"How many times have I told you not to have anything to do

with the King of Lanya?" she asked. "Can you understand the simple prudence of befriending those Her Majesty favors, shunning those she disfavors? Can't you see you are playing with fire? If you were not the father of our children, little would I care if you were sizzled crisp. Can you get through your mule head you can be involved?"

"In what?" asked Shaw.

"Anyone could accuse King of Lanya of treason."

"Treason? You know all these treason cases are merely an excuse to murder for gain. Why should Her Majesty trust the dispensation of justice to such a rapacious wolf as Chinzen?"

"Simple enough. To terrify the subversive elements into submission."

Shaw's voice became bitter. "And it does not matter that innocent lives are sacrificed?" He looked beyond his wife and reminisced, "the King of Lanya and I grew up together. I esteem him as my own brother. His well-being means a great deal to me." He turned suddenly and looked squarely at the Princess, "Is he in danger if he comes to the inauguration?"

The directness of the question took Princess of Peace by surprise. She hesitated before she answered, "How would I know?"

The hesitation clinched Shaw's decision. He would advise his cousin not to come. He sighed, and his face was lined with deep concern. He heaved himself up slowly from his chair and went to the door.

"Wait!" Princess of Peace called after him. Shaw paused, without taking his hand off the latch. "For the sake of your children and your ancestors, have nothing to do with the King of Lanya or any of the Kings," she pleaded in desperation.

"Our ancestors are even now turning in their graves."

"You will be digging yours if you do not heed my warning."

"You would not know there are such things as loyalty, justice, and righteousness!"

Princess of Peace picked up the ink slab and threw it at Shaw, but it crashed on the door he closed behind him.

[201]

26

The King of Lanya waited anxiously for his cousin's reply. He hoped his suspicion was unfounded, for he was an amicable man, and as long as he was left in peace in his own domain he had no intention of censuring the Empresss Dowager or interfering with her rule. If he disapproved of her domination over the Son of Heaven and her reign of terror, he kept such thoughts to himself. He would not think of taking any action that would rock the peace of the nation. Yet he was worried. He knew that from the Empress Dowager's point of view he and the rest of the kin were a potential threat to her reign. Her summons had brought home the vulnerability of his position.

Troubled in his mind, he tossed his book onto his desk and went to the veranda. There, along the railing, were the rarest and the most beautiful miniature trees, planted in shallow, tray-like containers, each representing an exquisite scene—a forest beside a meadow, a wind-swept tree on a crag, or an old trunk by a lake. He watered them, trimmed them, sheltered them in the shade, and did not trust his servitors to care for them. Now, as he gazed, he projected himself into the scenes as though he were the man seated on the tiny bench below the willow tree. He moved from scene to scene, again and again, and became a part of it, and an unaccountable solace came to him.

[202]

A servitor broke in on his reverie. "Your Highness, the messenger has returned from Loyang."

"Send him in . . . right away."

The King of Lanya tore open the letter the messenger had brought. As he read it his face became worried, and his hand trembled as he fingered the end of his swallowtail mustache. Shaw's letter confirmed his suspicion. He could tell between the lines that he was not the Empress Dowager's only target. His father, his uncle, his cousins—all were in her range. Confronted with this grave situation, he summoned his ministers for consultation.

After the letter was passed around the conference table, the Chief Secretary said, "There is danger either way. To obey is to be caught in the Empress Dowager's net; not to, is to revolt. The question is do we have the troops and the resources to revolt?"

"Judging from the letter, all the kin are involved," said the aged counselor. "While a single twig is easily broken, a bundle of twigs is another matter. Therefore there should be concerted action by the kin."

"Scattered as we are, is it possible to call a meeting to plan concerted action without arousing the suspicion of the Empress Dowager?" asked King of Lanya.

"Your Highness could send confidential messengers," suggested the Chief Censor, "to acquaint the Kings with the contents of this letter. They would see that for their own survival open rebellion is imperative."

"And attach a concordance," said the Finance Minister, "for pledges to enlist soldiers and accumulate armaments in secret. Then, on a designated date, all will meet at a certain place to march on the Capital and restore Emperor Jui Tsung to the throne."

"How big a force do we need to warrant success?" asked the King of Lanya of the Defence Minister, who remained thoughtful and silent.

"A considerable force, Your Highness," he said discouragingly.

"If each of the thirty-odd Kings contributes five thousand soldiers, it will be a force of one hundred fifty thousand," said

[203]

the Chief Censor. "Besides, once the purpose of the revolt is proclaimed to the nation, those who are now secretly against the Empress Dowager would openly join the insurrection, which will further swell the number of the force."

The King of Lanya turned to the Defense Minister again, "How is the guardsmen situation in our own territory?"

"There are only a thousand guards at present. The people of Chinchou and its countryside are law abiding; there was no necessity to have more. If Your Highness wishes, we could enlist more. However, the Empress Dowager's forces are formidable. Your Highness must consider the consequences before taking this irrevocable step."

"What other step would you suggest to meet this situation?" asked the King of Lanya. Getting no answer, he went to the black lacquered cabinet, withdrew a map from its shelf and spread it on the table, "Where would be a logical location for the forces to meet?"

"Then Your Highness has made your decision?" asked the Defense Minister.

"The decision is made by the Empress Dowager. I abhor bloodshed, but my hands are forced. If it is death either way, I choose to fight." Studying the map the King of Lanya said, "We need to choose a centrally located place of easy access by all the Kings."

Pointing to the center of the map the Secretary asked, "Could Sinyang be the place?"

"What is your opinion and how is its topography?" the King of Lanya asked the Defense Minister.

"The surrounding countries are flat, but to the west are hills and woods, possibly a good cover for the troops while waiting for the others to arrive."

"Then we will decide on Sinyang. Now the date . . ." said the King of Lanya.

"We should allow as much time as possible," said the aged counselor. "A revolution is a weighty matter. A premature uprising could spell failure."

"We have but little time," said the Chief Censor. "The

inauguration is on the first of the ninth moon. Besides, the longer we wait the more the chance there is of discovery. The Empress Dowager has eyes and ears everywhere."

"Then it cannot be later than the eighth moon," said the King of Lanya. "Only four moons for preparation—much too short a time. Will our Secretary dispatch the concordance as soon as possible and set the date on the twentieth?"

The Secretary sent four of the most trustworthy messengers to make secret deliveries of the concordance to the Kings. But keeping a secret from Chao was like keeping water in a sieve; for Hung had planted servitors in the Kings' households to report to him regularly.

In going through these routine reports, Hung noticed that the King of Lanya had sent a letter to each of the Kings.

"Something is brewing," said Chao, when informed. Have your men look out for enlistments, purchases of armaments, troop movements, and such things. Do not neglect to watch the kin's households in the two capitals, including that of the imperial son-in-law, Si Shaw." She shifted her trusted generals to strategic positions; issued orders to strengthen the fortifications, to re-examine the logistics, and to enlist more soldiers; then waited uneasily for the Kings to make their next move.

On the appointed date, when the King of Lanya marched out of Chinchou and the heavy gate swung closed upon the last soldier, the people gathered around the guards and asked, "Is there a war somewhere?"

"Have you read the King of Lanya's proclamation?" asked one of the guards. "He is fighting to restore our Emperor Jui Tsung to his throne and put the Empress Dowager in her place. She is much too ambitious, if you ask me. She plans to kill all the imperial kin and seize the throne for herself."

"She keeps the nation in peace and the barbarians off the border. That is good enough for me," said a carpenter on his way to work.

"Her tax is not exorbitant, and the conscription of labor still

[205]

twenty days a year, as it has always been," said a bearded merchant.

"Rebellion! Surely Her Majesty's wrath will fall upon our city. We are all in for trouble," said a scholarly man.

"Not if the King of Lanya succeeds," contradicted the guard.

"Do you expect an egg to crush a stone? How can these soldiers stand the mighty army of the Empress Dowager?" said the scholar.

The crowd scattered at the approach of the Captain of the Guards. "What is the rumpus about?" asked the Captain.

"They say that if the King of Lanya fails our heads will fall and Chinchou will be in for trouble."

When the Captain reported this to the Defense Minister, he said, "Close the wall-gate to the King of Lanya when he returns in defeat. Maybe it could save our heads and the city from the Empress Dowager's wrath."

The King of Lanya's hurriedly trained mercenary soldiers were decimated by Chao's seasoned troops in four short days. He struggled back with a few survivors. These, anxious to get inside the protection of the wall, shouted again and again, "Open the gate! It is the King of Lanya!" No response. Only echos came from inside the silent wall.

With the retreat thus cut off, the King of Lanya led his men toward the coast to embark for the East Ocean Island, now called Japan. By nightfall they were in a pine grove. Exhausted the men dropped to the ground and were soon fast asleep on the thick pine needles. But sleep did not come to the King of Lanya. Leaning against the stump of an old tree, he asked himself if it would have been better not to have revolted at all. He shook his head. He had no regrets. He hoped the other Kings would fare better than he. Then his thought turned to his wife and children, and tears blurred his eyes. His mind, too, became blurred as sleep finally overtook him.

The shimmering light filtered through the pine trees revealed a shadow moving stealthily towards the King of Lanya. There was a gleam of sword, a slash, and the King of Lanya's head rolled to the ground. The betrayer wrapped the head in his cape and tied the bloody bundle to his belt. Then he kicked his com-

[206]

rades and shouted, "Wake up! Let us go to the nearest magistrate to redeem our lives with the King of Lanya's head."

Among the Kings only the King of Lanya's father marched to avenge his son. He, too, was easily defeated, and the insurrection petered out in seven days. The quick rout of King of Lanya made the rest of the Kings lie low. But their prudence did not help them, for now Chao had a valid reason to punish them.

She put two of Kao Tsung's most powerful uncles on trial for treason. When the local judicial officials found no proof for conviction, she ordered Chinzen to retry the case. Chinzen's torture chamber easily extorted confessions from his victims and made them involve others until seven hundred families of Kao Tsung's clan were destroyed. The terrible slaughter stunned the court, but no one dared to defend the kin.

During the seven days' insurrection, each morning Shaw prayed to the spirits of the dead Emperors for the success of the march. When the news of its failure came, he was plunged into an abyss of despair. Then came the indictment of the kin. It made his heart bleed to see his uncles and cousins brutally killed and himself powerless to help.

Soon he, too, was sucked into the terrible vortex. He and his brothers were arraigned for storing armaments for the rebels. His brothers were beheaded and he, being the imperial son-in-law, was spared that disgrace but left in the prison to starve.

Chao kept Princess of Peace and the children in the Palace when Shaw was taken into the prison. "Waste no tears on the ungrateful cur," she said. "I shall see that your next husband is Yu-Chi, a Wu, whose loyalty we can count on."

Regardless of the sweeping slaughter of the kin, the inauguration of the Hall of Great Brilliance took place on the appointed date. Hordes of people entered the Palace to view the magnificent hall. Free wine and food were served to win the good will of her hundred-names, making it a gala occasion for all.

In addition to the prefectors, Chao summoned one elder from each village, town, and city to participate in the inauguration, and all of them returned home to brag of what they had seen. For a long time the subjects of discussion in the tea-houses were the Hall of Great Brilliance and the Empress Dowager's largesse. Few people cared—or even knew—about the tragedy of the kin.

However, the atmosphere in the court during that period was as tense as if a million arrows were darting in the air. Even the most stalwart officials lived in fear. Anyone, any day, could be accused of aiding the Kings, and if even the Princess of Peace could not shield her husband, who could expect to escape death?

Shensi and the other Wus swaggered about, confident that with the Kings obliterated their time for becoming the Imperial House was at hand. Shensi spoke to Chao in a conspiratorial tone: "Your Majesty, the plum is ripe. Will Your Majesty pluck it?"

Chao knew Shensi was alluding to the throne, and she said, "We shall wait till it drops into our hands."

27

When the dust had settled after the slaughter of Kao Tsung's kin, Chao summoned Shensi to the Palace.

"The hundred-names believe a sovereign is predestined by heaven," she said. "You shall fabricate a succession of divinations to prove that I am ordained by the gods to found a new dynasty."

Shensi's pale face flushed, and his crafty eyes sparkled. He had been urging his aunt to establish a new dynasty, but she had bided her time. Now, finally, came her order to proceed. He plunged into the scheme wholeheartedly.

Soon thereafter, during an audience, Chao noticed whisperings in the court. When she looked askance at the disturbance, an official said, "Your Majesty, a guard is here to say that the magistrate of Sung Yang has sent a man to present a white stone found in the Lo River. He says the Abbot of the Temple of Tranquil Heart has verified that the inscription on it is the writings of the gods."

"Aw-w-w?" said Chao, as if surprised. "Tell the man to await our pleasure." After examining the carved oblong stone with the inscription, "A Holy Mother has descended to earth to establish an everlasting dynasty," she handed it to the secretary to circulate among the ministers and then said, "We will hear the opinion of our ministers."

Shensi nudged the Judge next to him, who promptly petitioned, "Your Majesty, since the stone is the gift from the gods, your humble servant suggests that it be exhibited in the Temple of Tranquil Heart for the hundred-names to see."

"It shall be done," said Chao. "For presenting the stone we shall award the magistrate one hundred bolts of silk. We shall hallow the Lo River and build a temple at its bank."

A few days after this, a monk presented Chao with a four-volume Great Cloud Sutra, which included an augury that the Empress Dowager was the reincarnation of the Laughing Buddha, destined to supercede the Tang Dynasty. When Chao rewarded him with an abbotship, opportunists began to invent fantastic auguries for gain, and soon the nation was rife with omens.

Then, on a fine afternoon, Deputy Censor Foo led a large column of people to the Palace Gate to present a petition that since the omens indicated the Empress Dowager was ordained by the gods to rule, the House of Wu should be made the Imperial House, and the dynasty changed from Tang to Chou. Chao accepted the petition, promising to present it to the court for deliberation, then ordered wine, food and a cash reward to be distributed.

As the petition was read in the morning audience, a deadly silence greeted her. She realized that the court was not yet prepared for the launching of her course.

She retreated astutely. "We thank our hundred-names for their interest in our reign. We regret we cannot assent to their request."

She again indicated her predilection by elevating Deputy Censor Foo's rank several grades, thus generating another flood of petitions from other self-seeking officials. In the meantime, Shensi's helpers solicited signed petitions from leading citizens all over the nation to request the change of dynasty. The repeated reading of these petitions during the audiences so conditioned the court that they came to regard the change of dynasty as no longer unthinkable but inevitable. Only then did Chao

[210]

issue a proclamation that to accede to the persistent supplication of her hundred-names, she would mount the throne. The dynasty would be changed from Tang to Chou, and her youngest son, Dawn, would be her heir-apparent. Since tradition forbade a woman to desecrate the throne, she would ascend the throne as Emperor instead of Empress. Her name for her ascension would be *Wu Tse Tien,* meaning "Wu Is Heaven," and her imperial title was to be *Tse Tien Da Shen Huang Ti,* meaning "Tse Tien the Great Holy Emperor."

On the day of accession, Chao discarded her Empress Dowager's costume for the Emperor's. Her hair was combed into a knot on top of her head like a man's. Over it was a tightly fitted headdress of black lacquered gauze with open crown. Her robe was of white satin, overlaid with another of bright red silk gauze, thin as cicadas' wings.

In the Audience Hall each official took his prescribed place, with the Grand Preceptor and the Grand Commander in the forefront. They waited in reverent silence as the drum rolled and the bell tolled to announce the arrival of Chao. As she entered, the court knelt to the Son of Heaven who was a woman. Then the Grand Preceptor and the Grand Commander went to the vessel placed at the foot of the marble steps to perform the rite of ablution of hands. After that, they took the oblong crown and placed it upon Chao's head. The court hailed their new sovereign with "Wen Sui! Wen Sui! Wen Wen Sui!"

Chao retired to the east room to change into a black and pink sacrificial robe, embroidered in twelve symbols, with wide, sweeping sleeves reaching to the floor. Then she came to the altar in the open court, where the officials were already in array according to their ranks. She burned incense, poured wine into a three-legged cup and placed it on the altar table, reported to heaven that she was now the new Emperor, and prayed for blessing upon herself and the nation. Thus ordained, she experienced a sense of fulfillment. At long last she was Son of Heaven, founder of the Great Chou Dynasty, Sovereign of the Celestial Empire.

To share her joy with her people, she granted an amnesty and also remission of one year's tax. There was great rejoicing throughout the nation, and no one seemed to mind that a woman was now on the throne. To the people she was neither man nor woman but a semi-god, their Holy Emperor, the Son of Heaven.

In the Imperial Park that night, lanterns outlined the pavilions, bridges and the rock gardens, looped from tree to tree, and clustered on bushes like fireflies. Eunuchs shuttled back and forth with wine, food, and tea. Music came from hidden recesses. The sky was a kaleidoscope of fire works; the mood was gay, with stage plays, musicians, acrobats, and storytellers; and the colorful robes of the spectators were themselves a fantastic spectrum of colors.

A dance choreographed by Chao herself was being performed in the open court. Chao watched it at the head of the court, and the other three sides were crowded with other spectators. The dancers, in gray robes and gold headdresses, formed tableaus again and again, each featuring a word in a verse:

Holiness surpasses the ancient,
Virtue excels all kings.
Ten thousand years to the Emperor!
Great prosperity to the nation!

Chao noticed that Shensi was not among the spectators. Her eyes swept the court and saw him scowling by a column. She sent a eunuch to summon him. When he came, she said, "You have discharged your mission well. We are pleased. This is the time for rejoicing. Why the frown?"

"I did not realize I frowned," Shensi parried.

Chao had rewarded Shensi with a kingship, which with his cabinet post made him the most powerful man in court; yet, she suspected, it did not meet his expectation. "Speak out, Shensi. What is on your mind?" she persisted.

"As Your Majesty says, this is the time for rejoicing. Celebration is in order, so why talk about serious matters? It can wait till another day."

"We will not wait."

Thus pressed, Shensi lowered his voice and said, "Your

Majesty is well aware that it has taken a strenuous effort to establish the Great Chou Dynasty, and it is all the more reason that its continuity should be safeguarded. If Your Majesty wishes to perpetuate the Chou Dynasty, Your Majesty's heir should be a member of the House of Wu, for when Your Majesty's son succeeds to the throne, the dynasty would immediately revert to Tang, and all the pains of establishing the Great Chou Dynasty would come to naught."

"Hum!" Chao grunted. She did not need Shensi to tell her what she knew herself. She wanted the continuity of her Dynasty, but if she had made a Wu the Crown Prince instead of her son, she could not have established her Dynasty as smoothly as she had; likewise, she dared not change the succession so soon after her coronation. Later, when the court got accustomed to her being the Emperor, she would see how she could circumvent their objections.

But the seed Shensi had sowed sprouted in her mind; the next day, she summoned her ministers to probe their opinions. The Secretary of State Affairs spoke emphatically: "No one could have a better claim to the throne than Your Majesty's son. To bestow it upon Your Majesty's nephew would surely plunge the nation into a civil war. In fact, entrusting too much power to him would be a danger to Your Majesty's own self."

Chao turned upon him and said cuttingly, "You forget he is my nephew."

"Even an ambitious son kills his father for his throne," answered the Secretary.

Chao herself had perceived that Shensi was overambitious. Now, warned by the Secretary, she began to curtail his power. As to the question of succession, it could wait.

But Shensi could not wait. Time was not in his favor, for his aunt was sixty-seven, and he reckoned that the one person in his way was the heir-apparent, Jui Tsung. If Jui Tsung were dead and the other son, Tsung Tsung, in exile, his succession would be assured; but how was he to do away with Jui Tsung? He could slip an accusation in the receptacle to involve Jui Tsung. But for a conviction he needed the help of Chinzen. He was not sure Chinzen would fall in with his plan. After all, Jui Tsung was the heir-apparent. But what he was sure of was Chinzen's weakness for women. So he invited Chinzen to dinner with a few of his confidential Wus.

Before the meal was half over, musicians filed in and squatted upon the square mats on the floor. Then came the dancing girls. In mincing steps they imitated butterflies fluttering about a peony bloom, their wide, transparent sleeves swaying like gossamer wings. Then the butterflies flew away, and only the peony girl remained. Slowly she twisted her body and arms, simulating the opening of petals; then she pirouetted as though tossed in a storm. She came perilously close to Chinzen, her sleeves almost touched his face, sending waves of her bodily fragrance to his nostrils. Chinzen, mad with desire, gasped, "Beautiful!"

"If our honorable guest is pleased with her, accept her as an unworthy gift from your humble host. And with as many of the others as you wish to accompany her."

Chinzen, flushed with happiness, lifted up his cup to Shensi. "To my generous host," he said, and drained his cup in one draught. "My humble self is at Your Highness's service."

"Your gracious words encourage me to speak my innermost thoughts," said Shensi, and in a muffled tone he told Chinzen of his scheme to implicate Jui Tsung. With his heart set on the dancing girl, Chinzen agreed readily. He left in the darkest hour of the morning, the hour of the cow, with the Peony girl at his elbow and a cartload of dancing girls following behind.

When the incrimination of Jui Tsung reached Chao, she read it in disbelief. It was unlike the meek, philosophical Jui Tsung to contend for power so suddenly. Yet . . . yet he could be a pawn in some other schemer's hands. She brushed a decree for Chinzen to question Jui Tsung's eunuch-servitors.

While the rest were cowed by Chinzen's threat, one rough-hewn servitor fearlessly snatched a sword from a nearby torturer and called in a loud voice, "I will cut out my heart to prove the Crown Prince is innocent." He ran the sword diagonally across his chest, then swooned in a pool of blood.

When Chao learned of this incident, she had the man removed to the Side Palace and put him under the care of her own physician. As she went to thank him in person at the Side Palace, she tripped on a loose brick and stumbled. Catching hold of a sturdy arm and balancing herself, she said, "If it had not been for you, we would have a fall." She looked into the bronzed face of a seven-foot giant and was pleased with what she saw. "Have we seen you before? What is your name?"

"Chi Hsueh, Captain of Your Majesty's guards. May your captain escort Your Majesty to the Hall of the Sick?" he asked in a voice that rang like a bell.

Because Chao liked his voice, she kept the conversation going. "So you know where we are going."

"Your Captain keeps his eyes and ears open for opportunity to serve Your Majesty."

"Well said. What have your ears heard from the outside world?"

"Gossip that will amuse an ordinary person but too irreverent to repeat in Your Majesty's august presence."

"You have our permission to repeat."

"This year, the harvest is good . . ."

"That we know," interrupted Chao.

"So good that farmers are coming to the city to pick wild flowers."

"Aw-w-w?"

At Chao's amused smile, he boldly continued, "The low-class brothels are doing a roaring business. One country bumpkin flaunted his silver and tried to get into a first-class Singsong House. The mother, not wanting to have a fracas on hand, reluctantly let him in. She took all his silver but sent a serving woman to entertain him. He, of course, did not know the difference."

Chao laughed, and as they had reached the Hall of the Sick, she said, "We will hear more of your tales when we ride in the park tomorrow."

As Chao entered the sick chamber, the servitor tried to rise. She gestured him to lie down. "We heard what you did for the Crown Prince and we want to commend you on your courage and loyalty. We wish we knew how to thank you." Seeing the

[215]

tears in the man's eyes, she stepped closer and handed him her pink silk handkerchief. He crushed it in his hand and held it to his bosom.

On her way back to the Main Palace, Chao speculated on who had accused Jui Tsung. Was it Shensi, who wanted the succession for himself? She had better warn him that she would make her decision in her own time and would let no one force her hand. Perhaps she should caution Chinzen too . . . Then she shook her head. She needed him to lay bare the guilty. As to the innocent, "Genuine gold fears no fire."

Chinzen lay low for a time. When no repercussion came, he became exceedingly bold, and even entertained the thought of superseding the Wus. If he could get rid of them, he would be Her Majesty's only confidant. He began to scheme to implicate Shensi and the other Wus.

Princess of Peace was in constant communication with Purple Orchid. When the girl came to see her in a high state of tension, she knew something was afoot. "What is it?" she asked.

"Chinzen plans to accuse the Wus of conspiracy. I heard him discussing it with his henchmen last night."

"Hmmmm! So the snake plans to swallow the elephant. Do not breathe a word to anyone. Remember, after your father is avenged, you will come and live with me."

Princess of Peace immediately summoned the Wu clan to her house and told them of Chinzen's plot. "The brute forgets he is favored only because he is useful to the Wus in bringing about the Chou Dynasty. If he does not know how high is the sky and how deep the sea, then he shall have a potion of his own poison. Accuse him of treason before he accuses us. Who will drop the information in the receptacle?"

"I will see to that," said Shensi.

Informed by Chao's secretary, Princess of Peace managed to be in her mother's study when the accusation of Chinzen came to Chao's hand.

"Hum!" Chao grunted. "Read this." and she tossed the accusation to her daughter. "I suspected that one day someone would take vengeance on Chinzen."

"Vengeance? You mean you think he is not guilty?"

"You should know better. As far as treason is concerned, my left hand does not trust my right hand. What I mean is that nothing is so simple as it appears. Like an iceberg: there is always more under the water than above."

"I came to tell you of what I have heard, but I thought I would wait till you are through with your work. Now this . . ." She handed the accusation back to her mother.

"What have you heard?"

"I have a special friend in Chinzen's household. She told me that he intends to destroy all us Wus including Your Majesty's daughter so as to clip Your Majesty's wings."

"Aw-w-w? Then we shall order a thorough examination."

The day Chinzen was on trial, the gate of the Judicial Hall was swarming with people. Friends, relatives, and loyal servitors of those whom Chinzen had slaughtered vied with each other to testify to his crimes. The trial did not take long for there were enough witnesses to convict ten Chinzens and more. They swore that his purpose in killing loyal, guiltless ministers was to cripple the throne so that he could seize it for himself. When Chinzen was led out in chains the crowd booed and spitted. "Now you are tasting your own medicine," they said.

Chinzen swung the long chain hanging from his wrists left and right to get at the people. "Your mother!" he cursed. "Wait till I am back. I will grind everyone of you turtle spawns under my heels."

He swaggered up and down his cell, boasting to his cellmates, "You will see. I shall be out of here in no time. When I am back where I was, heads will roll. Your mother! I swear the cockeyed judge who dared to indict Lan Chinzen will have a good taste of my vengeance."

When this was repeated to the judge, he was worried, for already three days had passed and Chao had not signed the execution document. If Chinzen was reprieved, the horribleness of his own fate would be unimaginable. He sent an urgent message for help to his friend the Captain of the Guards in the Palace.

When Chi Hsueh came he asked, "What is so urgent that you wanted me here immediately?"

[217]

"I would not trouble you if it were not a matter of life and death. Chinzen boasts that he will be reprieved. If so, my head will fall. Could you possibly put in a word with Her Majesty?"

"If Her Majesty takes her usual ride in the Imperial Park. That is the only time I can get a word in."

The next day, while Chi Hsueh held the stirrup for Chao to mount, she asked as usual, "What news from the outside?"

"For the last few days the talk in Loyang is of Chinzen. They wonder why his head is not on the wall yet."

"Aw-w-w!" said Chao, noncommittal.

"The people hate Chinzen and cannot wait to tear at his carcass."

Not pleased with what she heard, Chao puckered her brow and said, "You may be excused. We wish to ride alone." She spurred her horse and cantered into the woods, then pulled it to a stop to collect her thoughts. She knew Chinzen for what he was, a tool and nothing more. She doubted that he was of the calibre to seize the throne, and she meant to reduce his sentence to banishment, for with death her weapon would be irretrievably lost. Yet . . . yet . . . was it wise to go against the wish of the hundred-names? Would she lose their allegiance by protecting a man they hated and wanted dead? Perhaps she should concede to their wish. With her decision made, she turned her horse around and rode to the Main Palace. Then, without further delay, she signed the document of Chinzen's execution.

28

There was an unusually long spell of rain that spring, and the constant "drip, drip" from the overhanging eaves made Wenyi seeth under the tedium of his eight years of captivity. He flung wide the door and stepped out. Even the water dripping from the roof seemed to wall him in. He turned at a discreet cough. The sight of Chao's messenger was like a tug on his leash. "You!" he roared. "What do you want?"

"Her Majesty desires Your Highness's presence," said the eunuch, wiping his wet face and shaking the rain down his thatched rain-coat.

Wenyi groaned. He was finding it harder and harder to make love to a woman more than twice his age. At times he had to close his eyes and imagine it was Autumn Fragrance he held in his arms. Now, with Chao dressed in an Emperor's costume, it was even harder. How was he to love a freak who was neither man nor woman? There were times when he wondered if it would not be better to let Princess of Gold put him in jail than to be the lapdog of a rapacious old vampire.

He dawdled in putting on his military costume. He wished he could be going to war instead of into the arms of an insatiate woman. He took his time admiring the scalelike metal armor and the embroidered tiger head that covered his middle. If there was one thing that pleased him in the ennui of his present life, it was his military status of a Marshall General.

He waved aside the sedan chair sent to fetch him and walked deliberately along the Thousand-Pace-Corridor. The rain had stopped, and the sky promised a bright tomorrow. He sighed. Sunshine or rain, what difference did it make to him?

A gust of wind brought a strain of music to his ears. With a mischievous smile tugging at his mouth, he walked toward the theatre, a short distance to the east. He shook loose the eunuch's detaining hand and quickened his steps.

The ladies were rehearsing a scene from "The Cowboy and the Spinning Maid," in which the daughter of a god came down to earth to bathe in the lake at night. The lady acting the part of the Spinning Maid was singing, while the eunuch teacher beat time with two long blocks connected with a cord hung over his thumb. Wenyi paused by the column and listened. When the song ended in a high note, he shouted *"Hao! Hao!"* (Bravo).

Indifferent to the astounded eyes riveted upon him, he strode to the stage and swung his lithe body onto it. He pushed aside the lady who played the Cowboy and took the role himself. As the Cowboy carried the Spinning Maid to his cowshed, Wenyi became his lecherous self, pressing his lips hungrily over her breasts. Suddenly he let the maid drop, for framed in the stage entrance was Chao, who had come at the eunuch's report of Wenyi's waywardness.

Chao motioned the others to leave. When the two of them were alone, she boxed Wenyi's ear. Wenyi glared at Chao. His one thought was to get away from the old witch, for Chao in her fury looked her full sixty-nine years. He jumped down off the stage, ran to the stable, got on his horse and rode to the White Horse Temple.

When they saw Wenyi throw himself in bed and stare at the ceiling, the squad leaders guessed that the lovers had quarreled again, and they nudged each other, each wanting the other to speak. Finally Pockmark said, "We come to remind our Abbot that a thirsty man does not plug the source of his spring. Our Abbot must not forget that the White Horse Temple depends upon Her Majesty's favor."

A monk knocked on the mother-of-pearl window pane and said excitedly, "Her Majesty is coming to the temple."

The leaders quickly pulled Wenyi out of his bed, straightened out his costume, and brought a hot towel to refresh his face, all the time recommending reconciliation.

Wenyi exhaled a long, resigned breath and reluctantly went to the gate to welcome Chao. They strolled to the garden of the ginkgo tree, where they often had their tea. Chao glanced at Wenyis' surly face over the edge of her teacup and said, "If I forbid you to mingle with the ladies, it is because I love you and want you only for myself."

"If I wandered into the theatre it was because I was bored. A man must have something to do with his time. Let me do a man's work. Let me lead an expedition."

"Going to war certainly is not the work of the Abbot of the White Horse Temple."

"It is of the Marshall General."

"That . . . that is a sinecure for rewarding our Abbot. We do not expect you to fight."

"I do. I want to."

"You realize you might get killed?"

"I would rather die by the sword than by the slow poison of boredom."

To avoid another quarrel, Chao postponed the issue by saying, "We will see, when there is an expedition to lead."

A year later, when the Mongolians rebelled, Wenyi reminded Chao of her promise.

"How can you want to go to such a place? There is nothing there but deserts and nomads. No houses, no civilization—and they live in tents and eat nothing but mutton."

"Your Majesty promised that I was to lead the next expedition," Wenyi insisted.

"We refuse to expose our love to the barbarians. Besides, the climate of their land is a worse danger than the people. The ferocity of their windstorms is unparalleled, and sand dunes shift in the wink of an eye. People and goat herds are buried without leaving a trace of their existence. Your sovereign loves you too much to permit you to join such a war."

[221]

"Your Majesty promised."

Chao sighed. "It is against our better judgment, but if it is your wish, it shall be so,"

She ordered a seasoned general to accompany Wenyi, entrusting to him the actual conduct of the campaign and the safeguarding of Wenyi's life.

A month went by, and no word came from Wenyi. Chao eyed the pile of memorial brought in by the secretary and asked, "Any report from the Mongolian campaign?"

"Not yet, Your Majesty," said the secretary.

"No word. No word." Didn't he know she would be worrying about him? Longing for him? And the nights . . . they were interminably long. The curse of being in love! Since he had left, food had had no taste, flowers no fragrance, and she was sick and aching.

The Princess of Peace and Princess of Gold bore the brunt of Chao's short temper, as they were constantly summoned to the Palace to keep her company. One day on their way to the Palace, Princess of Peace said, "A heart malady needs a heart remedy. If only we could find Her Majesty another lover . . ."

"I know of a physician whose virility is the talk of the tea houses. In spite of a houseful of concubines, he still seeks amorous exploits with his female patients."

"Then mention it to Her Majesty," said Princess of Peace.

They found Chao brooding in her study, and Princess of Gold said, "Your Majesty, since the eunuch physicians cannot cure Your Majesty's illness, would Your Majesty consider summoning a physician from among the hundred-names? We have heard of a certain physician who is said to have a secret formula for a love potion. Do we have Your Majesty's permission to bring him to the Palace?"

The next day, Princess of Gold brought in a quiet, scholarly man, rather effeminate in comparison to Wenyi.Chao was disappointed, for she saw nothing in him to indicate an ardent nature. He stood with his head bowed, without once looking up at her. To put him at ease, Chao said, "Since we are your patient, we will dispense with formalities. You may sit down." She indicated a chair by her desk and he sat on the very edge of it.

[222]

As Chao stretched her arm across the desk and laid her wrist on a tiny embroidered cushion, he timidly placed three fingers on her pulse, then asked, "May your humble servant see Your Majesty's tongue?" As he looked up, he smiled. Chao saw a firework of passion explode in his eyes, and her pulse raced. He pressed her wrist a little more boldly, sending messages of love through her veins.

From then on Chao's simulation of illness was a daily incident.

29

When the Mongolian campaign drew to a close and Wenyi returned, Chao was as excited as a young bride on her nuptial night. She discarded her Emperor's costume for a flowing robe and had her hair up again in high puffs, as she waited for him at the Lotus Pavilion.

After two years of the rugged life in Mongolia, the luxury of the Wisteria Pavilion was a pleasant change. Humming an operatic aria at the top of his voice, Wenyi bathed in a crock of steaming water. Then, decked in his elaborate military costume, he headed for the Lotus Pavilion.

Chao met him at the veranda. Seeing him again after the long separation, she was at a loss to find words to greet him. All her yearning was in her eyes. Her radiance made her beautiful in spite of her age, and Wenyi's eyes softened with desire as he spread his arms to let her come into his embrace. She laid her head on his broad bosom, "I missed you. Promise me you will not leave me again." Wenyi tightened his arms around her and kissed her.

The rapture of reunion did not last long. A month after his return, Wenyi was bored. As he slouched in his chair, his thoughts drifted to the Mongolian desert. It was a wild, open country; when the wind whipped, the sand pricked his face like the point of a needle. But he liked the excitement, the danger, the freedom . . . yes . . . the freedom, and he yearned for it now. He closed his eyes and saw again the silent night, the vast stretches of sand, the long line of camels silhouetted against the sand dunes in the moonlight. He relived the night of the surprise attack, the fire-arrows darting into the Mongolian camp like a million shooting stars, the enemy tents burning like a bonfire, the sky a flaming vault and the sand an expanse of glittering gold.

Then, after the victory, how they had reveled in the wine and women! He liked raping the Mongolian women, who unlike their sisters of the central plain were uninhibited by the age-old teaching of women's purity and virtue and responded with the wild passion of the desert wind.

He liked the other general who was subservient to him; while here in the Palace he was subservient to an old tyrant. He wished he could lead another campaign. He felt that he could not stay in the Palace another moment.

He let his feet drop from the table with a loud thud and clapped for a eunuch. "Saddle the horse," he ordered.

"Where does Your Highness wish to go? In case Her Majesty wishes to know."

"The White Horse Temple, where else? Tell Her Majesty I shall be back tomorrow."

At first, Wenyi stayed over in the White Horse Temple one night at a time, then two nights, then three. The success of the campaign fired his ambition. He imagined how it would be if he were the ruler of a nation instead of a temple, and he worked feverishly to recruit more monks, to plunder for more money and more weapons, so that even the streets of Loyang were no longer safe.

The Gold Guards had stayed their hands so far. But one day, when the monks ambushed the Gold Guard for their arms, their Captain could no longer close his eyes, and he set a trap to catch the marauders.

On a moonless night, a decoy carriage heavily laden with baggage threaded its way through a wooded pass. When the monks swooped down from the hills to plunder, they were

[225]

greeted by a volley of arrows from the carriage. Then a swarm of Gold Guards encircled them like the walls around a well. They were caught like a school of fish in a fine net. Only their leader, directing the raid from a hill top, escaped. Straggling back to the temple, the leader was immediately surrounded by other squad leaders.

"What happened?" they asked. "You look as if you have seen a ghost."

"The Gold Guards—they caught us. Everyone except me."

"Are they trying to 'catch flies on the tiger's head'? Wait till our Abbot hears of this."

"I am not sure our Abbot is still the tiger he was before. I heard that Her Majesty has another lover."

"Does our Abbot know? We must tell him."

Wenyi looked up as the squad leaders came in. "Why the long faces?" When told of the disastrous encounter with the Gold Guards, Wenyi cursed, "The turtle spawns! What do they think they are? I will make Her Majesty cut every one of their heads off."

"Then our Abbot will go to the Palace . . . tomorrow?"

Wenyi frowned.

"The expedition to Mongolia took our Abbot away from the Palace too long. What if Her Majesty takes on a new fellow in our Abbot's absence?"

Wenyi scoffed at that preposterous idea; but then it struck him as strange that for the ten days he stayed away no summons had come while previously he had not been permitted to stay away a single day. He dismissed the leaders, hopped on his horse and dashed off toward the Palace.

The Guards at Chao's Resident Hall crossed their pikes over the entrance and told Wenyi that Her Majesty was unwell and no one was to be admitted.

"Have you no eyes to see that this is the Left Brave Guard Marshall General?" He thrust the pikes aside and walked in. In the antechamber the eunuchs again stopped him. Wenyi was furious. He had never been treated like that before. Could it be that Chao was with another lover? He shoved the eunuchs from the door and broke in. He found the physician seated beside

Chao on the couch, his arm around her shoulder, his hand holding hers, his prurient eyes shining full upon her face.

Wenyi stood at the door, a mountain of a man, his eyes murderous, his face muscles corded in hatred, his hands clenched, his stance like a cougar out to kill. For a moment all three were motionless, wordless, suspended in a heavy silence. Then Chao stepped calmly toward Wenyi. Her eyes riveted on him were like those of a trainer stalling a wild beast, and she asked in a steely voice, "Were you not told I was attended by my physician?" Then she softened her tone and said, "Go. Come back tomorrow."

Smoldering with rage, Wenyi stomped out without a word. She had deceived him, and there was nothing he could do. His anger so blinded him that he did not know where he was heading. He saw the glimmer of the oil lamp in the Temple of Heaven and he entered.

The temple had been built so that Wenyi could perform Buddhist rituals in the Palace. Its structure was as bizarre as Wenyi's nature. It was even higher than the Hall of Great Brilliance, but in the entire temple there was only a single Buddha, looming to the ceiling, with an open palm big enough to hold forty persons with ease.

Wenyi glared at the colossal image of gold. He was a pygmy beside that giant god, but the demon in him swelled to many sizes larger than the Buddha. He lighted a candle and held it to one of the embroidered panels hung on each side of the altar until it caught fire. Then he stamped across and held the candle to the other panel.

He stepped back to the center. With his arms akimbo, his feet wide apart, he stood and watched the tongues of fire leap up toward the ceiling. He stared at the Buddha's head, a ludicrous caricature with the gilt burnt off its face. Wenyi threw back his head and laughed deliriously, as if all his pent-up emotion were suddenly released. He rocked back and forth, unable to stop his hysteria. Then, choked by the smoke, he ran out to his horse and galloped away.

Once outside the city wall, his head cleared by the cool night air, he reined in his horse and looked back. The sky was a crimson dome, and smoke and fire were gushing upward as if hell had broken loose. Wenyi's horse snorted, shook its mane, and pawed the earth, but Wenyi remained transfixed. He could not take his eyes off the fire. What had he done? What if the whole Palace should burn down?

Back at the White Horse Temple, appalled at his own impetuous outrage, Wenyi could not sleep. His head throbbed as if a thousand hammers were pounding inside his skull. The thought that he was no longer indispensable to Her Majesty, that hereafter he would have no one to shield him from the Gold Guards, terrified him. Could his army of monks defend the White Horse Temple, or would they desert him too, now that he was no longer Her Majesty's favorite?

The quarter moon rose high in the sky, casting a bright sheen over Wenyi's room. The floor before his bed made panels of silver light, inlaid with lacy shadows of the ginkgo tree; the bells on the eaves tinkled with the wind. But, obsessed with fear, Wenyi could neither see nor hear. He moaned; he groaned; he sat bolt upright. Awake or asleep, he saw the giant Buddha made grotesque by the fire. He hid his face in his hands, but he could not hide from his own hallucination. To ease his stricken conscience, to atone for his sin, he wanted to perform a religious rite. He climbed to the bell tower and rang the bell of alarm, then ran down to wait for the monks. They trooped out of the dormitory half asleep, their robes thrown over their naked bodies, their feet bare.

"What happened?" asked Pockmark. "Fire? Gold Guards?"

"No," said Wenyi. "We will perform a religious rite in the Main Hall."

"Religious rite! At this hour!" said several monks together. "What madness . . ." But after one look at their Abbot's glassy eyes, they kept their silence.

They lighted the candles and the incense in the Main Hall, but none of the monks, including the Abbot, knew the sutra, since their priestly robes had never been more than a masquerade. They milled around with palms together in a farcical rite, mumbling the simple "O-me-to-fa," while Wenyi knocked his head on the floor, praying for remission.

After Wenyi had left, Chao felt remorseful to have hurt the one person she loved, the one person who had aroused in her the consuming passion that she had missed in her youth. Tortured with the guilt of an unfaithful wife, she wanted to make amends. She turned to the physician and said, "We regret this unexpected interruption. However, we believe it is best that we do not see our physician again."

She reached up and pulled out a jade bar that pinned her hair to the top of her head. One end of it was carved into a coiled dragon, the emblem of sovereignty. Paying no attention to her falling hair, she handed the bar to the physician. "A keepsake from your sovereign. If ever our physician is in need or in trouble, present this to any public official and it will come to our attention."

After the physician had left, she sat motionless. Except for the flutter of her eyelids she could have been taken for an oversized ivory figurine. The loneliness of that moment was the worst she had ever experienced.

Jasmine rushed in. "Your Majesty, the Temple of Heaven is on fire."

"On fire!" echoed Chao. "Get my cape."

As Chao reached the wall-tower, the fire had already lighted the Palace City into a brilliant glow. Looking down, she saw rows of eunuchs strung from the stream to the fire, passing water-buckets from hand to hand. But the puny buckets of water made no indentation on the wall of the blaze. Giant tongues of roaring fire lapped up the immense wooden structure like fodder, throwing up fire-crows for the wind to toy with and carry to the next building. Soon the magnificent Hall of Great Brilliance was also burning.

When the fire was spent, Chao returned to her study and summoned Hung. "How did it happen?" she asked Hung.

Hung hesitated, then said, "The Abbot set it on fire."

"Are you sure?"

"A eunuch saw him. . . ."

"Then silence him; and let it be known that the carelessness of the attendant was the cause."

The next morning she sent for Wenyi, and it was a contrite

Marshall General who crouched at her feet. "You should not have stayed away in that confounded White Horse Temple." chided Chao. "And what in the world made you set the Temple of Heaven on fire? Are you not afraid of the retribution of Buddha, even though Your Sovereign is ready to forgive for the love of you?"

"I will pray Buddha for mercy. But I would go crazy folding my hands and sitting in the Wisteria Pavilion with nothing to do."

"We will think of something. Perhaps we will rebuild the Hall of Great Brilliance . . . in time . . . but not now. In the meantime, our Abbot may divert himself in the White Horse Temple in the mornings but return to the Palace by the hour of the monkey."

30

The news of the fire and the trapping of Wenyi's monks got around and reached the Deputy Censor Chou. As a censor he was more concerned with the latter. He wondered if Chao would interfere with justice to protect her paramour. If so, how was he to censure Her Majesty without embarrassment to her and ill effect to himself? His forehead, much too broad for his small, lean face, was creased in deep lines as he draped the reins on the neck of his old horse and let it clump along the cobblestone street in a slow, deliberate motion.

As they approached the gate, the animal stumbled on a loose stone and almost unseated its rider. A man hurried forward to hold up the rein and patted the horse's flank reassuringly. "Are you the new groom here?" asked the Deputy Censor.

"No, Your Eminence. I work in the White Horse Temple. I came to visit my cousin, Your Eminence's gatekeeper."

"You handle the horse well."

"We have over four hundred in the White Horse Temple, and I am one of the grooms."

The Deputy Censor looked surprised. Why should a temple need so many horses? He probed the groom and learned of the martial training and the sham court Wenyi held in the temple.

The following day the Deputy Censor sent his gatekeeper to

[231]

return his cousin's call. "Keep your eyes and ears open and your mouth shut," he enjoined his gatekeeper. "Ask your cousin to take you around. Find out if there are arms stored in the temple and whether the horses are as many as your cousin said. Note the monks' doing and see if there is anything out of character with religious life going on. Report to me as soon as you return."

When the gatekeeper verified his suspicions, the Deputy Censor accused Wenyi of harboring rebellious intent.

Chao stomped to the Wisteria Pavilion and thrust the memorial into Wenyi's hand. "What do you have to say for yourself?" she stormed. "Armaments piling up in the storeroom, horses and monks trained for war—to revolt against the sovereign who gives you her love."

"Your Majesty, I swear I harbor no intention to revolt. My hands cannot reach to the White Horse Temple when I am shut in the Palace. For all I know the monks may have plundered the arms for gain during my absence."

Before Wenyi's stooped shoulders and worried face, Chao's anger was spent. Her memories overwhelmed her. Flashing through her mind were the rendezvous at the temple, the childish romping in the park, and the nights of sleeping in Wenyi's arms. She loved him and could not imagine a life without him. The thought of subjecting him to the supreme penalty of a rebel made her shiver. To punish Wenyi was to punish herself. She knew he was erratic and wild, like an unbridled horse, but treachery was not one of his traits.

Not wanting to believe him guilty, she grasped at the excuse he offered. Her voice was strained as she said, "We will disband the monks. As to the Abbot, we will see. In the meantime, our Abbot is not to leave the Palace."

When Chou was ushered in, Chao said, "We commend our Deputy Censor for his memorial. We have no reason to doubt its veracity. However, we have questioned the Abbot ourselves. He said that the monks probably pilfered the arms for gain without his knowledge and there was no intention to revolt."

"Your Majesty, in view of the seriousness of the offense, the Abbot should be questioned by the Judiciary. If the Abbot is innocent, there is all the more reason that he should be vindicated in the eyes of the public. What would the hundred-names and history say if Your Majesty should make an exception of him?"

Chao's brow creased in a fierce frown; then, after a menacing silence, she said, "In the years that our Deputy Censor has been in our service, we have always valued his advice. Therefore we shall send the Abbot to the Judiciary for question. However, it is our wish that the Abbot be treated with consideration and that no harm come to him"—thus making it plain to the Deputy Censor that the questioning was to be a mere formality.

Wenyi, however, refused to leave the Palace, where the arm of the law could not reach him. "How could Your Majesty send me to my enemies, who will surely make a meat paste of me?"

Chao saw a strange blankness in Wenyi's eyes. Thinking it was fear, she said, "Life and death is in my hand. No one can touch a single hair of your head without my permission. If the Deputy Censor knows no better than to harm our Abbot, then his head shall fall, not yours. I shall send the Captain of the Palace Guards to accompany our Abbot and to ensure your safe return."

On the day of the trial, Wenyi hid himself, trembling like a hunted animal. Then, all of a sudden, he emerged and rode out of the Palace with the Captain of the guards hurrying after him. At the Hall of Justice, he left his horse with the Captain and stalked to the bench alone. Staring at the judges with glassy eyes, he drew up the corners of his mouth in an idiotic smile, his face contorted into a hyenalike mask. Then he unfastened his garments, exposed his large belly and stretched full length on the floor. Before the judges could recover from their astonishment, he had run to his horse and galloped back to the Palace.

The Deputy Censor hastened to report Wenyi's strange behavior to Chao.

"The Abbot must be out of his mind," said Chao. "Leave the Abbot in our hands."

After the Deputy Censor left, Chao chuckled. How clever of Wenyi to feign madness and thus solve this delicate situation.

Chao waited for Wenyi in the Lotus Pavilion. As he came along the zigzag bridge, his incongruous attire told her some-

[233]

thing was very wrong with him. He was in his undergarment, yet on his head was the ornate Marshall General's headgear adorned with long pheasant plumes. He walked like a somnambulist, his eyes wide open but unseeing. At his approach, Chao backed away and motioned her eunuchs to be alongside of her.

Wenyi stepped into the pavilion and went into a pantomime of lighting the candle and setting the Temple of Heaven on fire again. When that was done, he lifted up his face and laughed a metallic, demented laugh. Then he sank into a chair and dropped his chin to his chest.

"Heaven have mercy! He is mad!" Chao began to see that Wenyi had not been himself since the night of the fire. In a voice laden with sorrow, she said to her eunuch, "The Abbot is sick in his mind. Take him back to his hall and summon the physician."

The following days, Wenyi got steadily worse. Chao blamed his madness on herself, for it was his jealousy of the physician that had made him set the temple on fire, and now Buddha was punishing him by taking away his reason. Oppressed with regret and loneliness, she drifted to the Lotus Pavilion. She sat on the bench looking out to the silent lake, thinking of her happy time with Wenyi. Preoccupied, she did not notice Wenyi's coming. She turned abruptly as she felt his hot breath on her neck; she saw his demoniac eyes glaring at her, his hands raised to close in on her neck. She screamed. The eunuchs rushed to the veranda at the same time Wenyi's attendants caught up with him. They subdued Wenyi and dragged him back to the Wisteria Pavilion.

Chao detained one of the attendants. "Were you not told to watch the Abbot? How did he get away?"

"The Abbot hid in a corner for hours," said the attendant. "But suddenly he sprang up, grabbed our necks and knocked our heads together. He was gone before our heads were clear. The night watchman said the Abbot roams the burnt temple ground in his sleep; but up to now he had not tried to hurt anyone."

Chao turned her eyes to the distance in infinite sorrow. Now that Wenyi's madness had become violent, she could no longer keep him in the Palace, but neither could she turn him out. She knew that what seemed cruel was in fact a kindness, but she could not harden her heart to issue the order to dispatch Wenyi. Sauntering to her Resident Hall, she was tormented by indecision. It was almost evening before she finally summoned Nurse Chang. "We have heard that the Abbot haunts the temple ground in his sleep. Dispatch him and make it look as though the monks have wreaked vengeance on him."

A crescent moon hung in a cloudless sky, shedding a pale light over the Palace City. A shadow lengthened as Wenyi sleep-walked to the ground where the Temple of Heaven had been. He was in his sleeping garment, yet insensitive of the bleak night air. He walked round and round, like a buffalo hitched to a watering-wheel. He stopped short and waved his arms as though struggling from the grip of the giant Buddha. He ran. He fell beneath a tree. He felt a host of fists mauling him, and he died believing that Buddha had taken retribution on him.

"Make sure he is dead," said Nurse Chang. "Take the body to the woods near the White Horse Temple."

31

A year had passed since Wenyi died. It was a lonely year. Chao was grateful that her mornings were occupied with the affairs of the nation, but the afternoons were empty and endlessly long.

"Is Princess of Peace not here yet?" Chao asked one day.

"No, Your Majesty," said Jasmine. "She says her son is ill."

"So her son comes before her mother. She is much too happy in her second marriage to think of others. And Princess of Gold?"

"She is still taking the herb medicine. She says her legs wobble like a newborn colt. She says that in her sickness, she promised a votive offering of a carved Buddha on the Dragon Gate Hill. She asks Your Majesty's leave to go there for its dedication as soon as she regains her strength."

"Hum! We shall see. If she is not well enough to wait upon her Emperor, she is not well enough to worship the gods.

The long day ahead galled Chao. She wondered who else she could summon. The wives of her nephews? The cringing lot. They bored her. She wondered why an hour was an eternity when she was alone, while the ten-odd years with Wenyi had passed like an arrow. She did not want to think of Wenyi, but he kept coming into her mind. She strolled to the garden, where the eunuchs were stringing colorful lanterns.

"What are they for?" she asked irritably.

"Your Majesty's seventy-third birthday," said the eunuch.

"Seventy-third! How the years had flown!" The thought that eventually her years would come to an end depressed her. She had sent Taoist priests to the highest mountains and the lowest valleys in search of the herb of eternal life. She had had a high terrace built in the Palace to pray for immortality. Yet, deep down in her heart, she knew she was fooling herself. Even the Holy Emperor must face that inevitable end, and each birthday drew her nearer to it. What was there to celebrate for? What was there to look forward to on her birthday? The congratulations from the court? The tributes from the prefectures? The gifts and wishes from the nobles?

The sameness of the Palace life irked her. She wished she were a commoner, free to walk the streets of Loyang unattended, to flirt with the first man she encountered, to chat with whomsoever she pleased. A sudden urge to shake off this restriction possessed her, and she stopped the eunuchs. "No celebration in the Palace this year. I shall worship on the Dragon Gate Hill on my birthday."

She called Jasmine excitedly, "Tell Hung to prepare a boat to the Dragon Gate Hill. An ordinary boat. I wish to travel incognito. Tell the two Princesses to accompany me. We will start as soon as the preparation is made. By then, both Princess of Peace's son and Princess of Gold should be well."

The imperial party sailed down the Lo River disguised as ordinary travelers, with only four boatmen plying the oars. Living a secluded life in the Palace, Chao had lost touch with the outside world. Now she looked about her as with the eyes of a child. The water was shallow and crystal-clear, and she could see the pebbles imbedded in the golden sand, colorful, like a mosaic fashioned by the hands of the water god. Here and there a boulder jetted above the water line, laced in foaming white; along the bank were the exposed roots of willow trees, and beyond, she saw a sleepy village, a billowing millet field, a forgotten grave. As they sailed past a cluster of farmhouses, a water buffalo treading at a wheel, a farmer on his way home, and a

[237]

pugnacious dog yelping at their boat, Chao envied the simple life of an unaspiring commoner.

That night their boat was moored beneath an overhanging bluff, where heavy vines hung from the cliff like serpents and naked roots clutched the precipice like giant claws. The moonlight heightened the fantasy, etching eerie shadows on the crags, casting a silver glow upon the water.

Chao listened to the hoots of the owls, the whispers of the trees, the rhythmic lapping of the river. Then, out of the night, she heard an exquisite melody of a moon-guitar, faint but clear, and mingled with the music were men's voices and laughter, young and carefree. Then came the heavenly song of a flute. Then all was quiet, as though silence had tucked the night in like a counterpane.

The next morning Chao wondered if what she had heard the night before had been a dream. But then, out of the medley of noises, she caught the lilting strain again. She stepped to the bow and saw a skiff skim by. At its stern were two handsome youths. One was playing the flute; the other was scrutinizing her curiously. As Chao's eyes met his, a sudden desire rose in her. She ordered the boatmen to row faster, but the heavy barge was no match for the light skiff, which glided off effortlessly like a swallow.

"Why fret, mother?" Princess of Peace said. "All the boats go to the Dragon Gate Hill. Surely we will run into them there."

The Dragon Gate Hill was a holy mountain covered with statues of the Buddha in all sizes, from pygmies to giants. Emperors and empresses had been carving statues on that hill to propitiate the gods for two hundred years, and with the people following their sovereigns' example, it had become a veritable forest of statues. Chao herself had had seven colossal statues carved on the mid-wall of the hill, an eighty-foot-high Varocana Buddha flanked by six Bodhisattvas of lesser height, and on the ground above the images were seven temples.

As the hill came into view, Chao stood at the prow, squinting her eyes to locate her statues. "You can see them even from here," she said with pride.

"Of course," said Princess of Gold. "Your Majesty's statues

[238]

are the largest and the finest. I am sure no other Emperor could ever carve a statue to equal Your Majesty's."

"I meant it to be that way," said Chao.

Accustomed to rising at the break of dawn, Chao was up at her usual time the next morning. She wandered from temple to temple to look for the man of the skiff. But besides a few pious monks, no one was astir. She clambered up the hill and prayed to the seven statues. Then she sat on the rough ledge to rest, her thoughts wandering inconsequentially. At the sound of footsteps, she turned and found herself face to face with the man she was looking for.

There was instant recognition between them. The man measured her furtively, speculating as to who she was. The mother of a wealthy merchant? The wife of a retired high official? Something in Chao's eyes made him revise his opinion. Perhaps she was just a "mother" of courtesans, making the pilgrimage to atone for the sin of her trade. With a knavish twinkle in his eyes, he sidled up to dally with her. "The honorable lady is a pious pilgrim to worship here so early," he teased.

"What brings a handsome young man to this holy mountain?"

"To enlarge the horizon of my eyes. To view the Buddhas dedicated by the Holy Emperor. I hear the Holy Emperor is a holy terror."

Chao shook with laughter. "I hear she is a lonely woman, who longs to have young men like yourself around her."

"If you ask me, Her Majesty should have man-concubines. A man-Emperor has three thousand in his Inner-Palace; why should a woman-Emperor have none?

"Would you want to be the man-concubine?

"Why not? What road to wealth and official position could be shorter? Perhaps the honorable lady knows someone who could recommend my humble self to the Palace?" he asked, half in jest.

"I do know someone," said Chao, and she gave him the address of Princess of Peace.

The man gasped. "Your ladyship knows the Princess of Peace?"

She nodded and left before he could probe her further.

The young man, known among his friends as the Sixth Lord,

was puzzled. Shrugging his shoulders, he returned to the temple where he and his brother, the Fifth Lord, were staying. He saw his brother sitting on a stone balustrade that circled the gold fish pond, and he stole upon him from behind and prankishly gave him a shove, as if to push him into the pond.

"You never grow up," chided his brother.

He laughed at his brother's fright, then sat down beside him and told him about the strange matron. "She looks . . . um . . . about fifty . . . fifty-four or -five . . . may be more, but still chic and desirable. I could tell by her dress that she is oozing with wealth. She says the Holy Emperor likes to have men like me around her. She says to go and see the Princess of Peace.

"Who is she?"

"I didn't ask. By the holy pagoda, she didn't know my name either."

"And you expect to see the Princess of Peace? You can't even get past her gatekeeper."

"I can slip a little silver up the gatekeeper's sleeves."

"Where is your silver?"

"We came on this trip without any silver."

"That is because our rich friend likes our company."

"This woman likes my company too, I can tell. Perhaps she will oil the gatekeeper's palm for me. You may have the brain, but I have the luck. Remember, the fortune teller said I should have a windfall of good fortune tumble into my lap."

"But he did not promise you a long life, and he warned you to be prudent."

"Who wants long life? Fun, pleasure, luxury—that is life. To be Her Majesty's bedfellow is just the thing."

Back in Loyang, the Sixth Lord tried his luck at the residence of the Princess of Peace, and to his surprise he was taken to the Palace. As he knelt at the Holy Emperor's feet and stole a sidelong glance, his eyes bulged, and his jaw dropped. "You! You are the Holy Emperor yourself!" Then he bowed his head reverently and said, "Forgive me, Your Majesty. I should die."

Chao smoothed his cheeks and smiled into his eyes. "We are pleased with you," she said. "And shall make you the Left Thousand Cow Lieutenant General, second in command of our personal guards. Our eunuch will take you to your new abode. Come to us as soon as you can."

The Sixth Lord's head was dizzy. Overnight he was in possession of a mansion manned by a horde of slaves, and of acres of land stocked with horses, camels, cows and sheep. He moved his brother to the mansion while he himself went to live in the Palace. There he was fawned upon by the Palace officials and eunuchs, whose sole duty was to satisfy his wishes. In this windfall of good fortune there was one drawback: he missed his brother. But no sooner was his wish made known to Chao than the Fifth Lord was also brought into the Palace.

When the two of them were together, they roamed the Palace like puppies off the leash. They stooped to the lowest conceivable means to amuse Chao. They acted the part of concubines to the Emperor by effeminizing themselves. They used face powder, carmine color, and fragrant water, and minced their steps disgustingly like a woman's. They took every liberty, tossing the Palace conventions to the wind. They told obscene stories picked up from the street and flirted with Chao more outrageously than common courtesans.

Their wantonness delighted Chao, and she made love to them openly, shamelessly. She let her mother's voluptuous strain in her have its full fling and abandoned herself to debauchery, cramming into her last years what she had missed in her youth.

Her two young favorites made her forget her age, and the feeling of rejuvenation was exhilarating. She delegated the senior guards, the older eunuchs and the gray-haired ladies to distant posts, for they mirrored too painfully her own impending decadence, which she wanted desperately to forget. She chose the young and strong to be around her, and she behaved as one of them. Life was a continuous merrymaking, with music, wine, games, and hilarious laughter. In time, this lightheartedness set the mood of the capital's social life, and merrymaking was the temper of the time.

The court, as well as the nation, no longer applied to Chao the precepts governing the conduct of women. They closed their eyes to her love life and her indulgences, as long as these things did not interfere with the affairs of the nation. As to the two brothers, the upright in the court regarded them as no more than Chao's parrots or sleeve-dogs. The sycophants, however, pampered them, hoping to worm their way into Chao's favor. They catered to the gay fancies of the brothers, from wild orgies to ball games and gamblings. And the two Lords did not care who their friends were as long as they were good losers.

Once, they pestered Chao to permit their merchant friends to play a dice game in the Palace. As the promiscuous group gathered around the Holy Emperor, yelling and calling boisterously over the tinkling of dice in a porcelain bowl, Minister Wai happened to come, to report on state affairs. He pushed the two brothers aside, knelt at Chao's feet and said, "It is the duty of your minister to remind Your Majesty that merchants of low birth are unworthy to be permitted in Your Majesty's presence." He signaled the eunuchs to throw them out.

"How dare you!" shouted the Fifth Lord, "Ordering the eunuchs around in the presence of Her Majesty!" and he spread his arms protectively over the merchants huddled behind him.

"The unheard-of impudence!" said the Sixth Lord. "Your Majesty, decapitate him!"

Chao, looked embarrassed, then thoughtful. The candid censure of Minister Wai was a breath of fresh air, clearing away the fog of dissipation and making her realize how far gone she was. To the astonishment of her two favorites, she said to the eunuchs, "Do as our Minister commanded."

Later the two brothers slouched on the couch and pouted, "I hate ministers," said the Fifth Lord. "Kill-joys, all of them."

"Just as I was winning, he has to spoil it," said the Sixth Lord. "Why do you permit him to do this to us?"

"Because he is right. No commoner is permitted in the Palace. The Son of Heaven is to be worshipped. Reverence and familiarity do not mix."

"But we are commoners," they said together.

"You no longer are; you are consorts of the Emperor. Mingle with your friends outside the Palace, if you wish, but do not bring them here."

"What fun is there? No this, no that!" pouted the Fifth Lord.

[242]

Chao came to sit between them, and she pressed her hands on their knees, "Cheer up, puppies. We can have some other game tomorrow. Hm-m-m," she said. "How about the strike-the-ball game? We shall summon the court, the nobles, the emissaries and their families to watch the game. And you can wager to your hearts' content."

32
𓆙

When the Sixth Lord woke up the next morning, he stretched, yawned, and asked, "What time is it?"

"The hour of the snake [9–11 A.M.]" said the eunuch.

"You fool! Why didn't you wake me earlier?"

"Your Lordship didn't say so. Your Lordship's usual time is the hour of the horse [11 A.M. to 1 P.M.]."

"Shut your stupid mouth," said the Sixth Lord.

He pattered barefooted to the west chamber of the Resident Hall and woke his brother. "How can you sleep like a pig when it is the day of the strike-the-ball game?"

"So what? The game is in the afternoon."

"So we'll go and watch the ladies practice. So we'll know which team to bet on."

"One of these days you'll bet your life away," said the Fifth Lord, yawning.

In the afternoon, waiting in Chao's antechamber, the Sixth Lord asked the ladies impatiently, "Is Her Majesty not ready yet?" Rubbing his palms he said, "I am itching to place my wagers. I shall be a richer man by tonight."

When Chao appeared, the Fifth Lord fluttered about her and said, "What a beautiful strike-the-ball costume. Your Majesty looks magnificent."

[244]

"Flatterer!" said Chao, patting his cheek.

They took her arms and escorted her to the horse. When holding the stirrup for Chao to mount, the Sixth Lord said, "Your Majesty, I wager you a hundred bolts of silk on the Phoenix."

"So be it," said Chao.

As the Sixth Lord saw Jasmine by the column he called, "Jasmine, shall I place a wager for you? It will make you rich."

Jasmine shook her head and sidled behind the column. She did not want Chao to see her. She knew Chao loathed to have old people around her. She did not blame her. Wrinkled, bleary-eyed, doddering, they did not make a pretty picture. She knew she had outlived her usefulness to her mistress, but she did not want to be sent away like the others. As long as there was a breath in her, she wanted to look after Chao. Who would remember to serve Her Majesty the ginseng tea if she were not around? She would keep herself in the background and attend to Her Majesty's well-being through the other ladies.

She smiled indulgently as the horses trotted away. What youth, what lively "puppies" the two brothers were. How good of them to make Her Majesty feel young and happy. How kind of them to want to wager for her; but what good was wealth to her? She rubbed her aching knees and limped to her quarter, thinking that yes, she was getting very old.

On the strike-the-ball ground, the colorful pennants flapped noisily in the wind, the gilded carved dragon and phoenix on the crossbar of each goal glistened auspiciously in the sun, and the warm air was pregnant with festivity and excitement. The spectators arrived, the men taking the benches to the left of the throne seat, the women to the right. They cheered as the players came to the field, the Dragon Team in blue and the Phoenix in pink, their hair tied in double knots on top of their heads. They rode on white ponies magnificently caparisoned in flowing saddle-clothes fringed with red tassels, their green breastplates studded with brass nailheads and their leather bridles lacquered in crimson. They paraded around the field, and then each team ranged itself in front of its goal and the riders dismounted to await Her Majesty's appearance.

[245]

Chao came on a white Arabian steed beautifully caparisoned in red, green and gold, its mane clipped close to its neck, its tail tied into a short stub. She sat straight as a tree astride the horse, a magnificent picture of a regal sovereign.

The drum rolled, the gongs reverberated, and Chao's crescent-headed rattan mallet struck the red leather-covered ball to start the game.

As Chao took her throne seat on the terrace of the elevated observation pavilion, the game started in earnest. The ponies thundered by, raising a cloud of dust above the smooth field. The players raced their mounts, their mallets flying. When a goal was made by the Dragon, the drum rolled three times and a flag was taken from the field to the observation pavilion to mark the score. Then the captain of the winning team waved her small red flag as a signal to resume the game.

The Sixth Lord yelled himself hoarse, boosting the Phoenix, and he was wild with joy when the final score went to his team.

"I have won Your Majesty's wager," he said.

Chao smiled dotingly, not telling him that she had ordered the Dragon to lose.

The sun was setting when Chao rose to leave. Red, gold, and purple splashed in bold spans across the celestial canvas. Chao watched the fiery globe sink in majestic splendor like the regal exit of a monarch. A pensive expression came to her face as she drew the analogy to herself. Like the sun, her own days were setting. Like the sun, someday, she would take her exit from the world; only there would not be another dawn for her, as there was for the sun.

Shensi, watching the nuances of expression on his aunt's face, surmised her thoughts, and he said, "Your Majesty's sun will never set, as long as there is a Chou Dynasty, as long as there is a lineal Wu to continue Your Majesty's heritage."

It was consoling that her dynasty and her name would live even if she died. And she smiled at Shensi, approvingly.

That night Chao was preoccupied. Thoughts of what Shensi had said kept recurring. She was getting on in age, and if she wanted to perpetuate her dynasty, she should make Shensi her

[246]

heir; yet she was undecided, and the indecision plagued her mind. The drum was booming the third watch, and still she was not asleep. When she finally closed her eyes, she dreamed that she saw a large Ying-Wu (parrot) with both wings broken. The bird spread its wings again and again but could not lift itself above the ground.

The next day Chao could not get the dream out of her mind. She was sure it was an omen, probably a bad omen. Why the broken wings? Why? Why? She summoned Ti, now the Prime Minister, to the Palace.

Ti prodded his way wearily down the long corridor to Chao's study. His joints ached and his snow-white head shook uncontrollably, generating a ripple in his long, flowing beard. His thoughts meandered back through the many years he had served under Her Majesty. Yes, he understood her as no other did—her ambition, her fears, her suspicion. He admired her intelligence, her indefatigability in work and play, and her administrative skill. He was grateful for her friendship to himself. Once, she had even ordered the Crown Prince to hold his bridle to calm his fidgeting horse. And because of his stiff knees she had excused him from kneeling. "It pains me more than you to see you kneel." she had said.

She had sent him the purple robe he was wearing, on which she embroidered, with her own hands, the laudatory words commending his loyalty. Yes, in spite of her many faults, she was a good sovereign to work for. But he was very old. He had petitioned many times to retire; but she had refused to let him go. Perhaps it was just as well, for there was one last duty to his nation that he wanted done. He wanted to see the succession settled on the lawful heir, Chao's elder son. He was speculating on how to speak to Chao about it when he found himself already in her presence.

Chao motioned Ti to a chair, then told him of her dream. "What is our Prime Minister's interpretation? Why the broken wings?"

Ti smoothed his long white beard thoughtfully before he spoke. "Your Majesty's name is Wu. Ying-Wu symbolizes Your

[247]

Majesty's self. The two broken wings are Your Majesty's two sons. If Your Majesty would elevate the two princes to their rightful places, the broken wings would be mended."

"Hum!" Chao grunted. Ti's reasoning was so logical that after a long silence she nodded her head.

Ti seized the opportunity to speak of the succession. "If it is not settled upon Your Majesty's elder son, to whom it rightfully belongs, there will be a mad scramble for the throne among Your Majesty's sons and nephews after Your Majesty ascends to heaven, and the nation will disintegrate into warring factions. Your Servant humbly advises Your Majesty to recall Elder Prince from exile to effect a reconciliation."

"We will see." Chao's impulse was to procrastinate.

After Ti left, Chao sat thinking. Death! So final and irrevocable! Powerful as she was, she had no power over it, neither could she project her will through it to the future. A civil war after her death, when her strong hands would no longer be there to prevent it, was unthinkable. Perhaps, for the unity of the nation, she should follow the counsel of her Prime Minister. Yet she let two months slip by before she issued the edict to recall Tsung Tsung.

In the third moon of her seventy-fifth year, Chao waited uneasily for Tsung Tsung to arrive. Fourteen years was a long time—long enough for her and her son to become strangers. Would he hate her, fear her, or be grateful to her that he was finally recalled? She herself had found that affection, once stunted, was hard to bring to bloom again. Her thought shifted to the day when this child was born. She remembered the small, round, bloated face, which later took the square shape of his father's.

Another picture flashed to her mind. Tsung Tsung was nine, and she had returned from her first audience in her full court robe. Noticing her pearl earrings, he had asked, "Will you give them to my wife when I marry?" She had laughed. That was twenty years ago. She still had those lovely pearls; lustrous, perfect spheres. She would give them to his consort as a gesture of her good will. She would do whatever she could to mend the broken relation. "Fetch my pearl earrings with the long pendants," she said to her lady-in-waiting.

Chao received Tsung Tsung in her center-chamber. He entered with his head bent, his eyes lowered. He knelt at her feet and said, "Your unfilial son humbly inquires after Your Majesty's health."

"Rise," said Chao. She noticed that he was now a middle-aged man, stout and bearded. "We are happy that you have safely arrived. How is your family?"

"They are well and are waiting at Your Majesty's pleasure."

"We shall be pleased to receive them," and she motioned the eunuch to summon them. When they came and the formal greeting was over, Chao took the brocaded box containing the earrings from her lady-in-waiting and handed it to Tsung Tsung's consort. "My son asked for these for his wife when he was nine —a childish whim which he probably no longer remembers, but his mother does. Take them as a token of your mother-in-law's good will."

Then she scrutinized Tsung Tsung's son, a young man of seventeen, and his four daughters. To each she gave a word of praise, a sentence of advice and a valuable gift. "We know you are tired from your long journey," she said. "You have our permission to retire. Come again tonight. We will have a feast to wash the dust from the travelers." To Tsung Tsung she said, "We have summoned your brother to meet you here."

After their formal greeting, the two brothers clapped each other on the arms, both trying to hide the tears that filled their eyes. They talked, laughed, and reminisced about the old days when they were children. "Remember," said Jui Tsung, "once you swallow a whole sweet-rice-cake and almost choked yourself. Your eyes kept turning up and up, all white and no pupils —frightened the wits out of me."

"You couldn't be more frightened than I. I thought I was dying," said Tsung Tsung.

Ti was announced, and Chao stepped out to meet him.

"Your Majesty," said Ti. "Your servant came as soon as he could. What is this urgent affair?"

[249]

"You will see for yourself," she said and preceded him to the center chamber.

When Ti saw Tsung Tsung, his bleary eyes were moist with joy. "Your Highness . . ." was all he could manage to say.

"Bow to our Prime Minister," Chao said to Tsung Tsung, "the staunchest advocate for your recall."

As Tsung Tsung bowed to Ti, Jui Tsung said, "Your Majesty, may I have a word in the presence of our Prime Minister? Since the elder son is by right the heir to the throne, I will renounce the Crown Princeship in favor of my brother."

"In this you have shown wisdom," said Chao. "We shall make your brother the Crown Prince as you have requested and shall proclaim to the nation your virtue in renouncing it."

With a nod of approval, Ti said, "Your Majesty has two good sons. Now that my last duty to the nation is done, your servant again petitions for retirement."

"How could I get along without you?" said Chao. "Who could take your place?"

"Your servant strongly recommends the Prefect Chang of Chinchou. He has the makings of a great Prime Minister."

"Later . . . when the need comes," she said.

In the evening, a three-table family feast was spread in Chao's Resident Hall, one for her and her two sons, one for the women, and another for the children. On the surface it was a happy reunion, yet Chao could feel an undercurrent, as her glance went to Tsung Tsung's consort now and then. She wondered what was behind that cold, distant face. Was she resentful for being pushed out of her throne? Was she counting each year as one less to wait? Chao chuckled to herself, thinking that her daughter-in-law would have a long wait, for she would live to a hundred just to spite that ambitious vixen.

Her thoughts were disrupted by the voices of the two Lords, who had had a party of their own and were not expected back so soon. They bungled in, and when they saw what it was, they made a face and tiptoed out. Chao's sharp eyes glanced around at her family. Her two sons' heads were bent, their faces flushed with embarrassment; the women pretended they did not see;

[250]

and the children giggled at the funny faces they saw. What riled Chao was the silent censure on her daughter-in-law's face. The look of contempt was impossible to ignore, and her earlier resolution to be conciliating dissipated into hatred.

33

It was snowing, and even with three braziers blazing in her sleeping chamber, Chao shivered. "Fetch my padded inner garment," she said. When the ladies came with the wrong garment, she blazed, "If you do not know where to find it, at least have the sense to ask Jasmine."

"She was sent to the ladies' court many moons ago."

"Fetch her back."

"She is ill. Her physician says she has not long to live."

"Why was I not told?"

"She did not want to trouble Your Majesty with the information."

In the silence that followed, Chao recalled the night she sent Jasmine away. She had dismissed the ladies and was reading alone when she heard a bowl knock against a saucer. She looked up and saw Jasmine with the ginseng tea in her unsteady hands. Jasmine's wrinkled face emerging from the shadow horrified her as if it mirrored her own. "Jasmine! Did I not tell you to stay out of my sight?" she shouted. The next thing she knew the hot liquid spilled and scorched her hands. "Get out! Do not ever come near me again!" she cried.

Now, she repeated incredulously, "Not long to live." She

forgot the inner garment and went to the ladies' quarter to visit Jasmine.

As she stood in the little courtyard, the years rolled back. It was in a court like this she had dwelled when she first entered the Palace. Now, standing in the snow, she heard again the shuffling feet of Old Uncle, the sobs of Phoenix, the chattering of Pure Jade and Peony, and her own cries of despair. Yes, she had come a long way, a very long way.

She parted the heavy padded curtain and stepped into Jasmine's room. She waved aside the chair the eunuch brought and stood looking down at the little heap of bones and skin huddled beneath the heavy counterpane.

Jasmine's parchment face lit up. "Your Majesty should not trouble to come," she said weakly.

"I would have come earlier if I had known. I have sent for my own physician to attend you. Jasmine, speak your wish and the Son of Heaven shall grant it to you."

"Your Majesty's presence has fulfilled my wish."

"Perhaps something for your family?" Chao persisted.

"They are content as they are."

On her way back, Chao weighed herself against Jasmine, who wanted nothing and got nothing herself. She wanted the utmost and got the utmost; yet both would go the same way. The visit depressed her. The thought that she, too, would someday face Jasmine's fate sent ice down her spine. She stepped closer to the brazier in her room, spread her hands over the fire, and sighed. Somehow the buoyancy of her pretended youth was over, and she felt old and tired.

The next morning, the snow stopped and the sky wore a big smile of sunshine. Blanketed in white, the garden was enchanting, and Chao wanted to see the Lamei grove, exquisite after a heavy snow.

"Get my cape and hood," she ordered.

"But Your Majesty, the ground is covered with snow," said her lady-in-waiting.

"Have I not eyes to see for myself?"

"It is bitter cold outside," said another lady-in-waiting.

"I know. I know." She glared.

"Will Your Majesty wait for the Fifth Lord and the Sixth Lord?"

"No," she roared. "Tell them to meet me at the Lamei grove."

Out in the open, she shivered. The sun was deceptive. Its brilliance had not warmed the air. But the piercing cold did not deter her. Her spirit was as high as when she was in her prime. A eunuch proffered a carved dragon staff. Chao threw it away in scorn, and it shot through the air like a golden javelin.

With her chin high she strode up the bridge. At the hump she turned to see if her eunuchs were shadowing her, as they were wont to do lately. She lost her balance and slid to the foot of the bridge. The eunuchs came running. The two brothers, catching up with her, helped her up and chided her as one would a child caught in mischief.

Back in her sleeping chamber, Chao's teeth chattered. Her ladies tucked her in bed under a pile of comforters. Still she shivered. The two brothers stripped themselves bare to lie on either side of her, but their body heat could not warm her from the chill that came from within.

Then came the fever, sudden and severe. A dry cough tore at Chao's throat, and her breath was short and difficult. The two brothers dressed in a hurry, then knelt by the dragon bed to feed her honey-water, spoon by spoon, to ease her throat. The physicians were summoned, and their diagnosis was inflammation of the air passage.

When the Crown Prince was informed, he came to the antechamber and sat nervously on the edge of his chair, his eyes glued on the door of Chao's sleeping chamber. It was his duty as Crown Prince to watch by the bedside of the ailing monarch; but never having felt at ease in his mother's presence, he dreaded this ordeal. Besides, being in the Imperial Chamber to witness the intimate relations between his mother and the two Lords was simply too humiliating, and his ineffectual face flushed with embarrassment.

His wife, son, and daughter were beside him on the mahogany couch. All three hated Chao. Although the daughter was married to Chao's grand-nephew, Extended Heritage, her loyalty remained with her father's clan. The nineteen-year-old son detested the old Dowager's lechery and looked forward to the day when the heads of the two loathesome knaves would fall.

When the Sixth Lord reported the Crown Prince's presence to Chao, she frowned. "Tell him he is released of his filial duty."

"Your Majesty's daughter-in-law, grandson and granddaughter are also here to inquire after Your Majesty's health," said the Sixth Lord.

Chao hissed through her nose. Jackals after their plunder, she thought, coming to find out how soon they could prey on her carcass. But she would live and disappoint them. "Tell them to go away. I wish to see no one."

As the Sixth Lord entered the antechamber the faces that turned to him were so hostile and scornful that he bristled. "Go!" he said, "Her Majesty wishes to see none of you."

Tsung Tsung involuntarily expelled a breath of relief, but the eyes of his wife, darting toward the Sixth Lord, were like poison arrows. The nineteen-year-old Prince whispered to his sister in a voice that was meant to be heard, "Some people do not know their days are numbered. Where will the clinging vine be when the old tree falls?"

This naked truth alerted the Sixth Lord to his precarious position. He beckoned his brother to the antechamber. Huddled in a corner, they talked in whispers. "They will kill us as soon as Her Majesty is dead," said the Sixth Lord. "What shall we do? You have the brain. Think!" he pressed his brother.

"Our only hope is that Her Majesty does not die," said the Fifth Lord.

"But she cannot live forever. She is eighty."

"At least it will give us time to plan. In this desperate situation, either we stretch our necks on the block or . . ."

"Or what?"

"Or gamble for a last throw of dice. Form a junto and seize the throne. When Her Majesty dies, we will be the first to know. We can repress the news till we have called in our band and disarmed the palace guards."

"Seize the throne!" echoed the Sixth Lord. The very thought prostrated him.

[255]

"It's a hazard either way. With the junto there might be a chance. But we need time and Her Majesty must get well."

They nursed Chao with painstaking care and watched her in turn, day and night. Chao herself was determined to live. Life was too good to give up without a struggle. One day, as if her sheer will to live had touched the compassion of the gods, her crisis was over, and the Sixth Lord said to his brother, "The tide has turned; her head feels cooler at last."

Chao, vaguely conscious of her two favorites' devotion in her delirium, now was clearly aware of their haggard faces and sunken eyes. "You look tired," she said. "Go and take a rest. Let the ladies wait upon me." From then on, Chao slowly recovered, although never to her old self again.

In the year that followed, the two Lords worked feverishly to form their junto. Through their influence with Chao, they sold official posts to get money for arms and recruits. This did not escape the eyes of Hung. But with Chao under the influence of her two favorites, he felt it was futile to warn her. Hung knew that in serving Her Majesty he had collected powerful enemies through the years who would surely demand his head when Chao was out of the way. To protect Chao and save himself, he decided to report the junto to the Prime Minister. He wished Ti were alive. He could speak more freely to him than the new Prime Minister. He waited till the New Year festivity was over; then he went to inform Prime Minister Chang of the junto.

"Have you told Her Majesty of this?" asked the Prime Minister.

"No, Your Eminence."

"Then repeat it to no one."

"Your Eminence can trust me to be discreet." Hung hesitated a moment, then said, "I have served Her Majesty faithfully these many years and will serve her to the end. But when Her Majesty ascends to heaven, may I be permitted to return to Anhwei, where my sister is?"

"Your bringing this to our attention warrants the granting of your wish. I shall personally intercede for you when the new Emperor comes to the throne."

In the spring of Chao's eighty-second year, she sank so low that the two Lords thought her end was near. They called up the squad leaders of their band and hid them in a hut at the outskirts of Loyang to wait for their word to storm the Palace. The long wait made the men fidgety. As they gathered under a circle of light shed from a lone oil lamp, one of them said, "The dragon had better die soon. I cannot hold my squad in check any longer."

"I see no sense in waiting. Storm the Palace anyway," said an impatient young leader.

"No," several horrified voices dissented. "It is agreed that we do not sally the Palace while the Holy Emperor lives. We are not ingrates, to do her ill in return for her good reign."

In another part of Loyang that same night, Prime Minister Chang sat alone in his study. Now and then he looked toward the door, waiting for the Deputy Director of the Board of Justice to come. Since Hung's secret warning, Prime Minister Chang had secured the pledges of several high officials and generals of the guards to forestall the two Lords' insurrection in the name of the Crown Prince. Tonight he sent the Deputy Director to the East Palace to secure the Crown Prince's consent and participation. The Deputy Director was late in returning, and the Prime Minister's nervous hand pulled at his beard as he frowned.

At a light knock, the Prime Minister opened the door to admit the Deputy Director. After a silent, secretive greeting, they sat at the square tea table, put their heads together, and talked in a low tone. "Does His Highness approve of our plan?" asked Prime Minister Chang anxiously.

"He does."

"Then we must act quickly. 'The longer the night, the more the dreams.' "

"How quickly?"

The Prime Minister fingered his beard thoughtfully, "Tomorrow . . . at the hour of the rabbit [5-7 A.M.]."

The next day, before the sun touched the horizon, the Deputy Director went with the Right Wing Guard General to escort

[257]

Tsung Tsung to lead the guards into the Palace. Tsung Tsung, at the last moment, demurred. "What if it fails?" he asked. "Would it not be safer to wait?"

"Your Highness," said the Deputy Director. "For twenty-three years Your Highness was shoved away from your inheritance. Now Her Majesty is too feeble to be in Your Highness's way. Would Your Highness waver and forfeit your heritage to the two knaves?"

"The rogues, no doubt, should be dispatched. But to kill them now would upset Her Majesty. Is it not better to wait?" he asked again.

"Why do you fear?" said Tsung Tsung's consort behind the screen. "Your mother is too sick to harm you further. Put yourself in the hands of these loyal supporters. Kill the two rogues. Mount the throne."

Tsung Tsung, thus encouraged, rode with the Deputy Director and the Wing Guard General to the gate of the Main Palace, where Prime Minister Chang waited with five hundred guards. With the Crown Prince in the lead, they marched into the Palace unopposed, for it was general knowledge that Chao's sun was setting. At Chao's Resident Hall, the Wing Guard General ordered his men to disarm Chao's guards. Then Prime Minister Chang led Tsung Tsung to the throne seat in the center chamber. Tsung Tsung looked uneasily at the Deputy Director and the Prime Minister. Then, in a hesitant voice, he ordered the Wing Guard General to arrest the traitors.

The two Lords were dragged from their beds and brought to kneel at the Crown Prince's feet. They looked at the drawn swords of the guards and shuddered. "What ... what ... is this?" they stammered.

"Your plot to seize the throne is exposed," said the Prime Minister, "and His Highness will decree your sentence."

"Decapitation," said Tsung Tsung uncertainly.

At the Wing Guard General's signal, the guards expeditiously dragged the Lords to the Side Palace to be beheaded.

The Lords' screams woke Chao and she asked irritably, "What is this commotion?"

[258]

"Your Majesty," said the lady-in-waiting. "The Prime Minister and some other officials are here."

"At this hour?" asked Chao.

"Your Majesty," said Prime Minister Chang, stepping into Chao's chamber. "We are here in obedience to the command of the Crown Prince. The two Lords' conspiracy to seize the throne is discovered and His Highness has ordered their execution."

For a moment, Chao was speechless, choked with pain and anger. She knew that she could not protect them after her death, but to kill them now was an unpardonable affront to her. The cowards! They would not dare if she were not weakened by illness. She ordered her lady-in-waiting to prop her up and to hold the candle to the circle of faces. She wanted to see who had perpetrated this outrage. In spite of her feebleness, her face was majestic and awe-inspiring. Her dark pupils blazed with rage as she surveyed the ministers crouched in front of her bed. As the candle flashed upon Prime Minister Chang, Chao said bitterly, "I personally placed you in this high office, yet you did this to me."

"It is in gratitude to Your Majesty's grace that this is done," said the Prime Minister, "that the throne may be preserved for Your Majesty's heir."

Tsung Tsung blinked as the candlelight flickered on his face.

"So it is you," said Chao.

Tsung Tsung lowered his eyes without a word, but the Deputy Director of the Board of Justice said, "Your Majesty, the court and the nation, deeply concerned with Your Majesty's health, request that Your Majesty abdicate in favor of the Crown Prince."

The audacity! Chao's old vigor flashed, but like the cinder of a dying fire, it glowed momentarily, then extinguished into ashes. All her life she had known when to advance and when to retreat. She was not going to struggle against the inevitable now. She knew she was approaching the end of her life journey. She could not fight destiny. "So be it," she said. "Serve your new sovereign well. He will need the guidance of your experienced hands." Then she dismissed them with a slight movement of her hand.

Later in the day, Chao retired to the Palace of Ascending Sun. For her, life ended on the day of her abdication, since her two predominant passions, power and love, were both strangled on that same day. Hence her mind and her heart were dead; only her body lived. She refused to receive her physicians, since she no longer desired to prolong her life. Only Princess of Peace was her constant companion.

Idling in bed one day, she saw her life stretch before her like a canvas brushed in daring strokes. It was a powerful but frightening picture. There were peaks of accomplishment, valleys of frustration, rivers red with blood, plains heaped with skeletons, paths strewn with bodies over which she had trod. She covered her eyes. What had she done with her life? What price had she paid for power? She wished the scene were different—a simple house warm with affection, a singing brook with a willow or two. She wished she could undo what she had done. She could not recall the dead, but she could at least make restitution to the living. She turned to her daughter and asked, "When is the Son of Heaven coming?"

"He comes every tenth day of the moon. That is tomorrow, mother."

When Tsung Tsung was ushered into her room the next day, Chao said, "We realize Chinzen was unjudicious in his trial of the treason cases, causing the innocent to suffer with the guilty. Therefore we want you to order a retrial. Also, pardon Chu Saliang and Chanson Wochi and reinstate their descendents. We also wish to rescind the title of Holy Emperor." For she knew that only as Empress Dowager would her soul tablet repose in the Imperial Temple of the Tang Dynasty.

After Tsung Tsung left, Chao closed her eyes and heaved a sigh. Peace was beyond her grasp, but at least there was one consolation; she had given the nation a good reign and handed to her son a heritage based on a solid foundation.

Six months after her retirement, Chao sensed her last hour was near, and she said to Princess of Peace, "Move me to the window. I want to see my beloved garden for the last time."

[260]

"No inauspicious words, Mother," said Princess of Peace, but she ordered the eunuchs to move the heavy bed to humor her mother. As Chao wanted the window open, Princess of Peace pulled the comforter up to Chao's chin and put a hood over her head, then signaled a lady-in-waiting to prop her up.

The brisk air pricked Chao's skin; the desolate scene pierced her heart. The frozen ground, the bare trees, the fallen leaves— how like death, she thought. Then the imminence of her own death made her eyes blur, her breath come short. Princess of Peace quickly closed the window and ordered the eunuch to move back the bed.

That night, when Princess of Peace was about to leave, Chao clung to her daughter's hand. As this was not her mother's usual wont, Princess of Peace stayed with her mother for the night. She sat by the bed till Chao was asleep, then sank in a chair by the charcoal brazier. Soon she dozed and nodded until the drum beat woke her. She listened. It was the fifth watch, almost day-break. She looked about her. The candle had burned low. The ladies were dozing on the floor, their backs against the wall, their chins on their bosoms. She rubbed her face and tiptoed to the bedside. The eerie stillness made her press her fingers on her mother's pulse. Not a quiver, for the soul had already taken its leave.

Bibliography

Changan Shih Chi Kao
長安史蹟考 － 足立喜六著，楊鍊譯

Ching Hsun Tang Ts'ung Shu
經訓堂叢書

Chiu T'ang Shu
舊唐書 － 劉昫等

Hsin T'ang Shu
新唐書　歐陽修

Ku Chin T'u Shu
古今圖書

Li Shih Hsiao Ts'ung Shu—Wu Tse Tien, By Li Tang
歷史小叢書　武則天　李唐著

Li Shih Wu Chung Ho Kan—Li chao-Lo
李氏五種合刊　李兆洛輯　皇朝輿地韻編，歷代地理沿革圖

Loyang—Ni Hsi-Ying
洛陽　倪錫英著

Loyang Ku Chin T'an—Li Chien-Jen
洛陽古今談　李健人著

Shu Fu
說郛　洛陽花木記，周氏；洛陽名園記，李廌

T'ang Hui Yao—Wang Fu
唐會要　王溥撰

T'ang Shu Ho Ch'ao—Shen Ping-Chen
唐書合抄　沈炳宸輯

San Ts'ai T'u Hui—compiled and edited by Wang Chi
三才圖會 - 王圻纂集

T'ang Tai Ching Chi Shih—T'ao Hsin-Sheng & Ku Chin Yuan
唐代經濟史　陶希聖　鞠清遠著

T'ang Tai She Hui Kai Lueh—Huang Hsien-Fan
唐代社會概略 · 黃現璠著

T'ang Tai Ti Fang Hsin Cheng Shih—Huang Shou
唐代地方行政史　黃綬著

Tzu Chih T'ung Chien—Ssu-Ma Kuang
資治通鑑　宋司馬光編集，元胡三省音註

Yen Li Pen Ti Wang T'u
閻立本帝王圖

Chinese Antiquities
  Edited by Yoshito Harada & Kazuchika Komai

Chinese Dress and Personal Ornaments, by Yoshito Harada

The Empress Wu, by Charles Patrick Fitzgerald

The Eumorfopoulos Collection, by R. L. Hobson

Four Thousand Years of China's Art, by Dagny Carter

History of World Art, by Upjohn, Wingert and Mahler

Polo, by Carrington Goodrich (Published in Horse and Horseman V19
  April 1938)

Names of Historical Characters

Hsu	許敬忠
Hsu (Justice)	徐有功
Kao Tsung (Emperor)	高宗
King of Lanya	琅邪王冲
Lan Chinzen	來俊臣
Li Chi	李勣
Li Hsiao I	李孝逸
Li Nien Fu	李義府
Liu Shih	柳奭
Loh Ping Wong	駱賓王
Loyalty (Prince)	燕王忠
Ming	明崇儼
Payi	裴炎
Prince of Dawn (Emperor Jui Tsung)	豫王旦即睿宗皇帝
Prince of Wisdom (Emperor Tsung Tsung) . .	英王哲即中宗皇帝
Princess of Gold	千金公主
Princess of Peace	太平公主
Princess of Wen Chen	文成公主
Si Shaw	薛紹
Si (General)	薛仁貴
Si Wenyi	薛懷義
Sixth Lord	六郎張昌宗
Tai Tsung (Emperor)	太宗
Ti	狄仁傑
Virtue (Prince)	雍王賢
Wai (Prime Minister)	韋安石
Way Yuan Chung	魏元忠